TIME CASTAWAYS
THE OBSIDIAN COMPASS

TIME CASTAWAYS
THE OBSIDIAN COMPASS

Fischer Middle School
Indian Prairie School District #204
1305 Long Grove Dr.
Aurora, IL 60504

To Fischer
Falcons,

[signature]

LIESL SHURTLIFF

KATHERINE TEGEN BOOKS
An Imprint of HarperCollins Publishers

Katherine Tegen Books is an imprint of HarperCollins Publishers.

Time Castaways #2: The Obsidian Compass
Copyright © 2019 by HarperCollins Publishers
ISBN 978-0-06-256818-2

Typography by Katie Fitch
19 20 21 22 23 PC/LSCH 10 9 8 7 6 5 4 3 2 1
❖
First Edition

For Mom, who taught me perseverance.
And for Dad, who taught.

1
The Disappearing Thief

Belamie, Age 5-15
1762-1772
Asilah, Morocco

It was a perfect day. At least in the beginning.

It began with blue skies, not a cloud in sight, and a calm, glassy sea.

No one understood where the storm came from, not even the old fortune-teller, who for decades had been a reliable source for most impending tragedies and doom. Stories abounded of course, as people will always search for answers and reasons. Perhaps some thoughtless sailor had whistled in the wind or stirred his tea with a knife, or maybe an ignorant passenger on a ship had unwittingly cut their nails. Reason or not, the storm blew in, quick and relentless.

The clouds rolled and rumbled into a dark foreboding mass. The first lightning bolt struck just before midday. The wind grew savage and the rain burst from the sky, pelting the water like a thousand arrows every second. The waves swelled to the size of small mountains, rising up and slapping down with brute, merciless force.

The little merchant ship did not stand a chance. The sailors did all they could, followed every order from their captain at the helm, but they knew there was no hope. In less than an hour the ship was sunk and every soul on board was drowned.

All but one.

A tiny girl, no more than five years old, miraculously survived the storm without so much as a scratch. She bobbed along the ocean in a small skiff, wearing only a thin nightgown, soaked and sticking to her like a second skin. The only other possession she had was a small dagger, which she held close to her chest like a talisman. She stared out at the water, now still and calm, as though waiting for something to rise from its depths.

A young sailor on a ship found the girl, floating among the wreckage. He spoke to her in English and then French, and when she didn't respond either time he assumed she couldn't understand him, but she could. The sailor argued with his companions over whether or not to rescue the girl. They seemed to be afraid of her for some reason. Perhaps they thought she had been the cause of the storm, that she would bring them bad luck. She had often heard sailors say that a female, even a little one, was bad luck on board a ship.

They left her in her skiff, lashed it to their ship, and tugged her all the way to the shores of Asilah, where the sunken ship had sailed from the day before. The girl did not speak or cry the entire way. She did not move.

When they had tugged the little skiff onto the beach, the sailors again argued over her, where they should take her, how she would survive. The girl didn't even register their words. She only watched the waves, now calm and gentle, roll upon the shore.

The young sailor gave the girl what little food he had on him, some biscuits and dried fish. He gave her a final look of sympathy and left her on the beach, still sitting inside her little boat, clutching the dagger.

The girl's name was Belamie Rubi Bonnaire. She knew her name as well as she knew that she was now alone in the world. Her parents were gone. Her papa, a French merchant with gentle hands, and her mama, a Moroccan beauty with a quick wit and captivating charm.

Though Belamie had been born in Morocco, her mother's country, she had spent most of her life at sea, sailing the world with her parents and their crew. There was no one to take care of her now. She knew of no other family or friends, no one who cared or even knew of her existence. She once overheard a member of her papa's crew say that her parents' marriage had been a crime, that they'd been disowned by both their families and lived on the sea because no place else would have them. At the time Belamie thought that was just fine. She preferred the sea to land anyway, and she didn't need anyone besides her parents. And now they were gone. They'd been swallowed by the angry sea, and they would not come back.

Belamie stayed with the boat. It was all she had left, and it would be her home and family now. She slept curled up inside of it that night, then sat in its shade all the next day. She didn't leave the boat until her food was gone and survival instincts kicked in and forced her to get up and seek food and water.

Belamie determined she would not steal. Her religious education had been spotty and vague, but once, when they'd gone to Paris, Belamie had tried to steal a doll from the fancy shop where her father had been doing business. She'd tried to hide it behind her back, but her father had caught her and gave her a long lecture. Stealing was a sin, he had said. It might bring some fleeting pleasure, but then damnation and hellfire. Her mother told her that those who steal get their hands cut off. This frightened Belamie so much she vowed to never steal again. But after a week of eating little more than the dust kicked in her mouth by unsympathetic passersby, she decided a radical change was in order. Damnation be damned, it was steal or starve.

It was painful at first. She got a stomachache after eating her first stolen melon, but eventually she developed a callus on her conscience, and it got easier. By the age of ten she wasn't ashamed to admit she found thieving to be quite fun, though she was always cautious. She learned it was best to steal from foreigners. Not only was it easier, it was safer too. The guards and soldiers were not concerned with protecting visitors. Even if she were caught, she'd likely only be made to give back what she'd stolen, perhaps spend a night or two in jail. That was far preferable to getting her hands chopped off. She'd seen it happen to thieves younger than her. She didn't relish the idea of eating like a dog.

Day after day, year after year, she carved out a meager existence as a thief. She slept and ate and lived in her little boat on the beach. Occasionally thieves tried to steal her boat, but Belamie had her dagger and, despite her smallness, she was alarmingly dexterous and skilled with a blade. Thieves soon learned to leave her and her little boat alone, and Belamie was quite content to remain alone, a petty thief until the end of her days. But fate, as it seemed, had other ideas, as it often does.

She was about fifteen when the strange man who would change the course of her life came to Asilah. The whole village was talking about him. The guard keeping watch from the ramparts (the great white wall that bordered the city along the sea) reported that he'd appeared on the beach out of thin air. They all swore it was true.

The man was a spirit, everyone said. One of the mysterious and powerful jinn. Some said he was a good jinni come to grant wishes. Others said he was evil, come to possess their spirits. Good or evil, there was one thing everyone could agree upon. The man was rich as a king. Gold and silver seemed to flow from his fingers.

That got Belamie's attention more than anything. She had little interest in the jinn, good or evil. Even if they were real, they would not fill her belly. But gold and silver could, and Belamie could steal from anyone.

She found him the next market day. He stood out like a fish on land. He was very different, even from all the sailors and foreigners she saw year after year. Belamie could not confidently discern where he was from. He wore loose trousers and a shirt with many buttons, and nothing around his neck. His head was bare, revealing dark hair streaked with silver. His back was to her, so she couldn't see his face.

Belamie moved a little closer, just enough to hear the man speak. She'd know where he was from based on his accent. She'd traveled the world with her parents before they'd died, and after so many years stealing from foreigners she could accurately detect most accents.

"Would you like some cinnamon, sir?" said the merchant. "There is no better cinnamon in the world." He held out a tiny sack, clearly eager to get some of the foreigner's famed gold.

"Oh, I don't know about that," said the foreigner. "I've had some delicious cinnamon in Brazil, but the cinnamon in Sri Lanka is very nice as well, though I suppose at this time it's not Sri Lanka, but Ceylon? What year is this again? 1772? Yes, it should be Ceylon now."

The merchant blinked at the man, still holding out the pouch of cinnamon. Belamie was utterly perplexed. The man spoke flawless Arabic, only the barest hint of an accent that she couldn't quite detect. It seemed to alter every other word. At first she thought maybe he was French, then English, then Russian.

"Some people think Ceylon cinnamon is the only real cinnamon," the man continued, "but then they probably haven't traveled to India. There, the spices are so pungent you can taste them in the air. Unfortunately, you can taste other less savory things in the air as well, so I don't recommend eating Indian air, but Indian cinnamon is divine."

The merchant nodded, his brow furrowed. He looked as though he didn't know whether to be impressed or offended by the man. "You have traveled very far, it seems. From what country do you hail?"

Belamie leaned in a little closer to hear.

"I don't claim any particular country of origin," the man replied. "I find such labels to be a bit confining and, quite frankly, misleading and unfair to everyone. If I say I'm a Spaniard, you'll instantly think me clever but haughty. On the other hand, if I tell you that I'm French, you'll find me an amiable fellow, but you won't trust me an inch. And yet, if I tell you I'm English, you'll think me a self-aggrandizing snob, though a fashionable one. But there is a real chance that all these things might be true, and so I prefer to give us both the benefit of the doubt and say I am from nowhere and everywhere. It's more accurate anyway. I'll take some cinnamon, since you say it is the best in the world." He pulled a thick silver coin seemingly out of thin air. The merchant didn't move. He stared, blank as a dead fish, until the strange man placed the coin on the table and took the cinnamon out of his hand. "I'll compare your cinnamon to the others and let you know if it is the best, if you like, so you can claim the title with complete confidence. Or drop it altogether. I always like to be accurate. Good day!" He turned away from the spice merchant. He tossed the little sack of cinnamon in the air, tucked it in his pocket, and walked right past Belamie, who was so lost in studying the odd stranger she almost forgot what she was about. She was supposed to be robbing him. Who cared where the man was from!

Belamie picked her way through the crowd toward the man. He was almost to the chicken merchant. That was perfect.

Belamie moved quickly and with purpose. She was just behind the man now, and she slipped her hand into his pocket, when without any warning he stepped out of her path. Belamie pitched forward, crashing into the stacked crates of chickens. The crates toppled onto her. The chickens exploded in angry squawks and a cloudburst of feathers.

Belamie tried to get up and run away, but again she tripped over one of the crates and went down in the dirt, knocking her mouth and chin on the ground.

"*Majnun!* Fool! Get away from my chickens!" cried a voice.

Belamie cursed herself for being so clumsy. She quickly stood, ready to run, but found herself face-to-face with the mysterious man, the very man whom she'd been trying to rob. For the rest of her life Belamie would think about the man's face. She would try to bring it to the surface of her mind over and over and she wouldn't be able to. His features were somehow indistinguishable, blurred, like a smeared painting. She blinked. A bit of dust or sand must have gotten in her eyes.

"Are you all right?" said the man.

He smiled at her, or at least she thought he did. There was a smudge of white in the general area of his mouth.

"You must pay for damages!" shouted the chicken man, waving a fist in Belamie's face. "My hens will not lay, and you have created more work for me!"

"It was my fault," said the foreigner. "I was in this young lady's way. Allow me." Coins appeared in his gloved hand. Belamie could not explain it logically. One moment they were not there, and the next they were.

He dropped the coins in one of the chicken cages. The

chicken squawked and flapped again as gold and silver rained down on it. The merchant did not complain. In fact, he thrust the chicken out of its crate, so he could gather the coins. It was more money than he could ever make in a lifetime selling eggs and chickens.

Meanwhile, the foreigner had his back turned to her. Belamie was in a most advantageous position. She could see a lump in his pocket, a purse with a tiny glint of gold. She deftly reached into his pocket and pulled out his purse, smooth as a fish swimming through water.

She turned to run but was violently pulled back. The man had chained his purse to him!

"Thief!" shouted the chicken merchant. "She is robbing you, sir!"

Belamie dropped the purse and tried to run, but before she could take two steps, she was faced by the guards. One was pointing a spear right at her neck. Belamie pulled out her dagger, ducked and swiped at the guard, but another one was right behind him. He grabbed her wrist and twisted, forcing her to drop her dagger. She struggled against the guard, tried to step on his foot, jam her elbow into his gut, but he shoved her to the ground, yanked her arms behind her back.

"Thief," growled the guard as he tied a rope around her wrists.

Belamie struggled once more until the guard kicked her in the gut and yanked her to her feet. A crowd had gathered to watch, all of them staring at her, some with expressions of shock, others with gloating glares, clearly glad to see she'd finally gotten what she deserved. The guard grasped her under both arms and began to lead her away. But the strange man, the jinni, was standing right in their path.

He was still blurry. Belamie could not read his expression, but he must be angry. Perhaps he wanted to punish her himself. Spit on her, smack her across the face. Turn her into a mouse and feed her to the chickens. He was holding something in his gloved hands. Her dagger. Perhaps he wanted to cut her hands off himself. The guards would probably let him, if he paid them enough gold.

"Release her," said the man.

"But, sir," said one of the guards. "She was stealing your gold, was she not?"

"No, no, no. This is all a big misunderstanding. We were in the midst of a trade. I wanted this knife. It's a very fine knife, and I took it, but then she never got her end of the bargain because we were attacked by chickens! Untie her at once!"

The guard quickly untied her hands while the man detached the pouch from the chain in his pocket. He held it out to Belamie. She looked down at the pouch, then at the dagger. Her father's dagger. It was all she had left of him in the world. The boat was more of a practical thing. The dagger was precious to her. She did not want to part with it. But she also did not want to part with her hands or her freedom.

She looked at the man. His face flickered and became clear, just for a moment. He looked at Belamie with a curious expression, a smile she couldn't quite read. Amusement? Fondness? It was almost like he knew her, but she couldn't think how. She had no family, no friends. No one in the world who cared about her at all.

The man pressed something into her hand, a small purse, the one she'd tried to steal from him just minutes ago. "See you soon," he said, and then he dissolved, like a pillar of salt in water.

The crowd gasped, a few screamed. The guards lifted their spears, though what good would they do against an invisible man? He was gone, nowhere to be seen.

Belamie knew that if she waited long enough, the crowd would take their fear out on her. They'd say she was connected to the man somehow, believe her full of evil and witchcraft, and throw her in prison, or worse, stone her to death. She took this moment to disappear herself.

She slipped through the crowd and ran all the way to the ramparts. She put the purse in her teeth and grabbed on to a rope, swung herself over and scaled down, jumping the last ten feet to the rocky beach and her little skiff tucked between the rocks.

Belamie pulled the skiff into the water, hopped in, and began to row. She rowed for maybe a quarter hour, then rested the oars and picked up the purse, weighing it in her hand and trying to make sense of what had just happened. Everyone would be talking about how he had disappeared, but that was the less confusing part of the story to Belamie. Why had the man saved her like that? He didn't know her. She guessed there must be at least ten pieces of silver, based on the weight. She could start a new life with that kind of money, maybe even leave Asilah, sail to the Americas where she'd heard fascinating tales from sailors and merchants of work and land and food, more than could be consumed.

Belamie opened the purse and reached inside. She frowned. It was not full of coins as she had assumed. She pulled out what looked like a strange watch or compass, or some combination of the two. Her initial disappointment was softened when she saw how beautiful it was. It was made of shiny black stone and had numerals, letters, and symbols etched and inlaid with gold in three layers of circles. She could get a good price for it from the jeweler in the market. Or the clockmaker. Or maybe she'd get a better price if she sold it directly to one of the sailors on the docks. It was a piece worthy of a captain. Her father would have loved it.

Memories suddenly rushed upon her, one after the other. Her father, holding his own compass, navigating at the helm of his ship. He told Belamie that one day she would be captain and his ship and compass would be hers. She had believed him, had looked forward to the day. Now it was all at the bottom of the ocean—the ship, the compass, and her parents. Try as she might, she could never quite remember how she'd survived or how she'd gotten inside the skiff. Did her father put her inside of it? Her mother? Why didn't they come with her?

Belamie shivered as a sudden cool wind gusted. A small wave rocked the boat. She studied the compass again. Such a strange thing. She wondered what the dials were for, what the symbols meant. She turned the outer dial. It made a soft clicking noise. Then turned the other dials, too, back and forth. The compass suddenly grew warm in her hands. The skiff plummeted at least a foot and the water around her began to hiss and bubble. Belamie dropped the compass. It fell to the bottom of the boat as she reached for the oars, but they were no help. She was already traveling far faster than she could possibly row.

Marius Quine, the so-called jinni, watched from the beach as Belamie Bonnaire and her little boat disappeared. His heart skipped a beat when it happened, even though he knew it would happen. He'd known this moment would come for years, and yet he couldn't help the rock that formed in his throat, the mixture of excitement and panic. He almost wanted to go after her, make sure she would be all right. But he knew she would be fine. For a time anyway. The danger, and the sorrow, would come later.

He wiped a bit of sweat off his forehead and removed his gloves like a farmer who had just finished sowing the seed in his fields and now only needed to wait until harvest. It had not been simple or easy, getting to this moment. There were so many threads, so many years and places and lives all circling and spiraling around each other. There were so many opportunities for mistakes, and so little room to get it right, but he knew this was how it all began.

"Mr. Quine?" a voice called behind him. It sent prickles up his neck, and he felt his features begin to sharpen and pull into focus. He fought against it, felt his face flicker in and out, like an intermittent radio signal. He was getting interference from present company.

Slowly, he turned around and faced the boy.

And this was how it all would end.

2

Doppelgänger

THE NEW YORK TIMES
April 28, 2019
Mayhem at the Met

ON FRIDAY, APRIL 26, AT APPROXIMATELY 5:00 a.m., an MTA bus careened down Fifth Avenue and crashed into the Metropolitan Museum of Art, effectively breaking in. Though it appears no art was stolen, several artifacts and displays were damaged, some beyond repair.

The incident is still under investigation by the NYPD and FBI, and reports are hazy and incomplete, but all sources have named a single family at the center of the chaos. Matthew Hudson, director of museum archives, and his wife, Belamie Hudson, a freelance restorationist recently contracted by the museum to curate a special exhibit, were reported on the scene within minutes of the crash, only to find their three children in the wreckage (Mateo, age 11, Corey, age 11, and Ruby, age 11). Injuries were minor, according to an EMT on the scene. A police report filed yesterday afternoon stated that the Hudson children had been abducted by an unnamed suspect who has yet to be apprehended. The children were abducted in the early hours of the morning, but fought with the man, which caused the crash. The abductor and his accomplices took off shortly after a violent skirmish in the Arms and Armor exhibit. The abductor is described as five foot eleven, medium build, dark hair and beard, wearing all black with red Converse. He supposedly carries a white rat in his pocket. (The police officer stated this detail was supplied by one of the Hudson children.)

Police and FBI are searching extensively for the suspect and asking the public to come forward with any information, though the Hudsons have not been ruled out as possible suspects themselves. A reliable source says that Mr. Hudson, upon entering the scene, did not follow the museum's standard emergency protocol.

"I heard the crash," said Bartek Kowalski, a night guard at the museum. "I was in the upper gallery. No alarms went off. They were disabled for some reason. When Mr. Hudson and his wife showed up, they told me they'd handle it and I should go get a cup of coffee. I didn't like it, but he is my boss, so what could I do?"

Mr. Hudson has been put on unpaid leave for the foreseeable future, and Mrs. Hudson's contracted work has been canceled. Damages to the museum are estimated at $1.3 million.

The Hudsons did not respond to a request for comment.

May 3, 2019
Hudson River Valley, New York

It was a quiet, peaceful spring day on the Hudson family vineyard. The sky was clear and blue. The squirrels and birds chattered in their nests while the wind whispered through the big willow tree by the pond full of singing toads. The grapevines were draped artfully in straight rows and sparkled silver in the afternoon sun. It was a lovely scene, something an artist would paint in a picture, but the Hudson children—Mateo and twins Ruby and Corey—couldn't have cared less. They weren't even outside enjoying the fine weather. They were all cooped up in a small room, crouched beneath the window, heads hovering over a vent.

"Ouch, Corey, move over," Ruby demanded in a whisper. "You're stepping on my fingers!"

"Move your fingers, then," said Corey.

"Shh!" said Matt. "Be quiet! If they hear us, this is all over." Matt was quite uncomfortable himself. The corner of the windowsill was jabbing into his side, and his back and legs were cramped from crouching for so long. Additionally, he was holding a notebook and pen and was trying to position himself in such a way that allowed him to both write and hear well at the same time, which resulted in a rather awkward sort of yoga pose. His parents' voices were muffled, and they weren't talking all that loudly, but if he really focused, he could understand what they were saying.

"Is that it?" asked Mrs. Hudson. "It looks like he's in Siberia."

There was a dull rustling sound, the jostling of thick sheets of paper.

"They're looking at the map!" whispered Ruby. "They're tracking the *Vermillion*!"

Yes, Matt thought Ruby was probably right. Up until last week this map had hung above their dining room table in their Manhattan apartment. Matt had always thought it was just another one of his father's old maps, but now he knew it was much more than just an old piece of paper with borderlines and countries and capitals. This map had the power to trace the whereabouts and when-abouts of a certain time-traveling ship called the *Vermillion*.

"No," said Mr. Hudson. "See, the mark isn't blazing, but it's dark enough so we know it was recent travel, at least according to our timeline. Wrangel Island?"

Wrangel Island. Matt wrote it down in his notebook.

"Why would Vincent travel to Siberia now, and so far back?" Mr. Hudson asked.

"Probably discarding old crew," said Mrs. Hudson.

Matt paused his writing and sucked in a breath.

"Jia . . . ," whispered Ruby.

Jia was their friend on the *Vermillion*. She and Matt had grown especially close during their time there. She had even betrayed Captain Vincent to help them get home. Matt tried not to imagine what might have happened to her, but sometimes he got flashes in his mind and it turned his stomach.

"Here," said Mr. Hudson. "He's in Chicago right now, in 1893. That's the year of the World's Columbian Exposition. Why would he be there?"

"It's one of the coordinates given on Quine's letter," said Mrs. Hudson. "I traveled there myself once, but the mission was . . . disrupted, and then we met, so . . ."

Matt felt a flutter in his chest. He quickly wrote down *Chicago, 1893*. He'd been pestering his parents all week to tell him what was going on, but they kept putting him off. "We'll let you know when something important comes up," his mother said, which Matt thought was incredibly unfair. They got to decide what was important and what was not, which meant he, Ruby, and Corey knew very little. But what could they do? They were just kids. The parents held all the power.

Until yesterday, that is, when Matt heard their voices

coming up through the vent in the kids' bedroom. He, Corey, and Ruby had practically been glued to this spot ever since. They'd learned more in a few short conversations than they had all week.

"Are you *sure* you haven't seen him in New York these past weeks?" Mrs. Hudson's worried voice traveled up to them. "Anywhere near at all?"

"Not since the day he took the kids," said Mr. Hudson.

"If he comes," said Mrs. Hudson, her voice quivering, "and we don't notice . . . if he gets the kids again . . ."

"He won't," said Mr. Hudson firmly. "We won't make the same mistakes as last time, and the kids won't either. They know now. We're all on our guard. It's going to be okay, Belamie, I promise."

Matt thought he heard his mom sniff back tears, and he felt just a bit sorry for his parents. He was beginning to understand the weight and worry they'd carried on their shoulders, not only in the past few weeks, but for years, especially his mom.

One week ago (according to their kitchen calendar at least) on April 26, 2019, Matt, Ruby, and Corey broke their number one family rule and boarded a subway train in New York, alone. The next thing they knew they were in Paris, France, in the year 1911. Unbeknownst to the Hudson children, the train they had boarded was not a train at all, but a transforming time-traveling ship called the *Vermillion*, powered and steered by the Obsidian Compass. The *Vermillion*'s mysterious leader, Captain Vincent, and his ragtag crew of time pirates had taken the Hudson children all over the world and throughout history, performing thrilling heists and daring missions. They thought they were having the trip of a lifetime, until they realized that Captain Vincent had plans of his own that did not include returning the Hudson children home.

With a bit of luck and a lot of help, the children had managed to escape Captain Vincent and get home to New York, only to discover that their own mother had once been a time pirate herself and was not on the friendliest terms with Captain Vincent. The Hudsons had managed to defend themselves and stick together, but Captain Vincent and his crew had escaped with the Obsidian Compass and the *Vermillion*, leaving the Hudsons vulnerable to future attacks. That's why they had fled upstate to stay with Mr. Hudson's mother on the family vineyard. It was safer than the big city, teeming with people and traffic. You can't accidentally board the wrong train if there's no train to board.

His dad started talking again. Matt leaned in to hear.

". . . possible the compass stopped working?" Mr. Hudson asked. "You said you could never travel past 2019. Maybe we're past that point?"

"He still has a few weeks left."

"Do you have an exact date?"

Mrs. Hudson did not reply. Matt's heart suddenly started to beat a little faster. He wasn't sure why.

"Tell me, Belamie," said Mr. Hudson. "I need to know."

Mrs. Hudson whimpered the answer, but it was clear enough. "June first."

Matt felt his stomach drop. Ruby and Corey both leaned back and looked at him. June first was his birthday, just a few weeks away.

Mr. Hudson let out an exhale loud enough so Matt could hear it. "Why didn't you tell me?"

"I didn't think it really mattered," said Mrs. Hudson. "It's only a coincidence."

"Belamie, how can you say that?" Mr. Hudson's voice rose. "You know it *must* matter. You know Mateo is—"

"What are you kids up to?" said a voice behind them.

Matt dropped his notebook and lost his balance. He fell back on his bottom as their grandmother walked into the room with a basket of laundry. Corey grabbed Matt's notebook, placed it over the vent and sat on it, while Ruby jumped up and shouted, "Nothing! We were just playing a game!" entirely too loud and chipper to be innocent.

Matt picked himself up. He had half a mind to shove Corey off the vent and try to hear what his dad was saying right now. He had been about to say something important. Something about *him*. "Mateo is what?!" he wanted to scream into the vent. But it was no use now.

Grandma Gloria, affectionately known as "Gaga" (that's how Matt said her name when he was little), was a petite woman with silver hair, black square glasses, and hot pink lipstick. She wore jeans, a flannel shirt, and combat boots. Matt had always thought she was the coolest grandma in the world, but right now he found her thoroughly annoying. Why did she have to come put away laundry now?

"You three look delightfully guilty," said Gaga. "Eavesdropping on your parents, are we?"

"Eavesdropping?" said Ruby in a scandalized tone.

"Oh no, we'd never do such a thing," said Corey.

Matt looked longingly at the vent currently covered by his notebook and Corey's bottom. Whatever his dad was going to say about him was said by now.

Gaga just smiled. "I remember when your uncle Charles used to eavesdrop on your grandfather and me in that very spot," she said as she put their clean clothes in the dresser. "I never could figure out how he knew all the family secrets when he was only five, and then I figured it out, so that night, when I knew he was listening, I casually told your grandfather that I'd finalized all the paperwork to send Charles off to boarding school in Tanzania. I thought I was so clever. And then years later, Charles ran away. And where do you think he went? Tanzania! Sent me a picture and everything, little devil. He was always giving me a run for the wine cellar."

Charles was Mr. Hudson's younger brother. None of the

children had ever met their uncle Charles, though they'd seen pictures and heard plenty of stories about him from their dad. Matt thought he sounded a lot like Corey, always pulling stunts and pranks. He was a geologist or something like that, so he was always off on some expedition, hiking mountains and volcanoes. He hadn't been home in years. Last they heard, he was in Peru. Matt had seen a Polaroid stuck to the fridge of their uncle Charles at the top of a mountain, a younger, more mischievous-looking version of their dad.

"So . . . the moral of the story is," said Corey, "eavesdrop on your parents as much as possible so you know when it's time to run away?"

"Haven't your poor parents been through enough with you three nearly being kidnapped?" Gaga lowered her voice to a whisper. "By the way, while you were eavesdropping, did you hear any more about that maniac? Did the police catch him yet?"

Gaga knew nothing of what had really happened to the kids, and their parents wanted to keep it that way. They said things were complicated enough. It was best to keep others out of it, so for all Gaga knew the kids had simply been kidnapped by a maniac who used to know their mother, which was true. They just didn't tell her that the maniac was a time-traveling pirate from the eighteenth century.

"No," said Ruby. "The police are still looking."

"Well, you're safe with me. There are no maniacs here.

Just buckets of wine, bless that vineyard. It's heaven." Gaga laughed as she tossed underwear in a drawer, and then an engine rumbled in the distance and the sound drew steadily nearer. Matt stiffened. He looked to Ruby and Corey. They all three at once jumped up and dashed toward the door. "Gotta go, Gaga!" said Corey.

"Don't run down the stairs! That's how your father broke his arm!"

They all ignored their grandmother's advice and ran down the stairs just as their parents came rushing down the hall. Mrs. Hudson was brandishing a fire poker, and Mr. Hudson had a baseball bat.

"Stay inside, kids!" said Mr. Hudson, but they didn't obey their parents either. They followed them out the door and onto the porch. Ruby picked up a long, thin metal stick Matt had seen Gaga use to turn on her sprinklers and got in a defensive stance alongside Mrs. Hudson. Corey pulled out a slingshot from his back pocket. He loaded it with a marble and hopped onto the railing. Matt was the only one without some kind of weapon, but he didn't need one. If the *Vermillion* appeared, all he cared about was getting Jia.

"It's coming toward the house!" said Corey. "It's a white van!"

Matt moved to run down the porch stairs, but Mrs. Hudson snatched him back by the collar and held him tightly to her with one arm while still holding out the fire poker.

The rumbling of the engine grew louder, and a moment later an unmarked white van appeared through the trees. The van pulled up to the house and squeaked to a stop. A man stepped out. He had dark hair and a beard. Mrs. Hudson tightened her grip on Matt's shoulder, so he could feel her nails digging into his skin. He didn't blame her. Captain Vincent had dark hair and a beard, too, but this was not Captain Vincent. He was shorter and heavier, and he wore glasses. He whistled as he opened the side of the van and pulled out a box full of groceries, but when he turned around and caught sight of the Hudsons he stopped short and went silent midwhistle.

"Hello?" he said. "I have a delivery for . . ." He glanced down at the clipboard in his box. "Gloria Hudson?"

"That's our grandma," said Corey, his slingshot still cocked and ready to launch.

"Okay . . . may I approach please?"

Mrs. Hudson nodded, but she didn't lower the fire poker, and she didn't loosen her hold on Matt. Ruby still had the sprinkler stick pointed toward him. Only Mr. Hudson seemed to have relaxed at all. He set down his baseball bat. "Here, I got it."

He stepped down and took the box from the man, who then quickly backed away. "Have a nice day!" he squeaked, and hopped in his van. He drove away much faster than he had driven up.

"I told you it was nothing," said Mr. Hudson, hefting the

groceries onto the porch. "Poor guy probably thinks we're all lunatics."

"We sort of are," said Corey. "Aren't we?" He released his slingshot and hit a tree.

"We're not lunatics," said Mrs. Hudson. "We're being cautious. All vehicles that approach the vineyard must be treated as a threat."

"I just wonder how cautious we can be before we scare away every delivery truck in the county," said Mr. Hudson.

Matt scanned the surrounding property. He'd seen very few cars in all the times he'd come to visit. The only vehicle in sight was an orange, rusty Volkswagen bus that sat in the empty field on the other side of the vineyard. It belonged to Chuck, Gaga's old farm manager. It didn't run, hadn't in decades, but Chuck refused to get rid of it. He was an odd duck, from what Matt had heard. The kids had never actually met him. They'd barely seen him from a distance since they'd come. Their dad said he was a bit of a hermit. Anyway, Gaga hated Chuck's orange bus, said it was a blemish on her beautiful vineyard. Matt had seen his mom glance nervously in the bus's direction more than once. Perhaps it was the hood ornament. It did look eerily close to the symbol of the *Vermillion*. Even Matt had given it a double look when he'd first seen it.

Other than that, there were no other cars in sight, working or otherwise. Gaga didn't drive and had all her groceries and supplies delivered. The Hudsons had rented a car to drive to Gaga's and promptly had it picked up by the rental company upon their arrival.

Matt couldn't help but feel a sting of disappointment that it hadn't been the *Vermillion* coming toward the house. It's not that he wanted to be kidnapped by Captain Vincent again, but if he did come, they'd have a chance to change things. They could steal the Obsidian Compass back from Captain Vincent. They could rescue Jia.

But he was stuck, useless, powerless. They couldn't do anything except wait and wonder and worry.

Matt rubbed at his wrist where he used to wear a bracelet. The stone in the bracelet had some mysterious connection to the *Vermillion* or the Obsidian Compass. Once, he'd been able to call the *Vermillion* back after he and Corey and Ruby had been discarded themselves. But he had lost the bracelet during their fight at the museum.

"What if Captain Vincent *does* show up?" Ruby asked. "What then?"

"Attack!" said Corey, standing on the porch railing. "I still think you should let me get a gun. We won't stand a chance in battle without one." Corey had tried every method possible to convince their parents that he should have a gun, to no avail.

"We will *not* attack," said Mrs. Hudson. "If there's *any* indication that the *Vermillion* is approaching, then you will do exactly as your father or I say. Is that clear?"

"Aye aye, Captain!" said Corey. He swung around the porch column and saluted Mrs. Hudson.

"So next time, when we tell you to stay inside, you stay inside," said Mr. Hudson.

"Aye aye . . . other-Captain!"

"Corey, get down from there before you break your neck."

Corey jumped down and saluted again. "Aye—"

"And please don't call me captain," said Mrs. Hudson. "I'm your mother, thank you very much."

Corey slumped. "Okay, if you want to be boring, I guess . . ."

"Where is Captain Vincent?" Matt asked. He figured this was as good a time as any to get some questions answered. "Are you keeping track on Dad's map?"

Mr. and Mrs. Hudson shared a look, which annoyed Matt. It was like they had their own silent language now, one he'd never be able to learn.

"The *Vermillion* hasn't been anywhere near us since it left the museum that day," said Mr. Hudson. Matt thought he was avoiding saying Captain Vincent's name on purpose, like it was a curse word or something.

"But where did he go right after he left us?" Matt asked. If Captain Vincent discarded Jia, he wanted to know exactly where and when. Not that he could do anything about it.

"It's not always easy to tell," said Mr. Hudson. "Especially if he comes and goes rather quickly. The markings tend to fade more quickly then. He did travel somewhere in West

Africa. Fourteenth century. Mali Empire."

"What's he doing there, do you think?" Matt asked.

"Probably stealing more of Mansa Musa's gold," said Mrs. Hudson, bitterly.

"Who's Mansa Musa?" Corey asked. "He sounds cool."

"King of the Mali Empire back then," said Mrs. Hudson. "One of the richest men to have ever lived. Probably *the* richest man to have ever lived. He had so much gold he gave it out like candy."

"Yeah, I knew he sounded awesome," said Corey.

"What do you mean Captain Vincent's stealing *more* of Mansa Musa's gold?" Ruby asked, looking pointedly at her mother. "Sounds like you have knowledge of this happening before. Did you ever steal some of it?"

Mrs. Hudson raised her eyebrows at her daughter. Mr. Hudson chuckled. "She takes after you, Belamie. Can't sneak anything past her."

Mrs. Hudson straightened herself. "I stole from Mansa Musa, yes. I stole from a lot of people."

Ruby gasped. "Mom!"

"What? I was a very different person then. And I'm not so sure you have room to get all high and mighty about it, missy. Are you telling me you didn't steal anything while on board the *Vermillion*?"

Ruby's face heated a bit. "That was different. *We* weren't in charge. And besides, you're our *mother*. No one expects their *mother* to be a thief."

"Pirate, actually," said Corey. "And a total badass with a blade."

"Corey!" said Mrs. Hudson.

Mr. Hudson put one of his large hands over Corey's head and shook it a little. "Hey, watch your mouth, mister."

Corey put up his hands in surrender. "What? I'm just trying to give Mom some dignity!"

"Thank you, *chéri*," said Mrs. Hudson. "Remember when I wash out your mouth with soap that I'm just trying to give you some manners."

"Manners-shmanners," Corey mumbled. "No one wants to have any fun around here."

"Speaking of blades," said Ruby, holding out her sprinkler stick. "You *still* haven't given me any sword lessons and you promised!"

"I'm sorry, Ruby," said Mrs. Hudson, "it's just . . . I've been a little distracted, trying to get everything settled here and at home and with work. Besides, I'm not sure how I would explain to your grandmother that I've suddenly become a fencing master. That's not a piece of background information your father shared with her before we married."

Mr. Hudson snorted. "That and a few other minor details."

"At least you can trust your mother," grumbled Ruby. "My mother is a thief *and* a liar." Ruby had been asking Mrs. Hudson for a fencing lesson at least twice a day since they'd returned from the *Vermillion*, and every time their mom put it off, Ruby got just a tad more sassy with her. Matt thought she was walking a fine line, possibly crossing it.

"Ruby," said Mr. Hudson, "cut your mom some slack, please. She's an excellent mother. She feeds you and clothes you and, despite her shady past, has taught you right from wrong, which ironically is why you're giving her such a hard time now."

Matt felt the conversation was slipping. There was so much he wanted to ask, so much he needed to know. "So why are you afraid Captain Vincent will come after us again?" said Matt.

"Excuse me?" said Mrs. Hudson.

"Well, he already got what he wanted, didn't he? He got that letter, so why would he come after us again?" During their battle at the Met, Captain Vincent had sent one of his crew to break into their mother's safe and steal a box that contained a letter. A letter from the inventor of the Obsidian Compass, Marius Quine. Matt assumed that's what he had been searching for all along and now that he had it, he'd leave them alone, but their parents' behavior would suggest otherwise.

"Because . . . ," said Mrs. Hudson, clearly stalling to answer, "the letter doesn't give enough information for him to get what he wants."

"And you have the rest of the information?" said Matt.

Mrs. Hudson pursed her lips. "I don't," she said. "But Vincent will think otherwise."

Matt stared at his mother until she looked away. He didn't think she was lying, but he was certain she wasn't telling him everything.

"And what *does* Captain Vincent want?" asked Ruby. "You never told us. Like what is his end goal?"

Mrs. Hudson fumbled for words. "He's looking for . . . something."

"Something to fix the Obsidian Compass," said Matt. That had been their main mission while on board the *Vermillion.* They were to help Captain Vincent find something or someone to make the Obsidian Compass work properly.

"No, it's something different than the compass," said Mrs. Hudson.

"What is it?" Ruby asked.

Mrs. Hudson took a deep breath, held it, and then let it out slowly. "He's looking for a . . . powerful *thing.* Something that will supposedly give you . . . more power than just the Obsidian Compass."

"Wow, Mom," said Corey. "That was, like, so illuminating and yet . . . not."

Matt glanced at Ruby who rolled her eyes. Was it any wonder why they'd resorted to sneaking around and eavesdropping? Matt thought. Their parents had promised to be truthful, and yet Matt had gotten the sense that they were trying to tell them only as much as they absolutely had to. It seemed to be a game for them. Answer the question as truthfully as possible, but also as vaguely as possible.

"I'm sorry," said Mrs. Hudson, "but I don't have that much information to offer. I've never seen it. I don't even know what *it* is exactly, or if it even truly exists. We had very little to go off of when I was on the *Vermillion*. Like I said, the letter from Quine is incomplete."

"Wait a second," said Corey. "You mean *you* were looking for the 'powerful thing' too, before you quit being Captain Bonnaire?"

Mrs. Hudson pressed the poker into the porch and twisted, digging into the wood. "I did search for it, once upon a time, but I didn't get very far before I decided it was a fool's errand, and misguided, like searching for the Fountain of Youth or the Holy Grail. It *seems* important, but really, it's just a distraction from what's actually important. So I stopped searching."

"But what if Captain Vincent found the 'powerful thing'?" Matt asked. "Would it be important then? Would we be in danger?"

Mr. and Mrs. Hudson shared a brief look.

"Does Captain Vincent want to kill us?" Ruby asked in a soft voice.

"No!" said Mrs. Hudson. She embraced Ruby with one arm while still holding the poker in the other. "No, no, *chérie*, that is not what he wants."

"Does he want to kill Dad?" Matt asked. In all the fighting at the Met, it had come to light that not only had Mrs. Hudson been a time pirate and the captain of the *Vermillion*, she had also been involved with Captain Vincent. Matt didn't like to think of him as his mom's old *boyfriend*, because that was weird, but that's pretty much what he was. In any case, it was clear he did not take the news of her abandoning him to marry another man very well.

"He probably does want to kill me," said Mr. Hudson, "but I think he knows that wouldn't do any good. It wouldn't win back your mother."

"What if he killed you in the past?" Matt asked. "Before you and Mom met?"

Again, his parents shared a look. "I have a strong suspicion that he's tried," said Mr. Hudson. "So far it seems he was unsuccessful."

"It's not always wise to attempt such drastic actions anyway," said Mrs. Hudson. "It's tempting, of course. When you have that kind of power you think you can change the world. I thought so when I first got the compass, but I learned early on that sometimes when you try to interfere with what you know has occurred or will occur, you end up hurting more than helping. Vincent knows this."

Matt wondered what things his mom had tried to interfere with, what she'd hurt more than helped, but it felt like a personal question, and it wasn't what he was most curious about anyway.

"But what if Captain Vincent finds what he's looking for?" said Matt. "What if he gets the 'powerful thing'? Will he be able to change things then?"

His mom stumbled to answer, when suddenly the porch door opened, and Gaga poked her head out. She surveyed the scene curiously over her glasses. "Am I interrupting a family meeting?"

Mrs. Hudson seemed to release all the tension in her body, clearly relieved to have the interruption.

"No, of course not, Mom," said Mr. Hudson. "Is everything all right?"

"Yes, I just came to see if my groceries had arrived. Oh, there they are. Jerry usually brings them inside."

"We'll bring them in for you," said Mr. Hudson.

"Thank you, dear. I was just going to start on dinner."

"Oh, don't trouble yourself, Gloria," said Mrs. Hudson. "I'll take care of dinner."

Gaga eyed the fire poker in Mrs. Hudson's hand. "Were you planning to hunt and kill dinner yourself, dear?"

Mrs. Hudson lifted the poker and twirled it around as only an expert swordswoman could. "I was thinking about it."

"Fabulous! I'll get the wine." Gaga went inside.

"We can't talk about this right now," said Mr. Hudson in a low voice. "You know how my mother likes to eavesdrop."

"Yes, I do," said Mrs. Hudson. "We can discuss this later, kids. If you see or hear anything suspicious, anything at all—a strange person, vehicle, weird noises—come to us right away. You will, won't you?"

"Yes," all three kids chorused without enthusiasm, as though this had been rehearsed several times.

Mr. Hudson picked up the box of groceries, and Mrs. Hudson opened the door for him. "Why don't you three go swim in the pond while we get dinner ready?"

The screen door slammed in their faces before any of them could utter a reply or ask any more questions. Matt, Ruby, and Corey all stood facing the door.

"Well, that was a load of baloney," said Ruby. She threw the metal pole off the porch, so it stuck in the grass.

"Yeah," said Corey, sitting down on the porch steps. "Parents are the worst."

Matt wondered if his parents had brought them here not just to hide from Captain Vincent, but also so they wouldn't have to talk so much about anything to do with time travel. After all that had happened, after all they'd been through, Matt thought his parents would be a little more forthcoming. They'd promised to be honest, and though they hadn't necessarily lied (he didn't think), everywhere Matt turned, every question he asked, there seemed to be more and more secrets and more mysteries. Now there was some "powerful thing" that Captain Vincent wanted, something that might put them in even more danger, and there was the matter of the compass not being able to travel past Matt's birthday, and Matt having something to do with . . . something.

Of course Matt knew he would time-travel again eventually. When he'd been on the *Vermillion* there had been convincing evidence that his future self had traveled before him. His, Corey's, and Ruby's names were carved on the mast, and there had been mysterious messages that Matt could only explain as coming from his future self. So he *must* travel again, though how or when or for what purpose he had no idea. Matt wondered if his mom knew any of this, suspected that he would travel at some point. Had she ever seen their names on the mast? Would she have known what they meant? He didn't dare to ask her. Time travel was a touchy subject at the moment.

"If only we'd gotten the Obsidian Compass from Captain Vincent!" said Ruby fiercely.

"Yeah, if only," said Corey.

Matt, too, had lamented this unfortunate circumstance more than once. These days all his thoughts seemed to begin with "what if" and "if only." All regret and wishful thinking. It was making him miserable.

"Come on," said Corey. "Let's go swimming." He pulled off his T-shirt. He and Ruby were always in their swimsuits. They wore them practically all day, so they could swim in the pond whenever they wanted.

"You coming, Matt?" Ruby asked as she pulled off her T-shirt.

"Maybe in a bit." He hadn't spent much time in the pond since they'd come. He'd had a couple of near-drownings while on the *Vermillion*, and recreational swimming hadn't been the same since.

"Okay, don't jump on any trains, planes, or automobiles," said Ruby.

"At least not without us," said Corey.

Matt smiled at his brother and sister. "I'll give you a heads-up, I promise."

Corey ran down the porch and jumped over the railing. A moment later Matt heard him make a Tarzan call and then splash into the pond. Ruby followed and soon they were laughing and shouting as they splashed water in each other's faces.

Matt wandered toward the vineyard. He strolled up and down the tidy rows of sprawling grapevines, glowing gold as the sun lowered in the sky. He liked the vineyard. It was all at once artful and mathematical, a place where you could feel lost and found at the same time, all in a good way. It was a peaceful place where he could sift and sort his thoughts. There were a lot to sift and sort. Matt thought a great deal about the *Vermillion*, his time there and his return. He was still trying to gain perspective. He wondered about Captain Vincent, where he'd gone since leaving them and what he was doing now, or in the past, or in the future. He thought a lot about Jia. He kept seeing her face, pleading for help, fading away. He saw the captain throwing her out of a moving train, or a helicopter, or overboard a ship. He imagined her stumbling through a hot desert or freezing at the top of a mountain. He kept reaching for his bracelet that wasn't there. Every time he heard the rumble of an engine his heart raced, and along with the fear was excitement, always followed by disappointment when it turned out to be the mailman or a delivery or Chuck mowing the lawn. If something didn't happen soon, he'd go crazy.

"Matt! Dinner!" Ruby was calling him from the porch.

Matt looked up. Had he been walking and thinking that long? His perception of time seemed to be way off since they'd time-traveled, sort of like coming onto dry land after spending a lot of time on a boat. Sometimes it felt like you were still moving.

"Coming!" Matt started to walk back toward the house. He was halfway across the vineyard when he heard a *thump* and a grunt. There was some shuffling and rustling in the row right next to him and then a head popped through the vines.

Matt froze.

He was staring at himself!

3
Tinkering

"Oops!" said the other Matt, and he ducked down and ran away.

Matt, present-Matt, stood rooted to the spot. Was that it? Had he cracked? Or had he really just come face-to-face with himself?

You weren't supposed to see yourself, he knew. That was one of the rules of time travel. It could cause a glitch or a ripple in the timeline, which could then cause a storm or an earthquake. At least that's what Captain Vincent had told him, and Matt had seen proof this was true when he, Corey, and Ruby had accidentally run into their own father in the past. It had nearly cost the Mets the 1986 World Series. But seeing yourself, and seemingly in the not-so-distant future? That would surely cause a glitch on a much larger scale. Matt braced himself for some kind of explosion, for the sky to fall or the ground to open up and swallow him. But nothing happened. Not so much as a whisper of wind. Had he imagined it?

Matt heard voices, someone shouting, but he couldn't understand what they were saying. And he smelled something. He sniffed.

Peanut butter!

Matt's stomach flipped. The *Vermillion* always smelled of peanut butter. Jia always used it for repairs! Could it be here? Was Jia here? And who else?

Matt started to walk the length of the vineyard, slowly at first, carefully peering down each row. He heard footsteps coming down the row on the other side of him. Closer and closer. The peanut butter aroma grew stronger. Matt's heart thumped louder. He made a split-second decision, ducked beneath the vines and ran right into someone. But it wasn't himself, nor was it Jia, or any of the *Vermillion*'s crew. It was just Chuck, Gaga's old farm manager.

"Geez Louise!" Chuck shouted. "You scared the beetle juice outa me!"

"Sorry," said Matt.

"Oh criminy, there goes my sandwich." Chuck bent over and picked up a sandwich covered in dirt. A peanut butter sandwich. That explained the smell. Chuck tried to dust off the dirty sandwich and stuffed it in his shorts pocket. Matt had never seen Chuck up close before, only from a distance. He was kind of an old hippy. He had long wiry gray hair and a scraggly beard. He wore a tan fishing hat and a tie-dyed T-shirt with a purple peace symbol, and he was holding a golf club over his shoulder. He swung it down and held it out to Matt. "Found my putter."

"Uh . . . okay," said Matt. Should he congratulate him or something?

"Don't you want it?" said Chuck.

"Do I?" said Matt.

"Well, you said you did, didn't you? You came running right by here shouting, 'I need a putter! I need a putter!' Sounded pretty urgent, so I ran and got my putter out of Blossom."

"Who's Blossom?" asked Matt.

Chuck took a deep breath and then hung his head as he blew out in exasperation. "Blossom is my bus!" he said, pointing to the orange VW bus. "Anyway, this is a pretty good putter. Want me to give you some putting tips? The key is to lead with your hips." He jutted out his hip a little to the side as he swung the club.

"Oh. Yeah," said Matt, taking a few steps back. "I thought I needed a putter, but I don't anymore. Thanks though."

Chuck slumped and shook his head. "Geez Louise, kids these days change their minds faster than I can flip a flapjack."

Matt heard the door to the house open and slam shut, then open and shut again. "Mateo, where are you going?" he heard his mother call.

"Be right there!" someone shouted back, but not Matt. At

least not present-Matt. The voice sent a strange kind of vibration in his throat and chest, as if his vocal cords had been strummed like a guitar.

"Sounds like you're late for dinner," said Chuck.

Matt raced toward the house. He heard someone else's pounding footsteps too. He reached the edge of the vineyard just in time to see himself run around to the back of the house. Matt hesitated. He knew it was dangerous to see yourself. It could cause any number of disasters. But he *had* to know how he was traveling!

Matt decided to throw caution to the wind. When he reached the back of the house, he saw himself standing with something in his hands. Something round and silvery, like a watch or a compass. Or both. The other Matt was turning its dials. He looked up and locked eyes with himself. The other Matt smiled, and then he disappeared, like he'd been yanked between invisible curtains.

Matt stood rooted to the ground, staring at the spot where he'd just seen himself. All his senses were on edge, every hair on end. His heart pounded in his ears.

The back door of the house opened. Matt whirled around, but it was only his dad. "Matt, buddy, come inside. We're all waiting for you."

"Coming," said Matt.

"And hey, bring in that jar of peanut butter, will you?" Mr. Hudson pointed.

Matt looked down. Right between his feet was an open jar of peanut butter. He picked it up and put on the lid. He took one last look around the yard and went inside.

All through dinner Matt kept glancing out the window that looked out over the vineyard. Any little movement was like a little zap that made him want to jump out of his seat and run outside.

"I sent a letter to Charles," said Gaga as they all sat at the dinner table. "I told him he really should come home for a while, see you and the kids? Wouldn't that be nice?"

"He'll never come," said Mr. Hudson with just a touch of bitterness in his voice.

"Maybe if you wrote him he'd come for Matt's birthday!" said Gaga. "Wouldn't that be something, Mateo?"

"Uh-huh," said Matt, barely listening.

Mr. Hudson snorted. "He skipped town the day of my wedding, Mom. He barely stuck around to watch me get married. His own *brother*. Do you really think he's going to come to a birthday party for a nephew he's never met?"

"He might," said Gaga, a tad defensively.

Mr. Hudson took a sip of wine and glanced briefly at a picture hanging on the wall of him and his younger brother standing in the vineyard, laughing while holding a bunch of grapes over their open mouths. Mr. Hudson was probably Matt's age in the photo, and so Charles was maybe six or seven.

"Matty, dearest, don't be bitter," said Gaga. "You know Charles has always had a wandering heart, much like your father."

"Yes, let's just hope he doesn't follow in *all* of Dad's foot-steps." Mr. Hudson drained his wineglass. Matt never knew his grandpa Hudson. He had died on some hiking expedition years ago, when Mr. Hudson was about Matt's age. That had been hard enough, but then Mr. Hudson's younger brother, Charles, left when he was in his early twenties to go on his own hiking expedition and hadn't been back in years. Matt wasn't sure how long, but he'd never met him either. Charles sent the occasional postcard or email, but that was it. Mr. Hudson had never quite forgiven him for abandoning the family.

Matt saw something move out of the corner of his eye. He whipped his head back toward the window, but it was only Chuck walking through the vineyard. He still had the putter over his shoulder.

"Mateo, are you all right?" said Mrs. Hudson, eyeing him closely.

"Yeah, fine." Matt settled back down.

Mrs. Hudson looked at Matt curiously. She looked out at the vineyard, then back at him again. "Did you see some-thing?" she said.

Matt looked at his mom. *Yes*, he almost said. *I saw myself, and then I disappeared before my very eyes.*

"No," said Matt. "It was only Chuck." He tried to take a few bites of food and act as though all was well and normal. He was not sure how his parents would react to the news that his future self had just appeared and disappeared before his eyes. He was guessing not great. But Matt was on the edge of his seat with excitement. He could barely keep still. He had time-traveled again! Of course he knew he would, but he never expected it to come so soon! His future self hadn't looked at all different than he did now. What was he doing here? Where had he come from? From how far in the future had he traveled? And just plain *how*? Did he have the Obsidian Compass? Or had he figured out another way . . .

He'd been holding something. Not the Obsidian Compass, he was pretty sure, but something similar, like another time-traveling compass. Where did he get it? When?

That night Matt's dreams were more vivid than ever. He was almost convinced they were truly happening. He dreamed of Jia being discarded again and again, dropped in a barren desert, thrown in an angry ocean, or left on an icy mountain to freeze. Jia would plead with Captain Vincent not to leave her, and Captain Vincent would say, "Find Mateo. He's the only one who can save you now," and then Captain Vincent would turn to Matt, only then it wasn't Captain Vincent. It was someone else. Someone blurred, like the camera in his dream was out of focus, except only on the man. Everything else was sharp and clear.

"Help her!" Matt cried. "Don't let him hurt Jia!"

"You heard Captain Vincent," said the blurry man. "Only you can save her, Mateo."

"But how?"

"Your compass, Mateo, use your compass."

"But I don't have a compass!"

Matt woke drenched in sweat, shaking and breathing hard, like he'd just sprinted a mile in his sleep.

Someone turned on a lamp, and Matt flinched at the sudden light.

"Did you have a bad dream?" Ruby asked softly.

Matt wanted to say no, but he was still shaking. Ruby padded over to his bed and sat next to him.

"It's okay," said Ruby. "I have them too. Sometimes I dream that we're on the *Vermillion*, but we can't get home. Or sometimes I dream that we're still stranded on that island with no food or water, and we can't even try to catch fish because we're surrounded by sharks." Ruby shivered a bit.

Matt hadn't given much thought to how Ruby or Corey had been handling things since they'd come home. They seemed fine, but then maybe he did, too, and it was only his insides that were all a mess.

"I keep seeing Jia," he said. "I should have gotten her off the *Vermillion*. I shouldn't have just left her there."

Ruby put her hand over his. "It's not your fault."

Matt took his hand away. "It *is* my fault though. I convinced her to help us. I asked her to betray Captain Vincent so we could get home. And we got home. But she . . ." Matt couldn't finish the sentence.

"We'll find her, Matt," said Ruby.

"What if we don't?" said Matt, choking on the words.

"We will," said Ruby firmly. "Where there's a will, there's a way, right? I mean, before we boarded the *Vermillion*, we never thought we could possibly time-travel, did we? But we did. And then when we were time-traveling, we never thought we'd get home. But we did. And now we're just at the next 'never thought.' It seems impossible, but somehow we'll figure it out. You're the scientist. You should know that better than anyone."

Matt nodded. He should know that better than anyone. The impossible was only impossible until someone broke the bounds of possibility.

Matt thought maybe he should say something about seeing himself in the vineyard. He had meant to tell them right away, but he never got the chance, and now he wasn't even certain that it had really happened. It almost felt like a dream to him now, and even if it did happen, what did it change in this moment? It proved he would time-travel again, he supposed. It wasn't over, so what should he do? Just wait around for something to happen? Or was he supposed to *do* something?

Ruby sat with Matt a while longer, until he stopped

shaking. Eventually she lay down on his bed and fell asleep again. Matt couldn't go back to sleep. He sat in his bed. He looked at the clock. It was just after four a.m.

He looked at his nightstand. There were several books there that he'd brought from home—Einstein, Stephen Hawking, time-travel theory, and a few novels, but at the top of the pile was his notebook. It was warped and many of the pages stuck together, the ink blurred and faded. It had been through a lot, including a dip in the ocean. He picked it up and opened to the page where he'd made notes about his parents' conversation.

Wrangel Island

Chicago, 1893

You know Mateo has something *to do with . . .*

He flipped to the middle of the notebook. Weeks ago, while he'd been on board the *Vermillion*, he'd made several sketches of the Obsidian Compass. He'd wanted to learn how it worked, or at least what dials did what. It ended up being a big part of the reason they were able to get home. The centerpiece looked much like a regular compass and was surrounded by dials with notches, numerals, and symbols.

Matt rummaged through his backpack and found his own compass. It was a simple aluminum compass his dad had given to him when he was little. He used to send Matt, Ruby, and Corey on little treasure hunts and instead of clues he gave them coordinates to follow.

Matt placed his compass on his notebook next to the drawing of the Obsidian Compass. He grabbed a pencil and started sketching around it. He scribbled out some formulas and equations. He didn't notice the sun come up. He barely noticed Corey and Ruby rise and get dressed and say, "Good morning."

"Good morning," he said.

"Whatcha doin'?" Corey asked.

"Just doodling," said Matt.

"Ha-ha, he said *doodling*," said Corey, but Matt didn't reply.

When he came downstairs and his mom offered him breakfast, he said no thank you and went straight to Gaga. She was sitting at the kitchen table with her coffee and a book.

"Gaga, can I use some of the things in the basement?"

"Of course, sweetie, what do you need?"

"I'm not sure. I'm in an experimental stage." Matt had never actually been down to the basement. Gaga said it was full of nothing but junk, mostly their grandfather's tools and things that she'd never gotten rid of.

"How lovely! I love experiments. You feel free to use anything you want down there. Just don't blow the house up, that's all I ask."

Matt agreed to the terms and went directly to the basement, notebook and compass in hand.

Matt rummaged through piles and boxes, unearthing old

clothes, electronics, tools, and memorabilia—old pictures of his dad and Uncle Charles; some of their dad, Matt's grandfather; and some of the whole family. He found a dinosaur of a computer, a broken gold watch, a box of tarnished jewelry, a television that was probably from the sixties, an antique radio, and an old record player. He found plenty of tools too—screwdrivers, chisels, hammers and clamps, and even a blowtorch with heavy leather gloves and a mask. He tested it and a white-blue flame shot out. He got a flash of excitement. That would definitely come in handy with this project. He knew his mom wouldn't approve. She was always nervous about him getting hurt, but Gaga *did* give him permission to use whatever he wanted down here, so he decided it was fine. He'd just take Gaga's request to heart and not blow up the house.

Matt began by dissecting everything, removing wires and nuts and bolts, screws, cogs and gears, links and clasps. He didn't take apart the record player, though, because he found a stack of records and thought some background noise might be good. So he dusted off the record player and plugged it in. He pulled out one of the records from its sleeve and set it on the player. He placed the needle and it screeched and crackled, then came to life. First guitar, then vocals and drums, sounds from decades past.

His dad came downstairs, followed by his mom and then Corey and Ruby.

"What are you doing?" his dad asked over the blaring music.

"Tinkering," said Matt.

"Ha-ha," said Corey. "He said *tinkering.*"

Mr. and Mrs. Hudson looked at each other like they were trying to decide if this was okay or not. Matt paid them no mind. The wheels in his brain were turning. He laid everything out on an old card table like pieces in a jigsaw puzzle. He wasn't sure what he was doing, exactly, but he decided to just start piecing things together, making little patterns and designs, and soon he got into a flow. He felt his hands take over, like he was building something that was already inside of him, digging it up like an archaeologist digs for bones out of the ground. It wasn't science, exactly, but it wasn't just guesswork. He had a gut feeling. Maybe he was foremembering, that feeling like déjà vu that comes when you're thinking or doing something that hasn't yet happened.

Matt worked all day. He didn't come up for lunch, and he only came up for dinner when his mom insisted. He wolfed down his food as quickly as possible. He wanted to get back to work.

"May I ask what you're up to?" his mom asked.

"I'm just experimenting with different things," said Matt. "It's nothing, really."

"You're not doing anything dangerous, are you?" she asked.

Matt shook his head. "I'm being careful." He wiped his mouth with his napkin and stood up. "May I be excused?"

His mother looked at him like she wasn't quite sure who he was. "Rinse your dish, please."

As he headed back to the basement, he heard his mom say, "Is something wrong with him, do you think?"

"Oh no," said Gaga. "This is typical teenage-boy behavior. Right around twelve or thirteen they descend into a dark dungeon of the mind and don't emerge until they're twenty or so. Don't worry, hon. It's perfectly normal."

For the next few weeks, Matt practically lived in the basement, building and torching and welding. He listened to his grandfather's old records while he worked—Aerosmith, Led Zeppelin, Janis Joplin, Joni Mitchell, Queen, Pink Floyd, and The Who. Matt decided he'd been born in the wrong decade because he liked his grandfather's music much better than most of the music the kids at school liked. Maybe it was because he wasn't used to it, but it felt more original, unexpected, eccentric even, but precise and inspired. It was the perfect accompaniment to his work. It gave him the feeling of escaping to another time and place, which of course was exactly what he had in mind.

His parents gave up on making him come up for family meals. He was hardly present anyway, so they left him in the basement. Corey and Ruby brought him food on occasion, which he didn't always eat. They pestered him with questions about what he was doing, and he evaded them with vague answers. He wouldn't show them.

Matt started sleeping in the basement, too, if he did sleep. He'd unearthed a puke-green, moth-eaten couch where he'd crash when he was too sleepy to focus anymore.

He lost track of the days and hours. He never knew what time it was, barely noticed if it was day or night. He torched, pounded, sculpted, welded, connected. He ran tests and experiments. Then he'd pull everything apart and start again. He scribbled more formulas and equations in his notebook, sketched new designs, found new pieces and ways to connect them all. It was like he was in a giant maze, feeling his way through. When he came up against a dead end, he'd just turn around and go the other way. He kept going and going and going until he couldn't go anymore, until his brain was fuzzy, and his eyes betrayed him and closed without his permission. Then he'd always dream of Jia. Jia alone, afraid, lost . . .

4

Spying

Over a century and a thousand miles away, the city of Chicago was hosting the World's Columbian Exposition, celebrating the four hundredth anniversary of Christopher Columbus's arrival to the new world in 1493. The air was hot, humid, and tingling with magic.

White classical buildings had been built right on the edge of sparkling lagoons that flowed into Lake Michigan. Great ships and yachts of differing design dotted the shoreline. Among all these, resplendent in black with gold trim and three tall masts with white sails, was the magical, time-traveling ship *Vermillion*. At the top of the mainmast was a black flag emblazoned with a white compass star and a red V at the center.

Jia sat cross-legged in the crow's nest of the *Vermillion* looking out toward the magnificent city that seemed to have been fabricated out of clouds and dreams. Her favorite was the big white wheel, suspended in the air and rotating slowly in the sky. It was called a *Ferris wheel*, she had learned, named after the man who had designed it. She'd overheard Captain Vincent tell the crew in a scornful tone that it had been built to rival the Eiffel Tower in Paris.

Jia felt a sting just at the thought. It reminded her of the Hudsons. She brushed her fingers over their names carved in the mast of the ship, as she had done a hundred times since they'd gone. Mateo, Corey, Ruby. Paris had been their first mission together, stealing the *Mona Lisa* from the Museé de Louvre in 1911. They'd become her friends. She'd never had real friends before. Before she'd come on board the *Vermillion*, she'd scarcely dared hope for a kind word. Captain Vincent had been kind, at least at first. He had given her food and clothing and purpose. She almost forgot about her life in China, and she thought she'd never want for anything ever again. And then the Hudsons came along. She didn't know how wonderful it would be to have other children on board who she could talk to and play with. Albert was about her age, but he had never been one to play or even talk much. He was far too serious. And Pike was sweet, but she was quite a bit younger than Jia, and she never talked at all. The Hudsons were different. Especially Matt. She'd never felt like anyone truly understood her until she met him. He was smart and a little bit odd, just like her. He liked to build and experiment and invent things just like her. Jia smiled as she remembered the day she and Matt spent trying to wire the *Vermillion* with electricity. They had zapped themselves until their hair was standing on end.

But now they were gone. Jia herself had betrayed Captain Vincent to help them get home to 2019 New York, despite knowing how important the Hudsons were to the captain's mission. His wrath had been a hurricane. The moment he'd discovered her duplicity, he'd hit her in the head hard enough to knock her out. She'd missed everything that happened in New York, which she had since learned was quite a lot. When she finally came to, she saw Matt for only a moment, chasing after her and shouting, but her brain was fuzzy and slow, and Captain Vincent had already turned the dials of the compass. The *Vermillion* started to transform, and then it disappeared, leaving the Hudsons behind.

Jia knew she would be discarded immediately. The *Vermillion* seemed to roar as it transformed into a train on a long stretch of barren wasteland, no trees or shrubs, just dry grass and dirt. She couldn't begin to guess where they were. Captain Vincent grabbed Jia by her vest and tossed her over the back of the still-moving train. She screamed and clung to the railing. Captain Vincent pried away the fingers of her left hand, then began working on the right. And that's when she saw it. Dangling from the rail right in front of her face was Matt's bracelet! The one he always wore with the Chinese character etched on the stone. *Take it!* the voice in her head told her. It was almost as if the *Vermillion* wanted her to find it. She didn't think twice. She snatched the bracelet with her left hand, just as Captain Vincent ripped her right hand away from the rail. She fell hard and tumbled in the dirt and grass. She clutched the bracelet tightly to her chest as she rolled and rolled. Finally she came to a stop, but she kept her eyes closed. She didn't want to open them because then she would be truly alone.

But when she opened her eyes, the *Vermillion* was still there, puffing steam and growling like an angry bull. The *Vermillion* had stopped. Captain Vincent was standing on the caboose of the train from which he'd just thrown Jia, cursing and furiously turning the dials of the Obsidian Compass, but nothing happened. And then he saw her.

Captain Vincent dragged her back on board, boxed her ears, and told her if she had any will to live she had better repair the *Vermillion* and fast. Jia didn't say a word. She went all over the train, checking the engine and the gears, every possible thing. Nothing was wrong from what she could tell, but she gave the appearance of making repairs, pulling out her hammer and wrench, tightening nuts and bolts, and the next time Captain Vincent turned the dials, the *Vermillion* traveled without a hitch.

Jia thought she might be safe then, that Captain Vincent might have let off some steam and would let her stay on the

Vermillion, but no. Captain Vincent tried to discard her again. This time he dropped her in the middle of the ocean, just like he had the Hudsons, only there was no nearby island, nor any land that she could see. As soon as she hit the water, the *Vermillion* disappeared. Jia couldn't swim. She had thrashed in the water in a panic, convinced she would drown. She almost did. Her vest full of tools was like a weight to aid in sinking her to the bottom. She clawed at the water, kicked her legs as hard as she could, but it was no use. She went under, convinced this was the end, but just as she was ready to give up and let the sea have her, she was caught in a net. It pulled her out of the water and she was hauled up onto a fishing boat and dumped on the deck.

Jia coughed and cleared the salt water from her eyes. Brocco and Wiley, her longtime crewmates and friends, looked down on her. She silently begged them to protect her.

"You know something, Captain?" Wiley had said, his pipe bobbing up and down in his mouth. "I'm starting to think the ship don't want to let go of her just yet."

"Yeah," said Brocco. "Seems like the *Vermillion*'s got some affection for Li'l Hammerhead."

"She's sabotaging the ship somehow," said Captain Vincent, giving Jia a rough kick in the ribs. She cried out in pain.

"Well, it's a smart move if you ask me," said Brocco. "If you don't want to be discarded, that is."

"Sho' is," said Wiley. "Make yourself indispensable and

you won't get left behind."

"Indeed," said Captain Vincent. "But such betrayal cannot go unpunished. I will not tolerate it." He pulled out his sword. Jia curled up inside the tangled net. She squeezed her eyes shut. She winced as there were a few slashing sounds, but she felt no pain. When she opened her eyes, she found the net had been cut, and also a good chunk of her black hair. "Fix the ship," said Captain Vincent, and he walked away.

It wasn't until later that Jia started to guess why Captain Vincent hadn't been able to discard her. She hadn't sabotaged the *Vermillion*. There was nothing wrong with any part of the ship. But Jia still had Matt's bracelet. She'd held on to the bracelet for dear life, and the bracelet had saved her. That was the only explanation. She remembered when the Hudsons had been discarded, the *Vermillion* had done the same thing. The captain had dropped them and moved the dials of the compass. They started to travel and then they were whipped back as though the *Vermillion* had been caught on a fishing line. Jia had always thought it had something to do with the Hudsons, but what if it was something else? Something the Hudsons had? Could Matt's bracelet be connected to the *Vermillion* somehow? Or the Obsidian Compass? Had Matt somehow left it for her protection?

Not that it offered much protection in the end. She wasn't discarded, but true to Captain Vincent's word she was punished. She was shunned and ignored by the crew, overworked and half-starved. She had nothing but scraps from the table, and she was not allowed a room of her own. She was forced to sleep on the deck of the ship, even in the rain, and sometimes the *Vermillion* would transform and toss her about like a rag doll. Some days she almost wished to go back to China, to take back the choices and blind promises she'd made. It had all seemed right and good at the time, but now she wished she'd never come on board the *Vermillion*.

Jia had no idea where or when the *Vermillion* traveled. Not only was she excluded from any missions, she was also excluded from any conversations. She tried to spy on Captain Vincent and the crew, to try to figure out what was going on, but Captain Vincent had probably told Santiago, his super intelligent pet rat, to keep an eye on her. Every time she came near enough to hear conversation, the white rat would appear suddenly and hiss and glare at her with his creepy red eyes. Then Captain Vincent would tell her to go scrub the deck or patch the sails or clean the toilets. She thought about sabotaging the plumbing as revenge. It was *her* design, after all, but she knew it would do her little good. Captain Vincent had the upper hand. He had all the power. She was stuck.

She could run away somewhere, try to make it on her own, but the thought of being stuck in one time and place without a friend in the world terrified her, and she had just a tiny ray of hope that somehow she'd see the Hudsons again. Jia didn't regret helping the Hudsons. She was only sorry she hadn't been able to escape with them. They were her friends now more than ever, even if they were miles and years away. If she could go back, she'd do it again. She assumed Captain Vincent would be traveling back to New York to get them, and when he did, Jia would be ready. She'd run away, find the Hudsons, warn them about Captain Vincent's plans, and then maybe, just maybe, they'd invite her to stay with them. She could offer to repair all their gadgets and things, like their refrigerator, and those little toaster boxes, and their electricity. She could be the official Repair Master (and family friend) of the Hudsons.

But so far, for whatever reason, Captain Vincent had made no attempt to travel back to New York. They'd gone back to Nowhere in No Time for a little while. There Captain Vincent had locked himself in his office for two days, with no company except Santiago. Jia could only guess what they were scheming. After that they'd traveled to two or three different locations, though Jia couldn't tell where or when, exactly. She thought she'd overheard Captain Vincent talking to Wiley and Brocco about picking up some new crew member, but hadn't seen anyone besides the regular crew, so she must have misheard.

Then, out of the blue, they'd come to Chicago in 1893 where a big fair was happening. The World's Columbian Exposition. Jia had heard much about this fair. Wiley had read several books about it, and she'd overheard him telling the captain and crew all about the buildings and gardens, the exhibits and shows and food. It lasted for six months and millions of people attended from around the world. Jia thought it was magnificent, magical. It was also extremely warm, the air so thick and humid you didn't breathe it in so much as swallow it down. There were tens of thousands of people on the shore of the lake, swarming the beach like a colony of ants. Jia had never seen anything like it, and she had seen a lot.

They'd arrived in Chicago early in the morning. Captain Vincent had sent Brocco and Wiley out on some mission hours ago, but they had not yet returned. She'd seen very little of Albert or Pike, but Captain Vincent was now at the helm of the ship, looking out toward the city.

Santiago poked his head out of Captain Vincent's coat pocket and climbed atop his shoulder. Captain Vincent said something to the rat and the rat appeared to answer. Jia knew that sometimes Captain Vincent spoke to Santiago as if he were a trusted adviser. Only to the rat did the captain divulge all his secrets and future plans.

Jia quietly climbed down from the crow's nest and tiptoed over to where Captain Vincent stood. She hid behind some crates but was close enough to hear what he was saying.

"They call this the White City, Santiago," said the captain. "You'd fit in well here, no?"

Santiago gave a noncommittal squeak.

Jia poked her head out from behind the crates. Captain

Vincent held the Obsidian Compass in his hands, circling his fingers around the dials. "I will need your help with this mission, Santiago," said Captain Vincent. "I trust no one but you now. We must work together, you and I."

Santiago squeaked, almost as if he were speaking real words. Captain Vincent seemed to be able to understand. Jia used to think it was interesting and magical. Now it just felt creepy.

Someone shouted in the distance. A gondola was coming toward the ship. Wiley and Brocco were clumsily rowing together, each with an oar. Their strokes were uneven and out of sync, so the gondola made slow and crooked progress.

"We got news, Captain!" said Brocco as he struggled to push his oar through the water. He was wearing a red velvet coat and top hat. The top portion of the hat was shredded, as though he'd set a bomb off on top of it. His clumpy hair was crawling over the edges like a bunch of hairy spiders.

Wiley was in his usual brown suit and fedora, his pipe bobbing up and down in his mouth as he rowed. When they finally boarded the *Vermillion*, Brocco bowed to the captain like a subject to his sovereign. Ever since Jia's betrayal of Captain Vincent, Brocco had been trying to prove to the captain that he was completely loyal and trustworthy. It seemed to be having the opposite effect on the captain, however, for he gave Brocco such a look of derision, even Jia could see it from her narrow hiding space behind the crates.

"Well?" said the captain. "I hope you have something of value to tell me this time."

"Yes, sir," said Brocco. "We found 'em! The Hudsons are here!"

Jia's heart jumped into her throat. Mateo? He was here? Now? And Corey and Ruby?

Captain Vincent squeezed the Obsidian Compass in his fist. "And? Where are they?" he demanded, the impatience in his voice rising. "I gave you express instructions to bring me Mateo!"

"We tried, Captain," said Brocco, "but someone else got to 'im first."

"What do you mean *someone else*? Who?"

"Some little lady with a gun! She nearly shot my hand off, and she ruined my new silk hat!" He pointed to his busted hat.

Captain Vincent was silent. He gazed out across the lake to the gleaming city on the shore. "Brocco," he said quietly. "Get your best guns and plenty of ammunition. Armor might not be a bad idea either."

"Are we going to *war*?" Brocco clapped his hands and rubbed them together.

"We're already at war, Brocco," said Captain Vincent. "We're going to battle. I need Mateo. I expect you to procure him for me at all costs."

"Okay, but what do I do if the mother gets in the way? You know how protective she can be."

Captain Vincent looked blankly at Brocco. Jia thought his eyes looked empty, dead. Cold stone had more life than his eyes. "Kill her if you must. Kill them all. I don't care. Just bring me Mateo."

Jia gasped, then covered her mouth. No one seemed to have noticed, thankfully. Brocco gulped, eyes wide. He looked sideways at Wiley, like he was hoping he'd have something to say.

Wiley removed his hat and pipe, which Jia knew meant he felt strongly about whatever he was going to say. "With all my respectfulness, Captain, I don't think this kind of violence is necessary," he said. "It was just one little lady with a rifle. Surely we can get the boy without *killing* anyone?"

Wiley was a skilled pickpocket and seemed to have no qualms stealing for Captain Vincent, but he had always been a bit squeamish about violence, especially guns. He thought all problems could be solved with words and books.

"When we are met with violence, we must respond in kind, Wiley," said Captain Vincent. "An eye for an eye. That's in the Good Book itself, isn't it?"

"Sure," said Wiley, sticking his pipe back in his mouth. "Though I think Gandhi said something like, 'An eye for an eye leaves the whole world blind.' Hard to steal anything without eyes."

Captain Vincent gave Wiley a cool gaze. "Your wisdom is always appreciated, Wiley. Of course I don't expect you to shoot any guns. Your skills are of a different variety and will be needed elsewhere."

Wiley gave a short bow. "Sure, Captain, whatever you need." But Jia thought maybe Wiley wasn't feeling quite so enthusiastic about his job as he had in the past. He, too, felt the shift. Ever since the Hudsons had left, the balance had been upset. What balance, Jia wasn't sure. All she knew was that things were not stable. Something was going to topple soon, and she had a growing dread it was a big something.

"Prepare yourselves now," said Captain Vincent. "We must get to the Hudsons at once, before it's too late. Send Albert and Pike to me, will you?"

"Aye aye, Captain!" said Brocco, saluting, and he and Wiley went belowdecks.

Jia watched as Captain Vincent paced back and forth on the deck, fingers continually circling the Obsidian Compass. A few minutes later Albert appeared, followed closely by Pike in her pillowcase dress lined with safety pins and cinched at the waist with a knotted and frayed rope. She looked curiously up at Captain Vincent. Jia didn't know what to make of Pike anymore. She had always thought Pike was more loyal to her than Captain Vincent. She had even helped the Hudsons break into Captain Vincent's office when they'd been trying to get home, but in the end, it seemed she really was loyal to the captain. Only Jia was the traitor.

Albert was still dressed in a long nightshirt. There hadn't

been much of a schedule on board the *Vermillion* in the last few weeks. Captain Vincent roused the crew at all hours, day or night, and traveled without warning. You had to sleep when you could. Albert hastily put on his spectacles over sleepy eyes.

"Yes, Captain?" said Albert eagerly as though he'd been waiting to be called, like a dog to his master. Jia was disgusted by him. She could not believe she'd ever considered him a friend. He didn't know the first thing about friendship or loyalty. Captain Vincent knew this, too, Jia realized, and he would use it to his advantage.

"You see the Ferris wheel?" said Captain Vincent.

Albert glanced uneasily at the giant, rotating wheel in the distance. He nodded. Jia knew he didn't like it. She'd heard him say it was the devil's device and would topple over in the wind and kill a thousand people.

"I want you to go ride it and keep watch for our friends, the Hudsons."

Albert didn't even attempt to hide his disgust. "The *Hudsons*? I thought we'd gotten rid of them for good."

"No," said Captain Vincent. "It seems we have unfinished business, and I need you to keep a lookout for them. The best views of the city are from the Ferris wheel."

Albert swallowed and stood straight, trying not to look scared. "Can't Jia do that?"

Captain Vincent stiffened, his nostrils flared a little.

Albert flinched and stuttered. "I j-just mean . . . she has better eyesight, sir. She'd spot them easier, and she's better with strange contraptions. What if it breaks while I'm at the top?"

At this Pike looked directly toward Jia, as if she knew exactly where she was. Jia pulled back.

"Yes, but I can't trust Jia anymore, can I?" said Captain Vincent. "Her loyalties appear to be with the Hudsons, and I can't risk her interfering, giving us away. *You* are the only one I trust to fulfill this mission, Albert."

With these words Albert squared his shoulders and puffed out his chest. "Yes, sir, I won't let you down."

"Good. Now go change into something suitable. It won't be nearly as satisfying to thwart your nemesis while wearing your nightshirt, will it?"

Albert flushed but nodded and went belowdecks. Jia remained hidden as Captain Vincent stood on the deck, his fingers circling the compass.

"It's only a matter of time, Santiago," said Captain Vincent. "Soon we'll be unstoppable. No . . . *invincible.* How do you like the sound of that? Vince the Invincible. Ha! That's what they'll call me throughout the world and beyond, perhaps. But first, we must find Mateo Hudson."

Santiago hissed, baring his long white teeth. At first Jia thought he had spotted her, but then she realized he wasn't hissing at her. He was hissing at the mention of Matt.

"Yes, I know he isn't your favorite," said Captain Vincent.

"He's not mine either. He has a weak stomach, and he lacks charm, but we can't mistake strength or charm for importance or usefulness. He *is* important, perhaps even essential to our cause. It was wise of our Bonbon to keep the letter hidden from me."

Jia wondered what letter he was speaking about. What did it say? What did it have to do with Matt? And what did Captain Vincent mean by *invincible*?

Captain Vincent turned the dials of the Obsidian Compass. The water rushed around the side of the ship, and the *Vermillion* started to transform. Jia braced herself as the floor beneath her began to shrink. The sails lowered and folded in on themselves, sinking into the deck of the ship while water shot up all around. The *Vermillion* plunged into the lake and then reappeared on land.

The ship had turned into a streetcar. Jia was sitting on the back of it. The horn beeped as it drove through the crowds. She looked for familiar faces. There were so many people it overwhelmed her, but she would have to find Matt before Captain Vincent did. This was her one chance. She had to warn him and hopefully get away with him.

When the *Vermillion* slowed, Jia hopped down and slipped through the heavy throng. She was so busy searching for her friends, she didn't see the white rat scurrying behind her.

5
Birthday Surprises

June 1, 2019
Hudson River Valley, New York

"Wake up, brother!" Matt woke to Corey jumping on top of him like a giant puppy. He groaned and tried to shove him off, but it didn't work. He just kept bouncing. The old couch he was sleeping on in the basement was very bouncy.

"Corey, get off of him," said Ruby. "It won't do any good to kill him on his birthday."

His birthday? Had that much time really passed? Matt had forgotten. He'd lost track of the date. He'd lost track of just about everything.

Corey finally rolled off of him. Matt sat up, his head spinning a little.

Ruby gasped. "Matt . . ." She stared at him like he was a ghost or something.

"What?" he said, looking all around.

"Bro," said Corey. "What *is* that?" He pointed at something. Matt looked down at his lap and realized what they were staring at.

"Oh. That. That's nothing." He tried to slip it in his pocket, but Corey was too fast. He snatched the thing away from Matt.

"Hey! Give it back!" Matt swiped at Corey, but he dodged him and jumped over the couch.

"Dude," said Corey. "This doesn't look like *nothing*."

"Matt," said Ruby, her voice full of reverence and awe. "You built a compass. I mean, like the Obsidian Compass."

"It looks just like the real compass, doesn't it?" said Corey. "Except not obsidian, obviously."

"Also, it doesn't work." Matt was finally able to snatch his compass away from Corey. "And it's not yours." He looked down at the hunk of metal. It did indeed look a great deal like the Obsidian Compass, made with a mix of metals—aluminum, titanium, copper, silver, gold.

"But maybe it could work," said Ruby. "I mean, we know the Obsidian Compass works, so why can't this one?"

"I don't know," said Matt. "Maybe because it's not magical?"

"Maybe you just need the magic ingredient."

"Har har," said Matt. He suddenly felt very grumpy. And stupid.

"So this is what you've been doing all this time," said Ruby. "Why wouldn't you tell us?"

Matt shrugged. "I didn't want you to laugh at me, I guess, or think it was stupid." Also he didn't want to talk about it or have to explain anything. It was supposed to be just for him. Something to keep his mind off things, give him hope, but now that Corey and Ruby had seen it, hope withered, and he suddenly felt foolish.

"Neither of us are laughing, bro," said Corey. "And that's saying something. You know I like to laugh as much as possible."

"And it's not stupid," said Ruby. "It's brilliant. If anyone could build a time-traveling compass, it's you."

"Yeah well, it won't work," said Matt, "and this is the last day the *Vermillion* can travel."

Corey and Ruby didn't say anything to that. They just let it hang in the air for a moment, heavy and full. A door was closing, and Matt didn't know how to keep it open. He was beginning to think he'd imagined seeing himself that day in the vineyard. It had been a hopeful hallucination.

Finally, Corey broke the silence. "Well, if it makes you feel any better, you definitely got the mad scientist look going for you. When's the last time you showered?"

Matt glared at Corey, but he was right. He couldn't even remember the last time he'd showered or changed his clothes or had a decent meal. He smelled something cooking upstairs and his stomach rumbled.

"Mom's making strawberry crepes!" said Ruby. "And we're

going for a hike. She says you have to come out of this hole and get some fresh air today, no matter what."

Matt guessed that was a fair demand. He also couldn't remember the last time he'd seen the light of day or breathed fresh air.

"So come on!" said Ruby, pulling Matt by the hand. "I want breakfast."

Matt slipped his compass in the pocket of his shorts, grabbed his Mets hat, and followed Corey and Ruby upstairs.

For some reason it didn't feel like his birthday. Maybe it was because he was away from home. If they were still in New York they would go for pizza in Brooklyn, see a Mets game, or if the Mets were away, they might play a family game in Central Park, then go for banana pudding at Magnolia Bakery. They couldn't do any of that here.

Or maybe the real reason it didn't feel like his birthday was because it wasn't, at least not in terms of the actual days, months, and years he'd been alive. If he were going by that measure, instead of the calendar date, he had likely turned twelve weeks ago, while traveling on the *Vermillion*. He remembered how Jia didn't really know how old she was exactly. He'd thought that was very odd at the time, but he was starting to understand. When you're time-traveling, timelines get a bit jumbled and confusing. He guessed he was experiencing that a little bit now.

After breakfast, the family packed some lunches and went out for their hike. There were several trails not far from Gaga's house, in the Catskill Mountains (or just *the Catskills*, as Mr. Hudson always called them). Mrs. Hudson had chosen a hike that would lead to a waterfall. Matt was surprised at how relaxed his parents seemed. If they were worried that something might happen today, they were hiding it well.

Matt was glad to have the sun on his face again. He was just beginning to realize how cooped up he'd been these last few weeks, how good it felt to get fresh air and move and make his lungs expand. The sky was blue and cloudless, and the air was refreshingly cool with just a faint breeze.

Finally, they reached the crest of a ridge and were faced with a waterfall cascading over stacks and layers of rocks covered in green moss and vines. A cool mist sprayed on Matt's face and arms. It was a beautiful place, and they were the only people here. It almost made him feel like he was in a different time altogether, or at least like time was removed.

They found a dry spot and spread out a picnic blanket. They ate fruit and veggies and sandwiches. It reminded Matt of picnics on the deck of the *Vermillion*. Sometimes they'd had food fights. Once Jia threw an entire blueberry pie in his face. The memory made him all at once happy and sad and confused.

After they ate, Corey and Mr. Hudson started playing catch, and Ruby was fighting a tree with her stick. Matt found himself alone with his mom, a rare thing indeed. He wanted to make the most of it, ask her more about Marius Quine, the Obsidian Compass, and this mysterious "powerful thing" Captain Vincent was searching for. But he didn't know how to ask about those things directly, not without rousing her suspicions.

"Mom?" said Matt.

"Yes, *chéri*?"

"Do you ever miss it? The *Vermillion*, I mean, and being Captain Bonnaire." He had learned only little bits and pieces of his mother's life as captain of the *Vermillion*. It wasn't like she told them grand tales of her adventures around the fire. Unless one of the kids had asked her a direct question, she'd hardly spoken of anything to do with time travel. Matt wondered if that's because it would surface memories she didn't want to relive. Maybe it was a life she wanted to forget.

"In some ways, yes," said Mrs. Hudson. "I miss the adventure every now and then, the magic of the ship and the compass. And I miss my friends."

Matt knew that the crew he'd known on the *Vermillion* had not been the same crew his mother had commanded when she had been captain, save for Captain Vincent and the moody French cook, Agnes. "What happened to them?" Matt asked.

Mrs. Hudson's face contracted ever so slightly, as though the very thought of her friends caused her pain. "I don't know," she said. "I thought I took precautions for them to be safe without me, but things did not go as planned. When I knew that Vincent had the compass, I feared the worst. He did not always see eye to eye with some of my crew, and naturally they would distrust him once I had disappeared. I hope they were safe and lived happy lives, but it's likely Captain Vincent discarded them."

Matt winced. In his head he knew the same was likely true of Jia. He just didn't know if he could say it out loud like that, so blunt and ugly.

His mom put a hand over his. "It's not your fault, you know, what happened to your friend? You mustn't blame yourself. I know it's hard, but you mustn't."

Matt nodded, but he felt a lump form in his throat, and he didn't think he could talk about Jia. He hastily changed the subject.

"You never meant for Captain Vincent to have the compass then?" he asked.

"No," said Mrs. Hudson. "I mean, I did intend it for him at one time. We were . . . close, but I had reasons to mistrust him, and when I finally decided to leave, I arranged for another member of my crew to take over the *Vermillion* and the compass, one whom I could trust to use it wisely. Or as wisely as possible, at least."

"Then how did he get it?"

"Truthfully I don't know," said Mrs. Hudson. "I thought

I'd planned everything so carefully, but even the best-laid plans can go wrong. I knew just after the twins were born. We were coming home from the hospital and a volunteer hailed us a minivan taxi. We almost got inside, the whole family, including Grandma Gloria, and then I saw the mark of the *Vermillion* on the hood, and I knew. It's funny, for a brief moment I was thrilled. I thought, Oh, the old crew's come to congratulate me! We'll have a little party, relive old times! And then I saw Vincent. I saw the hatred and anger in his face, and there was none of my old crew, and I knew it had all gone wrong. The moment he saw that I'd seen him he disappeared."

"Didn't you ever think about trying to save them?" said Matt. "Your old crew, I mean."

"How could I?" said Mrs. Hudson. "I had given up the compass."

"Couldn't you have gotten in contact with someone who could help?"

"Like who?"

"Like the inventor, Marius Quine. He'd be able to help, wouldn't he? I mean, he gave you the compass in the first place, didn't he? So he must be on your side."

Mrs. Hudson bristled a bit. "Maybe he is, but I have no way of contacting him. Any dealings I've had with him have been strictly on his terms. I've never been able to contact him or find him. He can only come to me."

"Who *is* he anyway?"

His mom was thoughtful for a moment. "I suppose he's a dreamer, like you."

"Me?"

"Yes. You've always had big ideas, big plans. I've always known you would do great things, Mateo. But keep in mind, try as we might, we all make mistakes. We all have regrets. Some we can fix, and some we can't. It's important to know the difference, understand?"

Matt nodded, though he wasn't certain he did understand. Was he supposed to give up? Move on? Was it just wishful thinking to believe their time-travel adventures weren't over? Would he never see Jia again? He reached for his own compass inside his pocket. He had felt hopeful while making it, and now he just felt sad and heavy. His optimism that it might work was quickly chipping away. He clutched it tightly, wondering if he needed to let go.

They cleaned up their picnic, took a few family pictures by the waterfall, and began their hike out. Corey sang "This Is the Song That Never Ends" about fifty times until Ruby threatened to end him if he didn't shut up, and then he started singing "99 Bottles" while Ruby plugged her ears.

Mrs. Hudson suddenly stopped in front of them on the trail and held up her hand. "Quiet," she said as she cocked her ear. Matt could hear a faint, steady beat. It got louder and louder. He suddenly felt his body lock up.

"Helicopter," said Mr. Hudson.

Matt felt like the world was spinning around him, like the earth was slipping beneath his feet. He was falling. Falling toward the ocean . . .

Someone grabbed him by the arm. His mom yanked him off the path and into the shelter of the trees. The Hudsons all huddled together. Matt was pressed against his mom, her arms wrapped tightly around his chest. The helicopter passed, and the beat of its rotating blades faded, and there was nothing but the sounds of birds and little critters rustling around in the shrubs.

Mr. Hudson told them to wait while he searched the area. Matt looked over at Corey and Ruby. They were huddled up against a tree, while Matt was still held tightly by his mother. He could feel her trembling. He searched his memory and suddenly realized that she always held on to him, not Corey or Ruby. Why? Did she think he was in more danger than them for some reason?

A few minutes later, Mr. Hudson returned and told them it was all clear. Mrs. Hudson loosened her grip on Matt, but she kept a hand on his arm for the next half mile, and he felt her twitch at every sound and movement. Finally, she let him go and told him to walk ahead of her, said that he should set the pace. Matt knew she just wanted to be able to keep her eyes on him.

* * *

When they arrived home, Gaga was waiting for them with a dinner of fettucine Alfredo, asparagus, fruit salad, and a big pitcher of grape juice for the kids and a bottle of wine for the adults. There was triple-layer cake sitting on the counter too. Chocolate with peanut butter frosting. Matt could smell it. All this peanut butter was making him nostalgic for the *Vermillion*. He imagined the crew bursting into the house. Wouldn't that be a sight?

"Twelve! Practically a teenager!" said Gaga, as they cleared the dishes. "Watch out, Matthew and Belamie, they can be pretty explosive."

"Not my Mateo," said Mrs. Hudson. "He's always calm, always makes good choices."

"Yes, I thought the same thing about my Matty," said Gaga, shooting a severe look toward her son, "and before I knew it, he was stealing cars and crashing them into barns."

Corey almost dropped a stack of plates. "Whaaaaat?"

"Mom!" said Mr. Hudson, his face flushing red. "I didn't *steal* the car! Chuck said I could borrow it any time I wanted."

"You stole Chuck's car?" said Ruby. "That rusty old bus?"

"It's a classic," said Mr. Hudson. "But a little more difficult to steer than I anticipated."

Mrs. Hudson put a hand on Matt's shoulder. "My Mateo will not be stealing cars or driving them, will you, Mateo?"

Matt shook his head. He didn't think he'd have a chance to drive a car even if he wanted to. His mother barely let him ride in one.

"You'll have to let them go someday, Belamie," said Gaga.

Mrs. Hudson stiffened and opened her mouth to make some retort, but Mr. Hudson jumped in.

"Let's have cake, shall we?" he said, jumping up from the table. "I'll get the lighter!"

Mr. Hudson lit the candles, and Gaga carried the cake toward Matt.

"Twins, get the lights!" she said.

Corey and Ruby went and turned off the lights. With the shades drawn it was quite dark except for the cake topped with twelve flickering candles. The peanut butter aroma wafted up Matt's nose. It almost made him dizzy. He felt like the room was shifting ever so slightly.

They sang "Happy Birthday." Mr. Hudson sang very off-key. He'd never been able to carry a tune, which always made the rest of the family laugh. Corey, however, sang opera-style and sounded surprisingly good, especially at the end when he raised the final three notes above the rest. Everyone clapped and cheered, and Corey took a bow.

"Make a wish, Mateo!" said Ruby.

Make a wish. What should he wish for? He reached in his pocket, grasped his compass. It was a silly wish. Nothing would come of it of course, but . . .

"Quick before the candles melt," said Gaga.

"Here, I'll help you," said Corey. He took a deep breath.

"Don't!" Matt laughed as he tried to push Corey away. But Corey was like an overzealous puppy. He jumped onto a chair and leaned over Matt as he tried to blow out his candles. Matt pitched forward and went right into the cake. The candles went out, and the room went dark, almost pitch-black.

"Aw, man, Corey!" Matt pulled himself up, cake and frosting all over his hands and shirt. And his compass. He'd been holding it when he blew out his candles, and now it was smeared with globs of peanut butter frosting. It would take him forever to clean it.

He tried to rub it off on his shirt. The compass made a small but distinct *click!*

"What was that noise?" said Mrs. Hudson. "Mateo?"

"Ruby, turn on the lights," said Mr. Hudson.

Matt couldn't speak. He felt a strange sensation overcome him, a faint tingling from head to toe. And then . . .

Thpt!

When the lights flicked on, Matt was gone.

6

Retro-Mom

When Matt was in third grade, he'd conducted a science experiment where he placed a boiled egg on top of a narrow bottle with a lit candle at the bottom. The heat expanded the molecules, creating a vacuum that then sucked the egg through the narrow opening. Matt now knew what it felt like to be the egg. He was currently being sucked through a very narrow bottleneck. He could feel it squeezing his guts, his brains, his eyeballs, until finally *phlp!* he shot out of the end.

It was dark and cold wherever he was, and when he tried to take a breath he started to choke and cough, but no sound came out. Only bubbles. He was in water. He saw weak gray light above, and with burning lungs and aching limbs he clawed his way to the surface. Matt gasped for breath and then coughed the water out of his lungs. He treaded water frantically, turning in all directions. Water, water, water, sky, sky, sky. Land! He was quite far from the shore, but there was a city with buildings and boats dotting the shoreline. Where was he? What had just happened? One moment he had been blowing out his birthday candles and the next . . .

Matt lifted his hand that had been holding his compass. Globs of frosting and a few cake crumbs were still stuck in the grooves. The frosting . . . it was peanut butter frosting. Peanut butter . . .

Peanut butter!

Matt laughed out loud and punched his fist out of the water, splashing himself in the face. Peanut butter was the magic ingredient! His compass worked! *It worked!*

And now what? Where and when had he traveled? Matt looked at the compass again and tried to decipher where he'd had the settings. He remembered while running tests on the compass, he'd put in different dates and coordinates. He'd written them down in his notebook, but he couldn't recall the last one he'd entered.

Something moved beneath him.

Matt flailed his arms as he momentarily went under water. He kicked his legs furiously. He pictured a shark coming after him. The theme music for *Jaws* played in his head.

He felt tremors from deep down. The water darkened beneath him. This was bigger than a shark, whatever it was. Maybe it was a whale, like in *Moby Dick*, or a giant squid, like in *Twenty Thousand Leagues Under the Sea*, sucking him into its giant tentacles. But then he realized it couldn't be any of those things. This water wasn't salty, it was fresh. He had to be in a lake.

The water began to bubble and churn. Matt grasped for the compass and frantically tried to turn the dials. He didn't think about where he would be going. He just knew he had to get out of here, but before he could complete the first turn, something caught his feet from underneath.

Matt shouted as he was pushed up and out of the water. A thick beam rose up between his arms and legs. Matt grasped onto it, whatever it was, as he was carried higher and higher into the sky.

It was a ship. He was holding on to a mast while white sails unfurled like giant wings all around him. A small platform appeared beneath him, then circular bars. A flag snapped out in front of his face. Matt's heart skipped a few beats. It was black with a white compass star and a red V in the center.

This wasn't just any ship. He was in the crow's nest of the *Vermillion*! There was his name carved on the mast, his and Corey's and Ruby's, just as they had been before.

Matt looked down on the deck. He didn't see anyone, but he wasn't sure if he should go down. What if this was a time when he was on the ship? He couldn't risk seeing himself. Then again, he already knew his past self on board the *Vermillion* never did see his future self, so he was pretty sure he was safe in that regard. But what if it was after he'd left? Then he was in an even more precarious position. Captain Vincent was his enemy now, and by extension, all the crew, except Jia, of course. Could Jia be here now? Was it possible that Matt had intercepted the *Vermillion* before Captain Vincent could discard Jia? He could rescue her. He could take her back with him to New York, assuming he could get back . . .

Matt waited a few more minutes. Still no one came above deck. Slowly, he climbed down from the crow's nest and landed on the main deck. He tiptoed quietly toward the stairs that would lead to belowdecks. It felt strange to be back on the *Vermillion*. It had only been a matter of weeks, but it felt like years, and somehow the ship *felt* different. It all looked the same, but it was different somehow. Perhaps it was after he'd left. Maybe the *Vermillion* could sense an intruder.

Bang!

Something whistled right past Matt's ear. He ducked down and covered his head.

Matt heard footsteps coming toward him, and then the heavy *click* of someone cocking their gun. "Who are you?"

Matt slowly uncovered his head and looked up. Whatever he was expecting to see, it surely wasn't a little girl aiming a rifle right at his head. But that's what he saw. She was young, probably only nine or ten. She was smaller than Ruby. She had long brown hair pulled into a messy braid. She wore a blue dress that reminded Matt of *Little House on the Prairie*, and she held a double-barreled shotgun that looked bigger and heavier than her, but she looked sure and confident. Matt was guessing she had good reason to be.

"I said who are you?" the girl repeated. "Where did you come from? You spying on Captain Bonnaire? No lies. I can always smell a lie, and liars deserve to be shot like a rabid dog."

Captain Bonnaire . . . This girl was one of his mother's old crew!

Bang!

Matt yelped as he felt the bullet rip through his hair. "I'm Mateo!" he blurted, holding his hands up in the air. "I'm Captain Bonnaire's son from the future!"

The girl lowered her gun and squinted at Matt, and then her eyes widened. "Is that Captain's magic compass? Is that how you got here?"

Matt looked at his hand. He was still clutching his compass.

"You *are* her son, aren't you? Is Vince your papa, then?"

Matt shook his head. "No. My father's not a time pirate." He slipped his compass back in his pocket.

The girl put her gun down. "Well, that's in your favor, at least. Might have had to shoot you if Vince were your papa, even if Captain Bonnaire is your mama."

Matt thought that was curious and couldn't help expressing it. "Why do you say that?" Matt asked.

"Because Vincent is a viper." She reached in her pocket and pulled out a couple of bullets. She placed them between her teeth as she opened her gun and loaded it. "He acts all gooey and lovey-dovey to the captain, but all he wants is her magic compass. I caught him trying to steal it once, when she was sleeping. I stopped him, nearly shot his head off. He swears he wasn't trying to steal it, and of course Captain believed *him* and not me, and I got in all kinds of trouble, but I *know* what I saw. He was trying to steal her magic compass, and he's gonna try to steal it again. But he must not get it, does he?" She said this as though she were just coming to this realization. "Not if *you're* here. I'll bet Captain Bonnaire finds him out and she discards him, doesn't she? Ooh, I hope he goes someplace terrible, like a black pit full of poisonous snakes. And then she gave the compass to you, and now *you're* the captain of the *Vermillion*, aren't you? Am I on your crew in the future? What is your time, actually? Or do you have no time? Were you born on the *Vermillion*?" She snapped her rifle back into place.

Matt shook his head. "No." He wasn't sure how to answer all the rest of her questions or contradict her assumptions, but it didn't matter, because there was some kind of commotion coming from belowdecks, and it was getting louder. Matt heard stomps and shuffling footsteps, accompanied by the clanking of metal.

"Oh great, here they come," said the girl.

"Who?"

"Captain—your mama—and Vince."

Matt started to panic. "She can't see me!" he said. "She's not supposed to see me!"

"But isn't that why you're here?"

Matt scrambled on the deck until he found some barrels stacked on the side of the ship. He ducked down and a moment later the girl joined him, just as two people came up the stairs from belowdecks, a man and a woman, clanking swords as they moved. Matt positioned himself so he could see between the barrels.

The woman laughed, and a chill suddenly ran down Matt's spine. It was indeed his mother, but long before she'd become his mom, long before she was Mrs. Hudson, so in a way this wasn't really his mother, not as he knew her anyway. This was Belamie Bonnaire. She looked to be in her early twenties. Her thick, dark hair was tied back, a few strands loose around her face. She was wearing black leather pants and boots, much like a typical pirate, but to his surprise and delight, her top was an old-school pinstripe New York Mets jersey, tied at the waist. It was just like the one his dad had hanging in his closet, even the same name and number on the back. Strawberry 18. Had his parents met already?

Around her neck she wore a gold chain that disappeared beneath her jersey. Matt guessed the Obsidian Compass was attached to it, hidden by her shirt. Matt's own compass grew warm inside his pocket, as if it recognized a fellow.

Belamie smiled as she sparred with Captain Vincent. Or just Vincent. He wasn't captain right now. He looked even more different than his mother did. He had no beard. His face was much younger, and his hair was longer. He wasn't wearing all black either, or his red Converse, just some old-fashioned trousers and boots and a loose-fitting shirt, open at the chest.

"You're getting better, Vince," said Belamie as she blocked one of Vincent's thrusts and then parried.

"Better than you?" said Vincent.

"Don't get ahead of yourself." Belamie sparred with one arm behind her back, eyes sparkling in such a way that told Matt she wasn't really trying her hardest, but Vincent was. His brow was furrowed in concentration and sweat ran down his face and neck as he wielded his sword, striking with all his might while the young Belamie met every blow with ease, each step a dance, until she pulled a quick move and Vincent dropped his sword.

Belamie pointed her sword at Vincent's chest. "Surrender, Vince, and admit that I'm the best!"

Vincent lifted his hands in the air. "I surrender, Captain. You are the best." He took a bow, then raised his head and smiled mischievously. With a quick motion he put the toe of his boot beneath his sword and kicked it up into his hand. Matt almost shouted at his mother to look out, but it seemed she was expecting this. She pirouetted behind Vincent and swung her sword around, stopping just short of his neck. Vincent immediately dropped his sword. Belamie picked it up and crossed the blades around his neck like a pair of open scissors. "When you're beaten, you're beaten," she said, her face close to his. "Don't try to push your luck."

Vincent smiled at Belamie in a way that made Matt feel a little bit squeamish. "One day, Bel," he said. "I'll best you one day."

"I look forward to it," said Belamie, removing the blades and handing Vince back his sword. "It gets a little boring being the best all the time."

"Really?" said Vincent, cocking one eyebrow. "Then why are you searching for the Aeternum? If being the best is such a bore, you'll be bored forever."

Matt's ears prickled. The Aeternum . . . It took him a moment to file through his brain and place the word. It was Latin, he was quite certain, and he had a vague idea that it meant something like "forever" or "eternity." Something like that, but it sounded like Vincent was talking about an object, not just some expression of infinity. Matt looked questioningly at the girl with the gun, but she just shrugged.

"Well, that's different, isn't it?" said Belamie. "When we have the Aeternum *we* will be the best *together*. Forever. And that won't be boring, will it?"

"No, it will not." Vincent leaned down toward Belamie. Matt closed his eyes. They were going to kiss. He could barely stand it when his own parents kissed in front of him. Just the thought of his mom kissing Captain Vincent twisted his stomach.

BANG!

Matt fell back, clutching at his ears. The girl had her rifle between the barrels. He'd almost forgotten she was there. Matt scrambled back to his feet and crouched again to be able to see his mother and Vincent.

"Annie!" shouted Belamie, looking all around. "I said no shooting while we're fencing!"

The girl, who was apparently named Annie, stood up so just her eyes and the tip of her rifle peeked over the barrels. "You wasn't fencing though," she said. "You was *kissin'*."

"No shooting during kissing either," said Vincent. "I'm sure you wouldn't mind shooting me, but what if you miss your mark and hurt the dear captain?"

"I never miss my mark," said Annie.

"Never say never," said Vincent. "It's bad luck."

"*You're* bad luck."

"Enough," said Belamie, putting up her sword and swinging it down. "Breakfast should be ready, and I want to meet with the entire crew. We've got a mission here."

"Where are we anyway?" Annie asked.

"Chicago," said Belamie. "Not too far from the time and place you were born, Annie."

Chicago . . . that's where Matt had gone. Now he remembered. His parents had mentioned Chicago weeks ago. Captain Vincent was supposed to have come here around this time, but then his mother said she'd come here, too, just before she left to be with his dad. By some stroke of fate, Matt had crossed paths with the *Vermillion* and its crew long before he'd boarded it for the first time.

Annie sneered. "I don't want to go anywhere near where or when I was born."

"I wouldn't either, if I were you," said Vincent. "What a horrible day."

Lightning fast, Annie aimed her rifle and pulled the trigger. The bullet hit the hilt of Vincent's sword and knocked it right out of his hand. Vincent jumped back, shaking his hand, and let out a slew of curse words that made Matt's ears burn.

"Annie!" Belamie shouted as she inspected Vincent's hand. "You could have shot his hand off!"

"If I'd wanted to shoot his hand off, then I'd have shot his hand off," said Annie, glaring at Vincent.

"I swear, Belamie," said Vincent, pointing at Annie, "if it were up to me, I'd take that little brat to the top of Mount Vesuvius and drop her in right before it explodes."

"It would be a waste, Vince," said Belamie. "You'll never find a sharpshooter with better aim. She *could* have taken your hand off." She shook her head at Annie, but with a smile behind her eyes. Matt saw just a hint of the mother he knew now. She was like a slightly older version of Ruby. "Come on, you two, let's stop quarreling and go eat breakfast. Agnes made some hotcakes and blackberry syrup just for you, Annie."

"Ooh, I love blackberry syrup!" said Annie, her anger forgotten. She flung her rifle over her shoulder and started to walk away, then stopped, glancing back to where Matt was hiding behind the barrels. "I'll be there in a minute," she said. "I have to clean my gun."

"Don't take too long," said Belamie. "We've got work to do." Belamie took Vincent's hand, and they went belowdecks.

As soon as they'd gone, Matt slowly stood up. He stretched his cramped legs. He took off his Mets hat, now itchy from the water, and shook his wet hair.

"See?" said Annie, walking back toward him. "I told you Vincent was a viper. Ooh, I *hate* him!"

"What were they just talking about?" said Matt. "Before you shot at them—"

"At *Vincent*," said Annie. "I'd never shoot at Captain Bonnaire."

"At Vincent," said Matt. "They were talking about something called . . . the Aeternum? What is that?"

"Oh, I don't know," said Annie. "They're always searching for some fancy treasure or something. I never pay any mind. I don't care a hoot about gold or diamonds. I just shoot at the bad guys, scare 'em off, and be grateful for a hot meal and a bed. Or a hammock, I suppose. It's more than I ever got back home," she said bitterly.

In an odd way, Annie reminded Matt of Jia. They were nothing alike in looks or personality, but Jia, too, had never questioned Captain Vincent's missions or commands, and she had also been grateful just to have food and a home, to have been rescued from the first life she'd been given. And he'd ruined that for her. It was going to be ruined for Annie as well, likely very soon.

"So?" said Annie, fiddling with a mechanism on her gun. "What happens in the future? Am I on your crew? Are you captain now or is your mama still captain? And what happens to Vince the viper? Does he get discarded in a pit of snakes?"

Matt considered what to say. He could lie, but then he remembered how Annie said she could always smell a lie and, somehow, he believed her. And maybe if he told her the truth, he could help her avoid a fate like Jia's. That was something at least. "Vincent gets the Obsidian Compass in the future," he said. "And the *Vermillion*. He's Captain Vincent in my time."

Annie's eyes widened. "But . . . then *you* get it, don't you? I mean, you have it now, or else how would you have traveled?"

Matt shook his head. He wasn't sure how much he could or should explain. How much would she tell his mom? He'd probably already said too much. "I can't explain everything," said Matt. "I don't think it's safe, but Captain Vincent still has the compass right now, in my time."

Annie set down her gun with a *thunk* on the deck. "So he does steal it from her, that filthy lying dirty rotten cheater! So what do we do? Are you on a mission to stop him? *Should* I shoot him dead?"

Matt considered. Should she? Would that solve their problems? His mind raced to calculate all the implications. He didn't really like the idea of killing someone, even Captain Vincent. Aside from the fact that he didn't think he had the guts to do it, it could have serious repercussions on his future and the future of his family. What would happen in his own life if Vincent died right now? Was it even possible? Matt was supposed to meet him in Vincent's future and his own past. If Vincent died before any of that happened, what then? Maybe his mom would never marry his dad. Matt wouldn't be adopted, at least not by his parents, and Corey and Ruby would never be born. He could seriously mess up all their lives.

"No, I don't think you should shoot him dead," said Matt. "Might do more harm than good."

"Well, what can we do then?" Annie asked. "We can't just let him get away with it. And what about me? Do you know what happens to me in the future? Am I with your mom? Does she take me with her?" Her voice had gone high and thin. She trembled a little, and with all her bravado gone she suddenly looked even smaller and younger.

What could Matt say? She hadn't been on the *Vermillion* with Captain Vincent when he had been on board. It was very likely that she'd been discarded, but he didn't have the heart to tell her that, even if it was the truth. Anyway, it was possible she could have gotten away before Vincent got the compass and took over the *Vermillion*. What if someone had warned her beforehand?

"Listen, Annie," Matt said. "I don't know all that happens in your future. All I know is that Vincent will be captain of the *Vermillion*, and you're not on his crew, and you're not with us. I think the best thing would be for you to get away from all this, from Vincent and the *Vermillion*. As soon as possible. Captain Bonnaire will take you home, won't she?"

"The *Vermillion is* my home!" said Annie.

"You heard Vincent, though," said Matt. "He'll discard you the first chance he gets, and you're not going to shoot him, or if you do, you miss."

"I never miss," said Annie, all stubbornness back.

"Then you're not going to shoot him," said Matt. "Because he has the compass in the future, and you're not on his crew when I meet him."

Annie's face went pale. "I can't go back home," she said, her voice wavering a little. "Mama bound me out to work for the most awful people, and I won't go back to those wolves!"

"Then don't go back to them. Go back to your mother. She'd be happy to see you, wouldn't she?" said Matt.

"She wouldn't. I'm just another mouth to feed, and she can barely feed herself and the little ones. Captain Bonnaire is the only one who's ever taken care of me!"

"I'll bet you could take care of yourself now. You're not the same little girl now as when my mom found you, are you?

You got your gun, and you never miss, right?"

Annie shook her head. "Never. I can shoot marbles tossed in the air."

Matt thought he might like to see that, but there wasn't time for sport here. "Then trust your gun," he said. "I'll bet you could feed your whole family if you wanted. Just don't stay here. When Vincent becomes captain, he'll discard everyone and get his own crew."

Footsteps were sounding from belowdecks. "I better go. I can't be seen by anyone else." Matt reached in his pocket for his compass. He moved to turn the dials, and then paused. If he traveled while on the *Vermillion*, would only he travel? Or would the *Vermillion* come with him? He wasn't sure his compass worked that way, but if it did that could be a real disaster, bringing past Belamie Bonnaire to future Mrs. Hudson. He decided it would be best to jump back in the water and travel back the same way he came, as terrifying and uncomfortable as it was.

He walked toward the side of the ship when someone came up the stairs from belowdecks. Matt ducked down behind the barrels again. He peered around the side and saw Vincent.

"Forgot my sword, which you so politely shot out of my hand," said Vincent. He picked up his sword, twirled it around, and swiped it across Annie's face, narrowly missing her nose. "Now get down to breakfast before—"

Vincent stopped speaking. He was looking at something

on the ground, his brow furrowed. He stabbed his sword at the ground and lifted it up in the air. Matt gasped and covered his mouth. Swinging from the tip of Vincent's sword was Matt's Mets hat! He'd dropped it. How could he have been so careless?

"What's this?" Vincent asked.

"Nothin'," said Annie. "I got a hat out of Priscilla's shop to shield my eyes from the sun, and then I dropped it in the water, and then I fished it out. . . ."

Matt put his hand to his forehead. Maybe Annie could smell a lie, but she sure couldn't tell one.

Vincent studied the hat, sniffed it, then turned around in a full circle, scanning the ship. Matt considered what to do. He wasn't that far from the side of the ship. He could probably run and jump. It wouldn't be that big of a deal if Vincent saw him from behind for just a moment. Or he could sit tight, count on Annie to cover for him, wait for Vincent to leave.

"I really don't think we should keep the crew waiting any longer," said Annie in a high voice. Vincent ignored her. He was heading toward Matt now, getting closer and closer.

"Golly, I sure am hungry," said Annie loudly. "We best be getting to breakfast, don't you think?"

Vincent was a mere ten feet from Matt. He was eyeing the barrels, his sword in hand.

Matt made a split-second decision. He made a mad dash

for the side of the ship, only to trip on a coil of rope! He scrambled to his feet, but it was too late. Vincent was upon him. He grabbed Matt by his hair and yanked him away from the side of the ship. Matt yelped and struggled to get free, but Vincent twisted harder.

"And what do we have here?" he said, pulling Matt's head back so Matt was looking at him upside down.

"Don't hurt him!" said Annie.

"You snuck him on board, didn't you?" said Vincent. "You'll most certainly be discarded now. Bel!" he shouted. "Captain Bonnaire, come *now*! We have a spy on board!" There was a rush of footsteps, more than just Captain Bonnaire's. Matt fought as hard as he could, but Vincent yanked his hair so hard, he thought his scalp might rip right from his skull. His eyes watered. This wasn't supposed to happen! He wasn't supposed to be seen by his mother or Vincent or any of them! He'd made a huge mistake. His heart beat faster and faster. He began to shake.

Captain Bonnaire came rushing up the steps, followed closely by three more crew members, and before Matt knew what was happening, he had a sword pointed at his neck. His own mother was pointing a sword at him. "Who are you?" she said.

"I'm, uh . . ."

"What are you doing on *my* ship?" The tip of her sword

pressed into his windpipe. It was a blunted edge, thankfully, but it still cut off his air so he couldn't speak, and he could barely breathe.

"A spy, most likely," said one of the crew, a tall woman with dark skin. "Children are always very useful spies."

"His clothes are most definitely from the future, Captain," said another woman. Matt couldn't see her face, but judging by her accent she sounded like she might be Indian. "Late twentieth century, somewhere."

"He dropped his hat," said Vincent. "That's how I found him out. The little brat was hiding him. She knew he was here the whole time! I told you she wasn't to be trusted. *She's* probably a spy too."

"I'm *not* a spy!" said Annie. "And I didn't let him on board! He was already here!"

"But spying for who?" Belamie asked, still studying Matt like he was some kind of puzzle she was trying to put together.

"Quine," said Vincent in a low voice. "He *knows* what we're after, Bel. He's trying to stop you. He's trying to infiltrate your crew."

Matt saw the blood drain from his mother's face. She looked afraid, and then angry. She lowered her sword and lunged. She grabbed Matt by the collar and twisted it, so it was fully choking him. "Who sent you? How did you get here?"

"Stop, Captain, stop! Don't hurt him!" Annie shouted.

Matt thought he was about to be murdered by his own mother (before she was his mother), and then suddenly she stopped and gasped.

"Ah!" She released him and clutched at her chest.

At the same time Matt felt a burning sensation on his leg. It was his compass. It was *hot*.

"Bel, what is it?" said Vincent.

Belamie pulled the gold chain at her neck and yanked off the Obsidian Compass. She dropped it to the ground where it started to smoke.

Vincent loosened his grip on Matt's scalp just enough. He twisted free and shoved Vincent as hard as he could. Vincent stumbled back. Matt ran, ignoring the smoke and searing heat coming from his own compass.

"Stop him!" shouted Belamie. "Annie, *shoot him!*"

Matt ran faster than he'd ever run in his life. He hurtled over the side of the ship, flailing as he dropped toward the water.

BANG!

A gunshot rang out just before he hit the water. For a second he thought Annie had tried to shoot him, but when he surfaced and turned around, it was his mother who held the gun.

Matt grabbed his compass and turned the dials. He didn't

know where he was going. He had no time to think. His mother blasted another shot. It hit the water just a foot from Matt.

"Don't shoot him, Captain!" Annie shouted, trying to grab the gun. "You can't kill him! He's your son!"

Matt made the final turn of the outer dial. Just before he traveled, he caught a final glimpse of his mother. She wasn't aiming the gun at him anymore. She stared at him with a look of total shock and disbelief.

Matt was jerked away, like a taut fishing line had been hooked right in his gut.

Phlpt!

He was sucked beneath the water.

7

Explanations

Matt hurtled through time and space like a bouncy ball. First, he landed in what looked like a field of wheat. It was quiet except for the gentle breeze rustling the stalks of grain, and then he was sucked away again, and rolled in the middle of a highway, and was nearly run over by several cars. He disappeared just as a semitruck was coming at him. And then he wasn't anywhere at all, or at least he thought he wasn't anywhere. Really, he was falling out of the sky, like a skydiver, except he didn't have a parachute. He stretched his mouth in a silent scream as he fell. I'm going to die, he thought as the ground came closer and closer. He shook his compass, turned one of the dials a couple of clicks, and just before he met the ground he was sucked back into the time-traveling vortex again.

Finally, he landed with a hard *thump*. All the air was knocked out of him, and stars popped out of the corners of his eyes, but he was alive and in one piece. He was pretty sure at least. When he was able to breathe again, he groaned and rolled over on the dirt. He looked around. He was in the vineyard. He could see the house. He'd made it back!

He pulled himself up and teetered a little. He grabbed on to one of the vine posts and then froze.

He was staring at himself!

"Oops!" He ducked and ran through the vineyard, hopping rows every few feet. Ha! He'd just come face-to-face with himself from a month ago! He looked at the dials of his compass. May third! He'd shifted the date dial to June first, but nothing happened.

"Come on!" he said, shaking the compass, but it wouldn't work. Why?

The peanut butter . . . It had all but washed off. He was guessing the compass needed more.

His past self was catching up with him. He looked toward the house. He could run in and grab some peanut butter, run out, and get back to where and when he was supposed to be. He would do it because he knew he had done it before. He ducked beneath another row and promptly ran into someone. At first he was afraid it was himself, but it wasn't, of course. He would have remembered if he'd run into himself before.

"Geez Louise, what in the heck is going on?" said Chuck, grabbing Matt by the arm to steady him before he fell over. "Is there a bear after you? Why are you running like a maniac?"

"P-peanut butter," Matt stuttered. "It just needs peanut butter!"

"What?" said Chuck. "You need a putter?"

Matt gurgled a laugh. A putter! That's why he'd given Matt a putter before!

"Yeah, yeah, a putter! Gotta go!" Matt hopped beneath a row of vines and ran toward the house. He ran up the steps and burst through the door that led directly to the kitchen. Gaga and his parents were there, preparing dinner. Matt dashed into the pantry and pushed the jars and cans around.

"Matt, buddy, what are you doing?" his dad asked.

Tomato soup, crackers, tuna . . .

"Mateo, no snacks now," said his mom. "We're just about to have dinner."

Beans, peaches, pears . . . peanut butter! He grabbed the jar and ran out of the kitchen, whirling past his parents.

"Mateo, didn't you hear me? And why are you all wet?"

"I'll be right there! Gotta do something real quick!" Matt ran out the door and jumped over the railing. He rolled as he landed, then sprang to his feet, ran to the back of the house, and crouched behind the lilac bushes. He unscrewed the jar of peanut butter, scooped out a glob with his fingers, and smeared it into the compass.

Come on, come on! He turned the time dial. He didn't need to go anywhere else, just travel a few weeks ahead.

He looked up and locked eyes with himself. His past self

looked like he was seeing a ghost. Matt supposed he was in a way. His own ghost. He smiled at himself, and then—

Phlpt!

Matt landed on his feet this time. His knees buckled beneath him, and he fell forward, landing hard on the heels of his hands. Dirt caked onto his sticky peanut butter hands and the compass too.

He was outside, he was pretty sure, and he was on dry land. The sky above him was dark and dusted with stars. The air smelled mossy. Crickets chirped, and someone not too far away was singing very off-key.

He stood up and swayed a little. His heart was beating very fast, and he was slightly dizzy. He was still in the vineyard, but had he come to the right time?

He heard the singing again. Where was it coming from? He turned around and saw Chuck's orange VW bus. The sliding door was open, and Chuck was sitting inside. He looked the same as the last time he saw him. Same scraggly beard, same fishing hat, same tie-dyed T-shirt with the peace sign, but that's what he always wore, so it didn't really give him any clue as to what day or time it was.

Chuck was singing some song about a piano man at the top of his lungs. Matt vaguely recognized the song, though he thought Chuck was singing pretty off-key. Chuck pulled out a harmonica and started playing. He turned just enough to notice Matt in his periphery. He jumped and dropped his harmonica.

"Good gravy, kiddo, what in the name of Peter, Paul, and Mary are you doing?"

"Sorry," said Matt. "Do you know what day it is?"

Chuck looked at him a little funny and then checked his watch. "It's uh . . . June first."

"And . . . the year?"

Chuck raised his eyebrows at Matt. "It's 1975."

Matt's heart skipped a few beats. Really? He'd gone that far off?

Chuck started laughing. "It's 2019, ya goof! I really had you there for a minute, didn't I?"

Matt heaved a sigh of relief. "Yeah, you did."

"Hey, I still got that putter. You want it?"

"Uh . . . ," said Matt.

"Mateo! Mateo!" Matt jumped and turned around. Someone was shouting his name. It was his mother. She sounded hysterical.

"Sounds like you're in trouble, kiddo," said Chuck. "Better run."

"Yeah, see you later."

Matt raced across the vineyard. His mother's voice got louder as he neared the house. "Mateo! You come out of hiding right this instant!"

"Calm down, Belamie, it's only a game," said Gaga.

"What kind of game of hide-and-seek is this?! We've been searching for an hour!"

An hour! He'd miscalculated the time he'd left. He'd have some explaining to do.

"It's a big house," said Corey. "Lots of places to hide. That's what makes it fun."

"Did you search the basement?" Mr. Hudson asked. "He's often in the basement, and there are lots of places to hide down there."

"He's not there," said Ruby. "I made a thorough search."

"That's it. I'm calling the police," said Mrs. Hudson.

"Belamie," said his dad.

"Matthew, something is not right."

"I'm here!" Matt shouted as he ran. "I'm right here!" He stuffed his compass back inside his pocket.

"I hear him!" said Ruby. "He's outside."

"Outside!" said Gaga. "Isn't that cheating?"

A thunder of footsteps sounded in the house and the whole family burst out of the front door as Matt ran up the porch steps.

"I'm here," he said. "It's okay. I'm here."

Everyone froze as they saw Matt. His mother had her cell phone out, ready to dial 911.

"There you are!" said Ruby, giving Matt a hard look. "We told you to come out! Didn't you hear us?"

Mrs. Hudson looked Matt up and down. "Why are you all wet?"

"I . . . uh . . . fell in the pond. It was dark, and I wasn't looking where I was going. Sorry." Matt tried to smile, but his teeth chattered. He started to shiver, even though it was warm and humid outside.

Mrs. Hudson put down her phone and slumped into the rattan chair on the porch. She closed her eyes, took a deep breath, and spoke in a slow, tired voice. "Go get changed into dry clothes, Mateo. Then we'll have cake."

"Okay, sure. Sorry." Matt hurried inside the house, keeping his eyes to the floor. Gaga sniffed as he passed. "Amazing," she said. "As soon as they become teenagers they start to smell like something that's crawled between the walls and died."

"I never smelled that way," said Mr. Hudson.

"Oh please, you *still* smell that way," said Gaga.

Matt went to his room, his shoes squelching with every footstep. He peeled off his wet clothes, then put on dry ones. It was difficult because he was shaking so much, whether from cold or the shock and excitement of all that had just happened, he couldn't tell. He suddenly remembered his compass and pulled it out of his wet clothes. It wasn't hot anymore. It looked like just a lump of metal with dirt and peanut butter stuck in the grooves.

But it worked. *It worked!* He'd time-traveled! He'd gone to the *Vermillion!*

Matt trembled as his mind raced with all the possibilities. He was no longer trapped. He could go back and get the compass from Captain Vincent. He could rescue Jia. He could fix everything now.

There was a soft tap on the door. "Mateo? Are you all right?" It was his mom.

"Fine!" Matt said, stuffing his compass back in his pocket. "Be right there."

His mission would have to wait until after cake. He couldn't leave right now anyway. He would have to talk to Corey and Ruby. He was certain they knew something to do with time travel had happened. They'd covered for him by saying he was hiding, but they would expect answers.

The second round of "Happy Birthday" was not as jovial as the first. They did not turn out the lights, and Matt's parents didn't let him out of their sight for a second. His dad kept a hand on Matt's shoulder almost the entire night, and his mom kept looking at him with a furrowed brow, as though she were trying to put together the pieces of a puzzle. Matt tried to act natural, but he was jittery with nerves and excitement. He kept reaching for his compass to make sure it was there. He was sure his parents suspected something had happened, especially his mom. Of course she did. She'd seen him in her past, after all. And Annie had told her he was her son. She *knew* he would be her son before he'd ever been born, and she knew he would time-travel to her past. Why did she never tell him any of this?

After they'd finished cake, and Matt had opened a few presents (a new baseball bat, a book about famous inventors in history), Ruby brushed up against Matt and whispered, "What happened?"

"Later," he said.

Corey brushed up on his other side. "Did your compass . . ."

"Not now," Matt said between gritted teeth. "Wait until we're alone."

But alone was a long way off. Mr. Hudson brought out a stack of games and said they were going to play every single one. They'd play all night if that's what it took! And he wasn't joking, apparently. Gaga dropped off at about ten o'clock, after a long game of Trivial Pursuit.

"Yeah, we should probably get to bed too," said Matt, eyeing Corey and Ruby.

"Oh yeah," said Corey, giving an exaggerated fake yawn. "I'm pretty tired."

"Oh no you don't," said Mr. Hudson. "We said we'd get through all the games! This is a family mission, and we shall fulfill it! Or are you guys a bunch of quitters?"

Matt exchanged looks with Corey. He was starting to think there was more to this than just getting through a bunch of games.

They played until well after midnight. It was only when Corey started to fall asleep while rolling dice for Yahtzee that Mrs. Hudson said enough was enough.

Finally, Matt thought, but it wasn't as though that gave them an opportunity to talk. Both Mr. and Mrs. Hudson supervised the kids to bed, watched them brush their teeth, and tucked them in like they were toddlers. Mrs. Hudson sat on Matt's bed and brushed her fingers through his hair.

"Happy birthday, *chéri*."

"Thanks," he said.

"Are you sure you're feeling all right?"

"Yep. Feeling great."

"Is there anything you want to talk about? Anything you want to tell me?"

Matt tried not to squirm beneath her gaze that seemed to be reading all his thoughts. There was part of him that wanted to open up, tell her what had just happened, show her the compass, ask his mom what he should do. But there was another part of him that felt she didn't deserve his honesty. *She* hadn't been honest with him. She'd never told him that she'd met him in her past, that she *knew* he would time-travel. Why would she keep these things from him? Whatever her reasons, it altered things for him. He wasn't sure how, but he felt just a little different toward his mom.

"No, I'm good," said Matt. "Just tired."

Mrs. Hudson looked at him with a searching gaze. Matt

yawned and tried to make his eyes look heavy. "Good night, Mom. Love you."

This seemed to appease her more than anything else. "I love you, too, *chéri*." She kissed his forehead, and she and his dad left the room, leaving the door open and the hall light on.

Matt listened to his parents retreat down the hallway. He counted to one hundred and then he flipped off his blankets and slipped out of bed. Ruby and Corey both sat up in their own beds at the same time.

Matt put his fingers to his lips. He clicked on his bedside lamp, then went to the door and silently shut it. He pointed to the vent. Very quietly all three children tiptoed over and crouched down to listen. It took a few minutes for their parents to start talking, but just as Matt was thinking they weren't going to talk in their room, he heard their voices.

"... something happened," he heard his mother say.

"I checked the map," said his dad. "Vince was never here. He's still in Chicago, 1893."

"There's something going on, Matthew. I know Mateo's not telling me the truth. I could see it in his eyes."

"Belamie, he's home. He's safe. Everything's okay."

"He was missing for nearly an hour!" said Mrs. Hudson. "Do you really think he stayed hidden in a game of hide-and-seek for an *hour*?"

"Well, our kids can be pretty competitive," said Mr. Hudson with a bit of a chuckle.

"Don't joke, please, Matthew. I'm not in the mood."

"I'm sorry. But look, it's past his birthday. The kids are in bed asleep. Vincent isn't anywhere near us. We don't need to worry anymore."

"Then why do I have this *feeling*?" said his mom, her voice starting to quaver.

"It's just adrenaline release," said Mr. Hudson. "You've been so worried these past weeks, for years, actually. So have I, but it's over. You said Vincent couldn't travel past Matt's birthday, and here we are past Matt's birthday, so what are you worried will happen?"

"I don't know! That's just it. I have no idea what will happen, but I know it isn't over, and I don't know what to do! I don't know where to look or run or hide, and I don't know how to protect the kids. If something happens to them, I don't think I can bear it. And you . . . if something happens to you . . ." She broke down into sobs. The kids all looked at each other. Matt couldn't recall ever seeing or hearing his mother cry in his whole life. She always seemed so strong, confident, unbreakable, but lately she was always on the verge of tears, ever since they'd come back from the *Vermillion*.

Their parents didn't talk anymore, at least not about anything of importance. Matt could hear his dad murmuring soft words of comfort, his mom shuddering through her sobs. Ruby closed the vent. Corey took some books off the shelf, plus an extra blanket, and covered it up to block sound going in or out. Matt padded over to his bed, and Corey and Ruby followed him over. All three huddled together on top of the blankets.

"So?" whispered Ruby. "What happened? You scared us half to death you know."

"We were afraid Captain Vincent had kidnapped you," said Corey. "Mom was going berserk."

"Yeah," said Matt. "Thanks for covering for me, though it sounds like she didn't totally buy it."

"Of course she didn't," said Corey, "but what can she do about it, force you to tell her the truth?"

"So what is the truth?" Ruby asked. "Does it have something to do with your compass?"

Matt reached in the pocket of his pajamas and pulled out his compass, grimy and sticky with dirt and peanut butter.

"It worked," said Matt. "I mean, it works. I *traveled.*" Saying it out loud sent a tingly shiver down his whole body.

Corey and Ruby stared at the compass for a few seconds, both with their mouths agape, and then Corey nearly shouted, "No freaking way!"

"*Shh!* Quiet, Corey! We don't want Mom and Dad to come check on us again."

Corey lowered his voice to barely a whisper. "Sorry. No freaking way. That's amazing."

"How did you figure it out?" Ruby asked.

"I didn't," said Matt. "Not directly anyway. It was my birthday cake, and also seeing myself in the vineyard. That made no sense until today."

"Hold up," said Corey. "You saw *yourself*? And you didn't tell us?"

Matt hardly knew where to begin or how to put this experience into words. It was like trying to translate a bizarre, discordant dream in a language he barely knew. He started with the tale of how a month ago he saw himself in the vineyard and how that was what inspired him to build the compass in the first place. He knew his future self must have found a way to time-travel. Instead of waiting around for it to happen, he decided to make it happen.

"Why didn't you tell us any of this?" Ruby asked.

"I'm sorry," said Matt. "But I wasn't sure about any of it, and I thought you would have thought I was crazy."

"Bro," said Corey. "Aren't we past crazy now? After what we've all been through, *nothing* could ever sound crazy to us."

Ruby sniffed the air a little. "Why do I smell . . . ?" She bent down and sniffed the compass. A huge grin split across her face. "It smells like peanut butter, just like the *Vermillion*!"

"Yeah," said Matt. "Would you be surprised if I told you that peanut butter is the magic ingredient that makes the compass work?"

"You're joking!" Corey pounded the bed and tipped back his head in silent laughter. "I take it back. That is crazy. And awesome."

"So your compass didn't work," said Ruby, "and then you put peanut butter on it and it worked."

Matt nodded. "Remember the frosting from my birthday cake? It was peanut butter frosting. When Corey knocked me over—"

"Yeah, sorry about that," Corey interrupted.

"—I fell in the cake, and then I got some of the frosting in the compass, and that's when I disappeared."

"Well, it sort of makes sense, doesn't it?" said Ruby. "I mean, Jia always used peanut butter to fix the *Vermillion*, didn't she?"

"I always knew peanut butter was magical," said Corey.

"Okay," said Ruby. Matt could almost see the wheels turning in her brain, the connectors trying to put it all together. He knew the feeling well. "Okay, so you built a time-traveling compass, and you time-traveled. Where did you go? What happened?"

"And how long were you gone?" Corey asked. "Did you see Captain Vincent or Jia or anyone? Brocco or Wiley?"

Ruby hit Corey. "Don't ask so many questions at a time. He can't answer them all at once."

Matt shook his head. "I'll just start from the beginning. Or at least from when I disappeared, okay?"

"Okay," Corey and Ruby said together, and they were quiet, mostly, as he told them all that had happened.

He told them how he landed in Chicago and how he came on board the *Vermillion* well before they'd boarded it the first time, before Jia's time, even. He told them about Annie, how she almost shot him, and then how he saw their mom as Captain Bonnaire, and how she was with Vincent.

"Did you see them *kiss*?" said Corey, his face twisting in disgust.

Matt shook his head vigorously. "No, but almost, and it was weird." He still had the picture of his mom and Vincent in his head, standing so close. He wanted to erase it. Shake it off.

"I heard them talking about some stuff, though," said Matt. "Stuff that sounded important. They were talking about something called the Aeternum. I'm not sure what it is, exactly, but it sounded important. It sounded like they'd been searching for it for a long time, and they were going to look for it in Chicago. I *think* it might be the thing that Captain Vincent is looking for."

"Is that the 'powerful thing' Mom mentioned?" Corey made little quotation marks with his fingers.

"Maybe," said Matt.

"So what is it?" Ruby asked. "Did they describe it at all?"

Matt shook his head. "Not really. Vincent kept talking

about being the best, and Mom said something about living forever, or being together forever, but I don't really know if that was just an expression or what. You know, like she was trying to be . . . romantic."

Corey made a gagging sound. "Gross. Yuck. I don't wanna know. But this Atter-noon thing . . ."

"Aeternum," said Matt. "A-*tear*-noom."

"Right. Whatever. It makes you like the Hulk or something? Or Captain America?"

"This isn't like one of your stupid comics, Corey," said Ruby.

Corey held up a hand to Ruby's face. "First of all, my comics are not stupid. Second of all, this is *exactly* like a comic, duh. We *traveled through space and time* on a transforming ship full of pirates. Our mom used to be one of those pirates and can somehow sword fight like freaking Zorro. Matt's compass is like an amulet with magical peanut butter powers. So tell me, sis, why *wouldn't* there be some magical thingy that makes you live forever?" Corey said this all with great pomp and authority. Ruby rolled her eyes and turned back to Matt.

"So is that it?" said Ruby. "Did anything else happen?"

"Well . . . ," said Matt. "It's possible that maybe some of the crew, including Mom, may have seen me?"

Ruby gasped. "They *saw* you? Mom saw you?"

Matt nodded. "She almost killed me. Good thing she used

a gun instead of her sword, or she might have."

Ruby put her hands over her eyes as though she were imagining the whole dramatic episode.

"That's awesome," said Corey. "Do you think Mom knows now who she saw then? I mean, do you think she looks at you now and thinks, Holy *bleep*, I almost killed my own son?"

"I don't know," said Matt. "I got away before they could question me too much. It was a long time ago for Mom, I think, probably twenty years ago, and I don't think Captain Vincent—or I guess just Vincent. He wasn't captain then. I don't think he saw me at all, at least not my face too much. He was holding me."

"How did you get away?" Ruby asked, her hands now resting on her cheeks.

"That's the weird thing," said Matt. "I mean, it's all weird, but when Mom came toward me, my compass suddenly grew hot. It happened to hers, too, I'm guessing. I think they were reacting to each other. Anyway, Vincent got all concerned for Mom and let me go. That's when I jumped ship and traveled back here. And that's it."

Silence fell between them. Corey and Ruby just stared at the compass for a while, like they were still trying to process everything.

"So now what?" said Corey. "I mean, we have a compass. We can time-travel, or Matt can at least. So what do we do?"

Matt had been thinking about this all evening, ever since he'd gotten home. He'd gone from feeling completely trapped to suddenly having too many possibilities. What to do, when, and how?

"We have to find Jia," said Matt.

"Yes, of course," said Ruby, "but we also have to think about Vincent and the Obsidian Compass. We can't just let him keep it and keep coming after us. I don't want to be in hiding for the rest of our lives."

"I thought he couldn't get to us now," said Corey. "Matt's birthday's supposed to be the furthest he could travel, right?"

"Yes," said Ruby. "But who knows what that really means? Who knows how things will be tomorrow? Or yesterday, for that matter. If he finds the . . . the Atter-whatever-it's-called-powerful-thing, then it might change everything, couldn't it?"

"You're right," said Matt. "We have to stop Vincent."

"Great," said Corey. "So let's go get him. We got our own compass now. We can take him."

"But where and when do we go to get him?" Ruby asked. "We can't go back to the museum, or any time when we were with them on the *Vermillion*. It's too risky. We're sure to see ourselves. And what about Jia? You don't know where or when Captain Vincent might have discarded her, so how are we going to rescue her?"

"Dad's map, obviously," said Matt.

Ruby's eyes narrowed. "So you're going to tell Mom and Dad, then? About the compass and everything?"

"Are you crazy?" said Corey.

"No, I'm not," said Ruby. "I think they might be really glad to see Matt's compass. You know how worried sick they are that Captain Vincent might show up at any moment. This way we can be on the offensive, head off Vincent before he gets to us. With our own compass we can stop him for good."

"Yeah, maybe," said Corey, "except do you really think Mom and Dad would let us come with them? They'd probably take the compass, go off on their own to save the day, and leave us here with Gaga."

"Well, maybe that's . . ."

"Don't say that's the *sensible* thing to do," said Corey. "It doesn't make any kind of sense. What if they don't come back? Are you okay with living with Gaga forever in this boring place? And don't rule out the possibility that Mom might crush the compass with her bare fists and lock us all up in a high-security prison, and then we'll *really* be stuck."

Matt clutched his compass. He was not okay with either of those possibilities. It was *his* compass. He'd made it, so he should be the one to travel with it. Not his mom. Just because she'd been captain of the *Vermillion* before did not give her the right to *his* compass.

Matt shook his head. "We can't tell them about the compass," he said. "Corey's right. Even if they do think we should go after Captain Vincent, you know they'll never let us travel with them. They're too protective. And they won't put the family at risk to rescue Jia, not like we will. We owe her. We have to do this on our own."

Ruby pulled at her hair and tipped her head back. "And what if *we* don't come back? Have you considered that possibility? What if something goes wrong? I mean, Matt only traveled once. His compass is still a big unknown. What if it breaks down in the middle of travel?"

"I'd be able to fix it," said Matt with confidence. "I mean, it's not perfect, I'll admit, but it works. I traveled, and I was able to get back home. I can do it again."

Ruby was still clearly apprehensive about the whole situation. "We promised we'd stick together, with Mom and Dad too. Have you forgotten what it was like last time, when we never thought we'd see them again? When we thought we were going to . . . going to . . ."

Tears were pooling in Ruby's eyes. Matt was suddenly flooded with feelings and images of when they'd been discarded on that barren island and thought they'd never see their parents again. They thought they were going to die.

"Hey," said Corey, placing a hand on Ruby's shoulder. "We got away last time, didn't we? And we didn't even have our own compass then. We're way more prepared this time. I say we—"

"Shh!" Matt put his hand up to make them stop talking.

They all sat still and listened. Matt heard the creak of old floorboards as someone walked down the hallway. Corey and Ruby scrambled out of Matt's bed and into their own. Matt switched off his lamp and lay down just as their bedroom door cracked open. Matt kept his eyes closed. But he knew it was his mom. Did she *ever* sleep? He could hear her sigh as she saw that all three children were in their beds. She stood in the doorway for a long time before she shut the door and left.

Matt listened to the creak of her footsteps as she walked away. He waited a minute before he spoke again. "Ruby, I get it," he said. "It's not an ideal situation, and it's good to be cautious, but we can't plan for every little thing that might happen. We're going to have to take some risks. But you need to decide right now whether you're in or you're out. You don't have to come, but we don't have time for a lot of debates. If we're going to do this, we're going to have to move fast, before Mom and Dad catch on."

"You know I'm in," said Corey. "A pirate's life for me."

"Ruby?" Matt asked.

Ruby didn't reply for several moments. He imagined she was biting her lip, mulling everything over in her brain. She was always cautious. She liked to be sure about things, and Matt liked that about her, but now was the time to make some big decisions. Jump off the cliff and grow some wings. Ruby took a deep breath. "Of course I'm in. It's all insane, but I'm in. For Jia's sake, if nothing else."

"Good." Matt thought the moment should have felt momentous somehow, like there should have been fireworks or trumpets or something, or a rush of magic that they all felt at once, but all Matt heard was the crickets outside, and the distant tinny sound of Chuck still playing his harmonica. It seemed like no one slept around here except Gaga.

"So what now?" Corey asked. "When do we leave?"

"We need to get Dad's map," said Matt. "It's the only way we can know exactly where and when the *Vermillion* went after we came home."

"What, do we just ask if we can look at it?"

"No," said Matt. "That will make them suspicious. They'll know we're up to something. Plus we should really have it with us when we travel. We need to steal it."

"Well," said Corey. Matt could hear him rubbing his hands together. "We've learned a thing or two about that in the last few months, haven't we?"

"We also need to run more tests on the compass," said Ruby. "We need to see if we can actually time-travel all together. If only Matt can do it, then that changes things."

"If that's the case, I vote we take turns," said Corey.

Matt felt a slight clench in his chest. He didn't want to be selfish, but he did feel a powerful possessiveness where his compass was concerned. Luckily Ruby voiced his thoughts for him.

"Only one person should hold the compass and that's

Matt," she said. "He built it. It's his. We're not going to take turns."

"That's bogus," Corey muttered, but he didn't argue the point any further, and Matt was silently grateful to Ruby.

They stayed up late into the night, or early into the morning, rather, making plans for their first mission. They had to steal their dad's map. Then, hopefully, they could rescue Jia and somehow stop Captain Vincent.

8
Signs and Symbols

Captain Belamie Bonnaire had enjoyed an illustrious and lucrative career as a time pirate since acquiring the Obsidian Compass a decade ago. Her private quarters were only a small glimpse into the life she led and the interests she'd developed. Clothes from all different eras and countries were stuffed in an open wardrobe and slung over the back and arms of an enormous golden throne she'd stolen from a Russian czar. (She never sat in it. Though it was majestic and beautiful, it was quite uncomfortable to sit upon.) Ornate silver and golden boxes overflowed with jewels and pearls.

Several paintings hung on the walls in gold-leaf frames, many of them from artists quite famous, including Rembrandt, Van Gogh, and Vermeer.

The rest of the walls were covered with swords and

daggers—heavy ceremonial swords with jeweled hilts, thin rapiers with little embellishment, and dozens of daggers, some ancient and some made hundreds of years after she was born. She was forever collecting blades and learning how to use them. She'd studied fencing and combat with every master throughout the world. If she were being honest with herself, she might admit she was trying to compensate for something, but she was rarely honest with herself. She was rarely anything with herself. Belamie was a self-escape artist. Everything she acquired, everything she did, was an attempt to escape her past, ignore the present, and avoid the future.

Sometimes she escaped into clothing, luxurious gowns, jewels, furs, and shoes. Other times she used art, theater, music, or books. She had hundreds of books in towering stacks around her cabin, a few art and history books, but mostly novels—adventure and fantasy and mystery and romance—from nearly every country, era, and language. She told herself it helped her with language learning, and it did, but the primary reason was escape, to slip into another world, become another person. Romance novels were her favorite, her guilty pleasure. This was a great secret. To her crew she appeared to be above such "nonsense," but deep down she was a romantic. Romance was the best escape of all.

But romance was far from her mind now. Nothing could help her escape the present situation (or past or future, whatever it was). Belamie paced around her cabin, holding a baseball cap in her hands, the one the boy had left behind. The boy . . .

Annie's words echoed inside her head.

"You can't kill him! He's your son!"

Her son . . . The boy was her son?

Impossible. Annie had to be mistaken, or she was playing some kind of trick. She never thought the girl capable of such an outlandish lie, but it was easier than believing that the boy was her son. Belamie may be a romantic, but her fantasies always stopped short of having children. She'd decided long ago, even before she'd been given the compass, that she could never be a mother. She'd barely had a mother herself. Both her parents had been torn from her when she was so young, and she wasn't exactly the perfect role model.

Vince, however, had a different reaction to the whole fiasco. He'd believed Annie's claim more readily than Belamie did, even though he despised the girl. In fact, he'd welcomed it. He immediately dropped all notions of any spies and rejoiced in the idea that he'd just seen his own future son, his heir!

This had annoyed Belamie for some reason, though she couldn't quite peg why. Maybe it was how happy he was about it, his complete joy and enthusiasm at the prospect of a son. At best, Belamie felt annoyed that the universe would suddenly plop a child in her midst without her permission. At worst, she was absolutely terrified.

Or maybe it was how Vince had called the boy his heir.

Not theirs. *His.* But heir to what? Vincent had no real title or property or inheritance (a definite sore spot for him). Belamie was master of the Obsidian Compass. She was captain of the *Vermillion*, but the way he spoke made it sound like it was *his* to pass on. Belamie felt a prickle of apprehension.

A knock came at the door. Belamie tucked the hat in the back of her waistband. "Come in."

The door creaked open and Annie peeked her head inside, her eyes wide and shining like a frightened doe. It reminded Belamie of when they'd first found her.

Belamie had found Annie about a year ago in Ohio in the late 1860s. They'd only stopped there as a resting point on a longer journey. It was never a good idea to travel too far in one go. It had been the dead of winter. (Belamie had gotten the timing off.) They were just about to leave for warmer weather when Belamie spotted a young girl carrying firewood in the freezing cold and snow. She wore a threadbare dress and no coat. She was shivering violently, her lips blue, and she looked half-starved. Belamie's heart nearly split in two at the sight of her. It was perhaps the closest she'd come to feeling any kind of maternal instinct. Without a thought she took the girl, wrapped her in her fur coat, and brought her on board the *Vermillion*. She gave her a cup of hot tea, a hearty meal, and told her she could stay as long as she wanted.

"Forever?" Annie asked, her eyes wide.

"If you want," said Belamie. "But you have to earn your

keep. No one dawdles on the *Vermillion*. I run a tight ship."

Annie wasn't afraid of hard work, only cold and hunger. Belamie had thought to teach her the sword. She was petite, but strong and agile, with dark, serious eyes that seemed to soak in every tiny detail. But Annie turned out to prefer guns over swords. Belamie had never cared for guns and only kept some on board the *Vermillion* as a means of precaution when they traveled to certain times and places, but one day Belamie found Annie on the upper deck with a rifle, shooting pewter goblets off the sides of the ship. Belamie would have been angry if she hadn't been even more impressed. Annie's aim was dead-on. She knocked over every single goblet from every which angle every single time. She was a natural sharpshooter, and Belamie knew she had a skill that could be very useful on many missions.

Annie grew bold and confident, and Belamie grew quite fond of her. She became something like a little sister. Belamie never could understand why Vince didn't like her, or why Annie didn't like Vince, though it wouldn't be the first time he'd clashed with one of her crew.

Now Annie was trembling almost as much as the day Belamie had found her in the freezing cold, all boldness and confidence swept away. "Are you going to discard me?" she asked in a near whisper, staring at the compass on Belamie's chest.

"Of course not!" Belamie quickly tucked the compass

beneath her shirt. "I would never do that to you."

Annie gripped her rifle tightly, her whole body tense.

"You're not in trouble, Annie," said Belamie. "You've done nothing wrong, but I need your help. I want you to tell me exactly what happened today with the boy, everything that was said. As much as you can remember."

Annie relaxed a little, but she still looked pale and frightened. "I don't know where he came from. I had him looking down the barrel of my gun, and I asked who he was and told him he'd better not lie 'cause I could smell a lie, and that's when he told me he was from the future and he was your son."

"You're sure that's what he said? He said he was *my* son?"

Annie nodded. "Yes! He said, 'I'm Captain Bonnaire's son from the future.' That's what he said exactly, I swear it." She crossed the rifle over her heart.

Belamie furrowed her brow. She was hesitant to ask her next question, but she felt she must. "And . . . did he say who his father was?"

Annie shook her head. "He didn't say who his papa was, not exactly," said Annie in a small voice. "But . . ." She looked at the floor and shifted uncomfortably.

"Yes?" Belamie coaxed. "Tell me, Annie. I need to know."

Annie looked Belamie straight in the eyes. "He said it's not Vincent."

Belamie let the words sink in a bit. "He said Vince was *not* his father?"

Annie nodded. "I asked if Vince was his papa, because that seemed reasonable, considering, but he said he wasn't. He said his father's no time pirate."

Something flared in Belamie's chest. Disappointment? Relief? Perhaps it was just her body telling her this was the truth. Vince was not the boy's father. But she was his mother. If it was true, what did it mean? Why wouldn't Vince be the father? Her mind began to spin. Maybe he gets lost in time somewhere. She searches the world over but fails to find him. She believes he's lost forever, and then after years of mourning she meets someone else . . . and they have a son together, and they're happy, but then the father tragically dies . . . and then, years later, she finds Vincent again, and he sweeps her in his arms and . . .

"He also said Vincent gets the compass."

Belamie snapped out of her daydream. "I'm sorry, what did you say?"

Annie scratched her leg with the butt of her rifle. "The boy. Your son? He said in the future Vincent is captain of the *Vermillion*, that he gets the Obsidian Compass."

Belamie's eyes narrowed. "But the boy had the Obsidian Compass, didn't he? If he came from the future, then surely he had the compass?"

Annie shook her head. "He had a compass, but this one was different. It wasn't the Obsidian Compass."

Another compass . . . that sounded like trouble . . . And Vincent, captain of the *Vermillion*? A memory surfaced in Belamie's head. It was more than a year ago. She'd taken the Obsidian Compass off to bathe. That was the only time she ever took it off. When she went to dress, there was Vince, holding her compass. He'd wrapped the golden chain around his wrist, his fingers circling the dials. Belamie had taught Vince the basics of how the compass worked. It had felt like the right thing to do, a precaution in case anything happened to her, but looking at him with the compass . . . she'd never forget the look in his eyes then. *Desire. Hunger. Possession.* It sent a shiver up her spine.

Vince played it off smoothly enough. When he saw Belamie standing there in her robe, he unwound the chain from his wrist and placed it over her head, gently setting the compass against her chest. He smiled and told her she was beautiful, but the compliment felt more cunning than romantic, and his smile did not reach his eyes. They still held a dark sort of hunger that she knew was not for her.

Belamie was startled out of her thoughts by Annie, who suddenly burst into tears. Alarmed, Belamie knelt down next to her. She'd never seen Annie cry. Not once. She was not sure what to do or how to make her stop. "Annie, it's all right," she soothed. "Everything's going to be fine."

Annie only sobbed all the harder. "No it won't. If Vincent gets the compass and becomes captain, he's going to discard me at the top of a volcano right before it explodes!"

"Annie, I'd never let that happen, and Vince would never do such a thing."

"He said he would!"

"He's only teasing you."

Annie took a few deep shuddering breaths. "I want to go home," she said.

"Home?" said Belamie. "You mean to Ohio?"

Annie nodded. "Your son said I should go home, and you said you'd take me back whenever I wanted."

"I did," said Belamie. "But, Annie, if I take you back to Ohio, you may never see us again. Are you prepared for that? Your life was not easy before you became a time pirate, you remember?"

"I remember," said Annie. "But I can take care of myself now. And Mama. I want to go home."

Belamie did not know all the circumstances of Annie's family, but she'd heard enough to know it was not an ideal situation. Her mother was a widow with too many children to feed and had sent two of them away to work for other families in order to relieve some of her burden. If Annie was asking to go back to her mother, she knew she must be truly afraid. The boy must have convinced her she was in danger.

"I'll take you home, Annie, but I want to be sure it is truly what you want. Will you sleep on it tonight?"

She nodded and used the sleeve of her dress to wipe the snot and tears from her face. "But only if you promise to take me home in the morning. If I come in the morning and say I want to go home, you'll take me?"

Belamie put her hand over her heart. "On my honor as a time pirate, you have my word."

Annie smiled, still trembling from head to foot. "Can I keep my rifle?"

Belamie put her hands on Annie's face. She wiped away the tears still spilling down her cheeks. "Of course you can," she said. "What would I do with it? You know I'm a terrible shot."

Annie laughed a little. "You sure are." She walked toward the door to leave, but Belamie stopped her.

"Oh, Annie, I forgot to ask. The boy . . . I'm just curious if he told you his name?"

Annie nodded, her eyes red and puffy. "He said his name was Mateo."

Belamie went stock-still. Her heart flared in her chest.

"Somethin' wrong?" Annie asked.

Belamie forced a smile on her face. "No. Everything's fine. Thank you, Annie. You may go."

After Annie left, Belamie locked the door and went to her bed. She knelt and pulled out a wooden box, intricately carved. This box was one of the few things in Belamie's possession she had not stolen. It had been a gift from none other than Elizabeth, the queen of England. Coincidentally, Elizabeth was another of her friends who did not care for Vincent. She had warned Belamie on more than one occasion to guard herself, to not share all her secrets with him. Belamie thought Elizabeth was being paranoid, but some part of Belamie must have believed her, for she had always kept one thing from Vincent.

Belamie reached inside the lining of her boot and retrieved a small golden key. She unlocked the box and opened the lid. Nestled in red velvet lay a small glass bottle with a cork. She uncorked it, reached in a finger, and pulled out a rolled-up piece of paper. The paper was thin and white with light blue lines drawn evenly across it, and an almost nonsensical scribbling of words, numbers, and sketches covering every inch.

This was the only communication she'd ever received from Marius Quine since he'd given her the Obsidian Compass. Though the ink was faded and the paper yellowing at the edges, the paper looked like it was from the future, and of course she had always assumed Marius Quine was from the future, though she didn't know for certain.

The writing had made little sense to her at first, partly because the bottom right portion of the paper had been ripped away, cutting off some key words and phrases, but the rest mostly looked like a jumble of meaningless words, dates, and numbers. But she'd found it at such a pivotal moment in her life, she had to believe it wasn't coincidence, that it had meaning. And now she had one more piece of the puzzle. She brushed a finger over a name printed toward the bottom of the page.

MATEO

The rest of the words were missing, torn from the page.

Belamie pulled the hat out from her waistband and studied it more closely. It was a baseball cap, one that came from the future, in New York. She only knew this because the symbol on the hat matched the symbol on the shirt she was currently wearing. She'd gotten it from the future, almost the furthest she'd ever traveled.

In her early days of time-traveling, Belamie had been reluctant to travel into the future. It felt too unstable, less knowable than the past, and the further into the future you traveled the more everything changed—the fashions, the food, the buildings, and the inventions. The contraptions in the future were especially mind-boggling. She remembered the first time she saw an automobile. She thought she'd gone mad. And then the first time she'd used a telephone, and electricity, and saw an airplane fly over her head, a great, roaring metal bird that had nearly made her choke on her own tongue. Once the *Vermillion* had even turned into an airplane. *That* was an adventure. She was certain if she didn't crash and die, she would die of fright. Luckily, she'd had the presence of mind to turn the dials of the compass before either happened. After that she vowed she would never travel to the future again.

Eventually, though, Belamie grew to really enjoy traveling into the future, and despite some drastic and sometimes perplexing changes, in some ways it was nothing new. Just like any time in the past there were wars and violence in the future. People fought for the same reasons—land, religion, money, and power. There were storms and earthquakes and hurricanes and volcanoes and tsunamis that swept away entire cities, killing thousands, and people responded in similar ways as they had in the past. Some people were kind and generous. Others were not. Some people kept hope. Others did not. It was all things she'd seen before, and yet the future also revealed some incredible things Belamie had never seen, groundbreaking discoveries that eradicated diseases, and inventions that changed the world sometimes for the better (indoor flushable toilets!) and sometimes for the worse (Spam. Ugh.).

She traveled decade by decade. She engrossed herself in every era's theater, literature, art, and fashions. She took in the future like a novel, turning the pages with a feverish and insatiable need to know what happens next, until quite suddenly and without warning, the future stopped.

She was traveling into the twenty-first century. She was less than two decades in and thought to jump ahead another decade or two. It was always fun to see. It was a very interesting time all over the world. She didn't know what it was, but when Belamie tried to go forward, the *Vermillion* was suddenly flung back to Nowhere in No Time. She thought maybe she had made a mistake with the dials, so she tried again, but again was thrown back, like she'd been put in a giant slingshot.

She tried again and again, traveling in shorter intervals, testing different locations, making bigger leaps in time. She'd hit blank spots before, pockets of time and locations where she couldn't travel, but this was different. She tried to travel to AD 2050, 2080, 3000, 3500, 4000. . . . It was like a great wall had been built in the twenty-first century. The year 2019, to be exact, and not just in one city or region, but everywhere in the world.

Belamie wondered what could have happened then that would prevent her from time-traveling beyond that point. Did the world end? Maybe there'd been a great war. She'd read about bombs in the future that could annihilate entire countries. Maybe everyone just bombed each other until there was nothing left. There had certainly been enough threats. Or maybe the earth was hit by a great meteor and everyone died, just like the dinosaurs.

But if she were really being honest, she didn't believe it had anything to do with bombs or meteors. She had a gut feeling that something else happened then, something to do with the compass. Perhaps it had something to do with the Aeternum, or Marius Quine. Or maybe it had to do with the boy, Mateo, her son (she could barely think it). It could have something to do with this ugly shirt and the hat with matching symbols. Maybe this was a clue, a sign. They were connected somehow.

Belamie went to a small desk covered in books and papers, opened a drawer and pulled out the big leather-bound book where she kept the record of all her missions, the dates and locations and details of the events. She'd learned early on the importance of keeping a good record, so they didn't accidentally return to the same time and place and cross paths with themselves. It was easy to get mixed up. It also helped if you needed to recall a past mission.

She flipped through a few pages and found the dates she was looking for.

New York, AD August 3, 1997, Supplies
New York, AD August 24, 1996, Broadway
Musical
New York, AD January 15, 1998, Supplies

On one of these trips, when Belamie had been testing the limits of the compass, she'd made a stop in New York, late twentieth century. The date didn't seem important or significant to her then. Belamie liked New York at almost any time. She found it exciting with all the crowds and noise and lights and movement, contrasted by the peace and tranquility of

Central Park. She also loved the hordes of shops and products and supplies. The ease and comforts of twentieth-century living were also incredibly tempting to her.

If I had to stay in one place, she thought, it would be here. She never said that to Vince. He did not care much for the future world, particularly America, and especially New York City. He said it had no class or charm, that Americans were crass and rude, just a bunch of discards from around the world, all the people no one else wanted. Belamie suspected the real reason Vince didn't care for it was how difficult it was to steal in the future world. There were cameras everywhere, and alarm systems, and locks and codes, and guards with guns.

This never bothered Belamie. She was plenty rich. Money was no object. Here, in the future world, she could spend her spoils. And spend she did. Belamie simply adored shopping in New York. She loved all the displays of beautiful clothes, ready-made. She loved that women could wear pants without anyone batting an eye, wear their hair long and loose, or even cut it short if they wanted, and maneuvered through society with much more ease and autonomy than women in other times and places in the world.

After she'd made the year of several eager salesladies and her arms were heavy, laden with bags, she stopped at a convenience store to grab a few supplies, some snacks and candy for the crew, and a few magazines. (She couldn't stay away from the British royal drama. Some things never changed.) The man at the cash register wasn't paying any attention, and there were very few people in the store, so she just tossed things in her shopping bag as she went down the aisles. (Small stuff was easier to steal in the future world than in almost any other era.)

As she moved toward the front of the store, she stopped at a shelf stacked full of romance novels, ones with scandalous covers she was shocked were allowed to be shown in public. She leafed through a few, reading the back descriptions.

That's when she felt someone watching her. She looked around and saw a man staring at her. He was tall and handsome in a grungy, studious kind of way. He wore glasses, and his dark hair was a little wild and unkempt. He was wearing some hideous shirt, white with thin blue stripes and blue and red letters and numbers that said *Mets 18*. He smiled at her, clearly amused. She looked around, trying to see if there was someone behind her that he was looking at, but there wasn't anyone else in the store except the cashier. Maybe the man had seen her stealing, or maybe he was interested in what she was currently holding. She looked at the book she'd picked up. *The Mistress of Lord Haversham* by Sadie Brookes. Lord Haversham was not wearing a shirt, hideous or otherwise.

Belamie looked back at the man, smiled, then boldly tossed the book into one of her shopping bags. The man's smile only broadened. She could have sworn he was laughing, like she'd just performed a magic trick.

I'll show you a trick, Belamie thought.

She reached for the compass, turned the dials, and, just to be cheeky, she winked and blew the man a kiss, right before she disappeared.

Belamie forgot about the man, until a few months later she traveled back to New York, but a year earlier than the last time she'd come. This time she took the entire crew. She wanted them all to see *Les Misérables*. She'd read the novel by Victor Hugo, in its original French, and she was curious to see how the literary masterpiece would translate into a Broadway musical in English. Just as they were walking into the theater, she saw the man again. He was wearing more regular clothing this time, no ugly striped shirt, but she was certain it was the same man she'd seen in the convenience store a few months back. He was scanning the theater crowds, squinting through his glasses. She knew he was looking for her. And then it hit her. This man, whoever he was, somehow knew who she was, or at least knew that she could time travel. Belamie wondered, How many times had this man seen her? What did he want? Was he a friend or enemy? She was curious, but her sense of self-preservation was stronger. She gathered the crew and they left the theater without seeing the show, but just before she got in the *Vermillion* (a white limo) she stopped. There was a rack full of shirts and hats and bags for sale on the sidewalk. One of them was the ugly shirt, just like the one the man had been wearing before. It said *Mets* on the front. Belamie picked up the shirt.

"That's fifteen dollars," said the guy selling the shirts. "Two for twenty-five."

She stared at it for a moment, and when she looked up the mysterious man was there. Belamie backed up a step, put her hand on the door of the *Vermillion*.

"Ma'am, you gonna pay for that?"

Belamie didn't even think. She jumped into the *Vermillion*.

"Wait!" she heard the man call.

"Hey!" The seller pounded on the window. "I'll call the police! I got your license plate number!"

"Drive!" Belamie shouted.

Tui was at the wheel. She pulled into traffic while Belamie wrestled with the compass. Her hands were shaking.

"What's wrong?" Annie asked, craning her neck. "Who was that man?"

"No one," said Belamie.

"What is that thing?" Vincent asked, nodding to the shirt in her hand.

"A shirt," she said.

"It's hideous," said Vincent. "Did you get it for Annie?"

"I'm not wearing that!" said Annie.

Belamie turned the final dial. As the *Vermillion* began to stretch and twist, she glanced in the rearview mirror and saw the man chasing after her. Waving for her to stop. The mirror twisted and folded in on itself, and then the *Vermillion* disappeared.

The morning after the incident with the boy, Mateo, Annie appeared at Belamie's cabin door. She wore her ragged, oversized coat, her rifle slung over her shoulder, with her little knapsack tied to it. She was ready to go home. Belamie again asked if she was certain this was what she wanted. Annie said it was, and Belamie did not feel she could hold the girl against her will. That was not the way of the *Vermillion*. A time pirate joined and remained on her crew by choice, never against his or her will. She'd only had one other crew member ask to leave. That, too, had been oddly connected to Vince.

Belamie took Annie back to Ohio AD 1870, roughly one year after she'd picked her up. She took Annie back in the spring at least, when the snow had melted, and green things were pushing out of the ground. A little more welcoming than the cold winter in which they'd found her.

"She was never up to the task of being a time pirate," said Vincent as they watched Annie walk away from the *Vermillion*, now a train.

"And what is the task of being a time pirate, Vincent?" Tui asked.

"Take over the world, of course. The girl might have deadly aim, but she's shortsighted. Now she's stuck in that hovel, and she'll never amount to anything."

"Never underestimate what a girl in a hovel can do," said Neeti, and everyone laughed. They had found Neeti living in complete squalor in a small village in southern India. At the time, Vince had advised Belamie against bringing her on board. He had sneered at her ragged state, her seeming lack of skill or manners. He could be a bit of a snob about such things sometimes, what he called *breeding*. But Belamie disagreed. She had seen something in Neeti that reminded her of her own unfortunate background, and she wanted to give her a chance. She was glad she had. Neeti had become a valuable member of the crew and a good friend. Later, Vince had praised Belamie for bringing Neeti on board. He said it was a smart move to find someone in a completely desperate situation and rescue them. "People are like dogs that way," he had said coldly. "Rescue them and they'll be your loyal servant for life."

This remark troubled Belamie for a few reasons. For one thing, she had not "rescued" any of her crew with the idea of making them feel obligated or loyal to her. She'd simply sensed something in each of them that might add value to her crew. Yes, their circumstances had moved her to compassion, but it had more to do with her own past than anything else.

But that was only a minor bother to her. What really struck a nerve was the fact that Vince was the only member of her crew whom she had not rescued in any way. In fact, he had rescued *her*. Early on in her time travels, she'd appeared in the middle of a naval battle. She'd almost been blown up by a ship's cannon, and then Vincent swooped in and rescued her, and the rest, as they say, is history. It had been wild and very romantic, she thought. Definitely something that would happen in a romance novel. But she wondered, if Vince's words were true, were her feelings toward him rightly earned? Or was *she* a dog?

Belamie kept her gaze on Annie as she grew smaller and smaller, just a little speck on the wide, flat plains of Ohio.

Annie's words again echoed inside her head.

"Mateo."

"He's your son!"

"Vincent gets the compass."

Belamie had this strange feeling all of a sudden, like she could feel the world rotating beneath her feet, and the stars realigning themselves in the heavens.

Belamie clutched at her chest. She suddenly felt cold and empty, like there was a hole in her heart that was growing larger every day, and if she didn't find what it needed to be filled, the void would consume her.

"He's your son."

Belamie gasped and reached out. Tui caught her.

"Captain," said Tui. "What is it? Are you ill?"

"No, no, I'm fine. I just . . . I will miss Annie."

"Poor *Bonbon*," said Vince, putting an arm around her. "You have such a large heart. Let's get you out of this god-forsaken place. Shall we head back to Chicago?" He gently tugged at the chain around her neck. Belamie jerked away and placed her hand over the compass. Vince held his hands in the air, his brow knit in confusion. A hush fell among the crew. They were all looking at her like she was a wild animal.

"Excuse me," she said, stepping away from Vincent, her crew. "I just need a moment to . . . relieve myself. Go get ready for travel. I'll be there in a moment."

She walked until she found a thick copse of shrubs that would adequately cover her. She glanced over her shoulder to make sure all the crew had gone back inside the *Vermillion*. They had.

Quickly, Belamie pulled out her compass. She'd come to a decision. She needed answers, and she couldn't wait for the answers to come to her. She had to *know*. She began to turn the dials. When she'd made the final click of the outer dial, she was sucked into a void of space and time, and the next thing she knew she was rolling on hard cement spotted with old gum and littered with garbage. Feet tripped over her.

A man cursed at her after he'd kicked her in the gut. A woman threatened to sue her for almost running over her baby. A few people stopped and asked if she was all right and helped her up. Yes, she was in New York, the city that contained the best and worst of humanity.

She brushed herself off, apologized profusely to her victims, thanked those who had helped, and turned down a street.

And there he was. The man from the theater and the convenience store. His hair was a little windblown, his face flushed, as though he'd been running. His glasses were slightly crooked on his nose, and he was wearing the Mets shirt. The same one she was wearing.

He caught sight of her and smiled. Belamie's heart skipped a beat or two. Her knees were a little wobbly as she walked toward him.

"Nice shirt," he said.

"I heard it was the latest fashion and jumped on board."

The man's eyes danced with amusement. "Join me for a cup of coffee?"

Belamie accepted his offer.

9
Driver's Ed

June 2, 2019
Hudson River Valley, New York

Stealing their father's map turned out to be much simpler than Matt had anticipated. At breakfast the next morning Ruby asked Mr. Hudson to tell her more about what he studied in college, because she was interested in possibly studying the same thing. Mr. Hudson was thrilled. He went on and on about how ancient trade routes shaped the modern world. He got so animated while talking about the Silk Road and its effects on Asia that he knocked over his mug of coffee. The coffee spilled all down Mrs. Hudson's very white blouse, while the mug fell to the tile floor with a crash.

Beautiful, Matt thought. He couldn't have planned it better himself.

Mr. Hudson looked down at the mess with his arms still

out in a dramatic gesture. "I got a little carried away, didn't I?"

"Just a little," said Mrs. Hudson, blotting her blouse with her napkin.

"Kids, why don't you go outside until we get this all cleaned up?" said Gaga. "I don't want you getting cut from any of the broken pieces."

All three children stood up from the table and moved to go outside. Corey walked behind Mr. Hudson just as he took a couple of steps back. He knocked into Corey.

"Sorry, bud," said Mr. Hudson.

"No prob, Dad," said Corey, slipping his hands behind his back. Ruby then came up close behind Corey.

"Oh, Ruby, don't go too far!" called Mr. Hudson. "We still need to discuss Middle Eastern trade. That's where things get really exciting!"

Ruby gave him a thumbs-up. "Looking forward to it."

Mr. Hudson gave his daughter a big grin and a double thumbs-up.

Once they were outside, all three kids ran through the vineyard to the other end and into the empty field where Chuck's old VW bus sat like a giant's forgotten toy gone rusty in the rain. The side door of the bus was slightly ajar, and inside Matt could see a little table and benches. He looked all around for Chuck but didn't see him anywhere.

"Let's go in here," said Matt, opening up the door. "I don't think Chuck will mind."

They all scrambled inside and sat at the table. The seats were white vinyl with orange lining, a little dingy and worn. A few places were patched with duct tape. Little curtains with blue flowers hung in the windows.

"This is pretty cool," said Corey, opening up the little cupboards across from the table. "Hey, there are snacks in here!" He pulled out some granola bars and cheese crackers.

"Corey, we just had breakfast," said Ruby. "And we've got more important things to think about besides food."

Corey grumbled as he put back the snacks and shut the cupboards.

"You got it, didn't you?" said Matt.

Ruby pulled out a thick, folded-up piece of parchment from her back pocket and set it on the table.

"Good thing Dad is such a nerd," said Corey. "That was crazy easy."

"He's just passionate about his work," said Ruby.

"That's just a nice way of saying he's a nerd."

"What's wrong with nerds?" said Matt.

"Nothing, I love nerds," said Corey. "I'm related to quite a few."

Matt looked back toward the house. They were too far away to see through the kitchen windows, but it was only a matter of time before they came looking for them. It was only a matter of time before their dad noticed the map was missing. Matt was guessing he looked at it at least once an hour.

He pulled the flowered curtains shut and sat down next to Corey at the table, with Ruby on the other side.

Ruby unfolded the map slowly. Matt had never paid too much attention to this map. It had hung on their dining room wall for as long as he could remember, a permanent fixture that you barely noticed, like the living room rug, or the kitchen faucet. Matt had often seen his dad stare at the map, and even trace his finger over some of the markings, but he'd never thought anything of it. Why should he? His dad was an expert cartographer. He had dozens of maps and thought each one was something special. How could Matt have guessed that the one hanging above the table where he ate dinner every night was actually a magical map that showed the location of a time-traveling ship that his own mother used to captain? To Matt it had just been something he used to help learn geography—his countries, states, and capitals. But now, looking at it, that seemed completely ridiculous. This map was clearly something more than just a piece of paper with lines and markings. It almost hummed with a current of energy. The lines of the map shimmered and faded in and out, as though they could disappear or shift position. There were markings all over the map, little compass stars of varying shades dotting both land and water.

"Do you think Quine made this map?" Ruby asked.

"That's a logical assumption," said Matt, "seeing as it shows the location of the *Vermillion*."

"The compass, you mean," said Corey. "It would follow the compass, wouldn't it?"

"Yes, I guess that's true," said Matt. "One usually follows the other."

"I wonder how Dad got this," Ruby said. "He never did tell us."

"Maybe Quine gave it to him," said Matt. "He gave the compass to Mom, remember?"

"I wonder why, though," said Ruby, "like what's in it for him?"

"I don't know," said Matt. He had plenty of questions about the mysterious Marius Quine, but he couldn't focus on him right now. He was concentrating on the map, studying all the little compass symbols. There were several in varying shades and brightness, all piled up on top of one another, but Matt couldn't see how his dad gleaned so much information from them. How did he know the date the *Vermillion* landed, and in relation to their own timeline? It seemed impossible to figure out.

Ruby put her finger over one of the compass symbols in New York, then gasped as markings appeared above it. She snatched back her finger, and the markings went away. She put her finger back over the little compass star and the markings appeared again. It gave a coordinate and a date.

Forty degrees north, seventy-three degrees west; April 26, 2019 . . .

"That's when we came home from the *Vermillion*," Ruby said. The marking was still quite dark and defined. She traced her finger over some of the other markings, and more coordinates and dates appeared, some that Matt didn't quite understand, like they were on a different calendar system.

"It looks like the brightness of the marking correlates to how recently the *Vermillion* traveled according to our timeline," said Matt, tracing his own finger over some of the markings. He found the time they went to Paris, August 21, 1911, when they'd stolen the *Mona Lisa* from the Louvre. Shortly after they'd returned home from the *Vermillion*, Matt had looked up the *Mona Lisa* to see if it was still missing. They had never returned it when he was on the *Vermillion*, but according to all the articles he found, the painting had been recovered in 1913, just as Jia had said. Vincenzo Peruggia was caught with the painting and admitted to stealing it and everything, with no accomplices. No story of anyone else stealing it. Somehow it had been returned to Peruggia before he was caught with it.

Matt moved his finger to other markings. Sometimes the land lines shifted, moving inward from the sea, or expanding outward, and sometimes country lines shifted or disappeared.

"Why is it doing that?" Corey asked. "Why are some of the lines changing?"

"Land changes over time, I'm guessing," said Ruby, brushing her fingers over the maps so the lines rippled like an animation reel. "There are some ancient cities that sank below water in earthquakes, and then of course wars and politics change land lines."

"Plus, continental drift," said Matt.

Matt found another marking that stood out to him. It was on an island just off the coast of northern Siberia. The marking was quite bright, just as bright as the marking in New York, possibly brighter, as though the *Vermillion* had traveled there quite recently. Matt's heart skipped a beat. He remembered the conversation they'd overheard through the vent, how his parents had said the *Vermillion* was in Siberia, possibly discarding old crew . . .

"Look at this one," he said, pointing. When he tapped his finger over the marking, a coordinate popped up, followed by more numerals and symbols that Matt wasn't sure he understood at first, but Ruby did.

"Thirty twenty-one BC!" shrieked Ruby.

"Whoa," said Corey. "That's, like, five thousand years ago."

"We can't travel that far!" said Ruby.

"But what if Jia is there?" said Matt. "This is exactly the kind of time and place Captain Vincent would discard someone who betrayed him, and look at the marking. It looks like he traveled there right after New York."

"But, Matt, your time sickness," said Ruby. "I doubt it's safe for any of us to travel that far back in time, but especially not you."

"She's right, bro," said Corey. "Remember how sick you got the first few times we traveled?"

"And that was only a century," said Ruby. "This is five thousand years!"

"I'll be fine," said Matt, even though his stomach did make a sudden lurch at the thought. "This isn't my first time traveling. I did get used to it eventually, and we can travel back gradually, so it's not such a shock. We have time for that, and I'll pack plenty of food."

"Yes, food," said Corey. "We'd better make a grocery run. Get plenty of Cheetos and Oreos and other medicine."

"How are we going to do that?" said Ruby. "Grandma always has groceries delivered. It's not like we can walk to the store. We're just going to have to take whatever we can get from the pantry."

Somewhere in the distance a door snapped shut. Matt crawled to the window and peered through the curtains. Both their parents were out on the porch. Matt couldn't hear what they were saying, but they looked upset. Their mom was looking all around, shielding her eyes from the sun.

Ruby and Corey came up beside him. "I think they figured out the map is missing," said Ruby.

"And they're looking for us," said Corey.

"We'd better show ourselves," said Ruby. "We don't want them to suspect we took it." Ruby moved to the table and started to fold up the map.

"Wait!" said Matt. "We need to write down those coordinates and the date, just in case." He pulled his notebook out of the back pocket of his pants. He'd started to carry it with him everywhere, but he suddenly realized he didn't have a pen.

"Either of you have something to write with?" Matt asked.

"Yeah, sure," said Corey, feeling in his pockets. "Oh wait . . . I forgot. I'm not a super nerd."

Matt shook his head. He could hear his parents calling for them now. "I'll just put the coordinates in my compass." He pulled out his compass and started to put in the coordinates for the island.

"Matt, be careful," said Ruby.

"I won't turn the other dials, I'm just entering the location. I won't go anywhere unless I turn all the dials." He peered through the curtains and saw his parents walking in their direction.

"We should go," said Ruby. "We shouldn't be caught hiding inside Chuck's bus. They'll think we . . ."

The bus's engine suddenly roared to life.

"What the . . . !" shouted Corey.

They all looked to the driver's seat, but there was no one there, and no keys in the ignition. Matt looked down at his compass.

"Oh . . . my . . . ," said Ruby.

"Matthew! The kids!" Mrs. Hudson shouted.

Matt looked out the window to see his parents sprinting toward them.

"Kids! Get out of the bus!" shouted Mr. Hudson, running to keep up with Mrs. Hudson.

"Busted," said Corey.

"Never mind them!" said Ruby. "Matt, the compass! Turn the other dials!"

"But . . . ," said Matt, now suddenly unsure. "We're not ready!"

"We'll never get a chance if we wait!" said Ruby. "It's now or never. Turn the other dials!"

Matt was so flustered he fumbled the compass and dropped it between the seats. "Argh!" he shouted, and glanced out the window.

Their parents were halfway across the vineyard now. His mom was running as though her life depended on it.

"Don't worry. I'll buy us some time," said Corey. He jumped into the driver's seat.

"Corey, this car is a stick shift!" said Ruby. "And you don't have a driver's license!"

"Don't worry! I learned how to drive stick at the arcade. It's not that hard." He jammed the stick forward and pressed his feet on the pedals. The bus roared, screeched, and lurched forward. Matt was slammed back into one of the seats and then thrown forward all the way to the front of the vehicle, so he crashed into the radio, which turned on and started shuffling through stations.

The compass was sliding around on the floor. There was the unmistakable *crunch* of Corey driving over one of the grapevines.

"Corey! Watch where you're going!" shouted Ruby. She was holding on to the front passenger seat and hit her head on the ceiling as they bumped along.

"I'm sorry," said Corey, "but this beast does not have power steering!"

"Stop! You all get out right now! Right this instant!" Mrs. Hudson shouted. Matt could see them in the rearview mirror, chasing after the bus.

Matt suddenly felt unsure about the current situation. "Maybe we should stop," he said. "Maybe we should talk this through."

"No way. Do you want to be g-grounded for-e-ever?" Corey said as they bounced on the grassy lawn, the bus tilting on its side.

Ruby fell back into one of the benches. "He's right, Matt, get the compass!"

Matt's mind raced. They were right. If they stopped, that was it. They might never get another chance. He thought of Jia, all alone on an island five thousand years ago. He couldn't do that to her. He'd never forgive himself.

Matt got down on the floor and searched. He heard it sliding around and finally caught it in his hand. "I got it!"

His heart was pounding, his fingers sweaty, but he held tight to the compass. "I need to see the coordinates again, and the date!" he shouted. Ruby moved to the table and held down the map. Matt found the marking and put his finger on it, so the numerals popped up. The bus swerved and bounced wildly, so he lost his balance. He righted himself, got to the map again, and found the date. But he wasn't sure how to enter it. He'd never traveled in the BC era, and he wasn't sure what all the numbers meant. He heard a thump on the back of the bus. Matt looked up to see Mrs. Hudson running behind the bus, looking straight at Mateo through the rear window wearing what Matt could only describe as her you-are-in-the-worst-trouble-of-your-life expression. "STOP THIS CAR RIGHT NOW!" she bellowed, pounding on the window.

"We've got to try," said Matt. He started to turn the other dials, doing his best to guess where they should go. This could be a real disaster, he thought, but he had to take the risk. Matt made the last turn of the outer dial. Either this worked, or they were grounded for life. Maybe both.

The bus started to make a strange, grinding noise, like it was shifting into a gear it didn't know existed. There was a big thud on top of the bus.

"I think it's working!" said Ruby.

Matt looked out the rear window. He didn't see either of his parents.

I'm sorry, he said in his heart.

And then it happened.

There was an explosion of light. The bus shot forward, accelerating to what felt like a thousand miles per second. Matt felt as though he'd been flipped inside out and upside down. The bus touched ground, bounced, and swerved. They were careening along a path with lots of people. Men in suits, boys in suspenders, women and girls in dresses and hats. They almost ran over a man with a bunch of balloons, and then they were headed toward a big red-and-white-striped tent.

"Where are we?" said Ruby.

They drove right into the tent and were nearly trampled by an elephant. Corey swerved sharply, and a man on stilts blew a stream of fire out of his mouth.

"Matt! This is a circus!"

Matt suddenly remembered the compass in his hand. He looked at it. No, this was not where he had put the settings, he was quite sure. He shook it a little, pressed the dials. A tiger leaped toward them, roaring with claws outstretched. Everyone screamed, and then it was gone. They shot into the void again and touched down to earth in the midst of a sea of soldiers fighting with swords and bayonets. A cannon shot and exploded a barricade, and then it was gone again. They sped through time and space as though they were on a film tape in rewind. Every now and then the VW bus paused to see where they were before speeding off again. He caught glimpses of things—trees, mountains, buildings—and for a brief moment they looked to be coming in first in a chariot race, until they were whipped away again.

Finally they bounced down, and whether they'd arrived at their destination or the bus had simply had enough, they screeched to a stop.

10
New Crew, Old Crew

February 21, 3021 BC
Wrangel Island

Matt slammed back on the seat, his neck cracking a little.

Ruby groaned beside him. "Did we make it?"

Matt looked out the windows. The landscape was all white and gray. No buildings or people. He could feel cold air seeping through the doors. "I think so," said Matt.

Corey unwrapped his hands from the steering wheel. "That was crazy," he said breathlessly. He was quite pale.

"I thought we were going to die," said Ruby.

"We're okay," said Matt. "We're fine. We made it."

The three children just sat there for a moment, taking in the stillness and the silence, allowing their discombobulated brains to settle.

The side door of the bus flew open.

Matt's jaw dropped. There was his mother. Her long dark

hair was ratted and tangled, and her normally tan face was ashen. Matt started to shiver. He wasn't sure if it was the cold air or the rage on his mother's face.

"We might die now," said Corey, his voice cracking.

A pair of legs dropped down from the top of the bus, and their dad fell to the ground. He grunted, then pulled himself up on the footboard of the bus, gasping for breath. His hair looked like a porcupine with quills flared outward, and he was breathing very hard and fast.

"Get out," said Mrs. Hudson in a low growl that made Matt's neck hairs stand on end. "Now."

The children all got out of the bus quickly but cautiously, like they were moving around a wild beast that might rip them to pieces if they made any sudden moves. Mr. Hudson clutched at his chest and leaned against the side of the bus. He looked like he was about to have a heart attack, but Mrs. Hudson didn't seem too worried about that. She stood in front of her children, fists clenching, jaw pulsing. Matt thought she looked taller than he remembered.

"Explain," said Mrs. Hudson. "No excuses. No lies. You tell me the truth right now." Matt looked at Corey and Ruby, but they were both looking at him. Of course this was all his doing.

Matt reached for his compass and held it out for his mother to see. It was all greasy and sticky with peanut butter. It looked more like a toddler's teething toy than some powerful, magical object, but he knew she knew what it was the instant she saw it. Whatever explanation she was expecting, Matt was fairly certain she was not expecting this. "What. Is. *That?*"

"I . . ." Matt's mouth suddenly ran dry. He couldn't talk. He looked to Ruby, pleading for help.

"It's a compass," said Ruby. "Matt made it."

Mrs. Hudson blinked. "He made it?"

"That's what he's been working on in Gaga's basement all this time," said Ruby.

"And it works!" chimed Corey. "Isn't that amazing? He's like . . . like Iron Man and Doctor Strange all in one!" He was clearly trying to make this sound like it was all good news, something to be celebrated. Matt did not think it was working.

Mrs. Hudson looked around at the snow and ice, like she was just realizing that they were no longer in New York, and it was definitely not summer. "A compass," she said. "You built a time-traveling compass . . ."

Mr. Hudson had now composed himself enough to put his glasses on and observe their surroundings. The bus had landed on top of a cliff jutting out over an icy ocean. The shore was peppered with some kind of animal lazing on the icy rocks, dipping into the water. Walruses, Matt was pretty sure. He could see their large tusks, and their barking snorts and grunts filled the air. A few polar bears also roamed the beach.

Behind them, the land looked mostly barren, only a few

pitiful plants on the snow-covered ground. The rocks and crags were covered with giant icicles. There wasn't a building in sight, nor any other signs of humans. In the distance were a few mountain ranges, and roaming on the plains was a herd of large, furry animals that Matt could not quite make out. Maybe buffalo? They moved up and down like a dark wave on the white horizon.

"Matt," said Mr. Hudson, keeping his eyes on the creatures. His voice sounded strange. "What year is this?"

"Oh. Uh . . . we're somewhere in 3021, I think."

Mrs. Hudson's eyes nearly bugged out of their sockets. "I'm sorry? Did you say 3021 *BC*?"

"Give or take a year or two?" Matt hoped he wasn't off by too much. If Jia had been discarded here, he didn't think she'd survive very long. He looked around, hoping to see some sign of her. A trail of footsteps. A flag signaling for help.

"We traveled over five thousand years in one shot?" shrieked Mrs. Hudson. "Mateo! You're not supposed to travel that far that fast!" Mrs. Hudson groaned and clutched her head. She started muttering in Arabic. Matt heard her say she had a headache and they were all going to be sick. Matt was feeling a bit queasy himself, but he wasn't about to admit it to his mom right now.

"We have to get out of here," Mrs. Hudson snapped. "Everyone back to the bus. Matt, give me that . . . that *compass*."

She held out her hand. Matt reached for his compass. It was practically a reflex to obey his mother's commands, but Ruby reached up and stopped him.

"It's *Matt's* compass," she said. "Only he should be allowed to use it."

"Yeah, that makes sense," said Corey. "The maker is the taker."

Mrs. Hudson blinked, clearly taken aback. "I understand Mateo *made* the compass," snapped Mrs. Hudson. "But that doesn't mean he automatically knows how to use it. We could have all died traveling the way you did."

"It doesn't mean you'd do any better," said Ruby, defiantly. "It's not the Obsidian Compass. It might work a little differently. You might not even know how to work Matt's."

Matt couldn't believe how bold Ruby was being. The expression on his mom's face made him want to bury himself beneath the snow.

"You children think this is a game," she said. "You're lucky we didn't all die on the way here. You have no idea what you're dealing with."

"Why do you say that?" said Ruby. "Why do you assume that because we are children we don't know what we're dealing with? Don't you remember that we've time-traveled too? We traveled dozens of times. Do you think Matt could have even built the compass if he didn't have an idea of what he was dealing with?"

Mrs. Hudson pressed her lips together and took a deep breath. "Matthew," she said, turning to her husband. "A little help?"

Mr. Hudson bent down toward Matt. Matt flinched and clutched his compass to his chest. "Don't worry, I'm just looking," said his dad. He pulled his glasses to the tip of his nose, studying the compass. He sniffed. "Smells like . . . peanut butter."

"That's the magic ingredient!" said Corey. "Isn't that awesome?"

"Peanut butter? Ha!" Mr. Hudson laughed. "Incredible. *Genius.*" Matt took a breath. Maybe he wasn't in so much trouble, but then his mom started talking again.

"Yes," Mrs. Hudson snapped, sneering at her husband. "It is incredible. *C'est magnifique!* But what's even more astonishing to me is that you decided not to tell us that you'd built such a compass in the first place. Instead you steal a bus, nearly run us over, and travel five millennia in the past! What on earth were you thinking?"

"I just . . . we wanted to find Jia," he said.

Mrs. Hudson's expression softened just a little. "Jia?" she asked. "Your friend from Vince's crew? Why do you think she would be here?"

"Well . . . ," said Matt, digging his feet into the hard snow, "we sort of borrowed Dad's map."

Mr. Hudson whirled, his eyes blazing, all warmth gone.

"*You* stole my map?" he said. "Where is it?"

Alarmed by Mr. Hudson's sudden flash of temper, Ruby very quickly produced the map. Mr. Hudson snatched it from her. "You had no right to take this. If you had wanted to know something, you should have asked."

Ruby stood up a little taller, pushing back her shoulders. "And you would have told us?"

"Of course we would!" said Mrs. Hudson. "Did it ever occur to you that we might be able to help you? That I have just a little more experience time-traveling than you do? That your father is the only one who really knows how to read that map? What you did was reckless and foolish! What if something happened to you? What if you had gotten stuck? What if Vincent were to—"

Mrs. Hudson's lecture was interrupted by a strange rattling. The Hudsons all whirled around. The rusty VW bus was bouncing and shaking like there was a wild beast inside. The hatch popped open.

Mr. and Mrs. Hudson both jumped in front of the kids and took a protective stance, spreading out their arms. Matt peered over his mother's arm to see someone roll out of the bus and flop on the frozen ground with a loud grunt. "What the beetle juice?" came a grizzly voice. It was an old man, rough and bearded, wearing shorts and a tie-dyed T-shirt with a brimmed hat and a pair of dark, circular sunglasses.

"Chuck!" said Mr. Hudson, lowering his arms. "I'm so

sorry. We had no idea you were in there." He bent down to help Chuck off the ground.

"I guess I fell asleep," said Chuck, leaning heavily on Mr. Hudson as he got to his feet. "I was up late last night. Got a little caught up in the starry night sky." He looked up at the sky as though he were expecting to see stars. He frowned at the gloomy gray.

Matt wondered how they could have missed Chuck sleeping inside the bus the entire time they'd been in it. Even if he'd been covered by the back bench, Matt would have thought they'd at least hear him snoring or breathing. And how could Chuck have possibly slept through everything? It wasn't as though their travels had been particularly smooth.

Chuck put his hands on his hips and bent backward, cracking his spine, then stretched his arms and yawned. He shivered and wrapped his arms around his body. "Good golly, it's freezing. Did I hibernate through summer and fall?" He went back to the bus, opened a board in the floor, and pulled out a brown-and-yellow crocheted blanket. He wrapped it around his shoulders. Matt started shivering. It was freezing, and he was only in a T-shirt.

"I got more blankets if anyone wants one," said Chuck, "plus some other winter stuff."

Chuck pulled out blanket after blanket from the floor of the bus, like a magician pulling scarves out of his sleeve, and tossed them to everyone. Ruby got a colorful checkered one, Corey got rainbow waves, and Matt caught a blanket with purple flowers all over it. He wrapped it around himself, glad to have some protection from the cold. They certainly hadn't thought about clothing and gear for this mission. They hadn't thought about a lot of things, he was beginning to realize.

Mrs. Hudson pulled a blanket around her that reminded Matt of candy corns, and Mr. Hudson got a blue one with puffy pink pom-poms all over it.

"Where did you get all these?" Corey asked.

"I made them," said Chuck. "I like to crochet in my spare time. It helps me relax."

Chuck then pulled out some hats, gloves, and scarves, which he passed out among them. Corey put on a hat with flaps that made him look like Elmer Fudd. Matt peeked over Chuck's shoulder to see what else he'd stored inside his bus. There was a thermos, a pocketknife, Band-Aids, matches, toilet paper, and some granola bars and cans of food that looked like they were probably as old as Blossom.

"You keep all this stuff in your car?" asked Ruby.

"Sure, why not?" said Chuck, filling a small backpack with some food and supplies. "Always be prepared, I tell myself. You never know where you might end up, and that appears to be very true today. Where in the name of *The Godfather* are we?" Chuck swung the pack over his shoulder and looked all around at the ice and snow and the ocean below the cliffs.

"Uh . . . we're on a movie set," said Mr. Hudson. "Some epic fantasy film."

"Pretty realistic set," said Chuck. "Especially for summer in New York."

"It's a little hard to explain," said Mr. Hudson. "I'm afraid our kids made some bad choices and . . . accidentally stole your bus."

Chuck's bushy eyebrows rose above his circular sunglasses. "Accidentally? How do you *accidentally* steal a bus? Especially one that doesn't even start. Blossom hasn't worked in twenty years."

Everyone looked at Matt. He fumbled with his compass in his pocket. "Uh . . . I sort of fixed her, I guess?"

Chuck lowered his sunglasses to take a look at Matt. "*You* fixed her? Well, golly gee, I think that makes up for the stealing part. I never thought I'd live to see the day Blossom rode again. Thanks a heap!"

"Sure, no problem," said Matt.

"Yes, well, I do believe we're trespassing on this movie set," said Mrs. Hudson, "so let's all just get back in the bus now and we'll get you home right away!"

"What the . . . ," said Chuck, squinting toward the mountains. "Is that . . . ?"

Matt turned around. The animals he'd seen earlier were much closer now, so that he could clearly see what they were.

They were definitely not buffalo. They looked like elephants. Brown, furry elephants with huge curved tusks.

"Woolly mammoths!" shouted Corey. "It's a whole *herd* of woolly mammoths!"

"It's all part of the movie set," said Mrs. Hudson, grasping to make this all somehow reasonable. "It's set in the Ice Age. It's a documentary."

"Dad said it was an epic fantasy," said Ruby.

Mr. Hudson put his hand over Ruby's mouth and pushed her behind him.

"I can see a little baby mammoth!" said Corey. "Aw, he's so cute!"

"Good golly," said Chuck, scratching at his beard. "This is a pretty elaborate movie set, isn't it? High budget."

"Chuck," said Mr. Hudson, "I know this is all a bit strange. . . ."

"A bit? I went to sleep in a New York summer and it looks like I woke up in the Ice Age."

Snow began to fall. Fat flakes floated down from the sky, landing soundlessly on Matt's nose and cheeks. The plausibility of the movie set explanation was growing thinner by the moment.

"All right, very strange," said Mr. Hudson. "I can explain. Sort of. But we will get you home and pay for any damages to your bus."

"Yes, we'll get you home right away, in fact," said Mrs.

Hudson. "Kids, let's go. Chuck needs to get back to the vineyard. Us too." Mrs. Hudson reached for Matt, but he jerked away.

"I'm not leaving without Jia."

"Matt, she's not here," said his mom. "Look at this place! No one is here!" She waved her arm around, and as she did, Matt saw something. He blinked. Farther up along the cliffside he saw a pillar of smoke. It was thin, but unmistakably smoke from a fire. Matt started to walk toward it.

"Matt, wrong direction, bud," said his dad. "Chuck's bus is this way."

"It's Jia!" he said, breaking into a run.

"Mateo, wait!" his mom called after him. "It might not be her. It could be an indigenous tribe, you know."

"Jia could be with them!" Matt called. An icy wind rushed in his face as he ran, biting his nose and cheeks. The snow kept falling. Matt ran until he reached a grouping of jumbled crags and rocks. Smoke was rising from between the rocks. He walked around it, observing the ground. He looked up and down the cliffside, observing the rock formations.

"It's a cave," said Chuck. He and the rest had caught up to Matt. "We're standing on top of a cave. These cliffs are probably full of them."

Caves. Of course. The smoke had to be coming from inside a cave. Jia would have used that for shelter. Matt looked all around. He found a spot that descended more gradually down to the beach. He hitched up his blanket and started to climb down.

"Mateo, be careful!" said his mom, climbing down after him. "There's lots of ice here."

There was, and Matt slipped on it plenty, banged up his shins and arms a bit. He hopped the last five feet to the beach below. The rest of the group followed, including Chuck.

"Whoa," said Corey as they all stared upward. "This is crazy cool."

The cliffs were riddled with holes and caverns. Icicles hung down in front of them like a mouthful of sharp teeth. Matt couldn't see the smoke now, but it had to be coming from inside one of these caves.

"Jia?" Matt called, and waited. No one answered. There were only the barks and grunts of the walruses. Still, the hair on the back of Matt's neck prickled. Someone was here. He could feel it.

"Look at this!" said Ruby. She had stepped up to one of the cliff openings and was staring at the rock on the side. It was covered with tally marks. There were hundreds of them, row after row. If each mark represented a day, it was at least a year, perhaps more. Matt prayed that wasn't how long Jia had been stranded here. There was something else carved into the stone, too, Matt thought. A drawing or some writing, but he couldn't tell exactly what. His mom studied the writing up close, her brow knit.

A scuffling noise sounded inside the cave. Mrs. Hudson whirled around and pulled a dagger from the back of her pants.

Ruby gasped. A head peered around the edge of the cave, then disappeared. Matt's heart nearly leaped out of his chest. He saw the head for only a brief moment, but he was certain it was human.

"Jia!" he called. "It's Matt! It's the Hudsons! We came to rescue you!" He tried to run to her, but his dad grabbed him and held him back while Mrs. Hudson stepped forward and started talking. For some reason she spoke in Arabic.

"You can come out," she said. "We won't hurt you."

Matt waited, holding his breath.

The head appeared again, a dark face blinking in the bright light. Matt's heart sank. It wasn't Jia. The person stepped out of the cave fully. It was a woman. She looked young, in her late teens or early twenties, but her face was gaunt, cheeks hollow, like she was on the verge of starvation. Her eyes had that look of being too large for her head, and her dark skin had patches of frostbite. Her lips were cracked. She was covered with bits and pieces of furs and leather from a variety of animals, but even through all the bulk of her clothing, Matt could tell she was very thin.

Mrs. Hudson took in a sharp breath. She breathed out a

word that Matt did not understand. It sounded like "Two-ee."

And then the woman spoke.

"*Rubbana*," she said.

Matt didn't understand her at first, but then he realized she was speaking in Arabic too. She had called his mother "Captain."

11

Fatoumata

"Tui!" Mrs. Hudson broke into a run and swung her arms around the woman, hugging her so forcefully they both slipped on the rocks and nearly fell over.

"Am I dead?" said the young woman, still speaking in Arabic. "I had hoped the afterlife would be warmer, but I always imagined I would find you there, Captain."

"No, no, you're not dead, Tui! It's me. We're alive, and I'm here!" Mrs. Hudson released her and held her at arm's length. "But, Tui, I don't understand. Why are you here?"

"Why do you think? I came for a holiday."

Mrs. Hudson let out a gargled sound that was something between a cry and a laugh, and then stopped abruptly. She put her hand to her mouth. "Oh, Tui, no. No, he didn't leave you here. . . ."

Tui only stared at Mrs. Hudson, her eyes lifeless and empty as two black stones.

"I tried to stop him," said Tui, "but what could I do? He was strong, and when he got the compass . . . I could do nothing."

"What's going on?" Ruby whispered to Matt. "I can't understand a word they're saying. Who is she?"

"She was on Mom's crew," Matt whispered to her and Corey. "When she was Captain Bonnaire. Captain Vincent discarded her here, I think." Matt thought he recognized her somewhat, from when he'd been on the *Vermillion* before, though she'd looked fuller in the face then, healthier.

Mrs. Hudson looked at her friend, taking in her thinness, the tattered furs, like she was living all that she had been through, feeling her pain and suffering. "I'm so sorry, Tui," she said, her voice catching in her throat. "I did not mean for this to happen. I swear it. I thought you would be safe. Can you ever forgive me?"

"I've had my moments of anger, I admit," said Tui, her head held high. "But you are here now. I had almost given up hope, but you are here, and now I wish to serve my dear captain with all my heart." She squeezed Mrs. Hudson's hands tightly. "Though I see you have gathered more crew since we saw each other last." Tui turned her attention to Matt and everyone else in the party. "Maybe you do not have room for me any longer?"

Mrs. Hudson suddenly jumped and turned back to her husband and children. It was as though she'd almost forgotten they even existed. Her two worlds were colliding now. She laughed a little, wiping her nose on her sleeve. "They are a crew of sorts." Mrs. Hudson reached for her husband. He came to her side and took her hand. "This is my husband, Matthew."

"Husband?" said Tui as though she thought she may have misheard.

"And these are our children," said Mrs. Hudson. "Mateo, Corey, and Ruby."

Tui blinked down at the children like they were three little aliens. "Children? *Three* children? Captain Bonnaire a wife and *mama*?"

Mrs. Hudson laughed. "I know. I never would have believed it myself all those years ago when we were off playing pirates." Mrs. Hudson suddenly switched to English. "Matthew, kids, this is my dear friend, Tui. She was on my crew on the *Vermillion*, all those years ago. Tui, I'm sorry you will have to speak English with them. Only Mateo speaks Arabic fluently. The rest are too lazy."

"Hey!" said Corey. "We can't all be geniuses."

"I am very glad to meet you," said Tui in English. "My name is Fatoumata, but my friends call me Tui."

"Hi, I'm Chuck," said Chuck, stepping forward.

"Chook?" said Tui. "And you are part of the new crew?"

"I'm the neighbor whose vehicle they stole to get here, so I guess that does make me part of the crew, doesn't it? I'm very pleased to meet you." He shook Tui's hand vigorously. "So, where are you from? I'm guessing you weren't born around these parts, huh? Unless your parents are polar bears?" He chuckled. Tui pulled her hand away and straightened to her full and considerable height.

"I am from the great empire of Mali," she said. "I was born in AD 1308."

"You don't say?" said Chuck. "Wow. You look great for your age." He slapped his knee and cackled. Tui looked like she was ready to stab him with an icicle.

"Tui is the daughter of the great king of Mali," said Mrs. Hudson. "Mansa Musa."

The name tickled a part of Matt's memory for some reason, but he couldn't think why.

"Oh, so you're a princess then?" said Chuck. "And you say your real name is *Fat-mama*? That's an . . . unusual name. Does it mean something special in Mali-ese? Should I call you Princess Fat-mama?"

Corey laughed out loud until Mrs. Hudson slapped his back, and he turned it into a cough. Matt had to bite the insides of his cheeks, and Ruby stuffed her crocheted blanket in her mouth, shaking with silent laughter. Tui glared at Chuck, and for a moment Matt thought she was going to throw him to the ground, but then her face broke into a grin and she, too, started laughing. She tipped her head back and laughed and laughed. She wiped tears from her eyes and shook her head. "Oh, *Rubbana*. A husband . . . three children. I never thought I would live to see the day. But how is this possible? I did not think I had been here so long. . . ."

"More time has passed for me than for you, it would seem," said Mrs. Hudson. "It's been twenty years since I left the *Vermillion*. I'm quite a bit older now than when I was captain."

"And wiser," said Tui. "I can see that now."

Mrs. Hudson blushed and shook her head. "Not so wise, I don't think. I never was."

"It is always the wise who think they are not wise, and the fools who think they are," said Tui.

Matt watched his mother's eyes fill with tears. She looked so happy to have her old friend back but also sad for the years now between them, the time they'd lost that they could never get back. Matt remembered his own friend, the very reason they'd come here in the first place.

"Excuse me, Fatoumata?" said Matt, speaking in Arabic. Tui turned to Matt. "Is there anyone else here with you? I mean, another who was discarded by Captain Vincent? A girl about my age?"

Tui shook her head. "I have been all alone. I have seen no people in this godforsaken place. Only beasts and fowl and so much ice and snow."

Matt slumped. They had guessed correctly about Captain

Vincent discarding someone here, just not the right person. Not for him anyway.

"I have many questions," said Tui. "Some can wait, but how did you get the compass back from Vincent? Is he dead?"

Mrs. Hudson stiffened. "He's not dead," she said flatly. "He still has the Obsidian Compass and the *Vermillion*."

"But then, how did you come to find me? You are not discarded here too?"

Mrs. Hudson shook her head. "We have another compass." She glanced briefly at Matt. "A crude replica of the Obsidian Compass, but it was enough to get us here."

Matt felt a slight sting in his chest at the description of his compass. *A crude replica?* He grabbed the compass beneath his blanket and wrapped his fingers over the sticky, greasy hunk of metal. Maybe it wasn't so grand as the Obsidian Compass, but it worked, didn't it?

"So you can take me from this horrible place! Ah! When can we leave? You know how I hate the cold! Vince knew that too. Curse that evil man! I cannot wait to face him and give him what he deserves!"

"Yes, we'd all like that," said Mrs. Hudson. "We'll leave right away, this very moment!" Matt wondered where his mom intended to go. Back home to New York, still? Or did finding her friend from the past change things? Perhaps seeing Tui would make her realize that they couldn't just go home and live a normal life. Regardless, they still had to find

Jia. Matt wasn't going to give up on finding her.

"You have a ship for traveling?" Tui asked. "We can leave now? All together?"

"Yes, Chuck's vehicle is just right over there, up on the bluff," said Mrs. Hudson, pointing toward the jutting cliff where the rusty orange bus sat like an abandoned toy. "Oh my . . ."

The herd of woolly mammoths was now roaming the cliff-side. One gargantuan mammoth had discovered Blossom. It toyed with it with its trunk, nudging it with its giant tusks. Blossom teetered back and forth.

"Hey!" Chuck shouted. He started running down the beach, waving his arms and shouting. "Get away from my bus!" He picked up rocks and threw them at the mammoth. They didn't even reach halfway up the cliff, but something about the commotion or noise must have roused the mammoth. It suddenly lifted its trunk and blew, then shoved Blossom toward the edge of the cliff.

"No! No! NO!" shouted Chuck. "Back! Go back!"

The mammoth dug its huge curved tusks under the bus like a forklift, and with one heft it tossed it up and over the edge of the cliff. Chuck skidded to a halt. The mammoth stomped and snorted as the bus crashed down on the beach and rolled and tumbled over rocks and ice.

Chuck ran toward Blossom. Everyone else went after him. Matt stood next to his dad, and Corey came up beside him.

The bus had miraculously landed on its wheels, but that was about the only lucky thing about it. All the windows were cracked; one had been completely shattered. Dozens of dents had been pounded into the rusty orange metal. The bus hadn't been in the best shape before, but now it looked like a crushed soda can.

A few walruses had worked their way up the beach, all of them barking, grunting, and snorting like they'd found a new toy.

"Get away!" shouted Chuck, trying to kick at the walruses, but they just bellowed and blustered. One roared and snapped its long tusks at Chuck. He might have been impaled had Mr. Hudson not yanked him back. The walrus then dug its tusks into one of Blossom's tires. The tire let out a pitiful squeak and deflated, making the bus a bit lopsided.

"Chuck, I'm so sorry," said Mr. Hudson. "We'll pay for all the damages when we get home. I promise."

Chuck just kept staring at his bus. "Will we get home?" he asked. "I mean, I got a spare tire in the back, but I'm guessing there's some other stuff that might need repairs."

"I can fix it," said Matt. "Jia taught me a lot about auto mechanics while I was on the *Vermillion*."

The snow started to fall in thicker drifts. The wind picked up.

"We will not be able to fix it tonight," said Tui. "A storm is coming."

"You mean we're going to spend the night here?" said Ruby, shivering beneath her blanket. She looked around as though hoping a hotel might suddenly pop up in the midst of all the ice and snow.

"My cave is warm and safe," said Tui. "I promise you will be comfortable."

"Hey, a campout's always fun," said Chuck. "Let me get some supplies from Blossom. I think I got some food in the minifridge." The walruses barked and retreated as Chuck forced open the rusty, dented door of the bus.

After Chuck had loaded some food and supplies in a bag, they all followed Tui back to her cave. The snow grew so thick, Matt could barely see a foot in front of him. Everything turned white, and Matt could barely tell which way was up or down. It gave him a strong wave of vertigo.

When they reached Tui's cave, Matt was relieved to be out of the wind and then stunned as he observed the interior of the cave. He had been expecting a dark, cramped little space, but it was open and spacious and breathtakingly beautiful. Ice crystals were clustered all around, hanging from the walls and ceiling like chandeliers. Dim daylight filtered through the holes and patches of ice in the ceiling, casting a bluish glow.

Farther back was a smaller cavern, about half the size of the one they'd entered and more stone than ice. It was here that Tui had made her living quarters. In the center was a firepit. A small fire was burning, the smoke curling up to an opening in the rocks above. This was the smoke Matt had seen up on the cliffs. A few flurries of snow fell down from the openings in the ceiling.

Tui gathered two large handfuls of what looked like big grassy clods of dirt and dropped them on the fire. They smothered the flame at first, and then the coals flickered and the flames grew, casting light and shadow over the cavern walls.

"What is that you're burning?" Corey asked.

"Mammoth dung. It burns very well," and then when Tui saw the look of disgust on their faces she added, "but don't worry. It smells like grass, mostly."

Matt was surprised to see how cozy the cave had been made. The walls and floor around the fire were covered in furs. Some large stone blocks served as a table and bench. There were crude dishes made from stone, and tools and weapons that looked to be made of bone. A spear and a small ax leaned up against the wall. The space smelled strongly of smoke and sweat and game.

Ten minutes later they were all eating cold hot dogs and marshmallows. (No one was quite brave enough to roast their food in the mammoth dung fire.) Mrs. Hudson and Tui chattered away. They couldn't talk fast enough as they caught up on all that had happened since they'd seen each other last. Tui had very little to tell about her time spent in the Siberian Ice Age, but she had many questions for Mrs. Hudson about her past twenty years. That was one of the strange things about time travel, Matt decided. People's timelines didn't always line up. You could be the same age at one meeting, and then very different ages at another. Matt wondered, What if the next time he saw Jia she was much older than him, or he was a lot older than her? They would still be friends of course, but it wouldn't be the same. It gave him an unsettled feeling in his stomach. He didn't want to find her twenty years later. He wanted to start back up where they'd left off.

Mrs. Hudson told Tui about how she'd met Mr. Hudson, their marriage, their jobs, living in New York, and raising children. She told Tui about how Captain Vincent had kidnapped them, and how they'd escaped. Tui was clearly shocked and outraged by it all.

"That man . . . he is pure *evil*, Captain. I swear it on all the riches of my father, I will hunt him down and he will pay for what he has done. To all of us."

Matt was curious about how his mother would respond to this declaration, but she said nothing about it. She had just as many questions for Tui about what had happened before she'd been discarded here, how Captain Vincent had gotten the compass from her, what had happened to the other crew members. "I know Agnes is still on the *Vermillion*," she said.

Tui blew out a puff of air. "I am not surprised. Vince is probably too afraid to discard her. I hope she will chop off his head."

Mrs. Hudson laughed, then grew serious. "But what of Neeti and Demetria? Do you know what happened to them? Where he took them?"

Tui shook her head. "I do not know. I was first to go. I do not doubt he discarded the others in equally horrible places."

"What about Annie?" Matt asked without thinking. "What happened to the little girl with the gun?"

Mrs. Hudson whipped her head around to Matt. "How do you know Annie?"

"Oh . . . I . . . uh . . ." Matt suddenly realized his mistake. He still hadn't told his mom about the first time he'd traveled with his compass. On his birthday. His mom put it together though. He saw the wheels turning in her brain, practically heard the clicks of it all coming together. She paled and put her hand to her mouth. "It happened," she said. "You went to the *Vermillion.* . . . I saw you . . . *years* ago . . . I . . ." She shook her head. "When did this happen?"

"On my birthday," said Matt.

"I *knew* it," snapped Mrs. Hudson. "Hide-and-seek, my foot!" She glared at Corey and Ruby, who both shrank back a little.

"What is going on?" said Mr. Hudson, looking back and forth. "What am I missing?"

Mrs. Hudson didn't pause to answer her husband. "Mateo, you *must* be more careful! Time travel is not a game. There could have been serious repercussions!"

"I think there were," muttered Corey. "Matt saw you *kissing* Captain Vincent! Talk about scarring for life!"

Mr. Hudson started choking on a marshmallow. Chuck patted him on the back. "You okay, buddy?" He coughed, his eyes watering. Mrs. Hudson's face was beet red.

"And if that wasn't bad enough, you almost *shot* Matt!" Ruby added.

Mr. Hudson, now marshmallow-free, sat straight up. "What? Belamie, you never told me any of this! You saw Matt? Before *we* ever met? And you almost *shot* him?!"

"It wasn't something that I could easily explain," she said. "It all happened so fast, and I didn't know who he was. I mean, yes, Annie said he was my son, but that was after I almost shot him!"

She took a deep breath and looked back at Matt, flustered, bewildered. "I'm sorry, Mateo," she said, her voice suddenly soft, almost a whisper. "That must have been very frightening for you, to be attacked by someone who should only ever protect you. But don't you see? That is just *one* of the many dangers of time travel. You can't just go wherever and whenever you like. Things must be planned and thought out very carefully, or you could do *serious* harm." She shook a little, and Matt wondered if she was speaking from experience more than hypotheticals.

Matt wrapped his arms around himself and looked down at his shoes, unsure what to say. "So . . . did Captain Vincent discard Annie?" Matt asked. He was eager to change the focus.

"No," said his mom. "I took Annie back to her home in Ohio before I left. She asked me to take her home that very day you met her, in fact. I was very surprised. She had such an unhappy childhood, but she insisted. She was convinced that Vincent was going to get the compass in the future. You had told her that, she said." She spoke all this as though it had been buried deep in her memory and it was only now coming to the surface.

"Yeah," said Matt. "I told her she should go home. Was that wrong? Did I mess anything up?" He was suddenly worried that anything he'd done or said at that time could have caused some major catastrophe.

"You saved her from much pain and suffering," said Tui. "Vince hated Annie. He would not have been merciful, child or no."

"She knew what he was then," said Mrs. Hudson. "She knew he would get the compass. I should have listened to her. Trusted her more."

"Our past is always clear," said Tui. "Our future always clouded." She patted Mrs. Hudson on the arm. "Now, can I have another of those hot dogs? Those things look disgusting, but they are quite delicious."

Mrs. Hudson snorted and reached for the hot dogs and buns. "That is a true statement for many modern-made foods.

There's no getting around the stomachaches and headaches they cause, though."

"There is no worse stomachache than hunger," said Tui.

"Except a guilty conscience," said Chuck. "That's the worst."

Tui nodded. "Very true, *Chook*."

The evening continued with more hot dogs and marshmallows and stories. Chuck played a few songs on his harmonica, then dozed on one of the furs. Matt felt quite exhausted himself, but he didn't want to miss anything. Tui and Mrs. Hudson were reliving old times, and it was a side of his mother he'd never seen before. She seemed . . . *young*, full of vibrant energy and life.

Unsurprisingly, she'd met Tui while she was on a mission to rob her father, Mansa Musa, who was apparently the richest man to have ever lived.

"He has so much gold we are practically drowning in it!" said Tui. "So when I catch your mama stealing from him, I think, what is the harm? There are more valuable things than gold, no? I help her steal more gold in exchange for her promise to let me come with her. She helped me escape on the eve of my wedding. I was not much older than you three."

"We're only eleven!" said Ruby. "Matt just turned twelve."

"Yes, I was exactly your age when I was betrothed, and I was to marry at age thirteen."

Ruby made a face like she'd just eaten a sour piece of fruit. "That's horrible!"

Tui simply shrugged. "It was the way of things at that time. It is the way of things in many countries throughout the ages. Women are property to be sold off and bred like cattle."

"Thank goodness I don't live in those times and places," said Ruby, her face still full of disgust.

"Yes, and I am glad your mother invited me to be a part of her crew," said Tui. "I do not think I would have been happy marrying a strange man and having babies. But then what does your mother do? She abandons me, and what for? To get married and have babies!" She shook her head, laughing.

"Yes, but the difference is, you didn't have a choice in the matter," said Mrs. Hudson a little defensively. "You would have been made to marry a man you did not choose and have children whether you wanted to or not. There is great power in choice, wouldn't you agree? When we have the freedom to choose, we live our lives with more purpose and passion. I wanted this life. I chose to marry. I chose my children."

"Yes," said Tui, a smile on her face that did not entirely reach her eyes. "Choice is powerful. So is love. In fact, I can only imagine the greatest of love could have enticed you to *choose* to abandon your ship and crew, leave us all behind like dust in the wind."

Any warmth in the cave suddenly evaporated. A chill settled over them that made Matt shiver.

"Tui, I swear I never meant for any of this to happen," said Mrs. Hudson. "I was trying to do what I thought was right for myself and my own future, but I wasn't careful. I didn't think. I harmed you—and all the crew."

Tui waved her away. "I do not blame you. If there is anyone to blame, it is Vincent." A shadow came over her face.

"How *did* Captain Vincent get the compass?" Ruby asked. "Did he steal it from you?"

Tui shook her head. "Not exactly, no. It is difficult to explain. That night is a blur in my mind. It all happened so fast. We were in California. Los Angeles, I think it was?"

"LA?" said Matt. "But you left in New York."

Mrs. Hudson shook her head. "I decided it would be safer to disappear somewhere else, try to throw Vincent off my trail, just in case he did suspect something. Clearly it didn't work."

"Your plan worked as far as I was concerned," said Tui, "though I knew something was wrong the minute you give me the compass. You told me if anything should happen to you, that the compass belonged to me. I could not understand it. You never took off the compass, never let anyone else touch it, except Vincent sometimes. We all thought if anything ever happened to you, the compass would go to him, but we never think anything will ever happen to you. And then you died right before my eyes. No one could have believed you survived such an explosion."

"An explosion?" said Corey, now keenly interested. "What kind?"

"I was on a boat," said Mrs. Hudson. "Your dad arranged it all."

"It was a movie set for a film that was in production then," said Mr. Hudson. "I had a connection with someone who was on the crew, an old friend from grad school. He's a pyrotechnics specialist in Hollywood."

"How come I haven't met this friend?" said Corey.

"Anyway," said Mr. Hudson, ignoring Corey's question, "he helped us out. It was really quite simple. They had several boats that were rigged with explosives for multiple takes. The boats all had escape hatches in the bottom. The idea was your mom would go on board the boat as though she were trying to steal it, and thirty seconds later . . ." He made an exploding sound.

"And then you were gone," Tui said, shivering.

"And the compass?" Ruby asked. "How did Vincent get it if my mom gave it to you?"

"I don't know," said Tui, shaking her head. "It all happened so fast. It was dark and raining. There was lightning and thunder. When the boat exploded, I must have dropped the compass. Must have, because the next thing I see, Vincent has the compass. He's holding it in his hand like God himself come down and give it to him."

Silence fell. Matt shivered. He did not like the idea that

God would want Vincent to have the compass. Everyone else seemed to be feeling the same.

"But it is all in the past," said Tui. "We can fix everything! Now that you are here, we will find Vincent, steal back the Obsidian Compass, and discard him at the top of the highest mountain in the world ten thousand years ago."

"Tui . . . ," started Mrs. Hudson, but Tui was clearly not finished.

"No, no, that is too kind, I know. And too risky. You found me, didn't you? Who's to say someone else at some other time couldn't go back and save Vince. I will kill him. I will kill him with my own two hands."

"Tui, I'm sorry for what you've been through, truly, I am," said Mrs. Hudson. "If there is anyone to blame it is me. Not Vincent. Chasing after him—killing him—that is not the answer."

Tui looked at Mrs. Hudson like she'd just sprouted antlers. "Then what is the answer, *Rubbana*?"

"We leave him alone," said Mrs. Hudson. "Leave the compass. All of it. We go home."

Tui's eyebrows arched so high they nearly disappeared into her hair. "Home? What *home*? To Mali? To my *father*? And to do what? Get married and have babies, like you?"

"If you want," said Mrs. Hudson, keeping her voice even and calm. "Or don't. I'll take you wherever you want to go, and you can live your life as you choose. Or you can come with us to New York. You would be welcome. But leave Vincent out of it. Leave him in the past. You can't change it."

Tui's face darkened. "Maybe I cannot change the past," she said. "But *you* cannot stop Vince in the future. We must get the compass from him and keep him from doing more harm, to us, to your children!"

"I disagree," said Mrs. Hudson. "The best thing we can do to keep Vincent from harming us, from harming anyone, is to stay away from him. To go back to our lives."

"But what about Jia?" said Matt. "We still have to rescue her!"

"Yeah! We do!" Corey shouted. "If it hadn't been for Jia we never would have gotten home. We can't just leave her."

"We *owe* her," said Ruby.

Mrs. Hudson clasped her fingers together and pressed them against her forehead like she was praying. "Listen to me, all of you. I know how much your friend means to you. I know how responsible you feel. Believe me, *I know.* But there is no way to rescue her without crossing paths with Vincent or ourselves or both. It's all equally dangerous."

"*Rubbana,*" said Tui, her frown deepening to a scowl. "This man left me to die here. He kidnaps your children! And now an innocent child, a child who helped save *your* precious children, suffers because of Vincent, and you will do nothing?"

Mrs. Hudson shook her head, fighting back tears. "I'm sorry," she said. "I don't know how many times I can say it.

I'm *sorry*. I know it is difficult to do nothing when those you care about are suffering, when you want revenge upon those who have made you suffer, but some things cannot be fixed. Sometimes doing nothing is the wisest course of action."

Matt opened his mouth to argue, but Tui suddenly stood up, eyes blazing. She towered over them all. "No," she said. She spoke quietly, but there was a rumbling in her voice that shook Matt's very bones. "Doing nothing is the course for *cowards*. You want to leave your past, pretend it never happened. I see that now. But your past is catching up with you, *Rubbana*. It will not leave you in peace. Because *I* am here now, and I will not let you walk away! You say this is a game? It was your game first! You *started* this game. You pulled us all in. Are you such a fool to believe Vincent will allow you to stop just because you choose to stop? He will strike even if you don't. He will rip your precious family to shreds to get what he wants. Yes, I *know* what he is after. I heard you two whispering in dark corners, thinking the rest of us do not hear. I was not your greatest spy for nothing. I know what you two used to search for day and night. You may have given it up, but *he* has not. And if he succeeds, there will be no time or place you can hide from him."

Mrs. Hudson went pale. Matt thought she was trembling a little. She opened her mouth, but no words came out.

"What are you talking about?" Ruby asked, looking between her mother and Tui. "What exactly is Vincent after?

Does this have something to do with the letter?"

Neither Tui nor Mrs. Hudson answered. They both just stared each other down.

"Are you talking about the Aeternum?" Matt asked. His voice was barely above a whisper, but Mrs. Hudson's head whipped toward him so fast he flinched.

"*Where* did you hear that word?" she snapped, her voice suddenly a feral growl. "Did you travel to *another* place and not tell me?"

Matt winced and recoiled from his mom. For a moment she had transformed into another creature altogether, savage and fierce. "N-no," he stammered. "I heard it from *you*. When I traveled to the *Vermillion*. I heard you and Cap . . . Vincent talking about it. You talked about when you get the Aeternum, how you would . . . live forever."

Mrs. Hudson looked so tense, Matt thought the veins in her neck might burst. "You must tell them, Captain," said Tui.

Mrs. Hudson looked at each of her children, and finally to her husband, a silent plea for help, but he just sighed and put his head in his hands. He ran his fingers through his hair. His face looked tired and worn. "Clearly they're going to get certain information one way or another, Belamie," he said. "They might as well get it from us."

Mrs. Hudson's shoulders fell in defeat. She took a deep breath, her eyes closed. "All right," she said. "I will tell you what I can."

12

The Aeternum

"The Aeternum," said Mrs. Hudson, speaking slowly, "is *supposedly* another invention by the same inventor of the Obsidian Compass."

"You mean Marius Quine?" Matt asked.

Mrs. Hudson nodded. "There were rumors, only vague rumors, mind you, that the compass was just the beginning of his genius, and the Aeternum was his crowning achievement. It's his magnum opus."

"Where did the rumors come from?" said Matt.

"From Quine himself," said Mrs. Hudson. "Things he wrote down that I obtained at a significant cost." Matt wondered what that cost might be, but he didn't think now was the time to ask.

"You mean the letter inside your safe?" Ruby asked. "The one Captain Vincent stole?"

Mrs. Hudson nodded. "The compass was only a stepping-stone. It's powerful but limited. The letter expressed intentions for something on a far grander scale. It's called the Aeternum."

"That's the Latin word for *forever*," said Matt. His mom nodded.

"So what does it do, this Atternoom-thing," Corey asked, "make you immortal? Like Thanos?"

Ruby rolled her eyes, but Mrs. Hudson did not contradict him. "More than immortal," she said. "Immortality only assumes you can't die, but you still live within the confines and laws of this world, save the law of death. But avoiding death does not necessarily mean you'll avoid pain and suffering, and it doesn't necessarily equate to power or control. Some would argue immortality is more of a curse than a gift. But the Aeternum is different. Not only will it grant you immortality, but time itself becomes obsolete. Time is something that only comes with beginnings and endings. It's a product of this world. Eternity is another realm altogether, and when you live in the realm of eternity you have no beginning, no end, no past, and no future. You simply are. With the Aeternum, time is not a reality, and if time is not real, then you have the power to make your own reality. You can change anything you want, shape the past or the future however you like. You could make certain people go away, or split people apart, or make it so certain people don't exist at all." Mrs. Hudson's words got caught in her throat. Mr. Hudson reached for her hand, and she grasped it so tightly her knuckles turned white.

Matt felt his stomach drop. He didn't have to imagine very far to think what Vincent would do to their family if he had such power. They wouldn't *be* a family. He looked to Corey and Ruby and read the same thing in both of their eyes.

"We have to stop him," said Matt. "We can't let Vincent get the Aeternum. You know what he'll do to us."

Mrs. Hudson composed herself. She wiped away her tears and shook her head. "But that's just it. *Not* interfering is the best way to stop him. Even if the Aeternum is real, Vincent cannot hope to succeed without my help. He *wants* us to find him."

"How?" said Matt. "How can you help? He already got the letter. Doesn't it tell him how to find the Aeternum?"

"Instructions of sorts," said Mrs. Hudson, "but it's not enough. There are missing . . . pieces. Information he doesn't have."

"What about Quine," Matt asked. "Where is he in all of this? If this Aeternum is real and Quine made it, doesn't he have it? And so can't he just make everything the way *he* wants, in the past and future?"

"And isn't he on our side?" Ruby asked. "I mean, he *did* give you the compass, didn't he?"

"I know very little about Marius Quine," said Mrs. Hudson, "least of all his motives or intentions. What little dealings I have had with him have left me with more questions than answers. There have been times when I was sure he was on my side. Yes, he gave me the compass, but then that was probably after he'd already invented the Aeternum, so he had no use for it. It meant nothing to him to give it away, unless he had some ulterior motive for giving it to me." She shook her head. "I can't fathom the reasons. One thing is certain. Marius Quine is powerful, maybe mad, possibly dangerous . . . the problem is I don't understand what it is that he wants. I can't guess at what he'll do. Vincent, on the other hand, is predictable. I know *exactly* what he wants, and can guess more easily what he'll do, where he'll go, who he'll target. Believe me, the best thing we can do is to stay away from him."

"Why?" Matt asked. "I understand Vincent wants the Aeternum, but what does that have to do with us? Do you have something else that he needs? Besides the letter?"

"No," said Mrs. Hudson, quickly. Too quickly, Matt thought. "He *thinks* I have something that he needs, but I don't." His mom and dad shared a brief look, and he saw something exchanged there. There was something they weren't telling them, he was certain, but he was equally certain that whatever it was, they weren't going to share it with them. Not now anyway.

"Look," said Mrs. Hudson. "I will not pretend we aren't

vulnerable in any way, but I promise staying away from Vincent is far safer than any other plan. With just the Obsidian Compass, Vincent can't get to us past the date we came from, and if he can't get to us, he has no hope of getting the Aeternum. And that is the only way we all stay together. Safe."

Matt tried to think of something to say. He understood his mom's logic but . . . *Jia*. If she were with them now, if they had rescued her from Captain Vincent, then maybe he would agree with his mom. Maybe he'd be fine to let it all go. But she wasn't here, and he didn't think he could let it go. Matt wrapped his hands around the compass.

"We *have* to rescue Jia," he said with as much finality as he could muster.

"Mateo . . . ," his mom started, but he cut her off.

"We can travel back to that day at the museum and rescue her before Captain Vincent can take her away."

Mrs. Hudson paled. "That would be extremely foolish, and you'd regret it."

"Then we'll find another way."

"No," said Mrs. Hudson, her voice hard and final.

But Matt felt something break in him. His obedient nature, perhaps. "I'm not asking for your permission," he said between gritted teeth. "I'm telling you. I'll go by myself if I have to."

"No, you won't," said Corey. "Because I'll go with you."

"Me too," said Ruby.

Their parents gaped at them, stunned by this complete rebellion by all three of their children.

"And if you steal Matt's compass and lock us up, then you're no better than Captain Vincent."

Both Mr. and Mrs. Hudson looked as though they had just been slapped across the face. Clearly, the comparison to Vincent was below the belt.

"That's enough," said Mr. Hudson. "*We* are not the enemy here. And, Mateo, put that thing away, and all of you stop being ridiculous. You're not going anywhere. You don't have the first clue where to look for Jia, not without my map, and guess what? *I'm not sharing.*"

The fire of rebellion Matt had felt a moment before was quickly extinguished. His dad was right. He had no idea where to search for Jia. Without the map they were stuck.

Mr. Hudson dragged his hands down his face, stretching his skin so he looked ghoulish and then just extremely exhausted. His eyes were red rimmed and puffy. His usually tousled hair was even more of a mess. Matt thought he looked old, all of a sudden, like he'd aged two decades in a single day. "Can we all just take a minute? Can't anyone in this family stay in one place for *five minutes*?"

Chuck snorted and sat up. "Are we there yet?" he asked in a sleepy voice.

"No, Chuck," snapped Mr. Hudson. "Go back to sleep."

Chuck obeyed and started snoring again.

No one said anything. Matt glanced at his mother. She stared back, her eyes full of panic. Matt lowered the compass. His mom breathed.

"Okay," said Mr. Hudson, like he'd just managed to keep a bomb from going off. "Okay, we'll figure this out, okay? Let's just . . . get some rest. We can talk more tomorrow."

Matt suddenly felt the full force of his exhaustion overcome him. His entire body ached. He could barely keep his head up.

Tui helped them all set up their beds. She had plenty of furs for everyone, and in a few minutes Matt was warm and cozy between two fur pelts. Mr. Hudson put more mammoth dung on the fire. It smothered the embers at first, dousing them in darkness, and then the flames flared and spread warmth. Matt was extremely drowsy. The final dregs of his energy dried up. He snuggled down between the furs, ready to fall asleep in a half second.

Something cool touched his cheek and he started. His mother was crouched down next to him. Matt reached for his compass and braced himself for another fight, but his mom didn't make a move for it. "Hey," she said. Her voice was calmer now, her eyes softened. "You know I love you, right?"

Matt nodded. He waited for the *but*. *I love you,* but *I'm in charge.* But *I don't trust you.* But *you can't go find Jia.* But the *but* never came.

"You know what changed my mind about being a time pirate?" his mom asked.

"What?"

"You."

"Me?"

She nodded, brushed her fingers through his hair. "When you visited me in the past—years ago for me and just a day ago for you—that's when my old life ended and when my true life began. It was you."

Matt squirmed a little beneath the furs. He didn't know what to say. The experience of seeing his mom before she was his mom hadn't been such a momentous, emotional experience for him. It had just been . . . weird. He suddenly realized that there were things he couldn't possibly understand about his mom, but then he thought just the opposite was true. There were things about him that she couldn't possibly understand either.

"Here." His mom reached beneath the collar of her shirt and unclasped the gold chain she always wore. "You shouldn't keep your compass floating around in your pocket." She handed Matt the chain. He took it, then tentatively pulled out his compass and looped the chain through some of the metal. He clasped it around his neck and tucked the compass beneath his shirt. He shivered a little at the cold metal against his warm skin.

"Thanks," he said.

His mom leaned down and kissed him on the forehead. She did the same to Corey and Ruby on either side of him, and before Matt could so much as mutter a *good night*, he fell into a sleep so heavy and deep it felt more like a coma.

13

Impasse

Matt woke to the smell of coffee, pancakes, and maple syrup, and the sound of someone whistling a tune. When he opened his eyes, he saw Chuck standing in front of a camp stove pouring pancake batter on a griddle. Matt gazed around. They were still inside Tui's ice cave, and he was toasty warm beneath the furs.

Mr. and Mrs. Hudson were sitting by the fire, furs around their shoulders and cups of steaming coffee in their hands. Corey and Ruby were both eating stacks of pancakes drenched in maple syrup.

"Pancakes, Matty?" said Chuck.

"Um, sure," said Matt. He didn't hate the name Matty, necessarily, but no one ever called him that. That's what Gaga always called his dad.

"Did you get all this from inside your bus?" Matt asked as

Chuck handed him a stack of steaming pancakes and poured syrup over the top.

"Yeah," said Chuck. "I didn't even know Blossom had one of these griddles. I found it this morning. She was always a good bus, but she's just full of surprises lately."

Matt wondered if Blossom had somehow connected with his compass like the *Vermillion* did with the Obsidian Compass, shifting and providing supplies according to where and when they were traveling. He wondered if they traveled in her a great deal, if she'd one day be able to make transformations like the *Vermillion*, if somehow she would evolve. He was eager to run some experiments, but he had a hunch if he were to so much as turn a dial on his compass, his mom and dad would tackle him to the ground. No one brought up the conversation from the night before, though Matt felt it sitting in their midst like a ten-ton woolly mammoth.

Chuck filled the awkward silence by chatting up Tui, asking more about her life in Mali, her travels, her favorite movies and music. He claimed you could always really get to know a person through their taste in music. Did she prefer jazz or blues? Country or rock? Led Zeppelin or Grateful Dead? To which Tui asked what kind of music could rocks make, and why would anyone be grateful to be dead? Matt stifled a laugh. For all her time traveling, she clearly had not been immersed in modern pop culture, at least not in the latter twentieth century.

Matt looked over to see that his dad had pulled out his map and was studying it with his brow furrowed.

"Do you know where the *Vermillion* is now?" Ruby asked.

"No," said Mr. Hudson. "The map is being a bit difficult for some reason, maybe because of how far we traveled. I've only ever used it in New York, so perhaps it needs to recalibrate to this time and location."

Ruby scooted over to get a better look at the map. Mr. Hudson gave her a wary look, but he didn't close the map. "What about there?" Ruby pointed. "Is that it?"

"No," said Mr. Hudson. "The map seems simple to read, but it's actually quite complex. It's difficult to keep a timeline for a time-traveling ship and know when and where it is in relation to your own time and place. Here's an example." He pointed to a faded mark on the map. "We know the *Vermillion* traveled to Rome in 44 BC, but how long ago according to *our* timeline did it go? Ten years ago? Twenty? The map is calibrated to the timeline of whoever is in possession of it. The brightness of the mark is only an estimate, but I'd say it was there, oh about twenty-five years ago in my own timeline."

"That would have been when Mom was still captain," said Ruby. "Before you met her."

"Yes," said Mr. Hudson, "but I already had the map by then. I studied it obsessively."

"Where did you get it?" Matt asked. "And who made it? Was it Quine?"

"No idea," said Mr. Hudson. "I bought it in a flea market in London."

"You don't remember who from?" Ruby asked.

"No, unfortunately. I wish I did, but my memory is very fuzzy on that point. I paid for the map and I left."

"How much did you pay for it?" Matt asked.

"Fifty pence, less than a dollar. I knew it was probably worth a lot more than that, and I just figured the guy selling it had no idea."

Or they did, Matt thought. Maybe the seller wanted his dad to buy it for some reason. He rubbed at his wrist where his bracelet used to be. Like his father's map, it had also had some connection to the Obsidian Compass and the *Vermillion*, and also like his father's map, they had bought it for cheap off of a street vendor. There had to be some connection. These items had not made their way into their hands by chance. They were all chess pieces in some larger game.

Matt scooted cautiously toward his dad to get a better look at the map. It looked different than the last time he'd seen it, before they'd traveled here. There were different borderlines and land masses. Matt spotted the pinkie-sized island off the coast of Siberia that he knew was their current location, but there was no mark showing that they were there. So the map was connected to the Obsidian Compass and the *Vermillion* specifically.

"Anyway," continued Mr. Hudson, "the map will show

the *Vermillion*'s travels in relation to your own timeline. The mark will glow blue like the base of a flame, but right now it seems to be . . . wait a moment. . . ."

Suddenly the map started going haywire. Land lines faded and shifted back and forth. The symbol of the *Vermillion* popped up all over the map and then disappeared like a game of whack-a-mole. Dates and coordinates appeared, too, flashing on the map one after the other, faster than they could read them.

"Why's it doing that?" Ruby asked.

"Probably from the travel," said Mr. Hudson. "It just needs to recalibrate." He lifted the map off the ground a little, shook it, then put it back down on the ground, but it was still going berserk. He stood up with the map and walked away from the group a little, like he was trying to find a spot with a good signal. "There. It's better now."

They all came toward it again.

"Stop," said Mr. Hudson, putting up a hand. "Stay back. It's like you're causing interference."

"Maybe it's the compass," said Mrs. Hudson, glancing at Matt.

Sure enough, every time Matt got within a few feet of the map it went haywire. When he stayed away, his dad was able to read the map but could not find the *Vermillion* anywhere. "She must be in Nowhere in No Time."

Mrs. Hudson frowned. "That doesn't make sense."

"He is hiding," said Tui.

"Why?" Ruby asked. "I thought he wanted us to find him."

"Not if he knows I am with you," said Tui, flashing a wicked grin. "Then he knows he is dead."

Mrs. Hudson cleared her throat. "We should take a look at Chuck's bus now, right? See if we can get it working again."

And then what? Matt didn't dare to ask the question.

The day was bright, clear, and, in Corey's words, "booger-freezing cold," a description that no one could refute. They all carried a load of mammoth dung from Tui's cave and built a bonfire on the beach near Blossom, both to keep from getting frostbite and to keep the polar bears and walruses away. Blossom appeared to be the new cool hangout for Siberian Ice Age animals, but once they got the fire going, they kept away.

Chuck and Corey made friends with some of the walruses by feeding them pancakes. They were trying to teach a little one to do tricks until a big walrus with giant tusks bellowed and chased them away. It wasn't very fast of course, but it was still funny to watch Chuck and Corey jump.

Ruby finally convinced Mrs. Hudson to give her a fencing lesson using icicles for swords. Their ice swords broke about once a minute, but that appeared to be part of the fun. They'd just go pull off another one from a nearby rock and start again.

While that was going on, Matt moved around Blossom,

inspecting her and making all the repairs he could. Most of the damage seemed to be fairly minor—tightening nuts, reconnecting wires, adjusting the timing belt. Probably their biggest problem would be getting it to start in this cold. Tui stood and walked past him. She appeared to be watching Ruby and Mrs. Hudson fence, but every now and again Matt saw her glance toward him. He guessed his mom had asked her to keep an eye on him, make sure he didn't bolt away with his compass after he fixed the bus.

After the tenth or so ice sword broke, Mrs. Hudson called it quits. She wanted to talk to Mr. Hudson, who was crouched by the fire with his map.

Ruby ran over to Matt, her cheeks and nose bright red, her breath coming out in clouds. "Can I help?" she asked, smiling.

"Sure," said Matt. "You can help me change the flat tire."

"Okay!" Ruby said as though this were the most exciting thing in the world. She assisted Matt with the jack and removing the nuts. She chattered about her sword lesson with their mom, what a good teacher she was, and the different techniques she'd taught her.

"It's different than what I learned with Captain Vincent," said Ruby. "I mean, he always wanted me to hold my sword a certain way, but Mom showed me a different way that really does feel much more natural."

"That is because your mama is the best swordswoman in

the world," said Tui from behind them. "No one can compare with her."

"I wish she'd show us more," said Ruby. "It's like pulling teeth to get her to give me a lesson."

"It brings back memories for her, I think," said Tui. "Memories she'd rather forget."

"You mean like when she was Captain Bonnaire?" said Ruby.

Tui nodded. "Yes, when she was with Vincent. Fencing was something they always did together."

Matt got a flash of his mom and Captain Vincent fencing on board the *Vermillion*, the light in her eyes, the color in her cheeks, how close they'd been. It made him feel queasy.

"I am happy for your mama's new life. I am," said Tui. "But she wishes to shed a past that will not be so easily shed. Vincent will not let you be. I know it. Your mama knows it. I think we all know what is true, deep down, but we don't always want to listen. Truth is sometimes painful to face."

"What do you think we should do?" Ruby asked.

Tui shook her head. "It is not my place," she said. "I am sorry, I should not speak so freely. Your mama is a good captain, but she is afraid, and fear makes people blind, sends them in the wrong direction, and I fear your mother will soon regret not taking action in order to protect those she loves so dear."

Matt felt a chill run through him that he was certain had

nothing to do with the bitter cold. He looked over at his parents, their heads together. His dad brushed his mom's hair out of her face and whispered something in her ear. She laughed and kissed him. Watching his parents kiss always made Matt feel squirrelly but also sort of . . . safe, like no matter how crazy things got, their love would endure and hold them all together. But now he wondered if that was a childish fantasy, a fairy tale. The reality was Vincent could appear any moment and rip them all apart.

"Oh!" Tui exclaimed, clutching her head as though she were in pain. "If only I had gotten the compass, as was meant to be! I go back to that day in my mind over and over again. I think how I could have kept Vincent from getting the compass. We all could have been spared. We would have lived in peace. Even your friend. But it is too late. We cannot go back."

Matt tightened a nut on the tire, then took another from Ruby's cupped hands. She was staring at Tui in a strange way. He could practically see the wheels turning in her brain.

"When exactly did Captain Vincent get the compass?" Ruby asked. "Do you remember the date?"

"As though it were yesterday," said Tui. "AD 1998. March tenth."

"Huh," said Ruby. "And it was in LA."

"Yes. San Pedro Bay. Your mama was supposed to steal a boat there. She said there was something important in it.

That is what she tells us, and we never see her again and everything goes bad."

Matt finished up with the tire and moved on to other things while Tui and Ruby continued talking. He lost track of the conversation.

"Let's take a break, yes?" said Tui. "We will eat now. Maybe Chook has more of those hot dogs and what do you call those sticky fluffs? Mash . . ."

"Marshmallows," said Matt.

"Ooh, yes, those are delicious!"

"How are the repairs coming, Matty?" Chuck asked as they ate more hot dogs and thawed themselves by the bonfire on the beach. Matt's fingers and toes ached with cold.

"Okay," he said. "Nearly there, I think."

"Excellent! Do we have a destination in mind when we're ready to go? I have a list of suggestions if you need them. Woodstock is at the top of my list, of course. We could also witness the creation of the Seven Wonders of the World, both ancient and modern. I've always been curious about Stonehenge. Maybe we could see how they built it and why? But probably first stop, we wanna go someplace warm. I think Princess Tui would especially like that, right, Princess? How about Jamaica? Warm, sunny, plus great music!" He pulled out his harmonica and started playing a song. Matt recognized it as "Coming in from the Cold," by Bob Marley. He'd listened to the record in Gaga's basement while making his compass.

After lunch, Matt went back to work on Blossom, trying to figure out how he might repair the engine. Ruby and Corey joined him this time. Chuck sat in a camp chair near the bonfire, crocheting another blanket and singing "Do You Believe in Magic." He didn't think anyone could be more tone-deaf than his dad, but Chuck was definitely a contender.

Their parents and Tui were also by the fire, having what looked like a tense discussion. They were probably arguing over what to do once they got Blossom up and running again.

"Man, I thought they were going to come to blows last night," said Corey. "Totally disappointing."

"Maybe they will now," said Matt, watching as Tui's hands flew into the air and Mr. Hudson tensed up. He got in front of Mrs. Hudson.

"What do you think's going to happen?" said Corey.

"I don't know," said Matt. He didn't even know if he could fix Blossom to the point where they could all travel anywhere. He couldn't think beyond the here and now. He was tired and his head pulsed with a dull ache.

"I think we have to steal the Obsidian Compass back from Captain Vincent," Ruby suddenly blurted.

Matt dropped the screwdriver he'd been holding. It fell

down between the starter and the alternator. He cursed under his breath. He was never going to get that back.

"What the heck are you talking about?" Corey stared at Ruby like she'd just sprouted tusks.

"Okay . . . how?" Matt asked. "We don't know where he is, and you know we can't go back to any time we were on board the *Vermillion*. Also, Mom and Dad will never go for it."

"I know," said Ruby, her eyes blazing. Matt knew that look. It was the look she got when she wanted to do something and would never back down about it. "But we know where Vincent was when he *first* got the compass, and we can make sure he never gets it at all."

Matt's mouth dropped open as what she was saying settled into his brain.

"Are you joking?" said Corey. "I mean, you've never had much of a sense of humor, I'll admit, but this sounds very much like a joke."

"I'm not joking," said Ruby. "This makes total sense if you think about it, and I've thought about it. We travel back to the time when Mom left the *Vermillion* for good. We get the Obsidian Compass before Captain Vincent steals it from Tui. We travel on the *Vermillion* to some remote place, far in the past, discard Captain Vincent, then give the Obsidian Compass to Tui, explain the situation, and then get back home with your compass. If Vincent never gets the compass, then we don't have to worry about him coming after us or getting the Aeternum at all."

"But I thought we can't change the past," said Corey. "Right? Isn't that basically what Captain Vincent always told us? Otherwise he would have stopped Mom and Dad from ever meeting in the first place."

"That's not what he said," said Ruby. "He said it's *unlikely* that you'll change major events, things that involve uncontrollable forces and the decisions of lots of people, but we *have* changed our own past, or at least Matt has, and more than once."

"Me?" said Matt. "How?"

"The message you left yourself on that island when we were discarded? We would have died there if your future self hadn't done that."

That was true, Matt thought. He still had yet to do that. He wondered when it would be.

"And what about when you traveled back to Mom on your birthday? I heard what she said to you the other night. *You* were the reason she left the *Vermillion*. When she found out you were her son, that's when she changed her mind about everything. If you hadn't traveled to see her, Mom and Dad never would have gotten married. They wouldn't have adopted you. Corey and I wouldn't even exist."

Matt tried to think that one through. Could there be other reasons why his mom might have left? Could that encounter really be the only reason she became his mother in the first place? If so, that did change things. Could he have that effect on other events as well?

"It's really quite simple," said Ruby. "Captain Vincent stole the Obsidian Compass. But it was always meant for Tui. If we give it to Tui then everything else is essentially the same. Mom still leaves. She marries Dad. We're still their kids. The only difference is Captain Vincent won't have the compass and so he won't be able to come after us."

"Which means we'd never board the *Vermillion*," said Matt. "We'd never even know about it."

"Not necessarily," said Ruby. "If Tui's captain of the *Vermillion*, it might be an even bigger part of our lives, and not in a threatening sort of way. Mom only wanted to make *Vincent* believe she was dead. She might not be so secretive if he were out of the picture. Her old crew would be like our extended family. If Vincent weren't a threat, Mom would be much more relaxed about the whole thing. We might even time-travel for all our family vacations!"

Matt tried to imagine the whole family packing up to spend their summer on board the *Vermillion*, traveling around the world and visiting different eras. It sounded incredible, like the kind of life he'd always dreamed of having, but there was one important thing Ruby hadn't mentioned.

"But what about Jia? If Captain Vincent never gets the compass, she'll never board the *Vermillion*, and we'll never meet her. She'll be stuck in China, in the orphanage." Matt knew that to Jia that was a fate worse than being discarded.

"Don't worry," said Ruby. "I've thought of that too. We simply tell Tui to get her. We can tell her to get everyone else, too, if we want. Wiley, Brocco, Pike, Albert."

"Not Albert!" said Corey. "That nincompoop can rot in England for all I care."

Ruby snorted. "Nincompoop?"

"Yeah. Emphasis on the *poop*. He stinks, and nobody wants to be around him."

"And Captain Vincent never even picked up Pike," said Matt. Jia had told him she had just appeared in a storage closet one day. They didn't even know where or when she came from.

"Whatever," said Ruby. "We can tell Tui to get Jia for sure. The rest are optional. It doesn't really matter."

"To us," said Matt. "It might matter a lot to them." He didn't mind meddling when it came to his own life, but he wasn't sure how comfortable he was meddling in other peoples' lives. That didn't seem right or fair.

"Look," said Ruby, "I know this is risky, and maybe some things won't work out the way we want, but can we all agree that going home and doing nothing is a terrible idea? We need to *act*, and I think this is the best course of action. If it doesn't work out, then we try something else. Come on, I can *feel* it. Will you trust me on this one?"

Matt's mind was spinning. There was just so much to

consider. He was trying to do all the calculations, think of every possible outcome, all the risks, everything that could go wrong, but the possibilities were endless, and he started to feel dizzy. Could they really change things around? Make it so Captain Vincent never got the Obsidian Compass? And if that succeeded, what would happen to them? Would their memories be altered? Would they exist in a separate reality than the one they were living in now?

He definitely agreed with Ruby on one thing. They couldn't sit around and do nothing. No matter what his mom said, he was not convinced that was the right course of action. Ruby's plan was bold and certainly risky, but it was the best solution he'd heard yet. And they did have pretty solid evidence that they could change things. Matt's visit to their mom in the past. He had changed her course back then, who was he to say that he couldn't do it again? For the good of everyone? (Except Captain Vincent, maybe, but wouldn't he be getting his just deserts?)

"Okay," said Matt. "I trust you, I guess." He put a fist out.

Ruby beamed and bounced a little. She turned to Corey.

Corey hesitated for a few seconds. He glanced at Matt, uncertain. "I have a few questions first," said Corey.

Matt couldn't have been more surprised if Corey had grown a second head. He was always the one who jumped without looking. Act first, ask questions later. Ruby was always the careful one. It was like someone had swapped their brains or something.

"If we're not going to steal Blossom, how are we going to travel?"

"Well, Matt didn't travel with any vehicle the first time," said Ruby. "I was thinking if we're attached to him, we could all travel together. Would that work, Matt?"

Matt thought about it for a moment. "It's possible, but fair warning, it might be pretty uncomfortable, and also risky. What if one of us gets lost in transit?"

"We'll tie our arms and legs together," said Ruby. "We'll make sure we can't be separated."

Matt thought that sounded like it would be painful and possibly dangerous, but he didn't want to argue with Ruby right now. She was so determined, and personally he was glad she was taking the lead on doing *something*. He admired her boldness and zealous determination. It gave him courage to take the risk. Corey, on the other hand, seemed less sure, which was surprising as Corey always wanted to do dangerous and risky things. Matt guessed that was only when it was his idea, not when someone else suggested the risky thing, especially his twin sister, who was his opposite in almost every way.

"I still think this is a little bit nutso," said Corey, "but then again just about everything that has happened to us in the last few months has been pretty insane. This is just another drop in the bucket." He stuck out his fist. "Okay, I'll go along with it, mostly because I can't think of a better plan, and I do not want to go home and be bored out of my mind."

Ruby smiled. "Good enough for me." She put her fist on top of Matt's and Corey's, and then she pulled out a wad of yellow yarn from her pocket. "Found this inside Blossom, thought it might come in handy." She began to wrap it around all their wrists and arms.

"What are you doing?" Corey asked.

"Binding us for travel," said Ruby.

"What, we're going *now*?" Matt's voice squeaked a little.

"*Shh.* . . ." Ruby looked around. Their parents and Tui were still talking and Chuck was still singing and crocheting. "No time like the present," said Ruby. "If we wait, we might never get another chance. Do you really think once we get home Mom and Dad will let you keep your compass and travel whenever you like?"

Matt thought about it. No, they most certainly would not. Most likely they'd confiscate it until he was eighteen, and who knew what they would do with it between now and then? Lose it, destroy it . . .

Ruby wound the yarn every which way around their wrists and then up their arms, pulling it so tight Matt started to lose feeling in his fingers. He also felt a little light-headed, but he wasn't sure that had anything to do with the yarn.

"You feeling well enough to travel, Matt?" Corey asked. He looked a little pale himself.

"I guess," said Matt.

"Matt, you need to set the compass to March tenth, 1998, eleven p.m. Thirty-three degrees north and one hundred eighteen degrees west."

"Whoa, slow down," said Matt. "How do you know exactly where and when we need to go?"

"Tui," said Ruby. "And Dad's map. I found the symbol of the *Vermillion* in LA, and the date matched what Tui had said, so I memorized the coordinates. Let's go!"

Matt fumbled to get the compass out of his shirt. "It's kind of hard with one hand," he said.

"Here, I'll hold it, you turn the dials." Ruby grabbed hold of the compass and held it toward Matt.

"Okay," said Matt, taking a breath. This was all happening so fast he didn't have time to sort through all the details in his brain, make sure everything lined up and made sense, but Ruby was right about one thing. This might be their only chance to fix everything, including saving Jia, and he wasn't willing to waste it. He started to turn the dials.

"Here goes nothing," said Corey.

"Relax," said Ruby. "We'll be there and back before the parents even know what's happening, and when we do return, they won't be angry, because everything will be as it always should have been."

Matt hoped Ruby was right, because if this mission went south, he wasn't sure he wanted to return and face their parents anyway. He turned the last dial very slowly. The compass made a final *click*.

Nothing happened at first. Matt wondered if maybe it wouldn't work with all three of them. Maybe it was confusing the compass. But then he felt a small vibration just beneath his feet. It traveled up his legs, his arms and neck, reached over his head. It felt like some invisible net was being woven around all three of them. Matt started to panic. He suddenly wanted to stop. They hadn't thought this through. How would they know where to go after they'd taken the compass? If they succeeded, their parents wouldn't still be on Wrangel Island, would they? Were they supposed to go to New York? When, exactly? But there was no time to answer these questions or stop the compass. Suddenly the invisible net was cinched tight. Matt was jolted forward, like someone had shoved him hard in the back. The same thing must have happened to Corey and Ruby because their three heads were suddenly smacked together and . . .

Thpt!

They disappeared.

A few minutes later, Mrs. Hudson and Tui came walking arm in arm toward the place where the children had been. It appeared they had made peace.

"Where are the kids?" she asked.

Mr. Hudson looked around. "Oh, they're around here somewhere. I just saw them."

"Probably just playing hide-and-seek again," said Chuck.

Belamie Hudson's stomach clenched. Her heart raced. She called out for her children, but they did not respond. She had a horrible feeling. . . .

14

As It Always Should Have Been

Belamie, Age 17

It was Vincent's idea, or at least he had given the idea to her. She remembered feeling foolish for not thinking of it herself. Perhaps it was because she hadn't thought of her parents in so long. She had buried the memory of them so deep within her, it was almost as if they had never existed at all.

She knew she had parents, of course. Everyone did, but this was only a fact. She felt no emotional attachment to it. Even when Vincent had first asked about her parents, she simply told him they'd died long ago and expected to be done with it. He never brought them up, not for a while at least.

And then one day, quite unexpectedly, he asked the question.

"Why don't you go back and save them?"

That was all it took. That one little question unlocked something inside of Belamie, and the memories came rushing to the surface—the rich brown of her mother's eyes, the rough warmth of her father's hands, the sound of her name on their tongues. Her heart suddenly expanded in her chest. It ached. It was like it was beating for the first time in years. She felt light-headed. Why hadn't she thought of this before? If she could travel through time and throughout the world, do as she wished and take what she liked, couldn't she also change things she didn't like? What was to stop her from making things exactly the way she wanted? Why couldn't she change her own life? Belamie felt a surge of hope that she hadn't felt in some time. She would rescue her parents, and then everything would be as it always should have been.

15
Fingerprints

March 10, 1998
San Pedro Bay, Los Angeles, California

Matt thought traveling on his own without a vehicle was bad enough, but time-traveling without a vehicle while tied to two other people was far, far worse. It was like being tossed around in a dryer, ripped to shreds and twisted up, all while being punched and kicked and elbowed in basically every sensitive area of your body over and over. It probably only lasted less than a minute in real time, but it felt like a torturous few hours.

Thpt!

Matt crashed down onto cement and rolled, all tangled up with Corey and Ruby, until they hit a wall. The three kids lay in a heap on the ground. It was dark outside. Matt could barely discern up from down.

"You guys okay?" Ruby asked. She was breathing hard.

Matt nodded. He couldn't find his voice yet. He was alive, at least.

"I think all my body parts have been rearranged," said Corey. "Ruby, can you untie us, please?"

There was quite a bit of groaning and wincing as they all struggled to sit up enough for Ruby to unwind their arms. It took quite a bit more time than the initial binding. Once Matt's arm was released, he shook it out and rubbed the raw skin around his wrist. They were all pretty bumped and bruised. Ruby's hair was a tangled mess. She had dark smudges on her forehead and cheek.

"Ooh, you're gonna have a black eye," said Corey to Matt.

"Your nose is bleeding," said Matt.

Corey wiped at his nose with his sleeve.

Matt was already dreading traveling back in the same fashion. He hoped, if things went according to plan, that Tui could give them a ride back on the *Vermillion*, or maybe they could borrow a vehicle themselves.

"Where are we?" said Corey.

Matt looked around. It was hard to tell in the darkness, but it looked like they were in some kind of shipping yard. They were surrounded by stacks of giant crates, but at the end of the crates he saw sparkling black water and a few boats and cargo ships.

"I think we're in the right spot," said Ruby. "We've got to find the *Vermillion*. Come on."

They all got up and started to walk toward the water. Ruby winced and faltered as she took a step.

Matt caught her by the arm. "You okay?" he asked.

"Fine," Ruby said, but she was definitely limping like she'd twisted her ankle.

The air was balmy, only a slight breeze, which carried the scent of oil mixed with seaweed.

They came to the edge of the port where the cement ended abruptly and the water began. Several yachts and boats were docked to buoys. A cargo ship in the distance blew its horn. A large cruise ship moved slowly toward the open sea.

A swift wind swept through, and the temperature dropped at least ten degrees. The sky clouded over, and it began to rain. Matt looked to Ruby.

"Sometimes weather is just weather," she said. "Not every little rainstorm is caused by time travel. Look for the *Vermillion*. It could be anything, a yacht or a cargo ship. Look for the symbol."

Matt searched all the vessels for the symbol of the *Vermillion*. It was difficult to see any details on the boats in the dark. He thought maybe he saw the symbol on the side of a yacht, but it turned out to be a picture of an anchor inside a life preserver. They waited and searched for what felt like a long time, at least an hour.

"Maybe we got the wrong day," said Matt.

"Did you enter everything into the compass as I told you?" said Ruby.

Matt double-checked. He confirmed that everything had been entered just as Ruby had told him.

"Then we're right where and when we need to be," said Ruby. "I gave us a little time to be on the safe side. Just be patient."

Matt tried to be patient, but he was cold and wet, and he was starting to feel this plan wasn't a very good idea after all.

"There!" Corey pointed. Matt squinted and saw a little tugboat chugging right toward them. It looked like any other tugboat, but when the lightning flashed it illuminated the flag whipping in the rain, black with a compass star, a bold red V at the center.

"Let's get out of the way," said Ruby. They all backed up to hide behind one of the big crates. Matt crouched down, and a few rats suddenly appeared from underneath.

"Ah!" Matt shouted as one of the rats scurried over his foot, then disappeared beneath another crate.

"Shh! Here it comes," said Ruby.

The *Vermillion* pulled right up to the edge of the port and came to a smooth and silent stop.

A woman Matt didn't recognize appeared at the front of the boat and scanned the area. She must be an old member of his mother's crew, Matt realized, someone who Captain

Vincent had discarded. If this worked, then they'd be saving this person's life.

"There's Mom!" Corey said.

Ruby put her hand over Corey's mouth. "*Shh!* Could you just pretend we're in a spy movie?"

"Sorry," Corey mouthed.

Matt couldn't see his mom very well. It was dark, and she was wearing a hoodie, but he could tell it was her by her build and her smooth, athletic movements. But perhaps the biggest giveaway was the man beside her, dressed all in black. Captain Vincent. Or just Vincent for a little while longer, and if they succeeded, never captain at all.

The wind picked up, and the rain grew heavier. Matt started to shiver.

"I wish Mom had chosen a different day to change her life," said Corey, teeth chattering.

"This will be over before you know it," said Ruby. "Hang on."

Their mom turned toward some of her crew and said a few words, and then they all moved into different positions on the boat. Vincent lingered, whispered something in her ear, and then gave her a quick kiss and left.

Their mom watched him go, and then she pulled the Obsidian Compass off from around her neck. Lightning flashed. Matt saw her expression for a brief moment as she looked down at the Obsidian Compass in her hand. She looked somber, but resolved, like she was saying goodbye to a close and faithful friend.

Matt felt for his own compass inside his shirt. He wondered what would happen to it once they gave the Obsidian Compass to Tui. Would he still have his own compass? Or would it disappear? Without Captain Vincent he would have never built his own compass. Or maybe he would have, just for different reasons. He hoped that would be the case. He hated to think that all of that would be erased, but he was willing to sacrifice his compass if that's what it took to fix this, to save Jia. He'd built it for her in the first place.

Another crew member appeared next to their mother. Tui. Captain Bonnaire was speaking with her. Matt couldn't see their expressions. All he could see was Tui shaking her head. Belamie pressed the compass into her hands, then lowered a ladder over the side of the *Vermillion*. Tui shouted something as Belamie climbed down. Matt couldn't understand her words, but they sounded angry.

"It will be fine, Tui!" Matt heard his mom shout. "Just do as I told you and everything will be fine!" She jumped the last few rungs of the ladder, landing in a crouched position. She sprinted toward another boat anchored at the edge of the port, a gleaming white yacht.

"We gotta get on board now," said Ruby. "Let's go."

The wind swirled around them, lashing rain against Matt's face and blocking his vision. He shivered with cold, or maybe with something else. Nerves, that was all. Adrenaline.

They ran to the *Vermillion* and climbed up the ladder their mother had used to climb down. As Matt neared the top, he felt a gentle tugging from beneath him. He looked down to see a rat scurrying up the ladder. Matt tried to kick it, but the rat just hopped on his foot and climbed right up his leg, scampered up his back, and crawled on his head. Matt squealed and slapped at his hair. The rat jumped off, but Matt lost his balance in the process and nearly fell backward. Ruby reached up and grabbed his arm.

"Calm down, Matt!" Ruby hissed. "It's just a rat!"

Just a rat, Matt, just a rat. Matt pulled himself over the side of the boat. His heart was racing. He saw a scaly tail disappear around the other side of the bridge. He decided he hated all rats.

The *Vermillion* began to pull away from the port. "Come on," said Ruby. "Tui went to the other side."

They all crawled on hands and knees to the other side of the boat where Tui stood with two other crew members, both of them female as far as Matt could tell. Tui gave the other two some instructions, and they moved toward the back of the boat.

Thunder rumbled, and a flash of lightning illuminated Tui. Her back was to them, but Matt saw the Obsidian Compass in her right hand, the gold chain dangling. Vincent was nowhere to be seen. He must be in the bridge, Matt thought, driving the boat.

The *Vermillion* moved slowly through the water, slipping between other boats, moving toward the yacht their mother had boarded. The *Vermillion* made a sharp 180-degree turn away from the yacht, then backed up.

Lightning flashed. The sky rumbled. The rain was sharp needles on Matt's skin. He could just see the silhouette of their mom standing on the bow of the yacht, waiting. One of the crew members at the back of the *Vermillion* pulled the winch, unraveling a length of the cable. When they were just a few feet from the yacht, she tossed the cable to Belamie, who hooked it to the railing of the yacht. Once it was secure, she gave a signal and the crew member whistled. The *Vermillion* began to pull forward. The winch unraveled until it reached the end, and then there was a jolt as they began to pull the yacht behind them. Belamie gave a brief wave and then she walked to the other end of the boat and disappeared from view. Tui watched all this while holding tight to the compass.

"We have to get the compass now," Ruby said. "Mom's boat will explode any minute, and then Vincent will appear and take the compass from Tui."

They started to move closer. Matt's skin suddenly crackled with static electricity. His hair stood on end. He felt a push on his chest, almost as if his compass were repelling something in its path, like reverse magnetism. He remembered how his compass had reacted when his mother had grabbed him, how it burned against his skin.

"I can't get any closer," said Matt. "My compass . . . it's reacting to the Obsidian Compass."

"I got it," said Ruby. "You two wait here."

Ruby moved silently toward Tui until she was crouched right behind her, just beneath the Obsidian Compass. She slowly reached up and grabbed ahold of the chain.

BOOM!

The yacht exploded with fiery plumes of smoke.

"Captain!" Tui screamed. She yanked up her arms to her face. Ruby was able to pull the compass out of her hand, but the force of the blast caused her to also let go.

The Obsidian Compass went flying into the rainy night. It landed on the deck of the boat and slid right toward Matt. He backed away, feeling the hair rise on his arms, the compass at his chest getting warmer. He couldn't touch it.

The door to the bridge opened, and Vincent jumped over the railing to the main deck. "Bel!" he shouted. He ran to the edge of the boat and jumped on the rail.

"What are you doing?" Tui said, grabbing his leg.

"The compass!" he shouted. "I have to get the compass!"

The compass . . . It was still sliding toward Matt, but at the same time repelling him. Ruby was scrambling after it on her hands and knees. Corey was closer, but he slipped and fell.

And then there was that crazy rat!

The rat was scurrying toward the compass. Matt was the closest. They didn't have a moment to confer or decide. He braced himself, dove for the compass, and clasped his hand around it just as the rat reached it.

A fiery jolt shot through Matt's entire body, and the compass burned in Matt's grip. A bolt of electricity shot out of the compass, and at the same time lightning came down from the sky and the two connected in a jagged, twisted beam of light. Matt convulsed as the electricity shot through his hand and up his arm to his shoulder.

The rat was still on top of the compass. The bolt of lightning enveloped its body, and the rat screamed and writhed, its tail whipping madly. Its dark fur was on fire, fading from black to white. Its eyes also paled, first to a fiery blue and then red. The rat looked directly at Matt and hissed.

Matt pulled back his arm and flung the rat as hard as he could, like he was pitching a fast ball at a championship game. He had meant to get rid of the rat. Only the rat. But his brain wanted to get rid of the pain, too, and he accidentally let go of the compass. The rat soared into the rain-soaked night sky. It twisted and flipped through the air like an acrobat, holding tight to the compass still crackling with electricity. The rat and compass slowed and then paused, suspended in midair. Matt almost thought they would just stay that way, but gravity eventually remembered its job. The rat and compass came down. Before they hit the deck of the boat, a hand shot out and snatched the chain, and the rat and compass came to an abrupt halt.

Vincent pulled the compass toward him, gazing at it with reverence and awe. He paid no mind to anything else, not the other crew, or the three strange children huddled on the other side, or the boat in flames. He didn't even flinch as the white rat scampered up his arm and perched on his shoulder. It curled its tail around its body, stared out toward Matt with glowing red eyes, and hissed.

Matt backed away, staring in openmouthed horror at Vincent holding the compass, and the white rat on his shoulder.

Santiago . . .

"We have to go," said Corey. Matt hadn't noticed that he and Ruby were now crouched beside him.

"The compass," said Ruby. "We have to get the compass."

"It's too late," said Corey. Vincent was already turning the dials of the compass. Tui and the others were yelling at him, pointing to the burning yacht, but he ignored them. Corey grabbed on to Ruby and Matt but let go of Matt when he received an electrical shock. Matt could feel it coursing through his body still, especially his arm. His veins felt like they were high-voltage wires.

"Come on, Matt!" said Corey. He'd backed up to the side of the boat with Ruby. The boat was transforming now, lengthening and widening. A large wooden pole split from beneath the deck and grew like a tree in fast motion. Ruby climbed on the edge of the boat and jumped. Corey cannonballed himself over.

Matt walked backward toward the edge of the boat, still keeping his eyes on Vincent and the white rat on his shoulder. Water shot up all around the boat, like a dozen geysers. Their time was up. Matt jumped overboard just before the ship shot down into the ocean. When he hit the water, he was momentarily sucked down into the funnel. He spun around and around, reaching wildly for anything to hold on to, to pull him to safety, but there was nothing. He thought he would be sucked into a time vortex. Or drown.

The *Vermillion* disappeared, and the funnel suddenly closed in on him. The water rose like two towering walls and crashed down on Matt's head. Matt clawed his way to the surface and gasped for air. He struggled to keep above the churning water, but then he saw Corey and Ruby holding on to a buoy. He gathered what little strength he had left and swam to them. They both reached for him. Whatever electricity had been running through his veins must have faded because he didn't shock them. The three children stared at the spot where the *Vermillion* had been, the last waves disappearing.

The rain continued. The remains of the yacht smoked and burned on the water. Sirens sounded in the distance. Of course someone would have seen the explosion and called 911.

Matt saw a dark shape bob to the surface, not far from the burning yacht. It was their mom. She was wearing diving gear, a mask, a snorkel, and a tank of oxygen. She swam toward a small speedboat tied to a buoy. Matt saw the silhouette of a man standing on the back of the boat. He was fairly certain it was their dad. He reached down and helped their mom into the boat. She pulled off her mask and they embraced.

Matt looked away. Not because he felt uncomfortable. He'd seen his parents kiss plenty of times. But they weren't getting the happy ending that they thought they were, and it was his fault.

Ruby shivered as she watched their parents. It was difficult to tell in the rain, but Matt thought she was crying.

"Let's get out of here," said Corey.

"No," said Ruby in a choked voice. "We can't go now. We have to get the compass. We have to . . ."

"Ruby, it's over," said Corey. "We didn't get the compass, and we're not going to. Matt, turn the dials."

Matt pulled out his compass.

"Wait," said Ruby through chattering teeth. "We need to tie ourselves together." She pulled out a sopping tangle of yarn. The sight of it made her cry all the harder.

"Let's just hold on to each other, okay?" said Corey. "I'll hold on to you, Ruby, and you hold on to Matt. Matt will hold on to his compass. We get all smashed together anyway, so

I don't think the yarn is necessary. We won't be separated. We'll stick together, okay?"

Matt nodded. Ruby kept crying and shaking.

"Come on, bro," said Corey. "Get us out of here."

Matt turned the dials of the compass. The water warmed and bubbled around them, and then they were all shoved together and sucked under, leaving their young and unsuspecting parents in each other's arms on the back of a boat, and traveled toward their older and far more cautious parents who were now frantically searching for their three children in the Siberian Ice Age.

16
Past Faults

February 22, 3021 BC
Wrangel Island

Matt, Ruby, and Corey landed in a sopping heap on the frozen ground, shivering and clinging tightly to one another.

"Ev-v-veryone ok-kay?" Corey asked, teeth chattering.

"Yeah," said Matt. "R-ruby?"

She didn't answer. Matt shot up and looked around, his heart racing. What if she'd gotten left behind? Or worse, lost in transit? But he found her. She was curled up in a ball on the icy ground, shivering and crying.

"Ruby . . ." Matt went to her and put a hand on her shoulder. She kept her eyes squeezed shut. Matt looked to Corey, wondering what they should do. Corey just shook his head. There was nothing to be done. They'd made a mess of things, and there was no fixing it.

Footsteps sounded behind them. Someone took in a sharp

gasp of air. "Captain! They're here! I found the children!" It was Tui. A minute later their parents came running.

Mrs. Hudson came first. She rushed to her children, knelt down in the snow beside Matt and Corey. Mr. Hudson ran to the other side next to Ruby.

Matt braced himself. He was certain his parents were about to start shouting at them, as they had when they'd landed here the first time. This was even worse. They had deliberately disobeyed them. They had done exactly what their mother said they should not do, and for that Matt knew they all deserved to be severely punished—screamed at, berated, grounded for life. But when he saw his mom and dad, saw their faces, he knew they weren't going to yell.

Briefly he thought of the two young people he'd just left behind, embracing on the back of a boat, free and innocent. These were not those same two people. The years had changed them, and the weight and worry of family, work, and life was clearly etched on their faces. He saw the wisdom that had been forged through time and experience. They'd dishonored that, he, Corey, and Ruby. They'd thought they knew better.

"Ruby." Mr. Hudson scooped up his daughter's shivering little body and held her to his chest. She clutched at his shirt.

Mrs. Hudson took Corey's face in her hands, then Matt's, searching them over. Matt winced as his mom brushed a bruise on his cheek, and then she gasped as she touched his right hand. For a moment he thought he'd shocked her.

"Oh, Mateo, what happened?" his mom asked.

"Whoa, b-bro," said Corey. "Your ar-arm . . ."

Matt gazed at his arm and almost felt a jolt himself. His hand and arm had been badly burned, but the burn marks looked like an intricate system of tree roots branded on his flesh from the tips of his fingers all the way up his arm, disappearing beneath his shirtsleeve. He turned over his hand and found the origin point at the center of his palm. An angry pucker of red flesh. "It's from the compass," he said.

His mom frowned. "Your compass did this to you?"

"No," said Matt. "It was the Obsidian Compass. I had it. I was holding it, but then it burned me. . . ."

"The Obsidian Compass," said Mrs. Hudson. "What are you talking about? What happened?"

Ruby began to sob all the harder then. "It's my fault!" she wailed. "It was my idea!"

Mr. Hudson held her close and tried to calm her. Mrs. Hudson put both her cool hands over Matt's burned one. "We'll talk later," Mr. Hudson said, without even a hint of anger. "We need to get you three warm and dry."

Their dad carried Ruby, still sobbing, while their mom helped lift up Corey and Matt, holding them close to her as they walked slowly back toward Tui's cave. Tui built up the fire until the cave was practically an oven. Their parents didn't say a word. They asked no questions, only wrapped them in furs and tended to the children's scratches and Matt's burns.

Corey looked drained. His eyes were sunken and blood-shot. Matt felt sucked dry, and now that the shock was wearing down, the pain from the burns on his arm was set-tling in, intensifying every second.

Chuck found a small first-aid kit inside of Blossom. It wasn't much, just a few Band-Aids, some ointment, and med-icine for pain. Mr. Hudson gave the medicine to Matt. The Band-Aids weren't big enough to cover his burns of course, so Chuck brought over an old Led Zeppelin T-shirt filled with snow. Mrs. Hudson rubbed the snow on Matt's burns and gently pressed the T-shirt around his arm. He sighed with relief at both the cold on his burns and the warmth every-where else.

Ruby continued to sob into her father's shirt. Mr. Hudson tried to comfort her, get her to calm down, but it only made it worse, and finally it all came spilling out. Between racking sobs, Ruby confessed everything.

Mr. and Mrs. Hudson did not speak, they only listened. Matt saw his mom's jaw tighten and her nostrils flare at moments, but to her credit she didn't yell. She didn't even reprimand them.

"I—I'm s-s-so sorry," said Ruby, through her shuddering sobs. "It was a-all my idea. I planned everything, and I t-told the boys what to do. I thought it would be okay, but we made a m-mess of everything. It's my f-fault Vincent got the compass." She looked at Tui when she said this. "It's my fault he d-discarded you."

"Oh no, child," said Tui, reaching out to touch Ruby's cheek. "You must not blame yourself. This is no one's fault except Vincent's."

"And mine," said Matt. "I was the one who had the compass, and then I threw it right at Vincent." He gently touched the T-shirt over his arm. It was already warm. His skin was pulsing.

"If anyone is to blame, it's me," said Mrs. Hudson. "I should have told you before. I should have been more open with you." She pulled her knees up to her chest and hugged them.

"Told us what?" Ruby asked.

"I made a very similar mistake once myself, only the consequences were far worse, I'm afraid."

"You did? When?"

"A long time ago, about two years after I received the compass. I tried to go back in time and save my parents. I failed." Her voice was cold and hollow, like someone speaking from the grave. "Worse, I was the reason they died. My presence . . . there was a storm. . . ." She didn't need to finish. They all understood. Her time-traveling had caused the very storm that took her parents' lives.

"How did you survive?" Ruby asked.

"I saved myself," said Mrs. Hudson, and then she let out a derisive laugh. "Your mother has always had a keen sense of self-preservation."

"At least you survived," said Corey.

"Yes, but I hated myself," said Mrs. Hudson. "For a long time, I loathed my very existence. But I learned. Oh, I learned a very hard lesson, and I did not make that same mistake again. I was very careful to never cross paths with myself or anyone I knew in my present in the past or future."

They all sat in silence for a minute and let these things rest and settle around them and inside of them, like waves on the sea after a storm.

"So I guess we really can't change the past," said Ruby, "at least not the way we want."

"Which is totally bogus," said Corey. "What's the good of time travel if you can't change all the garbage in the past?"

Chuck stroked his beard and looked unusually pensive and wise. "What good would it be to change the past?" he said. "What would be the purpose of life without regret? All the wisdom in the world from the beginning of time has been acquired by mistakes. They may leave us bruised and scarred for life, but they also make us more whole, more beautiful. And sometimes good things come out of bad. Just think how much pain, how many mistakes have brought us together in this moment right here? I would not change the past for anything."

Chuck stopped speaking and gazed into the crackling fire.

"Chook," said Tui. "You have spoken great truth."

Chuck bowed appreciatively. "Thank you, Princess Tui."

"Yes, thank you, Chuck," said Mr. Hudson. "I too am grateful for all our past pains and mistakes that have brought us together."

"Hear! Hear!" said Corey.

Matt yawned and felt the final dregs of his energy drain out of him. He felt like he could sleep for a century.

Matt woke in the middle of the night. His arm was hurting. The burns pulsed with heat. He needed more snow or ice, and he almost got out of his furs, but then he heard voices.

"I think we need to rethink our strategy here," said his dad. "We've got to work with the kids somehow. We can't allow something like this to happen again."

"We need to take the compass," said his mom. Matt started, fully awake now. "We should take it from him now, while he's asleep." He grabbed his compass.

"You could do that," said Mr. Hudson, "but he'll never forgive you."

"I can live with that," said Mrs. Hudson, "as long as it means he's safe."

"What does that even mean, Belamie? Safe. You know you can't protect them from everything, and even if you could, I don't believe you could live with Mateo's anger toward you if you take his compass. That completely defeats the purpose, protecting those you love just so they can hate you forever. Maybe you can live that way, but I can't."

"You're letting your emotions get in the way of reason," said Mrs. Hudson.

"And why shouldn't I?" said Mr. Hudson. "Why shouldn't we be *emotional* about this? This is our family, Belamie, not a crew of pirates!"

"I know that," said Mrs. Hudson, her voice tight.

There was a pause. When Mr. Hudson spoke again, his voice was calm. "How come you never told me Mateo came to you in the past?"

Mrs. Hudson let out a long breath. "It's hard to explain."

"Try," said Mr. Hudson. "I think I have a right to know."

"But that's just it," said Mrs. Hudson. "You *don't* really have a right to know something like that, to see your own child before you even know you'll have children, before you've even met the person you know you want to spend the rest of your life with. And then when you finally do and you're ready for the child to come, they don't come, and it makes it all the more confusing and torturous, because you *know* you're supposed to have this child, but you don't know when or how. . . ." She paused and took a long breath. "I guess I was just trying to spare you some of the pain and confusion."

"Wow," said Mr. Hudson. "Thanks for that. None of our life has been painful or confusing at all."

Mrs. Hudson stifled a laugh.

"We're running out of options," said Mr. Hudson. "Tui is right. The past is coming back to haunt us, and we can't run or hide from it. We're going to have to face it, Belamie. We're going to have to face Vincent."

"It's not Vincent that I'm afraid of," said Mrs. Hudson. "Not really. He's part of it of course, but he's not the biggest threat. It's Quine."

"You've told me so little of him," said Mr. Hudson.

"Because I know so little. I don't know what his end goal is, or if he even has one. I don't know if he is good or bad, if he's on Vincent's side or ours. I only know he wants Mateo."

Matt's heart pounded in his chest so loudly, he wondered that his parents didn't hear it. Quine wanted him? Why?

"Why?" his dad said, echoing Matt's thoughts. "Do you think it's because he built a compass? Maybe he sees that as a threat."

"That could be part of it, possibly," said Mrs. Hudson. "But I think it goes deeper than that."

"What? Like he's Mateo's biological father or something? His grandfather, his mad genius uncle?"

"I don't know," said Mrs. Hudson. "None of it makes any sense. That's what scares me so much."

Matt's parents didn't speak for a while. His heart was still racing.

"Then I think we have to find out what it all means," said Mr. Hudson. "We can't live like this, Belamie. The kids can't live like this, always in fear, wondering each night if when they wake up their family will be ripped apart. I can't live like that." Matt thought he heard his dad's voice catch in his throat.

"I know," said his mom. "I know."

They said no more, and Matt was left to his own thoughts. Quine wanted him for some unknown reason. He could be his father or some blood relative. Matt wasn't sure how to feel about that. His dad was his father. His mom, his mother. His adoption was simply a technical fact. He never considered who might be out there wondering about him, perhaps missing him. But if they missed him, why would they have given him up for adoption in the first place?

People can have regrets.

Yes, he knew that as well as anyone. It was a heavy load to process, especially when his brain was already overloaded.

The next morning, as they all sat around the fire eating stale granola bars, Mrs. Hudson made an apology.

"I've been selfish," she said. "And a coward." She looked at Tui, who gave Mrs. Hudson an encouraging smile. "I will not pretend I'm not frightened, but your father and I have agreed that we can't go home and go back to normal. No matter what

I say, we'd spend the rest of our lives looking over our shoulders. We don't want to live like that, and you children deserve better."

"What does that mean?" Corey asked, hopefully.

"It means we're on a mission. We're going to find Vincent and put a stop to him."

"Do you mean it?" Matt asked. "And Jia? We'll rescue her?"

Mrs. Hudson nodded. "I can't make any promises that we'll succeed on either front. But we'll do all we can."

Matt felt a knot loosen in his chest.

"I want to be clear," said Mrs. Hudson. "This is not a game. The risks are great. None of us can comprehend the dangers we might face, but if you are willing to face them, then I will face them with you."

"I'm willing," said Matt, eagerly.

"Me too," said Ruby.

"Me three!" said Corey. "When do we leave?"

"Hang on, not so fast," said Mr. Hudson, holding up a hand. Matt was a little surprised at how stern and business-like he sounded. "Before we go further, we need to get a few things straight. First, all of you place your right hand over your heart. It's time to take the Hudson Family Oath."

Matt, Ruby, and Corey all did as they were told.

"Now repeat after me," said Mr. Hudson. "I solemnly swear . . ."

"I solemnly swear . . ." the children droned.

"That I will listen to my parents and obey their every command."

"That I will listen to my parents and obey their every command."

"And I will *never* time-travel without my parents ever again."

"And I will *never* time-travel without my parents ever again."

"If I do . . ."

"If I do . . ."

"Then . . . uhhhh . . ." Mr. Hudson clearly had not thought of a punishment to fit the potential crime.

"May I be cursed to listen to pop country music for the rest of my life!" Chuck interjected, raising his pointer finger into the air.

"Uhhh . . . ," said Mr. Hudson. "Let's just say, 'Shame be upon my head forever more.'"

"Shame be upon my head forevermore," the children repeated.

"And, Mateo," said Mr. Hudson. He stood squarely in front of Matt and looked him straight in the eyes. "Your mother could steal that compass from you with her eyes closed and you wouldn't even know it. She has *allowed* you to keep it, and we will allow it now, out of respect for the fact that you did build it, but if I get even a hint that you might use it again without our express permission, you will wish you'd never made it at all. Do you understand me?"

Matt didn't think he'd ever seen his father more serious. It surprised him, not just because his dad was normally easygoing and friendly, but also because he'd been the one to object to his mother's proposal last night that they take the compass from him, and yet Matt had no doubt whatsoever that his father would follow through with his threat.

Matt nodded. "I understand."

"Good," said Mr. Hudson. It took a few moments for the tension to loosen a little, but then Ruby asked where and when they were going and how they were going to stop Vincent.

"We're going to Chicago first," said Mrs. Hudson, "to 1893. We believe that's where Vincent is now and has been most of the time since he left us in New York."

"Why there?" Matt asked timidly. He didn't want to seem too nosy or in charge at this moment, but since Chicago was the place he'd traveled when he first built the compass, and it was where he'd seen both his mother and Vincent decades in their past, he assumed it had some significance.

"Quine made a reference to it in his letter," said Mrs. Hudson.

"Is that why you were there when you met Matt?" Ruby asked.

Mrs. Hudson nodded. "I was searching for the Aeternum, but after I saw Mateo, and I met your father, my goals changed rather abruptly. But it does make sense that Vincent would go there after he got the letter."

"So he's looking for the Aeternum there?" Matt asked.

"He's following the trail," said Mrs. Hudson. "Our mission is to cut him off."

"And cut his throat," said Tui.

"Tui . . . ," said Mrs. Hudson in a warning voice.

"Sorry, *Rubbana*," said Tui. "I will try to keep my vengeful thoughts to myself until they can be of use."

"Chuck," said Mr. Hudson. "You've been so patient with us through all of this. We can take you back to New York first."

"What?! And miss all the fun?" said Chuck. "And what would you do without Blossom? Seems like you need her for your travels, and where she goes I go. We're a package deal, so I'm afraid you're stuck with us."

"Fair enough," said Mr. Hudson. "Thank you, Chuck. You're a good man."

"On to Chicago! The Windy City!"

Matt expected to come up against a lot of resistance and delaying tactics from his parents when it came time to actually travel. He feared that at any moment his mom or dad would steal his compass and take them all home. But to his surprise they were both efficient and businesslike in the preparations for their mission and showed no signs of hesitation or changing their minds. Mostly their parents reiterated that the children do exactly as they say, stay close by, and not attempt any stunts or heroics. "When we find Vincent, I will deal with him," said Mrs. Hudson. "Is that clear?"

"Yes," said Matt, Corey, and Ruby, all at the same time, like little soldiers.

Tui cleaned up her cave with great care, folding up the furs, placing her tools and dishes as though she were only leaving on a vacation and not forever.

As they were all loading up into Blossom, Matt got some more snow for his arm. The pain had subsided a little, but it was still pretty raw. He slathered some snow over his arm and wrapped the Led Zeppelin T-shirt over it. Before he got on the bus, Mrs. Hudson pulled Matt aside.

"A few pointers," she said. "Start by turning the dial for location first, then move outward. It always made the ride a little less jarring for the Obsidian Compass, at least. Of course it's different, and we're not traveling in the *Vermillion*, but it might help. Also pause for just a second before you make the final click of the outer dial. That helps too. And put the compass away during travel. Don't leave it in your hand to go flying around and knock into things. That disrupts the navigation."

"Okay. Thanks," said Matt.

His mom nodded. It was weird, taking time-travel advice from her when he'd been the one to build the compass, but of course she was far more experienced, and it must be difficult for her to not just take the compass from him and navigate herself. Matt knew she'd probably do a better job of it, but he felt it was important that he keep it. He was determined to learn and improve.

"One more thing," said his mom. She hesitated a little. "Please don't separate yourself from us for any reason. I may be captain of the crew, but you are the navigator. Without you, we'll be lost."

Her eyes were shining, and she swallowed a hard lump in her throat. Matt almost wanted to ask about what she'd said the night before, about Quine wanting him for some reason, but he didn't want her to be angry at him for eavesdropping, so he just nodded. "I won't leave you."

Corey and Ruby were already buckled into the seats on either side of the little table in the middle. Matt wished he could join them, but his mom steered him to the back bench, and he sat between his mom and Tui. Mr. Hudson sat in the front passenger seat with Chuck as the driver.

"Everyone buckled up?" Mr. Hudson asked, turning around in his seat. After it was confirmed that everyone was buckled, Mr. Hudson gave Matt the location, date, and time for their mission.

Matt started to turn the inner dial of his compass as his mom had instructed. As soon as he did, Blossom sputtered, coughed, and roared to life.

"Good girl, Blossom!" said Chuck, giving the horn a little honk.

Matt turned the other two dials and paused for just a moment before making the final turn. Blossom rolled forward a little, revved her engine, and then shot into the air like a bird taking flight. Matt reached out to grab on to something, and Blossom made a sudden turn that caused them all to shift sharply to the left. Ruby screamed.

"Put the compass away, Mateo," said his mom in a calm voice that did not match the turbulent chaos.

Matt slipped the compass beneath his shirt, and Blossom righted herself, and then there was a flash of light and everything went dark.

17

Sure Shot

July 4, 1893
Chicago, Illinois

The travel did feel different this time. Less jarring, yes, but also Blossom made some interesting sounds, rhythmic honks and taps and dings like she was beatboxing. Matt felt things shifting around him, the floor beneath his feet, the seats. The ceiling must have rolled back because he suddenly felt a rush of hot, humid air. He saw a smattering of light, and the next thing he knew Blossom plunged down into water and rocked from side to side.

"Well, hot Chicago dog!" said Chuck as Blossom steadied herself in the water. "Blossom turned herself into a boat! Isn't that something?"

She had indeed turned herself into a boat. Sort of. From what Matt could tell, she was essentially the same vehicle as before, only a little wider and the top half had been removed so they were exposed to the elements.

Matt looked around. They were floating in some kind of lagoon, surrounded by huge white buildings built in a classical fashion with pillars and arches and domes. There were statues and fountains and bridges, and little boats and gondolas floated in the lagoon.

"This doesn't look like Chicago," said Ruby. "Not like any pictures I've seen of it anyway."

"This is a special time for Chicago. They're hosting the World's Columbian Exposition," said Mr. Hudson, turning every which way, trying to take it all in. "It's to celebrate the four hundredth anniversary of Columbus's arrival in the New World. They built all this just for the fair. Can you believe that? It was an astounding thing in its time. It still is."

Matt had time-traveled plenty before of course, but he never lost any sense of awe by the newness of everything, the people and clothing from another era, the buildings and streets, the smell, the *feel* of being in a totally different time and place. He'd never been able to explain it before, but now he thought it was a little like being in a dream, but with more physical power and control. Misplaced, but present all the same.

The city was crowded with pedestrians walking between buildings and over bridges and walkways. They floated toward a place where other boats had been docked, but when they reached it Blossom didn't stop. She rammed right into the walkway.

"Chuck, stop!" said Mr. Hudson.

"I'm trying!" he said, clearly pushing on the brakes. "Sometimes Blossom gets a mind of her own." Chuck honked the horn and people screamed and rushed out of the way as the strange boat crashed onto the walkway. The engine roared and groaned, then made a series of clinks and clanks, and the next thing Matt knew, they were driving on the walkway. The crowd parted for them but watched in awe as this strange contraption moved along the fairgrounds, until a man in an official-looking uniform came marching up to them with a sword in hand. Mrs. Hudson whipped out her dagger, but kept it hidden from the guard's view.

"Say, what do you think you're doing here?" said the guard, tapping on the front of the bus-boat. Or boat-bus.

Chuck rolled down his window and without skipping a beat said, "Hello. The name's Chuck. I'm here to display this marvelous machine!"

The police officer looked over Blossom. "This some kind of newfangled streetcar?"

"Uh . . . yep!" said Chuck.

"Well, do you have a permit?" said the officer.

"A permit?" said Chuck.

"Permits are required for all displays."

"Oh, sure. Sure, sure, sure. Just let me find it. I know it's around here somewhere." He searched around, opening compartments and drawers. "Here we are!" He pulled out a four-by-six index card from a little compartment beneath the steering wheel. "Signed by the mayor and all!"

"Mayor Harrison?" The officer squinted down at the card. Matt could tell he couldn't see it very well in the bright sunlight.

"Says here that I, Chuck, am an esteemed inventor and have permission to showcase this here contraption"—he tapped the side of the car—"wherever I like in this here fair." Chuck began talking in an almost-Southern twang, like he was trying to put on some kind of act, but not very convincingly.

"Our instructions say each exhibit is to have a specific showcase location . . . ," said the guard.

"See here, Officer," said Chuck, "this is a *moving* contraption! She can go from water to land, and even fly!"

"Fly?"

"Yes! Fly! Like a bird!" Chuck flapped his arms. "I can't very well showcase her in a single location, can I? There's no sense in that. That's why it's signed by Mayor Hamilton himself."

"*Harrison*," Mr. Hudson muttered.

"That's right. Harry and I go way back. Back to the . . . revolution."

Mr. Hudson put his hand to his forehead.

The guard wasn't paying all that much attention, however. There was a commotion somewhere in the crowd, shouts and shoves. It looked like a fight was breaking out.

"Okay, move along," said the guard, and he took out his sword and marched toward the commotion. Matt thought he saw two men fighting. One was in a red jacket and top hat. The other had a pipe in his mouth. Matt squinted, trying to get a better look, but crowds overtook them, and he couldn't see.

Chuck quickly honked his horn, so people jumped out of the way.

"What did you show him for a permit?" Ruby asked.

"A recipe," said Chuck.

"Are you joking?" said Ruby. "All you showed him was a *recipe*?"

"Hey, it worked," said Chuck.

"What was the recipe?" Ruby asked.

"Tuna and Jell-O Pie."

"Hey! I had something like that as a kid," said Mr. Hudson. "My mom used to make it all the time. One of my favorite meals as a kid."

"Mine too!" said Chuck.

"What the barf?" said Corey. "Let me see that." He reached for the recipe card, but Chuck slipped it into the little compartment below the radio. "Sorry. Secret family recipe. Not allowed to share."

"Yeah, I was really hoping to steal that secret," said Corey.

They drove along, honking for the crowds to move as they rumbled over a bridge. The air was sweltering, like a humid oven, and it was baking and fermenting everything, all the body odors, the pungent spice of perfume and cologne, the grease of meat, and the musk of animals and waste.

"Almost smells worse than Elizabethan England, doesn't it?" said Ruby, covering her nose.

"So *hot*," said Tui. She started shedding all her furs, revealing a bright blue tunic beneath and a gold belt accentuating her slender waist. She uncovered her hair, revealing braids shaped into whorls and spirals. Matt thought she looked remarkably fresh after how long she'd been in the Siberian Ice Age, though of course she was still quite thin.

Smells aside, the sights of Chicago were incredible. They were driving around the lagoon now. Matt gazed at the fountains and bridges, and the gleaming white classical buildings with pillars, domes, arches, and elaborate sculptures and statues. At one end of the lagoon stood a huge golden statue of a woman in Roman-style robes holding a globe in one hand, with some kind of bird perched on top, the wings stretched, and a long staff in the other with a sign that Matt couldn't quite read. At the other end of the water's edge stood a magnificent fountain, with a sculpture in the center of a barge with people holding long oars and winged creatures with trumpets, and surrounding the barge were groupings of mermaids and horses. And in the distance was the Ferris wheel. It rotated slowly in the light blue sky.

"I'm sure there's an extra-large crowd here today," said Mr. Hudson. "Since it's Independence Day."

Blossom inched forward at a snail's pace. The crowds were growing thicker by the minute and weren't responding much to Blossom's honks and growls. There were likely so many unusual things to see at the fair, this was just one more exhibition.

"I think we should find a place to park Blossom and go on foot," said Mr. Hudson. "We'll move faster."

"No, it will be too easy for us to be separated," said Mrs. Hudson.

"Belamie, if we're going to confront Vincent, we're not going to be able to do it from the comfort of Blossom."

"Don't worry, Captain," said Tui. "I will take care of Vincent myself. No harm will come to your family."

Matt watched his mom clench her jaw, but she didn't have any rebuttal. "Park over there, between those buildings," she said. Chuck honked the horn and turned into a narrow sort of alley between two of the large buildings.

As everyone got out of Blossom, Matt tried to move out of the alley and into the open, but his mom pulled him back by his arm. "No wandering," she said. "We all must stick together. Come on." Mrs. Hudson took hold of Corey with her left hand, and Mr. Hudson took Ruby with his right hand, and they each had hold of Matt in the middle. Tui walked ahead of them, with Chuck traipsing behind.

The fair was certainly a place that drew people from all over, but no one looked quite so out of place as the Hudson crew. They got plenty of stares and guffaws at their jeans and sneakers and T-shirts. Chuck especially stood out in his shorts and bright tie-dyed T-shirt with the peace sign, and his fishing hat and sunglasses. One woman stopped them and asked where in the world they were from, and when they told her they were from New York, she looked confused and said, "I must visit New York next, then."

People pointed at Tui, too, though they didn't laugh or snigger. Matt thought she looked intimidating and regal, every bit a princess, and guessed people probably would have stared at her even if she were in her own time and country.

"Are we sticking out too much?" Matt asked his mom. "People are looking at us like we're from outer space. Isn't that dangerous?"

"Yeah, Brocco always said it was important to dress in the time period," said Ruby. "Otherwise won't we cause a glitch or get in trouble somehow?"

"Sometimes that's true," said Mrs. Hudson. "Dressing properly for the time period and culture is certainly the safe thing to do, but we should be fine here. People will always try to make sense of whatever they see, find some explanation. That's a natural brain response. We like to categorize and place things. But if they can't find a place for you, and if enough people begin to wonder if you're really from another world or time, or just don't belong here, then strange, inexplicable things can happen. But we should be okay here. We do stand out, but there are enough strange people and things that most simply chalk it up to the wonders of the fair."

And there were many wonders at the fair, Matt decided. So many, he could barely take them all in, and he almost forgot the purpose for which they had come. They were past the big buildings and exhibits now and were in a place with smaller exhibits. Some people displayed their art and crafts. Others were sharing songs or dances from their countries. They saw hula dancers in grass skirts, accompanied by ukuleles. A woman was surrounded by people, her dress decorated in bangles that tinkled as she moved and swayed. A belly dancer, Matt realized. Some of the women watching looked scandalized. Some of the men tried to look scandalized, but didn't fully succeed.

And food. There were stalls selling roasted corn on the cob, sausages, fresh fruit, and pies. Corey asked if they could get some of the food here, but Mrs. Hudson said they didn't have the proper currency for that. But then Tui pulled out a little pouch attached to her gold belt and shook it.

"Not for nothing is my father the richest man in the world," she said, and pulled out a gold coin that had a head stamped in the center, with letters and symbols around the edges.

"Oh, your dad rocks," said Corey, snatching the coin.

"Vincent let you keep a sack of gold?" said Mrs. Hudson, one eyebrow raised.

"He made no search when he discarded me," said Tui, "and it's not as though it would have done me any good in Siberia. The beasts there do not trade in gold."

"We'll have to exchange some of the coins," said Mr. Hudson. "I saw a money exchange back that way."

Just one of Tui's gold coins gave them enough money to buy everyone as much food as they could possibly want with plenty to spare. They got stacks of pancakes, cabbage rolls, and tamales. They also got Cracker Jacks, which the vendor said were a brand-new treat, as well as brownies, which Mr. Hudson announced with professorial authority and pride had been invented by some hotel chef in Chicago just for the fair.

The Hudsons traipsed through the fair, searching every face, which was a big job seeing as there were a lot of faces. Matt started to lag. It was so hot and smelly and crowded, and he was tired. They came to a huge stadium just outside the fairgrounds. A giant sign read:

BUFFALO BILL'S WILD WEST AND CONGRESS OF ROUGH RIDERS OF THE WORLD

Big posters on a wall displayed different acts and attractions, scenes of cowboys on their horses with their guns and lassos and Native Americans in feathered headdresses, shooting bows and arrows.

Another poster caught Matt's eye, one of a young woman with dark hair and sharp, penetrating eyes, wearing a cowgirl hat and holding a rifle. At the top of the poster in large letters were the words "Little Sure Shot."

Mrs. Hudson came up to the poster and stared. She brushed her fingers over the picture of the young woman.

"It's Annie, isn't it?" said Matt. "From your crew."

His mom didn't say a word, just stared at the picture.

Tui came and stood next to Mrs. Hudson and studied the picture. "That *is* Annie, isn't it?"

"Annie Oakley, huh?" said Chuck. "You know her?"

"*The* Annie Oakley?" squeaked Ruby. "Annie Oakley was a member of your crew?! How come you never told us that?"

"I didn't . . . I never . . ." Mrs. Hudson stumbled over her words. Matt was guessing she hadn't realized who Annie was while she was on her crew. He felt a bit silly that he hadn't drawn the connection before, but it hadn't crossed his mind at all when he'd met Annie just a few days ago. She'd been quite a bit younger when he'd seen her on the *Vermillion*. Here, she looked like she was maybe in her early twenties.

Mrs. Hudson peeled her eyes away from the picture. She walked over to a ticket counter and asked if she could buy tickets for the show. The ticket seller said the show was already underway, but Mrs. Hudson gave him a stack of bills that Matt was guessing were worth a lot more than was required because the man gave her seven tickets and told her to enjoy the show.

They didn't sit down when they entered the stadium. They didn't make it that far. They stood at the edge of the arena while a parade of horses trotted around in formation. Both rider and steed were in elaborate costumes, and not just your typical western cowboys and Indians clothing. There were representations of countries and cultures from all over the world, waving flags and wearing special costumes or uniforms.

There were reenactments of Wild West battles and demonstrations of skills. A cowboy showed tricks with a lasso, twirling it over his head and around his body; a man rode on four white horses at once, and Will Cody demonstrated why they called him "Buffalo Bill" as he shot down a huge buffalo, charging right at him.

A man shot his gun while standing on his head and bending over backward, hitting his mark every time.

Then a young woman came in riding atop a horse, rifle tucked beneath one arm.

Mrs. Hudson stood frozen, rapt with attention, as the girl shot her gun. She shot clay jars, bursting each to smithereens. The crowd cheered. The girl rode to another spot and shot a target fifty yards away. She dismounted her horse and stood in the middle of the arena while another rider rode in circles around her and threw disks in the air. She hit every single one. And then more riders came out throwing smaller and smaller items in the air for Annie to shoot until she was shooting nothing more than black marbles that burst into little clouds of dust when she hit them. The crowd went wild, and Annie blew kisses all around.

"Wowie!" said Chuck, clapping loudly. "She's something, isn't she?"

"I want her to teach me to shoot," Corey said.

"Yeah," said Matt.

Annie continued her act, splitting cards from the side, snuffing out candles. If she ever missed, which Matt had a hunch was intentional, she'd pout dramatically and then shoot something else.

A flash of red caught Matt's attention to his right. He looked over and did a double take.

A man wearing a red velvet coat and a black satin top hat was climbing over audience members in the stands, and with him was another man in a brown suit and fedora, a pipe bobbing in his mouth.

"It's Brocco and Wiley!" said Corey.

"Where is Vincent?" said Tui, drawing a knife.

Brocco pulled out a gun and aimed it right at them. Matt froze on the spot. He felt paralyzed. Mrs. Hudson shoved him to the ground so hard his knees cracked. Wiley yanked at Brocco's arm just before he pulled the trigger.

Bang!

"Oh, look at that, Margie!" said a man in the audience, pointing to Brocco and Wiley. "They planted shooters in the audience too!"

"How splendid," said his wife, looking through a pair of brass binoculars.

Brocco jumped over audience members. Wiley stumbled after him, holding on to his hat as he tripped over a woman, apologizing profusely for his rudeness.

"We have to get out of here," said Mr. Hudson. "Now." Matt was suddenly yanked up by his arm, and half dragged away. Brocco took aim again.

"Watch out!" said Corey.

Bang!

Brocco dropped his gun. He howled and hopped around, shaking his hand.

Matt looked out toward the arena. Annie was back on her horse, aiming her gun at Brocco.

Bang!

She shot Brocco's hat. Brocco ducked, grabbing at his head as the hat fell to the ground. Annie kicked her horse into a trot, riding toward the Hudsons, her rifle still in her arms. The horse jumped the fence.

"Whoa!" Annie pulled the reins. The horse reared onto its

hind legs and stopped just a few feet before the Hudsons. The crowd was going wild. Annie turned her horse around, took off her hat and bowed. Then she turned back to the Hudsons, peering down at them with dark, serious eyes.

"Annie," breathed Mrs. Hudson.

"Captain," she said, nodding in a very soldierlike manner. "Let's get you someplace safe."

Matt looked back at Brocco and Wiley. Brocco was inspecting his gun, which had clearly been destroyed. Wiley picked up Brocco's hat, then looked up and met eyes with Matt. Brocco grabbed his destroyed hat and shoved it on his head and glared in their direction, but they didn't dare come toward them, not with Annie Oakley in front of them with her gun.

Annie led the Hudsons and Tui and Chuck to her tent located behind the stadium. It was far grander than your average camp tent, more like a furnished room with a floral-patterned rug, a small bed and tables and chairs. The tables were covered in prize medals, boxes of ammunition, and pictures, mostly of Annie with her rifle, and some of Will Cody on his big white horse. A bicycle sat in one corner, as well as several more rifles, each of them polished and gleaming.

Annie silently lit a few lanterns inside the tent and then shut the flaps.

"Well, well, well," she said, a smile playing behind her dark eyes. "Look what the cat done drug in."

"Annie," said Mrs. Hudson, still clearly shocked to see her old crew member.

Annie broke into a broad smile, set down her gun, and held out her arms. Mrs. Hudson walked to her and the two women embraced for a long moment.

"Annie, look how you've grown! Quite a lady."

"Haven't grown too much," said Annie with a small laugh. "I'll never be as tall as you, I'm afraid." She stood on her toes a little. She was quite petite, no more than five feet, Matt thought, but that didn't seem to hold her back any.

Annie turned to Tui. "Hello, Tui," she said.

"Annie," said Tui, giving a curt nod. Tui did not smile. Matt wondered if there was bad blood between them for some reason, but he didn't have time to consider it much before Chuck jumped in.

"Hi, I'm Chuck!" he said, shaking Annie's hand. "I'm a big fan of yours, even if I'm not much of a fan of guns in general."

"Pleased to meet you, Chuck." Annie shook his hand graciously. "Well, Captain, it looks like you've been quite busy assembling a new crew." She gazed around at the children and Mr. Hudson.

"Annie," said Mrs. Hudson, taking her hand. "Allow me to introduce my husband, Matthew Hudson, and my children. This is Ruby and Corey and Mateo." She touched each of them on the head as she said their names.

Annie looked at each of them, nodded and smiled, and then her eyes rested on Mateo. Annie cocked her head sideways with a confused expression. "You look just about the same as I remember, but that was years ago."

"It was only a few days ago for me," said Matt, feeling like that was a wildly inaccurate statement even as he said it. So much had happened—seeing his mother in the past, traveling to the Ice Age, finding Tui, their failed mission to retrieve the compass from Captain Vincent, and now finding Annie Oakley at the Chicago World's Fair of 1893. It seemed impossible that it could have all happened in three days. It felt like years ago even for him.

Annie shook her head like she was trying to wake up. "Oh, I never could get used to those kinds of twisty time things in my head. I like clear straight lines. Easier to hit your mark that way."

"Tell me about it," said Chuck. "Time travel is a real mindbender, am I right?"

"Sure is," said Annie.

"I'm glad to see you're okay," Matt said, "that you got away from Vincent at least."

"I have you to thank for that," said Annie. "Don't know that I would have had the guts had you not said what you did. 'Trust your gun,' he said." Annie said this to Mrs. Hudson. "Well, that's exactly what I did, and I think it's worked out okay."

"I'm not surprised in the least," said Mrs. Hudson. "I only feel silly that I didn't realize before. . . . Annie Oakley." She shook her head, smiling. "I should have known that was my Annie, when I heard the stories."

"They tell tales about me in the future?" said Annie.

Mrs. Hudson laughed. "They write books about you, and movies and plays! Of course none of them truly do you justice. How could they? But you are a legend!"

Annie's eyes widened, and she blushed ever so slightly, which made her look more like the girl Matt had seen a few days earlier. "You were there for me when I needed it most, Captain," she said. "I don't think I ever thanked you. I didn't have any manners to speak of back then, and I never thought I'd see you or any of the crew again. It all faded with time, like a dream. I thought I was dreamin' when I saw you there in the stadium, but you're really here, and I'm guessing you're not here on vacation. Who were those men shootin' at you?"

"They're Vincent's crew," said Mrs. Hudson.

Annie nodded like she wasn't surprised. "So he did get the compass after all?"

Mrs. Hudson nodded.

"It was my fault," Matt admitted. "I tried to stop him from getting it, and that's the reason he got it." He glanced down at his arm, still wrapped in Chuck's T-shirt, but the burns on his hand were red and shiny.

Annie didn't hide any surprise at this. "I had nightmares

of such for a long time after I returned home. It gave me quite a bit of motivation to keep practicing with my gun. I kept my family alive, won all kinds of prizes, and then I joined with Frank and Will and the show and traveled the world. It almost felt like I was back on the *Vermillion* with a crew and all, except the travel was not quite as convenient." She laughed a little at this. "And then we came here to Chicago, to this fair, and it all came rushing back to me. This was the last place I'd come with you, remember? This was where we were when I asked to go home. I've been keeping an eye out for the *Vermillion*. I knew I couldn't go and see you, not with my younger self on board your ship, but I wondered if something else might happen here. I wasn't sure what, but this place seemed important for some reason."

Mrs. Hudson nodded. "It is important. We believe Vincent is here now, with the *Vermillion* and the Obsidian Compass, and he's trying to obtain something else, something even more powerful that would make him very dangerous indeed. We're on a mission to stop him."

Annie nodded. "I'll help all I can," she said simply.

"Thank you, Annie," said Mrs. Hudson. "I always felt a little safer with you on my side."

"Captain," said Tui, stiffly. "May I speak to you alone?"

Annie's eyes narrowed on Tui. She smiled a little, like she knew exactly what Tui was thinking. "You don't trust me, do you?"

Tui raised her chin a little. "Why should I trust a girl who abandons her captain and crew at the first smell of trouble? You were not loyal to Captain Bonnaire. You have not earned trust."

"Tui," said Mrs. Hudson. "She was only a child. You yourself said Matt did her a great kindness in telling her to leave. She might have suffered just as you did, had she not left."

"Perhaps," said Tui, looking in a calculating way at Annie. "Or, if she had stayed, perhaps she could have kept Captain Vincent from ever getting the compass in the first place. Things would have been different then."

Annie looked at Tui with a stoic expression. "You think I don't think about that? You think I don't have regrets? Some days I think I should have shot Captain Vincent right between the eyes when I had the chance. I'm willing to make up for it now."

Tui strode across the small space until she was six inches away from Annie. "You will not lay a *finger* on Vincent. *I* will kill him!" She towered over Annie and glared down at her, but Annie didn't even flinch. She held her ground and her gun and simply stared back at Tui, cool and indifferent as a cat settling down for a nap.

"As you wish, Fatoumata," said Annie. "I'll just come along and keep a lookout if you don't mind. Seems like you could use a little protection from some of Captain Vincent's crew. No telling what would have happened if I hadn't shot that man's gun out of his hand."

"Yes, thank you, Annie," said Mrs. Hudson, coming between the two women before Tui could say another word. "We will *all* appreciate your help very much."

Tui glared at Annie, her jaw pulsing, but she said no more.

Annie walked to a small chest at one end of her bed. She opened it, rifled through, and pulled out what looked like a pair of binoculars. "Best place to spot a strange visitor is the Ferris wheel," said Annie, stashing the binoculars in a little purse at her waist.

"Ooh, a Ferris wheel!" said Chuck, clapping his hands together. "I haven't ridden on one of those since I was a kid. This will be fun."

Annie went to the table where the ammunition was, dumped a bunch of bullets in the purse, grabbed her gun, and marched to the entrance of her tent. "We still got some daylight left. Let's go."

Matt had been on the Ferris wheel at Coney Island, once, but that was toy-sized compared to this one. This was like a circular skyscraper. The carriages of the Ferris wheel were enormous. Instead of hopping into a little seat two at a time as they came around, the entire crew walked right into the carriage like a small house, with dozens of other passengers.

As they ascended into the air, Matt could see the whole span of the city, the gleaming white buildings, the swarms of people milling about like ants in a colony, the lake and all the ships and boats floating in the lagoons and ponds, and the train yard full of trains, but Matt could not see that any of them were the *Vermillion*. He did not see the insignia of the compass star with the red V at the center. Mrs. Hudson was searching all around with Annie's binoculars. Her deepening frown told Matt she wasn't having any more luck than he was. Matt was starting to wonder if again they'd made a mistake with the map, if it was malfunctioning because of his compass, giving them faulty information.

After they had made a full rotation on the Ferris wheel, they exited. They were walking away when Matt felt the hair on the back of his neck prickle. He turned around, searching the sea of people, and his eyes landed on a plump blond boy, about Matt's own age, with round spectacles. He looked right at Matt, scowled, and then disappeared into the crowd.

Albert.

Matt scanned the crowd. If Albert was here, then the rest of the crew must be close by. His heart started to beat a little faster.

"Come on," said his mom, tugging on his hand. "Let's keep searching." But Matt didn't move.

"Wait," he said. "I just saw . . ." Matt's voice trailed away.

"What?" his mom asked, pulling him closer to her. She

searched all around. "What did you see?"

"Jia," he said in barely a whisper.

A girl with long black hair was looking up at the Ferris wheel. Her back was to them, but Matt was sure it was Jia. She was wearing her many-pocketed vest. And then she turned, and Matt's heart skipped a few beats. It was definitely Jia.

"It's Jia! Jia!" Matt shouted and waved his arms wildly above his head, jumping up and down. Several people in the crowd turned and stared at him, but not Jia. She didn't hear him. She didn't see him either. She turned in the direction Albert had gone and, in another second, was swallowed by the crowd.

"Jia, wait!" Matt broke away from his mom.

"Mateo!" his mom shouted. "Come back!"

Matt ignored his mom. He forgot about every promise he'd made to her before they came here. All he could think about was Jia. He pushed through the crowds like a bull-dozer, not hearing the angry shouts and reprimands. His heart thumped in his ears. Matt reached a bit of a clearing. He searched all around, and then he saw her. Jia was running toward the entrance of a building, the only one Matt had seen at the fair that wasn't white. It was painted quite colorfully, as if to signal it was somehow more special than the rest. At the center of the building, a magnificent layered golden archway stood over the large set of doors that Jia was now entering. "Jia!" Matt shouted, but still she did not hear him, and she disappeared once again inside the building.

"Mateo!" he heard someone shout behind him. He thought it was Tui.

Matt ran after Jia, and once he entered, he understood why Jia had not heard him. The building was a cacophony of hisses and clanks and rumblings. The building was full of old-fashioned cars and boats and even a train.

Jia was walking toward the train now.

"Jia! *Jia!*" he shouted as loud as he could, and finally she heard him. She turned and saw Matt. She froze in place, and Matt saw her mouth his name.

Matt's heart tripped over itself, and so did his feet as he ran toward Jia, and she ran toward him, and then they stopped abruptly, just a few inches apart.

"*Ni hao*, Matt," said Jia, beaming at him.

"*Ni hao*, Jia."

They stood there just smiling at each other, and Matt felt wonderful and ridiculous all at the same time. Jia was here! Standing right in front of him! She was alive, and she wasn't twenty years older than him!

"I can't believe it's you," said Jia. "Captain Vincent said you were here, but I didn't believe it. But *how* did you get here?"

Matt pulled out his compass from underneath his shirt. Jia's jaw dropped. "Matt . . . you . . . you made this?" She reached out as though to touch it but stopped short. "Oh, Matt, your arm. What *happened*?"

In the mad dash to catch Jia, the T-shirt had fallen away from Matt's arm, revealing the red, root-patterned burns beneath. "It's a long story," said Matt. "There's so much I need to tell you, but it can wait. We need to get out of here."

"I know," said Jia. "Captain Vincent is looking for you. He sent Brocco and Wiley to bring you back to him. You alone."

Matt froze. "Wait. What do you mean me *alone*?"

Jia hesitated for a moment but then said, "He told Brocco and Wiley that they could kill the rest of your family as long as they brought you to him."

Matt winced. Kill his family? Would Vincent really do that? And why him? Quine wanted him, and now Vincent. What for? Cold fear flooded his veins. "We have to leave. Now," said Matt. He pulled Jia toward the entrance but stopped short when he saw yet two more familiar faces that he'd already seen that day.

Wiley and Brocco.

Wiley saw him first. His eyes rested on Matt and Jia together, and his expression turned somber and grim, like he wished he hadn't seen them at all. Wiley had always been kind to the Hudsons, and while he might not go up against Captain Vincent outright, Matt suspected Wiley had enough of a conscience to feel that what he was doing to the Hudsons wasn't right. Matt thought he saw Wiley flick his head, like he was warning them to get out of there.

Matt swung around the corner of the train exhibit, pulling

Jia with him, but on the other side he spotted Albert and Pike, both of them searching. Jia tugged on Matt's hand and motioned toward the train. They both climbed up onto the caboose and crawled inside the car to hide. Matt lifted his head just enough to peek out the window. Brocco still hadn't spotted them, and Matt didn't see any sign of Captain Vincent. Where was he?

Then Matt saw his family come running into the exhibit—his mom and dad, followed closely by Tui, then Annie with her gun, and Chuck and Corey and Ruby.

"Mateo!" his mom and dad shouted at the same time, searching wildly around for him, which only alerted Brocco and Wiley to their presence. Brocco spun around and pulled out his gun.

"No!" Matt scrambled to the outside of the caboose. "Mom! Look out!"

Bang!

Matt squeezed his eyes shut. People started screaming. Matt peeked through the slits of his eyes, fearing what he might see. There stood Annie, her rifle smoking. Brocco was crouched down on the floor with his hands over his head. His gun lay a few feet to his left, right at the tip of Wiley's shoes. Wiley glanced down at the gun, then back up at Annie, weighing his options. He took a step back, pulled his pipe out of his mouth, and raised his hands in the air. "I ain't got any guns, lady," he said. "Don't want no trouble."

Bang!

Annie shot Wiley's pipe clean out of his hand. It splintered into a hundred tiny pieces. There were more screams, people running everywhere, looking for an exit. "Hey!" said Wiley. "Now that was unprovoked violence!"

"I didn't hurt you none, did I?" said Annie. "But if you don't leave my friends alone, I won't hesitate."

"Mateo!" Mrs. Hudson called. She ran toward Matt.

Matt took Jia's hand. "Let's go," he said, but Brocco had spotted him by then, and he pulled out another gun hidden beneath his jacket. He aimed right at Jia.

"Matt, get down!" screamed Ruby.

Matt shoved Jia to the ground and crouched over her as a bullet whistled past his ear.

"I see Li'l Professor, Captain!" shouted Brocco. "He's on the train!"

More gunshots rang out. There were shouts and screams and crashes. Matt didn't know what to do. He held tight to Jia's hand. And then there was a long, loud whistle and a hiss of steam. The train suddenly lurched. Matt's stomach lurched with it.

"Jia, we have to get out of here!" said Matt. "Come on. Jump!" He hopped over the railing and jumped down from the train, which was now slowly chugging away. He reached up to take Jia's hand, but just as he did another gunshot rang out. Jia screamed and ducked down.

"Jia!" Matt shouted. She stood up. She did not appear to be hurt, but the train was picking up speed, and when she moved to jump, another bullet whistled toward her.

Matt ran after her. The train was rolling toward the exhibit entrance.

Matt didn't know what he was thinking. He should have known better than to chase down a runaway train that wasn't even on tracks. All he knew was he wasn't going to let Jia down again. No way. He ran as fast as he possibly could after the train.

"Mateo!" he heard his mom call. "Don't!"

Matt jumped onto the caboose, grabbing hold of the rails, which were quickly melding into something else altogether. He rolled onto the train next to Jia and looked back to see his mom and Dad and Corey and Ruby all running after the train, all of them screaming his name.

"Mateo! Get off! That's the *Vermillion!*" Corey shouted.

"Mateo, jump!" cried Ruby.

The train burst through the entrance of the building. Matt ducked down as glass and brick exploded around him. When he uncovered himself, he noticed someone else was now with them. Brocco had jumped onto the caboose, shooting his gun toward the small crowd running in the wake of the train. Annie shot back. Brocco cursed and ducked behind the rails.

"Don't shoot, Annie!" screamed Mrs. Hudson. "You might hit Mateo!"

"No, I won't!" Annie shouted. She took aim, but Brocco was faster this time. He aimed his gun between the rails of the train.

"Look out!" Corey pushed Annie out of the way just as Brocco pulled the trigger.

"Noooooo!" Matt screamed as the gun exploded.

Corey stumbled back and clutched at his chest.

"Corey!" Matt screamed. He felt something snap inside of him. He grabbed on to Brocco's wrist and bit his hand as hard as he could. Brocco let out a slew of curses, backhand slapped Matt, then grabbed him by the neck, wrapping his fingers around the chain of his compass. A sudden jolt of the train made Brocco yank the chain so hard it broke off Matt's neck. The compass fell and tumbled across the floor. Matt was thrown against the back of the train and stars erupted in his vision. He shook his head. His compass . . .

Jia scooped up Matt's compass, but then Brocco came after her. She backed away and hit the rails. There was nowhere for her to go.

"Jia, toss it to me!" Matt held up his hands.

Brocco lunged and Jia threw the compass, but in her panic she overshot and went wide. Matt dove and caught it by the chain before it went overboard.

Brocco attacked Matt, pulling at his clothes and hair, trying to get the compass from him. Matt could feel the floor of the train melting and stretching beneath his feet.

He looked back at his family. Most of them had stopped to help Corey, and Matt couldn't see if he was okay or not. They were getting farther away.

"Mateo," his mom shouted, still running after him. "You have to jump! Jump now!"

She was fading from view, walls closing in from all sides. The scene was flickering in and out, growing smaller and smaller. Brocco was clawing at Matt, trying to snatch his compass. He wouldn't let him have it.

"Mom!" he shouted. "Mom! Take the compass!" He knew it was too late to jump.

"Mateo, no!" she screamed.

But this was all he could do. If he couldn't escape, he could at least give his family a way home. "I'm sorry!" he shouted. Matt stretched as far as he could over the edge of the train and let go.

The compass fell and faded with his mother. Dark walls closed in on him, and his family disappeared.

18
Quine's Letter

Matt bounced and rolled around as the *Vermillion* traveled. The floor and walls stretched or shrank, while pieces of furniture appeared where before there had been none. A small table sprang up where he was crouched on the floor, hitting him in the head, and he was knocked backward. He rolled until he came in contact with someone—Jia. She reached for his hand and held it tight.

Finally the transformation was complete. The *Vermillion* had turned into a motor home that looked like something out of a disco movie—green-and-yellow-plaid couches and chairs, a yellow Formica table. Judging by the decor Matt was guessing they were somewhere in the 1970s. The *Vermillion* looked like the much bigger and older sister of Blossom.

"Are you okay?" Jia said.

Matt nodded. "You?"

"I'm fine," said Jia, and then her voice got all choked up.

"Matt, I'm so sorry. I didn't know the train was the *Vermillion*, I promise."

"It's okay," he said, squeezing her hand. "We're going to be okay."

Brocco hobbled over to the plaid couch, grimacing as he cradled the hand that Matt had bitten. The hand that had shot Corey. Corey. Corey had been shot. Brocco shot him.

Matt wasn't sure what happened next. All he knew was that something exploded inside of him. Instinct overcame any reason, and the next thing Matt knew, he was on top of Brocco. He punched and slapped and scratched Brocco with a rage he didn't know he possessed.

"Hey! Get off—ah!"

"You shot Corey!" Matt shouted, raking his nails down Brocco's cheek. "You killed my brother!"

"I didn't mean to! He got in the line of fire! I can't help it if he gets hurt!"

Matt continued in his madness until someone came behind him and pulled him off. Matt fought against the person, too, but whoever it was held him tight, and then a low and gentle voice spoke in his ear. "Hey now," said Wiley. "There's no need for that. All this violence won't help nothin'."

"I'm sorry, Li'l Professor," said Brocco, "but we had our orders, and you know what happens if we don't follow."

"So you'll just do whatever he tells you no matter what?" Matt snarled. "You shoot an eleven-year-old kid and that's okay because someone ordered you?" Matt gave one final struggle and then gave up. He slumped in Wiley's arms. The room was spinning. Matt suddenly felt sick to his stomach, but he didn't think it was time sickness or his seizures.

Corey. His brother.

His family . . .

Jia knelt down beside him and gently covered his hand with her own. Her eyes filled with tears. "Oh Mateo, I'm so—" She flinched as a small door opened at the front of the motor home.

Captain Vincent appeared, Santiago on his shoulder. The white rat looked at Matt with his red eyes and hissed, his usual greeting for the Hudsons. Matt shivered as he remembered that, not only was he responsible for Captain Vincent getting the Obsidian Compass, he was also the reason Santiago was the way he was. Somehow the rat's interactions with the compass had made him super intelligent.

At the sight of Captain Vincent, Wiley released Matt and stood up. He backed against the side of the motor home and bowed his head. Brocco snapped to attention, a soldier to his captain, but he eyed Matt nervously, like he was afraid he might attack him again. Matt felt a small sense of satisfaction as he saw the deep scratch marks running down Brocco's cheek and into his neck. His hand was bleeding, too, where Matt had bitten him. Good. He hoped it got infected and fell off.

Only Jia remained with Matt on the floor, her hand still

covering his, though she kept her eyes to the floor.

"Mateo!" Captain Vincent spoke in his congenial but oily British drawl. "How glad I am to see you again. It's been too long, and yet no time at all."

Captain Vincent looked just as Matt had remembered, dressed all in black, except for the red Converse. His dark hair was combed, his beard neatly trimmed but a little longer than the last time he had seen him, Matt noticed, in an unsuccessful effort to cover a scar on his cheek. Matt was responsible for that wound, too. He had given it to Captain Vincent when they'd been fighting in the museum. He had slashed him right across the cheek with his mother's sword. Still, even with the scar, Captain Vincent was a handsome man with a friendly smile and gentlemanly manner. Matt could easily see why his mother would have found him attractive, and why he and Corey and Ruby had believed him to be their friend. And yet there was something sinister about him too. His eyes were flat and empty, two unpolished stones. Matt wondered if they had changed somehow, or if they had always been that way and he'd just never noticed. Maybe experience changes the way you see people, forces you to see things you ignored before. It made him wonder if devils lurked beneath other people he liked and trusted.

"Wiley, search him," said Captain Vincent.

Wiley didn't look Matt in the eyes as he searched all of Matt's pockets and patted down his arms and legs. He pulled out a box of Cracker Jack and handed it over to Captain Vincent, who dumped the contents on the table, like he was searching for something. Santiago hopped down from Captain Vincent's shoulder, sniffed at the caramel popcorn and started to nibble on it.

"If you're looking for my compass," said Matt. "It's not here. I left it with my mom."

Captain Vincent looked at Brocco, who cowered under his icy stare.

"He dropped it just before we traveled," said Brocco. "We could go back. I could still get it."

Matt got a tiny spark of hope. If they went back to try to get his compass, then there was a chance Matt and Jia could escape with his family.

"That won't be necessary," said Captain Vincent. "You got the most important thing."

Matt got a little jolt as he realized that *he* was the "most important thing." He glared at Captain Vincent. "My parents will find me," he said defiantly. "You know they can track the *Vermillion*." He remembered his father's map and was filled with hope. His mom and dad would track him down to the ends of the earth and all time, and with his compass they'd be able to travel to Captain Vincent wherever and whenever he went.

"Wiley, I'm assuming you did not fail to fulfill your part of the mission?" Captain Vincent asked.

"Yes, Captain," said Wiley. He looked briefly at Matt, then cast his eyes downward. "You know I never let you down." He produced a thick, folded-up piece of paper. Matt's heart dropped to his stomach. It was his father's map. Wiley must have stolen it from their father in the fight back at the fair.

That was it. Matt's last straw of hope snapped and fell away. His family would never be able to find him without the map. He would never see them again, never know if Corey was all right . . .

Captain Vincent took the map and tucked it under his arm. Santiago stuffed a few more pieces of popcorn in his mouth so his cheeks bulged, then hopped back onto Captain Vincent's shoulder. "Come with me, Mateo," he said, turning around. "Let's have a little chat in my office."

Matt didn't move. He looked back at Jia, but Brocco gave him a rough shove in the back so he stumbled forward. "You heard the captain," he said. "Don't keep him waiting."

Matt glared at Brocco but turned around and followed Captain Vincent.

Matt was surprised to see that Albert was driving the RV. He glanced at Matt through the rearview mirror, only for a moment, then returned his focus to the road. He was driving down a paved road lined with pines, snowcapped mountains towering in the distance. Matt searched for any signs that could tell him where they were but saw none. They could be any number of places in the world.

Sitting in the passenger seat was Pike, fiddling with the ropes and pins fastened to her pillowcase dress. She turned and gazed at Matt with her ghostly eyes, her expression unreadable. Matt still didn't know what to make of this pale, silent girl.

Captain Vincent's cabin looked (oddly) similar to how Matt remembered it looking when the *Vermillion* was in its original form as a frigate ship—rows of red Converse, swords in every corner, the desk and the bed and all the ruined paintings of the dark-haired woman that Matt now knew was his mother. He looked around for the *Mona Lisa*, but did not see it here. Either Captain Vincent had returned it, planting it back on the original thief, Peruggia, or Albert was keeping it in the *Vermillion*'s gallery where they kept all their stolen treasures.

An elaborately carved box sat on Captain Vincent's desk, a small gold key beside it. Matt instantly recognized it. It was the key they had retrieved from the back of the *Mona Lisa*, the one that had sent them on a quest to find whatever it unlocked. They had searched the world over, but in the end the box had been in Matt's own home, inside his mother's safe. Pike had stolen it while they'd all been fighting at the museum. Now here it was.

Captain Vincent sat in an armed chair, leaning back like an arrogant prince on his throne, Santiago perched on his shoulder. He was holding the map, studying it with mild interest, like someone browsing a newspaper. Matt wondered if it would work for him at all, or if the Obsidian Compass would interfere with it, like his compass had.

Matt stood there for what felt like at least five minutes before Captain Vincent finally looked up at him. "Mateo!" he said, as though he were seeing him for the first time. "Welcome back. It's good to see you." He folded the map and set it on his desk.

"Oh no, what on earth happened to your arm?" Captain Vincent asked, gazing at Matt's burns.

"I was struck by lightning," Matt said baldly. He had no energy for lies.

Captain Vincent blinked in surprise. "And here? Did you fall?" He grabbed Matt's chin and turned his face to the side. Matt winced, remembering how Brocco had hit him. In all the pandemonium he hadn't the presence of mind to feel anything but rage and despair, but now he felt the pain bloom on the left side of his face.

"No," Matt said between gritted teeth. "I resisted abduction." He glared at Captain Vincent with every molecule of hatred he could muster.

Captain Vincent let go of Matt's chin. "I know you must be very angry with me."

Matt snorted. That was the understatement of the universe.

"I don't blame you, truly. I know what you just went through must have been terrible. Believe me when I say if there had been any other way . . ."

"You mean other than kidnapping me?" Matt snarled. "And shooting my *brother*?" His voice cracked as a lump formed in his throat. His vision blurred.

"I am sorry about Corey," said Captain Vincent, and his voice did sound sympathetic. "That was an unfortunate accident, but now you must understand that we are not playing games. You are in the middle of something extremely dangerous and powerful."

Matt clenched his jaw and balled his hands into fists, ignoring the searing pain from his burns. "Yeah, I got that message loud and clear."

Captain Vincent stood up and walked to the one small window in his office. "I am not a perfect man, Mateo. I have my faults like all mortals. I admit, I did trick you and your brother and sister into coming on board, and I did use you to serve my own ends, but I did nothing that anyone else in my position wouldn't have done. Even your own mother, saintly as she makes herself out to be, is no different from me."

"She wouldn't have kidnapped someone else's children! She wouldn't have attempted to *murder* a child!"

"Oh, but she would have, and she did make such an attempt, if you recall."

Matt closed his mouth. His mother had tried to shoot him that time he'd been on board the *Vermillion*. It was fortunate that his mother's skill with a gun was not on par with her skills with a sword.

"That was different," said Matt. "She didn't know who I was then. And she's changed."

"Has she?" said Captain Vincent, arching an eyebrow. "I'm sure she'd have you believe that. She may put on a good matronly show for you, but some parts of a person can't be hidden or erased. I have seen your mother do things that would make your hair stand on end. They leave a mark, and the proof of who your mother really is, what she truly wants, leads right back to you."

"What do you mean?" Matt asked.

Captain Vincent picked up the small gold key sitting on the desk next to the wooden box and held it out to Matt. "Take a look inside."

Matt didn't move. He had wanted to know the contents of that box ever since Captain Vincent had stolen it. His mom had told him that it contained a letter from Marius Quine, the inventor of the Obsidian Compass, but she hadn't been very forthcoming as to what it actually said. All he knew was that it had something to do with the Aeternum.

Now, with the information at his fingertips, Matt wasn't sure he wanted to know any more. His mother must have had good reason to keep it from him. He almost opened his mouth to refuse, say he didn't care. But he *did* care. He had to know. With trembling hands Matt took the key and unlocked the box. The hinges creaked as he slowly opened it.

Inside, nestled in crimson velvet, was a small glass bottle

stoppered with a cork, and inside the bottle was a rolled-up piece of paper. It looked like the kind of thing someone would have tossed into the ocean, hoping someone might find it washed upon the shore. Matt uncorked the bottle. He pulled out the scroll of paper and unraveled it. The paper, though torn and brittle and yellowing at the edges, was not something from centuries past. It looked like modern college-ruled paper ripped out of your everyday spiral-bound notebook, but the contents were not at all ordinary. It overwhelmed Matt at first. It wasn't so much a letter as a jumble of numbers, letters, symbols, and sketches. There was a sketch of the Obsidian Compass at the center. It looked almost identical to the one Matt had drawn in his own notebook, except there were words written around the compass:

Forged in the fountain of faith.

He couldn't fathom what that meant. Written haphazardly in all directions around the compass were dates and locations and coordinates, some that stood out to him—New York, Asilah, Paris, Chicago, 2019, 1762, 1772, 1911, 1893. Others were meaningless. There were symbols and little phrases in various languages that popped out here and there, some he could translate and even recognized, like *Les yeux tiennent la clé*. "The eyes hold the key." That had been the phrase that led them to the *Mona Lisa*, and *video et taceo*, which was Latin meaning "I see and say nothing," and had been the clue on the *Mona Lisa* key that led them to Queen Elizabeth, who had once kept this very box for their mother.

At the bottom of the page was a poem. It was written in English in an untidy scrawl. Some of the words had been scribbled out and replaced. A few words toward the end of the poem were missing with the ripped page, but as Matt read it, his heart began to thrum in his chest.

永
The Aeternum
Will mend what is broken.
Reclaim what is lost.
The world will be yours
But it comes at a co
A sacrifice must be
To win th
Bring Mateo t
We are on
—Marius Quine

Matt's heart jolted inside his ribs as he read his name. "Bring Mateo t . . ." Bring Mateo to where? Or bring the what? And was it really talking about him? Of course Mateo wasn't a completely original name. It could be talking about some other Mateo, but he knew deep down that wasn't true. It was too much of a coincidence. And what did it mean when it mentioned a sacrifice? Filling in the words that had been ripped away, he was guessing it said "A sacrifice must be *made*." It almost seemed to imply that *he* was the thing that needed to be sacrificed. Sacrificed *how*? Like pay-a-ransom kind of sacrifice? Blood sacrifice? Burned-over-an-altar-as-some-offering-to-the-gods kind of sacrifice? And that would somehow produce the Aeternum and give eternal life and ultimate power? Or was he just a piece of the puzzle?

All these questions swirled in Mateo's brain, but the one that came out of his mouth first was "Where did my mom get this?"

"Did your mother tell you how her parents died? How they really died."

Matt nodded. "She tried to save them and failed."

"Miserably so," said Captain Vincent. "I could not help but feel responsible. It had been me who suggested we attempt it. We were young and naïve then. We did not understand the repercussion of crossing certain timelines and meddling in our own lives. The failed mission did hold one silver lining, however. I found this bottle floating along the shore."

"*You* found it?" said Matt.

"Indeed, I did," said Captain Vincent. "And I shared it with your mother because we shared everything back then. That's when we learned about the Aeternum. We searched for it together for years. Did she ever tell you that? It was our greatest wish to find the Aeternum and live together forever. We searched for *you* together, and then you appeared one day on the *Vermillion*. I did not know your name was Mateo at that time. It would be several years before I figured that out, but I'm guessing your mother did. She became strange after your brief visit. Secretive. She went on secret missions, visiting places and people for reasons I couldn't understand. She hid the letter. The letter *I* had found. And then she left. And she adopted you. Mateo."

Matt looked down at the paper again. "What does this mean?" Matt asked, pointing to a Chinese character at the top of the poem. It looked like a *K* with a slash at the top and a number seven to the left. Matt had studied a little of the writing system, but he didn't know what the character meant.

"That's the insignia of the Aeternum," said Captain Vincent. "The Chinese character for *eternal*. For several years I believed the Aeternum was somewhere in China. It's how I came to find Jia."

Matt felt a strange sense of gratitude toward Captain Vincent all of a sudden, and then a flash of guilt for feeling any kind of positive feelings toward him. He may have done a good thing but not for the right reasons. Matt needed to keep that straight in his brain. He wouldn't allow Captain Vincent to manipulate him so easily again. Matt wished he could keep the letter, but he knew that wasn't possible, and he needed to appear cool and unaffected. He took one last look at the page, focusing mostly on the poem, particularly the unfinished lines. He committed every last letter to his memory, then casually handed the letter back to Captain Vincent.

"I don't see what's so significant about this," said Matt, keeping his face and voice free of emotion. "So my mother named me after some fanciful person in a poem. Lots of people do that."

"Ah, but there's the catch," said Captain Vincent. "Your mother *didn't* name you."

"What are you talking about?" said Matt, his heart beating a little faster now.

"Look at the rest of the contents of the box."

Matt looked in the box and found another piece of paper. He hadn't noticed it before because it was pressed flat against the bottom, underneath the bottle. It was thin and felt soft and worn. He opened it. It was some kind of legal document, and he quickly discerned that it was something to do with his adoption.

```
NAME OF CHILD (LAST, FIRST, MIDDLE): Mateo
SEX: Male
BIRTH DATE: Unknown (Approx. June 1, 2007,
            according to medical exam)
BIRTHPLACE: Unknown
BIRTH PARENTS: Unknown
NOTES: Liaison   claims   infant's   name   is
```

Mateo. Requested name to remain in adoption terms.

"So you see," said Captain Vincent, "your mother is not the saintly person you imagine. She too has her secrets and her motives."

Matt felt sick to his stomach. His mother always told him stories about adopting him, of how she had waited and waited for a child, how they had tried so hard to adopt in the States, and then they found him. She always said she knew he was her son the instant she met him, and Matt had always felt that it had been meant to be, like the universe had meant for them to be together. But now, with what he'd just seen and read, all his idyllic fancies began to crumble. Why did his mother *really* adopt him? Because his name was Mateo? Because she thought he was the key to her quest for immortality and unlimited power? Was she only protective of him because he was an important piece in her game?

He looked at Vincent, who gazed at him with the barest hint of a smile, more like a conceited smirk. Matt could barely hold in his rage. He wanted to punch him in the face. Maybe Vincent had thrown him off, raised a few questions about his mother and his origins, but that didn't mean Matt suddenly wanted to help him. And his mom might have a perfectly reasonable explanation for all of this.

"So what?" said Matt. "What if I was already named Mateo

and she had been searching for me all along? How could that help her get the Aeternum? She'd already given up the Obsidian Compass. You had it then. It was all over for her."

"Of course it wasn't over for her," said Captain Vincent. "Nothing is over until it ends, don't you see? And you were just the beginning. As soon as she saw you, she knew she didn't need the compass, or the *Vermillion*, or her crew, or any of it. She knew *you* would lead her to the ultimate prize. All she had to do was wait patiently for you to make your own discoveries, forge your path to Quine and the Aeternum. She knew it would happen eventually. Why do you think she's been so protective of you in particular? Because you're her first child? Her favorite? Perhaps she feels some sort of affection for you, she's not completely heartless, but make no mistake. In the end you are a means to an end."

Matt was trembling so violently, he was sure he was about to have a seizure. Any moment he would black out, but he held himself together.

"So what's *your* big plan, then?" said Matt. He wanted to sound threatening, but his voice came out high and whiny. "I can't help you, even if I wanted to. I don't know anything about the Aeternum, or where it is, or how it works, so whatever reason you brought me here, whatever you thought I could do to help you, you're wrong."

Captain Vincent seemed completely unfazed at this information. "That may be true for the moment," he said. "But if

I've learned anything it's that time changes everything. It is not required that you know anything. And I don't need you to be on my side. All things will be revealed in their proper time and place, including your own role."

Matt felt a shiver run through him. *His role.* What was his role? He was starting to feel it wasn't anything too wonderful. Was he just a pawn to be sacrificed in this game?

"You're dismissed," said Captain Vincent. "Get something to eat, talk with Jia. She has not had many friends since she helped you escape last time. I'm sure she's very glad to have you back on board."

Matt held out the birth document, but Captain Vincent refused. "Oh no, you keep it. Your mother would certainly be angry that I even showed it to you, but I believe it belongs to you."

Matt folded the document back up and slipped it into his pocket.

Captain Vincent replaced the bottle inside the box and shut it. Santiago took the golden key in his tail, locked the box, then scurried down the desk and disappeared with the key still clutched in his tail.

19
Forged

As soon as Matt opened the door of Captain Vincent's office, he came face-to-face with Albert, who had the startled, guilty look of someone who's been eavesdropping.

"Spying are we?" growled Matt. Albert's pale face flushed, but he quickly turned it into a scowl.

"You flatter yourself quite important, I'm sure," said Albert, "but as one of the captain's *loyal* crew, I am privy to much more information than the likes of *you*."

"Good for you," snarled Matt. He knocked Albert in the shoulder as he passed. He almost wished Albert would swing a punch at him. He felt like fighting, breaking things. He wanted to *hurt* someone, but Albert just pressed himself in to the wall and let Matt pass.

Brocco was now driving the *Vermillion*, with Wiley in the front passenger seat, smoking another pipe. They were still surrounded by trees and mountains, but the land below them had opened up, and Matt saw wide swaths of green fields, dotted here and there with what looked like cows, but as they got closer Matt realized they were buffalo. He felt a small recognition for this place, like he'd been here before, but he didn't have a chance to dwell on it.

"Hey!" Jia called to him from the other end of the RV. She was waiting for him at the yellow Formica table with a plate of sandwiches and a pitcher of grape juice. Pike sat beside her, still working with some of her safety pins. She had hooked hundreds of them together into some kind of intricate metal net. Matt sank down across from both of them and stared at the plate of sandwiches.

"You okay?" Jia asked. "No, of course not. What a stupid question. I'm so sorry." She bit her lip and looked down.

"I'm okay," said Matt.

Jia glanced up at him. They had barely had a chance to say hello when they'd met in Chicago, and then everything had happened so fast, but now that things had calmed down some Matt realized there was something different about Jia. "You look . . . older," he said, and though he couldn't bring himself to say it out loud, he also thought she looked really pretty. Not that she wasn't pretty before, but the last time he'd seen her she was more of a girl, and now she seemed more like a young woman. It made Matt feel a little awkward for some reason, like he didn't know her anymore. Now that he thought about it, Albert had looked different too. He'd been about the same height as Matt the last time he'd seen him, but Matt had been looking up into Albert's face just now, and his normally round face had seemed a little more defined. Matt glanced at Pike, trying to see if she had changed any, but she looked the same from what he could remember. Pale, thin, and silent. "How long has it been for you?" he asked Jia. "Since that day at the museum."

"I'm not certain," said Jia. "Several months? Maybe a year. You know I've never been one for keeping track of time."

This surprised Matt. "I thought Captain Vincent would have discarded you right away," he said.

"He tried to," said Jia, "but he couldn't."

"Why not?"

"I'm not sure exactly, but I think it had something to do with this." Jia reached in one of the many pockets of her vest and pulled something out.

"My bracelet!" Matt exclaimed, grabbing it. "Where did you find it?"

"On the *Vermillion*," said Jia. "I found it just as Captain Vincent was about to discard me, like the *Vermillion* wanted me to have it."

Jia recited all that had happened to her since Matt had last seen her, how Captain Vincent tried to discard her several times, but the *Vermillion* wouldn't leave without her, and she believed it was Matt's bracelet that kept her safe. Matt tied his bracelet securely back onto his wrist and felt a kind of comfort wash over him, like he'd been missing a piece of himself and now it was back. He rubbed his thumb over the stone, feeling the familiar lines etched into it. "Captain Vincent didn't suspect at all?"

Jia shook her head. "Not the real reason," she whispered. "He thought I was sabotaging the ship so he couldn't discard me. He didn't even know I had your bracelet. I kept it well hidden. He just said he changed his mind and he had other plans for me, and that's when we went to Chicago. I'm so sorry, Matt. I knew Captain Vincent was after you. I was trying to warn you and your family, but I only led him right to you. You have to believe me. I *never* would have hurt you on purpose, even if he threatened to send me back to the orphanage in China!"

Matt knew this was quite possibly the worst fate anyone could bestow on Jia. "I know," said Matt. "I never doubted you for a moment."

"If there's anything I can do, Matt. *Anything* at all, you know I will help you, right? I'm on your side." Jia grasped his hand and squeezed it tight. Matt winced and pulled away.

"Oh, I'm sorry!" she said.

"It's okay," said Matt, shaking his hand a little. He'd forgotten about his burns, but now the dull throbbing had returned.

"You should let me put something on that. I have that salve from before. Let me see if I can find it. Sometimes the

Vermillion gives you what you need, even in transformation." She jumped up and started rifling through cupboards and drawers around the kitchen and finally found the little box with all the bottles and bandages. She pulled out one of the jars and brought it to the table. Matt reached for it, but she kept it. "Let me do it."

She opened the jar, releasing the familiar floral, minty smell. It reminded Matt of one of the last times they'd been together, before he'd gone home. Jia took Matt's hand, scooped out some of the salve and gently rubbed it into the rootlike burns on his hand and arm. He winced a little at first, but then it started to soothe the pain. He watched Jia's face as she worked in the salve. She glanced at him and smiled, and his stomach did a little flip. He looked away, hoping she wouldn't notice his face heat up. Why did he feel so awkward with Jia all of a sudden?

Jia cleared her throat. "What did Captain Vincent tell you just now?"

Matt had forgotten about his meeting with Captain Vincent for a brief moment, sitting here with Jia, but now it yanked him down like weighted chains around his ankles, and his face flushed for different reasons.

"You don't have to tell me," said Jia quickly. "I understand."

"No, I want to," said Matt. "It's just . . ." He glanced at Pike. She was still working on her safety-pin web, seemingly not paying them any mind. But Matt now suspected Pike paid attention to a great deal more than perhaps anyone realized, and he wasn't sure how much he wanted her to hear. She'd been helpful to Matt at one time, but she'd also been the one to break into his family's apartment and steal the box that had now spurred everything else. . . . He didn't hate her for it, didn't even blame her. She was just a little kid and was only doing what Captain Vincent told her to do, but for that reason he certainly couldn't trust her.

Pike looked up at Matt then, as if she could sense all the thoughts in his head. Without a word from anyone, she hopped down from the table and walked to the other end of the *Vermillion*. She tucked herself in a corner and continued with her safety-pin crafting.

Matt gazed around the *Vermillion*. Everyone seemed to be occupied and out of earshot, but Matt couldn't be so sure Santiago wasn't lurking somewhere, and that rat clearly had some creepy ability to communicate with Captain Vincent, so he leaned in close to Jia and whispered, "How much do you know about what Captain Vincent is after?"

Jia shrugged. "I knew he was looking for you for some reason, because you have something that he wants. Or your mother or father does, but I don't know much beyond that."

Jia had finished rubbing the salve into Matt's burns and was now wrapping his hand and arm in gauze.

Matt tried to explain to Jia as much as he could about the Aeternum and his mysterious role in it. He told Jia about the piece of paper in the bottle, the incomplete poem mentioning him, and showed her the document from his adoption.

Jia listened carefully, her brow knit in concentration. "It's all very odd, isn't it?" she said. "I mean, it can't be a coincidence that your mother adopted you, but do you really think she knew who you were before she adopted you?"

"And who am I?" Matt asked.

Jia made a final wrap around Matt's hand with the gauze, cut it with some scissors, and tucked in the end. "You're . . . someone important," she said. "Clearly you have something to do with the Aeternum and Marius Quine." Jia gasped like she'd suddenly come to a realization. "Matt, what if Quine is your father? I mean, your biological father?"

Matt couldn't pretend he hadn't wondered this very thing, though he'd been slow to let it rise to the forefront of his mind. There had to be some connection between him and Quine. His father, his grandfather . . . but then why would they have let him be adopted? Or had he? Maybe he had been kidnapped when he was a baby. Not by his mom, but by someone else. Now Quine wanted him back . . . but what did all that have to do with the Aeternum? What did Matt have to do with any of it?

The RV slowed and made a turn. Matt rose and looked out the window. The *Vermillion* pulled into a parking lot teeming with cars and people, all of them moving toward what looked like a large log cabin, and beyond it a patch of land that was brown and barren. Here and there puffs of steam and smoke rose from the ground, as though the earth were on fire.

"I know this place," said Matt.

Jia rose from her seat. "Oh!" she exclaimed. "This is Yellowstone, isn't it? We've traveled here before, haven't we?"

The memory now came back to Matt. When he'd been on the *Vermillion* before, with Corey and Ruby, Captain Vincent had traveled to Yellowstone National Park, where they'd spent a few days exploring the geysers and hot springs, the mountains and wildlife. Matt thought it had been only a vacation back then, an adventure, but then why would they come back now?

The *Vermillion* parked close to the lodge, and Captain Vincent emerged from his cabin, Santiago on his shoulder. "Everyone out." Albert moved toward the exit, but Captain Vincent pulled him back. "Mateo, you first."

Albert glared at Matt as he passed him. As Matt stepped down from the RV, he shielded his eyes from the sun. The sky was a bright blue, and the air was mildly warm and dry, a stark difference from the muggy heat of Chicago. Based on the greenness of the trees surrounding the geysers and the patches of snow in the mountains, Matt was guessing it was late spring or early summer.

Jia stood beside Matt as Wiley, Brocco, and Albert filed out. Lastly, Pike hopped down, her newly woven safety-pin web dangling from her pillowcase dress like a little metal apron. Albert kept his distance from Matt, which he thought was a smart move on Albert's part. Wiley barely looked Matt in the eye and gave him a somber nod that Matt found acceptably polite, but still acknowledged their conflict. Brocco, however, bounced out of the RV in a bright-yellow button-down shirt, green-plaid bell-bottoms, and a matching jacket. It looked like he'd made himself an outfit from the interior of the *Vermillion* in its current form. Brocco winked at Matt and flashed a smile, his diamond tooth sparkling in the sun. He opened his jacket to show the two guns holstered at his hips. Matt glared at him and ground his teeth. Had Brocco no shame at all?

"Come along," said Captain Vincent, starting toward the lodge.

Yellowstone was a magical place to Matt, brimming with scientific wonders. At one point there were wide fields spread like a soft green blanket, then the land abruptly rose into the sky and became forested mountains, then dramatically dipped into lush valleys gushing with waterfalls and rivers, which then starkly changed to dry, barren land dotted with sulfurous hot springs and steaming geysers that boiled and bubbled and spontaneously erupted. The entire park was a super volcano that, if it were to fully erupt, could obliterate half of North America.

Currently they were in a concentrated section of geysers

in the park, which included the famous Old Faithful. The crowds were mostly in that area, sitting on benches, waiting for the geyser to erupt. As it was, it didn't look all that impressive, just a mound of dry dirt with a bit of smoke coming out of it.

"What's our mission, Captain?" said Albert, hopping to keep up with Captain Vincent's long strides.

"Just a stop to stretch our legs and get a bit of fresh air," said Captain Vincent.

Matt was not sure he believed this, and by the look Jia flashed him, she did not believe it either. They could have stopped to rest in any number of places, and he wouldn't describe the air here as particularly fresh. The geysers gave off quite a stink, like rotten eggs mixed with skunk spray.

Matt walked beside Jia, trailing Captain Vincent and the rest of the crew. They walked along the wood-planked walkways, passing crowds ogling over spitting geysers and cerulean pools edged with rusty red and yellow and white. People snapped pictures with their clunky cameras. Captain Vincent was keeping a watchful eye but didn't seem all that interested in the geysers or springs.

"What do you think he's looking for?" Jia whispered to Matt.

"I'm guessing it's not what but who," said Matt.

"Quine?"

"That's my guess."

"Do you think that's why we came here before?" Jia asked. "Because Captain Vincent was looking for Quine?"

Matt shrugged. "Could have been a coincidence, but probably not."

"We came here at least once before you came on board," said Jia. "But we didn't perform any missions, as far as I'm aware. We just walked around a lot, like last time."

Matt frowned. There must have been something in Quine's letter that he'd glossed over, a coordinate or some kind of clue, that led Captain Vincent to this place. They walked all around the walkway twice, the captain's gaze continually scanning the crowds and the landscape, but nothing seemed out of the ordinary from what Matt could tell. The most exciting thing that happened was Brocco said he wanted to take a dip in one of the hot springs. He was about to step off the walkway, but a park ranger shouted at him to get back, then gave their whole group a stern warning that the springs could reach nearly two hundred degrees Fahrenheit, and people had died in them in the past, whether they fell in by accident or jumped in on purpose.

"I've jumped in them in the past," Brocco whined. "I didn't die. Felt like a nice hot bath."

Captain Vincent thanked the ranger and told him it wouldn't happen again. He held Brocco by the arm as though he were his unruly child.

The ranger then started to give a loud lecture on safety to

all the park patrons, issuing dire warnings about the dangers of not staying on the designated paths or ignoring other park rules, but everyone's attention was pulled away when Old Faithful started to erupt, and the crowds quickly moved in that direction. Matt followed the crowd toward the geyser, now spitting out sprays of water higher and higher, while white steam billowed out in bigger and bigger clouds. The crowd began to ooh and aah as the geyser's fountain arced into the sky. Just as it was really getting going, the geyser abruptly stopped, like someone had turned off the faucet. The steam cleared and nothing else happened. People started to mutter and mumble, wondering if something else would happen.

"That was it?" said a young man in denim bell-bottoms and a leather jacket. "That was pathetic. I thought it was going to explode!"

The earth suddenly let out a deep groan, like it was some giant beast waking up from a long slumber. And then Old Faithful exploded. And not just with water. Along with a spray of dirt and clumps of earth came a rusty orange Volkswagen bus.

Matt's heart flared in his chest. It was Blossom!

"Groovy," said the man who'd been complaining.

"Everybody back away!" shouted the ranger, but there was no need. Besides Matt and the rest of Captain Vincent's crew, everyone was running toward the lodge. The ranger whipped out his walkie-talkie and said, "This is Ranger Larry. Old Faithful here is exhibiting strange geothermal behavior. It appears to be spitting out . . . automobiles."

Blossom soared on the arc of the water and landed with a rattling thud. She groaned and screeched and then drove in a jerky zigzag path toward the wooden walkway.

Ranger Larry waved his arms at Blossom. "Stop!" he shouted. "This is a hydrothermal preserve! You cannot drive on it!" But when it was clear the bus was not going to stop, he tossed his walkie-talkie and ran away with the rest of the crowd.

Blossom screeched to a stop just before it hit the walkway. The doors flew open and out jumped Mrs. Hudson, clutching Matt's compass in one hand and in the other, a short sword that Matt thought looked mysteriously like the swords the guards had carried at the World's Fair in Chicago. Mr. Hudson came out after her, followed by Chuck with his harmonica, Tui holding a knife, Annie, clinging to her rifle. Then Ruby hopped out with another short sword in hand. And behind Ruby came Corey. Matt's chest expanded. Corey. He was okay. His arm was in a sling, heavily bandaged, but he was alive! In his good arm he held what looked like one of Annie's rifles.

"Relinquish our brother, you filthy rogues, or we'll shoot you straight between the eyes!" shouted Corey.

"Mateo!" his mom called. "Run!"

Matt tried to run toward them, but someone caught him by the arm. He winced as Captain Vincent's fingers dug into his burns.

"We're not finished, you and I."

Brocco pulled out both of his guns and aimed them toward Matt's parents, but Annie was faster. She shot both Brocco's guns clean out of his hands, first the right, then the left. She reached out a hand and Corey tossed her the rifle he'd been holding, then took her other one. Annie aimed at Vincent now, but Vincent pulled Matt squarely in front of him, using him as a human shield.

"Stop, Annie!" Mrs. Hudson shouted. "Don't shoot!"

"Brocco, go and get the *Vermillion*!" Captain Vincent commanded, holding Matt tightly in front of him.

Brocco started to crawl on his hands and knees along the walkway, but he couldn't get past Annie. First she shot him in the hair. One of his thick locks started smoking, but he kept going. Then Annie shot him right in his rear. Brocco howled and grabbed at his behind. He rolled off the walkway and writhed on the smoking ground.

"Albert," said Captain Vincent. "Go."

Albert looked hesitantly toward Annie, who was swapping guns again.

"*Now*, Albert!" shouted Captain Vincent. Albert didn't say a word, but ran as quickly as he could. Annie took aim.

"Annie, don't shoot," said Mrs. Hudson. "He's only a boy!"

Annie lowered her gun while Albert kept running in zigzag lines along the walkway toward the lodge and parking lot.

Mrs. Hudson started running toward Matt now, sword in hand, his compass now hanging around her neck. Captain Vincent didn't move. As his mom drew closer, Matt felt a rising heat around his shoulder where Captain Vincent's hand was holding him.

"Ah!" Captain Vincent gasped. He let go of Matt and reached inside his sleeve and pulled out the Obsidian Compass. It dangled from his wrist, smoking. The compasses were reacting to each other. Matt tried to use the distraction to get away then, but before he could take two steps Captain Vincent stuck out his leg, tripping Matt. Matt fell hard on his hands. He cried out as pain shot through his hand and up his arm. He was certain some of the burns had torn open.

"Mateo!" his mom shouted.

Matt looked up. His mom was clutching at her chest, wincing in pain. The compass was clearly burning her, but she pushed on toward Matt, refusing to stop. "Mom! The compass! Take it off!"

Mrs. Hudson pulled off the compass.

"Tui! Catch it!" She tossed it to Tui, who caught it neatly in both hands, but it was still burning hot. As soon as she touched it, she threw it right back toward Mrs. Hudson. "Captain!" she shouted, but Tui had overshot. The compass arced right over Mrs. Hudson's head.

"I got it!" Brocco reached out and caught the smoking compass, then immediately started doing a dance as he tried to hold on to it somehow, but he couldn't. He tossed it to Wiley, who tossed it back to Brocco like they were in a game of hot potato. Brocco caught it and tossed it up and down in his hands.

"Ooh! Eeee! Ha-haaah!" Brocco finally caught the compass by the chain and swung it around and around like a sling, then released it. The compass soared over Matt's head and through the air until it landed somewhere near Old Faithful.

Matt scrambled to his feet. Captain Vincent grabbed for him, but Mrs. Hudson was there now. She jabbed her sword at Vincent. She would have stabbed him through the throat if he hadn't jumped back as quickly as he did.

"Hello, Bel," said Captain Vincent. "Come to steal back your treasure? It keeps slipping away from you."

Mrs. Hudson snarled and slashed her sword down again, but Captain Vincent was ready this time. He rolled back and jumped up with his own sword in hand.

"Mateo, get back to your father," his mom shouted as Captain Vincent came after her and their swords clashed.

"Wiley, the boy!" shouted Captain Vincent. Wiley started to come after Matt, but Annie shot at him and he stumbled and fell. He writhed on the ground and yelled, grabbing at his shin.

"Jia!" Matt called. He searched around frantically for her, then found her running toward him, little Pike in tow. He grabbed her hand and they started running toward Blossom, but halfway there he stopped short and looked toward the place where his compass had been thrown.

"What are you doing?" Jia asked, tugging at his hand.

Matt made a split-second decision. He pulled his hand away from Jia's. "Go to my family. I have to get the compass."

"Matt! Come back!" Jia's shouts were mixed with those of his dad and Corey and Ruby. Matt sprinted over the hot, dry earth, dodging the bubbling springs and pockets of steam as he made his way toward Old Faithful. There! He could see his compass now, sitting just at the base of the steaming mound of earth. He raced to it and swiped it up by the chain, ignoring the searing heat on his skin, and started to run back.

He stumbled, though, as the earth suddenly began to shake beneath his feet. Old Faithful hissed angrily and emitted a forceful puff of steam. The geyser erupted again, but not with the typical white spout of water and steam. It exploded with a thick gush of bright-orange lava. Matt raised his arms, shielding his face from the heat and glow of the lava that bubbled and flowed in slow, thick streams over the steaming earth, right toward him.

"Matt!" he heard Ruby scream. "Run!"

Matt turned and started to run, but as if Old Faithful had called all the earth to action, other geysers and hot springs began to erupt, some with lava, others with steam and water.

The *Vermillion* RV came racing over the steaming land and screeched to a stop in front of the place where Captain Vincent was still fighting Mrs. Hudson. Brocco and Wiley both limped their way to the RV. "Captain, I think we'd better get out of here now," said Brocco. "This place looks like it's going to blow!"

The air was a smoky, sulfurous oven. Matt started to cough. His eyes burned. The ground crumbled and steamed beneath his feet. He could feel the bottoms of his sneakers starting to melt. It was like he was running on a hot chicken potpie. Pockets of earth started to pop open and erupt with smoke and steam. Matt nearly fell into one. His foot sank down into a steaming hole. He tripped and fell, landing just feet from a stream of lava. The searing heat washed over his skin. He picked himself up and started to move, then stopped. His compass . . . It wasn't in his hand. . . .

"No!" he shouted, and watched in helpless horror as the flow of lava slowly rolled over his compass, leaving only half of the chain exposed. He reached for it. He would have picked it up, burned his whole arm off, if someone hadn't stepped up beside him and grabbed his arm.

"Matt, don't!" said Jia. "It's too late."

Pike came up beside her. She was holding one of the little swords. Without any fear or hesitation, she slid the blade beneath the bit of chain sticking out from the lava and lifted it up. The compass looked like a molten ball of fire. Pike gently lowered it into her safety-pin apron. Matt was certain it would melt right through, but it held. Pike cradled the compass and ran toward Blossom.

Matt ran after her, looking over his shoulder to check on his mom. She was still fighting Captain Vincent, but then he jumped in the *Vermillion*, and it disappeared. Mrs Hudson ran toward Matt. "We need water!" Matt shouted as they moved their way toward Blossom, hopping over streams of lava and dodging spewing springs and geysers. Ruby disappeared inside Blossom, and when they arrived she was holding a plastic pitcher of what looked like cherry Kool-Aid.

"Put it in here!" she shouted.

Without thinking, Matt grabbed the chain of the compass from Pike's apron. He shouted as it seared his skin. He plunged his entire hand into the liquid, which hissed and steamed as it met the smoldering compass.

"Chuck, drive!" Mr. Hudson shouted. Blossom beeped her horn and rolled over the smoking, burning ground. Matt wondered if they'd be able to drive out of this, or if they'd get stuck here and burn. Bake to death. He thought he felt the floor beneath him tilt and stretch. Was Blossom transforming or melting?

A geyser shot up in front of them. Blossom sank into the earth. And then they were gone.

20

The Real Inventor

Nowhere in No Time

They were either dying or traveling. Matt wasn't sure which, but either way it was a weird, bumpy, painful ride. Everyone shouted, screamed, and grunted as they were all tossed around like bugs in a jar. Matt got an elbow to his jaw, a foot in his ribs. He was hurtled across the bus and slammed against the side. He felt the walls swelling and stretching beneath his squished face. Everything went pitch-black, and he felt they were moving very fast, lightning speed.

Blossom burst through the darkness. Water sprayed all around them, showering down on their heads like a cloudburst. Blossom rocked violently from side to side. Matt shielded his eyes from the sudden bright light. When his vision adjusted and he got his bearings, he looked around. Blossom had transformed into a boat again, but an even larger one than when they'd gone to Chicago. She was nearly the size of a small ship. A mast with two white sails had risen out of the floor. Ruby was inexplicably tied to the mast.

"Get me out of here!" she growled, struggling against the ropes that bound her to the mast. Mrs. Hudson stumbled over to her daughter and unwound the ropes.

"Just like the *Vermillion*," Ruby grumbled. She threw the ropes to the deck like she was trying to punish Blossom.

"Mateo? Corey?" Mrs. Hudson asked, looking all around. "Matthew? Jia?" She started calling names until she heard a grunt or a "fine." Everyone had been shoved in various corners or plastered against walls during their travels. Corey popped his head up from a hatch. He had somehow ended up belowdecks. Mr. Hudson was hunched over a bench, which was screwed into the floor. He looked like he was about to be sick. Matt suddenly realized that he was going to be sick too. His stomach churned. He leaned over the side of Blossom and vomited.

"Oh, Mateo, *chéri*." His mother rushed to him.

"I'm okay," said Matt. "I'll be fine in a minute." He closed his eyes and took a few deep, raspy breaths. His throat was dry and scratchy as sandpaper, and his lungs ached.

"Here. Drink this." Chuck handed him a can of club soda. He took a sip, cringing at the bitter taste, but it wet his throat and calmed his stomach some. A gentle breeze brushed his face. He opened his eyes and found himself staring at endless water. They couldn't possibly still be in Yellowstone.

"Where are we?" Matt asked.

"We could be in the middle of the ocean somewhere," said Jia, "but if I had to guess I'd say we're in Nowhere in No Time." Matt would have guessed that too. It felt like Nowhere in No Time. He wasn't sure why it felt different than just the middle of the ocean, but it did. He wondered how they had gotten here, what had happened just before. His brain was foggy, disoriented.

Pike came and stood beside Jia. Her normally white-blond hair and pale skin were dusted with soot and ash. Matt suddenly remembered how Pike had come running after him in Yellowstone, amid all the exploding geysers, how she'd saved his compass when it fell in the lava. . . .

"My compass!" Matt shouted, suddenly realizing that his compass was no longer in his hand. "Where is it?" He took a few steps, swayed and nearly fell. Jia caught him from behind.

"Matt, you should sit," said Jia.

Matt looked all around until he saw the pitcher wedged on its side between the cushions of a bench at the back of the boat. It was mostly empty. Just a small pool of liquid rested at the bottom, and Matt could see the dark shape of his compass and the chain dangling from the lip. Matt stumbled over to it. The Kool-Aid, which had been red before, was now a dark, smoky purple. Bits of ash floated on the top and puffs of steam rose off the surface.

Matt used his gauze-covered hand to grab on to the chain.

It'll be okay, he thought. He'd made it of strong metals that could withstand extremely hot temperatures, even lava. And he was right. The compass had not melted, but what came out of the Kool-Aid shocked him even more.

Jia let out a gasp and covered her mouth. Everyone else gathered around, closing in on Matt and the compass.

"What the . . . ," Ruby began.

". . . beetle juice?" Corey finished.

No one else said a word. They all just stared at Matt's compass, or what had been his compass. It was now completely encased in a smooth layer of shiny black rock. It dangled from Matt's hand dripping with sooty Kool-Aid, hissing softly as it let off small puffs of steam.

"Hey, look at that!" said Chuck. "Have you ever seen such beautiful obsidian?"

"I . . . I don't understand," said Matt. He looked to everyone surrounding him, hoping someone would explain. Everyone was speechless, all except Chuck.

"It's quite simple, really," said Chuck. "You see, obsidian is formed when magma cools very quickly. Your compass was coated in magma and then you immediately dunked it in iced Kool-Aid. Perfect process!" Everyone looked at Chuck. "Rocks are a bit of a hobby for me," he added.

They all went back to staring at the compass. His mom muttered something under her breath. Matt didn't catch it at first, but then the words somehow traveled to his brain.

"Forged in the Fountain of Faith."

Those were the words that had been written in Quine's letter, around the sketch of the Obsidian Compass.

"What does this mean?" Corey asked. "I mean, does this mean there are *two* obsidian compasses?"

"No," said Mrs. Hudson, staring at Matt. "It means Matt's compass *is* the Obsidian Compass."

Everyone went from staring at the dangling, steaming lump to Matt. Matt looked all around, faces that were so familiar to him, so dear, and yet they were looking at him like they'd never seen him before. Like he was some kind of alien, especially his mom. She looked more than confused or curious. She looked terrified.

"So . . . ," said Corey, "does this mean Matt is the *real* inventor of the Obsidian Compass? And not the Quine dude?"

"It must," said Ruby. "I mean, Matt definitely made that compass, and this appears to be the beginning of the Obsidian Compass. *That's* why they reacted so powerfully to each other when they came together. Not because they're similar, but because they're one and the same."

"Psychedelic," said Chuck.

"But I . . . that can't be possible," said Matt, looking back at his compass. "The Obsidian Compass is super old. *Quine* made the Obsidian Compass ages ago. He gave it to Mom before I was ever born!"

Ruby shook her head. "You're thinking in straight lines.

Remember how Mom said it's all a web? It doesn't matter when anyone was born or what year you made the compass. It *travels through time.* Quine must get the compass from you at some point in the future, maybe after you die, and then he time-travels back to Mom and gives it to her. Quine could be your great-great-grandson!"

"Or he could be *Vincent's* great-great-grandson," said Corey. "Maybe he *steals* the compass from Matt."

"Then why would he go back in time and give the compass to Mom?" said Ruby.

"I don't know. Maybe he's messing with us, or he needs her for some reason. To get the Aeternum! What if Matt invented that too?"

"But . . . I didn't," said Matt.

"Not yet," said Corey, "but sometime in the future."

Matt tried to sort everything in his pounding head. Quine, the compass, the Aeternum, the letter. Himself.

A sacrifice must be . . .

Bring Mateo . . .

He looked up at his parents. His mom flinched a little when he looked her in the eyes, and Matt felt his chest hollow out. She knew, had always known all of this, ever since she'd read that letter from Quine. She knew about *him* before she'd ever adopted him, knew he was the real inventor of the compass, that he had something to do with the Aeternum. And she'd never told him any of it. Matt's stomach churned.

He felt bile rising to his throat. He closed his eyes and pushed it down.

"How did you find me?" Matt asked. "In Yellowstone, I mean. How did you know where and when to go without the map?"

"Corey figured it out!" said Ruby.

Corey grinned sheepishly. "It was an accident. I didn't do it on purpose."

"Oh yes," said Ruby. "Total accident. We never would have found you on purpose." She grinned at Matt.

"What happened?"

"It's quite a tale," said his dad. "But let's sit, shall we? I'm feeling woozy."

"And thirsty," said Chuck. "Let me make us all another jug of Kool-Aid. Cherry or grape?"

They all sat on the deck of Blossom, cups of cherry Kool-Aid in hand, drifting aimlessly on the water in Nowhere in No Time. The sky was a clear blue, the air perfectly warm, only a gentle breeze. Matt sipped his Kool-Aid as he listened with rapt attention as his family and all the crew, each of them talking over the other, told all that had happened after he'd been kidnapped by Captain Vincent. It sounded like an exhausting, chaotic whirlwind. As soon as the *Vermillion* had disappeared, they'd raced Corey to a hospital, jumping over a hundred years in order to get him more modern treatment.

"Otherwise they might have just cut his arm off," said Annie. She insisted on coming along, for which they were all grateful as she was able to describe to the doctors in great detail what kind of gun had shot Corey, and the range and angle of the shot. Luckily his wound had not been life-threatening. He'd been shot in the upper arm. The doctors said the bullet had narrowly missed a major artery. Even so, the bone had been fractured, and he had to undergo surgery. He would likely have nerve damage, and there was always the risk of infection, especially when such an old gun had been used. Doctors put him on a series of antibiotics and monitored him closely for several days. They of course asked a lot of questions, to which Annie also readily supplied the answers. She told them she was a gun collector and the kids had gotten into one of her safes while visiting and, well . . . accidents happen. It must have been a common enough story because the doctors didn't question further, though she did get a sound scolding about gun safety. This rankled Annie, and she grumbled loudly that someone needed to teach Brocco about gun safety *and* grooming.

At the same time, they were all in a rage over Matt.

"Mom went berserk," said Ruby.

"I was perfectly rational!" said Mrs. Hudson. "All things considered."

As soon as she knew Corey would be okay, she left using Matt's compass, traveling anywhere and everywhere she could think Vincent might have taken him. She searched for days, but popped in and out of the hospital every few minutes, according to Ruby. She hopped back and forth in time, switching between fretting over Corey and frantically searching for Matt. Matt could tell just by their voices and the bags beneath their eyes that both his parents had been driven to the brink of insanity. His dad's entire body tensed every time his mom mentioned traveling to find Matt. Matt could only imagine how torturous it had been to watch his wife run off and time-travel without him, not knowing the risks she might face or if she would ever return. They had all been through a lot. He could almost see the frayed edges of their minds and hearts.

Mrs. Hudson searched for Matt until she had exhausted herself to the point where she could hardly stand. She'd traveled the world over, centuries and millennia, trying to find any trace of the *Vermillion* after it had left Chicago. In a final act of mad desperation, she'd even gone back to the Chicago World's Fair, just before Matt had been taken. It was a huge risk in more ways than one, they all knew. It was exactly the kind of thing she'd warned them against, but it was her last hope.

She tried to board the *Vermillion* before everything happened, so she'd be there when Matt was taken and could escape with him after he threw her the compass. She hoped it would be a smooth enough meeting of timelines, and it almost worked, except the compass had somehow backfired on her, and she been thrown back to the hospital, again without Matt.

"That was a low point," said Chuck. "Boy, we thought you were a goner for sure."

"What happened then?" said Matt. Though he appreciated knowing everything that had happened while they'd been separated, what he really wanted to know was how they finally found him.

"We fought a lot," said Ruby.

"We didn't fight," said Mrs. Hudson. "We discussed."

Corey and Ruby both snorted. "We fought," said Corey. "I got discharged from the hospital, and then no one could agree on what we should do next. Stay in Chicago. Go back to New York. Split up. Stick together . . ."

And though Corey didn't say it out loud, Matt guessed there had been an argument over whether they would fight to find him, or let go. Move on. Cut your losses. He didn't want to guess who had been on what side of the argument. He preferred to just skip to the part where they found him.

"So what happened?" Matt asked. "How did you find me?"

Ruby started to say something, but Corey put a hand over her mouth. "I get to tell this part!" He pulled out a pack of pink gum from his pocket. "Second magic ingredient!"

"Huh?" said Matt.

"One of the nurses gave Corey a pack of bubble gum before he left," said Ruby. "Of course he shoved half the pack in his mouth right away."

"Yeah," said Corey, "I was blowing bubbles the size of my face!"

"And then he was blowing them in *my* face," said Ruby.

"And Mom was like, 'Corey, cut that out!' And she swiped one of my bubbles with the compass and then the compass started going haywire, and Blossom started up, and before we knew what was going on we exploded out of Old Faithful! It was epic."

"Terrifying is what it was," said Chuck, shivering a little. "Scared the beetle juice out of me. And then everything was exploding all around us. Then I thought *we* were goners."

"So the bubble gum . . . made the compass travel to Vincent?"

"To the other compass," said Ruby. "Or the *same* compass. It's like it created some kind of magnetic charge or something."

"You know," said Jia. "In a weird way this makes complete sense. You know how I always use peanut butter and bubble gum for repairs on the *Vermillion*? Something about the combination of gum and peanut butter just helps everything stick together. It must have had a similar effect on Matt's compass, except it wanted to go right toward the Obsidian Compass, and then it *became* the Obsidian Compass."

Matt's mind was swirling. Everything that had happened, that he had learned in the last day, buzzed around him like a busy beehive, everything humming and constantly in motion.

"What about Vincent?" Matt asked. "If our compasses are one and the same, shouldn't he be able to find us here?"

"I don't think so," said his mom. "This place always seemed to be a void where no one else could follow."

"I never could see the *Vermillion* on my map when your mom came here," said his dad. "It would just disappear."

"And I don't think Vincent would come after us now anyway," said Mrs. Hudson. "Not after what happened in Yellowstone. He knows it's too dangerous. I think we're safe."

"For now," said Tui. "That man has many tricks up his big sleeves. We will have to prepare to face him again."

"You should have let me shoot him when I had the chance," said Annie, grinding her teeth at Tui.

"And risk killing *Rubbana*?" said Tui.

"There was no risk," said Annie. "I *had* him. I could have put an end to this whole mess."

"Yes," said Tui, her voice sickly sweet. "Little Miss Sure Shot never misses."

"That's enough," snapped Mrs. Hudson. "This argument will get us nowhere."

"We're already *nowhere*," said Annie. "And we have no way of getting out, do we?"

Matt looked down at his compass, or his lump of obsidian, rather. He couldn't fathom how it was ever going to work again. All the dials had been coated in magma, hardened to obsidian. He couldn't even turn them. But if it really was the Obsidian Compass, and he was the inventor, then somehow he would get it to work again, right?

After the initial shock and excitement had worn off and everyone started to settle down, Matt finally had a chance to introduce Jia to his parents. Mr. and Mrs. Hudson both warmly embraced Jia, thanking her for all she'd done and sacrificed to help their family, to which she blushed and told them she was happy to help. Pike remained her usual quiet self, but Mrs. Hudson patted her on the head and told her thank you too.

That evening, Chuck cooked everyone a meal of ramen noodles with bits of beef jerky. Corey and Ruby caught up with Jia, each of them exchanging stories.

Matt kept glancing at his mom. Every now and then she'd catch his eye, then quickly look away.

Matt's mind went in loops and spirals. He kept going over and over everything that had happened. His compass turning to obsidian. Quine's letter. The Aeternum. Words and letters swirled in his brain, pieces of a puzzle. He turned them over and shifted them around, trying to fit it all together.

Forged in the Fountain of Faith

A sacrifice must be . . .

Bring Mateo . . .

His mom whispered something to his dad. He whispered something back. Neither of them approached him, and he wasn't sure if he was relieved or upset at this. He wasn't sure he wanted to talk to them, but why wouldn't *they* want to talk to him? *He* wasn't the one who had lied.

They all slept above deck that night, snuggled up in Chuck's crocheted blankets, lying beneath the starry sky. Blossom gently rocked back and forth as the water lapped against the side of the bus-boat, lulling them all to sleep. It almost felt like "old times" to Matt. He knew they hadn't been on the *Vermillion* that long ago, but it felt like years and years that they'd been parted from Jia.

As exhausted as he was from everything that had happened, Matt had difficulty sleeping. Maybe it had something to do with Chuck's growling snores or Corey kicking him in his sleep. Or maybe it was simply that his brain would not turn off. He felt for his compass—the *Obsidian* Compass—beneath his shirt. It was cool now. He rotated it over and over in his hands.

A strange sound made Matt sit up. He looked around. Corey and Ruby slept on either side of him. Jia was directly above his head, sleeping on her side, her hands beneath her cheek. Pike was curled up next to her, cuddling her rope like a teddy bear. Tui slept on one of the hard benches. Annie was curled up with her gun against the side of the boat. His dad and Chuck were both snoring on the bow. His mom was the only one who wasn't asleep. She was standing at the very back of Blossom.

Matt took a breath. He needed to talk to her, get things out in the open. He couldn't live with the tightness in his chest. He most certainly couldn't sleep.

He climbed over all the sleeping bodies, careful not to step on anyone. His mom didn't even look at him as he came and stood beside her. She just looked out at the water, sparkling like polished obsidian.

"I always loved coming to this place," she said. "It felt like stepping outside of the world, leaving it all behind for just a while. It always helped me to gather my thoughts."

Matt definitely needed a gathering of his thoughts. "Vincent showed me the letter from Quine," he finally said.

Mrs. Hudson nodded, still not looking at him. "I figured he would."

"Why didn't *you* show me?"

"Because," she said. "I didn't know what it meant. I still don't. I don't know the repercussions of everything that's happened, nor can I predict what *will* happen, so I thought, why lay that burden on my son? Why worry him with things that we can't possibly understand?"

"Like the part where it says I'm supposed to be sacrificed?"

Mrs. Hudson finally turned to Matt, staring at him with

her dark, intelligent eyes. "We don't know if that's what it means," she said. "Remember it's not complete. Sometimes having partial information is more dangerous than having none. And anyway, it could be a lie. It's just a poem, after all."

Matt could tell by his mom's voice that she didn't really believe that.

Matt reached into his back pocket and pulled out the adoption paper Captain Vincent had given him. "And what about this?" He held out the paper. His mom took it, squinting at it in the dim starlight. Matt could not see her expression too well, but he heard her take in a sharp breath.

"You always said I was named after Dad," said Matt.

"You were," she said, "in a roundabout way."

"How can you say that? I had already been named!" He pointed to the paper. It was a struggle to keep from shouting.

"I didn't know," she said calmly. "I swear it. The adoption agency gave us no details when they matched us. I had no idea you'd already been named, not until we came to get you, and they showed me the terms of the adoption. It was then that I *knew* you were my son, knew it with every fiber of my being."

"Because you thought I'd help you get the Aeternum?" said Matt, not even trying to keep the venom out of his voice.

"No," said Mrs. Hudson, shaking her head. "Don't you see? Mateo, you *are* my Aeternum."

"What are you talking about?" said Matt. "You're saying

by being your son I'll somehow grant you eternal life and power? Are *you* planning to sacrifice me at some point?"

"No, *mon chéri*, think of the poem." She reached toward Matt. He stiffened as she slowly brushed her fingers through his hair and down his cheek. "The Aeternum will mend what is broken. Reclaim what is lost. The world will be yours." Her voice caught in her throat as she spoke. "You and your father, and Corey and Ruby, you all mended my broken heart, and reclaimed my lost soul. You became my whole world. I made many sacrifices. I had to give everything up. The Obsidian Compass, the *Vermillion*, my crew and friends, my whole life as a time pirate, and everything in my past. But it was a sacrifice I was willing to make in order to have a family again, to have the future I wanted. I could not have the family I lost before, but I could make a new one."

Matt felt something loosen in his chest, a knot that had been growing and tightening for who knew how long, days or months or years. Matt slowly leaned toward his mom and rested his head on her shoulder. She wrapped her arms around him and kissed him on top of his head.

"So does that mean the Aeternum isn't real? It's all just . . . a poetic metaphor?"

His mom let out a long breath. "I don't know," she said. "Like any poem, I've interpreted it for my own life and desires, but that doesn't mean that's what Quine actually meant. There is evidence that the Aeternum—at least the one

Vincent is searching for—is real."

"And I'm connected somehow," he said.

"It seems so," she said. "But this should not come as a surprise to you now, seeing that you *are* the maker of the compass, and the compass is connected to the Aeternum."

Matt reached inside his shirt for his compass. The obsidian sparkled in the starlight. "I don't even know if it will work again," he said.

"You'll get it to work," said his mom. "I have faith in you."

"But what if I fail?"

"Well then, we'll fail together. That's better than winning alone, don't you think?" She smiled down at Matt.

"I don't know," said Matt. "It still sounds like . . . failing."

Mrs. Hudson laughed. "Then don't fail. I command you, as your captain *and* mother, to succeed."

Matt smiled and felt a surge of confidence and determination run through him. He felt certain he could make the compass work again because that's what was *supposed* to happen. It was his destiny. He was the inventor of the Obsidian Compass.

The good feelings were short-lived. The next day Matt sat on the bow of Blossom with Jia, working on the compass. They had made good progress, or Matt thought they had anyway. Within hours they had managed to chisel away the obsidian around the two inner dials, even found a way to open it up. The inner workings had been miraculously untouched and undamaged by the obsidian. He needed to make only a few adjustments and calibrations, but still the compass would not work. Everyone kept telling him it would be okay, that he would figure it out, but he had his doubts, and they were all on edge, wondering how long it would take. How long would they be stuck in this nothing place?

It was blazing hot. Matt wiped the sweat from his brow, then gazed out at the horizon. They were sailing slowly in whatever direction the wind blew them. There had been no signs of land or any other boats or ships, but still the adults kept a watch. Tui was standing guard now. She paced up and down the deck of Blossom, keeping watch for any sign of Captain Vincent or the *Vermillion*. Matt gazed at his hand and arm. He had removed the bandages. It was too sweaty and itchy in the heat. His wounds were healing okay, no infection. The rootlike burns had darkened in the sun so they were almost black against his brown skin, almost tattoo-like. His mom had tried to rub sunscreen on him, but it stung like a thousand bee stings, so she told him to work on the compass belowdecks, out of the sun. He tried, but there wasn't enough light, and he felt claustrophobic in the cramped space. Finally, he resigned himself to just baking in the sun and keeping the scars forever. Corey told him it made him look cool, like an X-Men character. Matt wasn't sure that made him feel any better. Weren't the X-Men totally feared and ostracized from society? Matt had never been a popular social butterfly by any means, but he wasn't a total outcast. He'd have to wear long sleeves to hide his scars, and maybe even those weird gloves with the fingertips cut off.

But he knew that would do little good. Scars or no scars, everything was different now. *He* was different. He was still reeling over the idea that *he* was the real inventor of the Obsidian Compass. . . . He could barely wrap his head around it all, what it meant. He flipped back and forth from confidence bordering on arrogance to complete and utter terror. If he was the real inventor, then he was the cause of all the events that would take place because of the compass, for better or worse. And if the compass did all the things he already knew it had, then eventually it must leave his hands. Quine would somehow get possession of it, then his mother, then Vincent. Was that all by design or coincidence? Did Quine steal it? Or did Matt give it to him? Was he friend or foe? And what about the Aeternum?

Three days passed and Matt still hadn't gotten the compass to work. Everyone tried to give their insight and advice. Ruby found a jar of peanut butter, and Corey gave Matt the remainder of his bubble gum. Jia mixed the two together, creating the sticky concoction she always used on the *Vermillion*, and then Matt slathered it over the compass, hoping that would be the magic ingredient. It helped the dials turn smoothly. Otherwise all it did was make a greasy mess. His mom tried to fiddle around with it, which only made Matt tense. Annie wondered if a little gunpowder might make it work, and Chuck played his harmonica thinking some good music would do the trick. (According to him, good music was magic.)

None of it worked.

Matt knew he was missing something, some small detail that had slipped his notice, but he didn't know what. He couldn't think.

Another day passed, and another. Matt kept working on the compass, though he was running out of ideas. And patience, and energy, and optimism. Eventually he started just making it look like he was working on it. Picking up tools, making tweaks, turning the dials. Nothing. His head had been aching for two days now.

And he wasn't the only one losing patience and hope. The rest of the crew started to grumble, and though Blossom appeared to have plenty of food, water, and supplies, they knew it couldn't last forever.

It was Jia who figured it out. The next day she tried to coax Matt to take a break from the compass and come swimming with her, Corey, and Ruby. He refused, of course. He could never take breaks when he was trying to solve a problem like this. She was just about to leave him when she stopped.

"It looks like there's a piece missing," said Jia, pointing to the very center of the innermost dial.

"Yeah," said Matt. "I accidentally chipped it when I was cutting around the dials."

Jia furrowed her brow. "But the Obsidian Compass didn't have a missing piece, did it?"

Matt shrugged. "Maybe Vincent filled it in or something."

Jia continued to stare at it, her finger on her chin. "Matt . . . your bracelet."

"Huh?" Matt looked at his bracelet, then at the compass. The stone in the middle . . . it was very similar in size and shape to the hole in the middle of the compass.

Matt quickly untied his bracelet, then tried to yank the twine away from the stone. "I need scissors!"

But then Pike was suddenly beside him. She pulled the bracelet from Matt's hands and began to untie the knots, her fingers moving so fast they were a blur. In less than a minute, she had freed the stone. She held it out to Matt and dropped it in his palm, then ran away and disappeared somewhere.

"I'm starting to think she's not human," said Matt, staring down at the pile of string that had once been his bracelet, and the stone nestled in his cupped palm. He turned the stone over between his fingers. He picked up his compass.

He placed the stone in the center. Jia gasped. It fit perfectly. The compass made a small click and a light flared.

"It's fixed!" Jia shouted. "Everyone, Matt fixed the compass!"

Matt felt strange. Dizzy, but also like he was falling. He

was falling away, away from everything and everyone.

"Matt?" he heard Jia call, though her voice sounded far away.

He tried to shake his head, keep himself alert.

"Matt, you okay?" he heard Ruby say, but her voice was just an echo, like she was calling to him from the other end of a tunnel. And then everyone was gone. Or he was gone.

21
The Future Awaits

2070
New York City

Matt wasn't sure if he was dreaming or traveling. It felt different, like something in between, more real than a dream, but different than the physical world. It was . . . *meta*physical. There was no rush and roar in his ears, though he wouldn't call it quiet. There was an absence of sound. He felt very light, almost weightless, like he was without form but still some aspect of his physical self was there, like his atoms had all separated but were still aware of each other and had a kind of magnetic force keeping them in the same realm. And then Matt felt himself coming together; his billions of atoms decided they wanted to form what they knew made Mateo— his brain, his heart and lungs, his bones and muscles, his blood, veins, and skin. When his eyes congealed (there was no other way to describe it) and his vision came into focus, he saw that he was in some kind of room or apartment. There were books, paintings, and furniture. The walls dividing rooms were transparent glass, but they were cluttered with text—words, lists, and phrases in at least a dozen languages, maybe more. He recognized some of it as Latin, Spanish, English, Russian, Chinese, and Arabic. Most of the writing looked to be everyday mundane lists or reminders, but he gleaned very little as the text was continually shifting and bouncing around. He caught a small grocery list that started out ordinary and grew increasingly odd—pickles, toothpaste, bread, sodium chloride, cetyl alcohol, $BiClO$. There were chemical compounds and mathematical equations scribbled all over, ranging from short and simple to long and incomprehensible.

Strewn across the tables and chairs and stuffed in corners were tools and machines and gadgets, most of which Matt could not name or even recognize. A large brass telescope stood by a window that overlooked a cityscape. Matt wasn't sure what city it was, but clearly he was on a top floor of a very high high-rise overlooking many other tall buildings, some sleek and pointing straight to the sky, while others twisted and coiled sideways and around each other in architectural wonder. It looked like something out of a Dr. Seuss book, Matt thought. Not at all feasible. But as Matt studied the buildings and the land he started to see things that looked familiar, some of the straight skyscrapers, and a big rectangular park in the midst of all the buildings, with trees and walkways, a lake and several baseball diamonds. Matt knew that park like he knew his own home. It was Central Park. This was New York.

Something large zoomed past the window where Matt was standing, and he jumped back, heart hammering in his chest. Was that . . . ? Why yes, there was another and another. Flying cars! He could see at least a dozen right now, zooming between buildings, dipping and rising. He must have traveled to the future! How far into the future? Matt turned around and looked for any newspapers or magazines that might give him some idea as to the date. But for all the books on the shelves, there was very little paper elsewhere. All he found was a spiral-bound notebook, worn and warped, the pages yellow and curling. Something flared in Matt's chest, like the notebook was calling to him. Matt picked it up. It was already flipped open to a random page.

I look at myself
And see nothing
I look at you
And see everything
There is no me
Without you
Without us
We are without

The world
Together we have
永

The last line was not written in English. Rather, it was a single Chinese character. Matt recognized it immediately. It meant "eternity." It was the symbol for the Aeternum. Matt had seen it in the letter from Quine that Vincent had shown him.

"It's rather rude to rifle through a stranger's belongings."

Matt dropped the notebook and whirled around. "I'm sorry . . . ," he began, looking for the person who had just spoken. "I didn't mean to . . . I was just . . ."

"Curious?"

Matt jumped back. He still could not see who was speaking, but the voice sounded much closer now, almost directly in front of him. He felt a strange kind of buzzing in his ears at the sound.

"It's quite all right," said the voice. "We aren't strangers, really. I know you quite well, even if you don't know me."

Matt jumped around again. Now the voice sounded like it was coming from the window, but still he saw no one.

"Where are you?"

"I'm here," said the voice, still by the window, "and there," this time it came from the ceiling, "and everywhere." Now the voice seemed to be coming from all around.

"Are you talking through some fancy surround sound system or something?" said Matt. "Are you trying to pull some kind of Wizard of Oz trick?"

The voice chuckled. "It is a trick, and one of my more useful ones." The air in front of Matt *moved*, or rather the particles in the air that had been invisible suddenly became visible. It was just a shimmer at first, and then it looked a little like a fuzzy television screen that grew clearer and clearer every second until a gloved hand was floating in the air.

"How do you do?" The hand floated toward Matt, extending for a handshake. Matt was grateful it was a left hand. His right hand throbbed with pain from his burns and cuts. Matt tentatively reached out and shook the floating, disembodied hand. It felt like a real human hand, solid and warm, the fingers squeezing his own with just the right amount of pressure.

"Are you . . . real?" Matt asked. "I mean, is there more of you? I mean . . . do you have a full body?"

"Of course," said the voice. "But it's rather a lot of effort to pull myself all together, and to be honest, I'm not entirely sure I'm wearing pants. Best to remain invisible, I think."

Matt was too amazed to laugh, for as the voice spoke, the floating, gloved hand dissolved like a sandcastle in the rain.

"How do you do that?" Matt asked as he watched the particles continually divide and spread until they were no longer visible.

"We are made of trillions of cells, each one of them

sentient to some degree. I have trained them how to separate and spread, yet still function as a single unit."

"That sounds . . . complicated," said Matt.

"It's quite simple, really, but not easy. Do not mistake one for the other."

"Could anyone do it? Could I?"

"Of course. And you will."

"Can you teach me? Now?"

Matt thought the voice chuckled a little. "No, not now, but another time. I promise I will." Matt had been trying to place the voice, the accent. It was all at once familiar and foreign. It sounded American, and then he caught a few elongated vowels and it sounded slightly British, and then a bit of a guttural sound slipped in that seemed French or maybe German. He couldn't figure it out.

"Who are you?" Matt asked, though he thought he knew the answer already.

"Marius Quine, scientist, inventor, and amateur poet, though I'm less known for the latter. Actually, I'm not very known for the former either, but fame was never the goal. Highly overrated, in my opinion, and not always an accurate gauge of anything worthwhile. Wouldn't you agree, Mateo?"

"How do you know who I am?"

"This is the first time you've met me," said Quine, "but it is far from the first time I've met you."

A chill ran up Matt's spine. Vincent had said something

similar to him before, and given that he had turned out to be an enemy pretending to be his friend, Matt was wary.

"What do you want?"

"World peace would be nice, but I've time-traveled enough to know that's impossible. So now I'm just aiming for self-peace."

"Self-peace?"

"Yes, peace with one's self is almost as difficult to obtain as world peace. It's a constant struggle, but it is achievable. So sorry. I'm getting carried away. What can I do for you today?"

Matt had so many questions he wanted to ask about so many things, he barely knew where to start. He decided the beginning was best. "You gave my mom the Obsidian Compass. . . ."

Quine scoffed. "I did not give it to her," he said, clearly annoyed. "We made a trade."

This was news to Matt. His mom had never mentioned anything about a trade, only that Quine had given her the compass at a time when she needed it. "What did she trade you?"

"This." The hand formed again. Quine pointed to a dagger resting on top of a stack of books. He plucked it up and handed it to Matt. As soon as Matt took the knife, the hand dissolved again. "It belonged to your grandfather," said Quine. "Your mother's father."

"Oh," said Matt. The knife looked old, simple in design,

but well crafted with a silver hilt. The blade was shiny and sharp. "Sorry, I'm really confused. *I* made the Obsidian Compass, right? Not you?"

"You did," said Quine, "with some help from Mother Nature and peanut butter."

"So . . . how did you get it? Do I give it to you or something?"

"Something like that."

"Are we related?" Matt looked down at the dagger in his hand. "I mean, are you . . ."

"I am not your grandfather," said Quine.

"Are you . . ."

"I am not your father either."

"Are you . . ."

"No, I am not reading your mind. Not in the way you're thinking. You just think in highly predictable ways."

"I do n—"

"Yes, you do," said Quine, chuckling. "For instance, I know that after perhaps a few more inane questions you will bring up all the drama between your mother and Captain Vincent, and how he's trying to steal the Aeternum and destroy all your happiness. It's all rather boring and cliché if you ask me, but humans do delight in repeating history and telling the same stories over and over and over again. You and I are above such bores though, so let's skip it, shall we? Don't waste any time or breath. Both are precious. Ask me about something interesting."

"Fine," said Matt, exasperated. He did not like to be bull-dozed in this way, especially by someone who didn't have the good grace to show his face. He looked toward the notebook he'd dropped on the floor. He thought of the poem and the Chinese character. "That poem in the notebook," said Matt. "Did you write it?"

"I did."

"The Chinese character at the end . . . ," said Matt.

"It means 'eternity,'" said Quine. "One of the few subjects worthy of poetry. The other worthy subjects are love and food, in case you were wondering. A poem about all three would be epic, but I lack the skill to pull off such a feat."

"Okay . . . ," said Matt. He felt a little discombobulated by the conversation. He was feeling strange for some reason, a little fuzzy, like his brain was only functioning at 50 percent.

"I've seen that Chinese character with another poem," he said, "a poem about the Aeternum. Did you write it?"

"Perhaps," said Quine. "Recite it for me."

"I don't know all of it. I've only seen it once, and some of it was missing."

"Recite what you remember, then," said Quine.

Matt tried to clear his head and remember the words of the poem.

"The Aeternum will mend," Matt began, and Quine immediately interrupted him.

"Oh! I remember this one. It's one of my best works."

"Is it true?" Matt asked.

"Of course it's true!" said Quine. "Lies do not belong in poetry, even when it's abysmal. Poetry must always speak truth."

"So the Aeternum," said Matt. "It really exists?"

"Haven't you heard a word I've said?" Quine said impatiently. "*Yes.* I have it in this very room, though its power is currently dormant."

Matt's heart beat wildly in his chest. The Aeternum was real. It existed. He looked around, wondering where it could be, what it could be.

"Why is its power dormant?" Matt asked.

"Its full power can only be unleashed under very special conditions and circumstances. All the necessary details are in the poem."

"Oh," said Matt. "That's the problem. Some of the words in the poem got ripped off the page, so I didn't get to read every word."

"That's unfortunate. It's much more satisfying when read in full."

Matt waited for Quine to tell him the rest of the poem, but he didn't. "There's something written about me," said Matt. "Or at least my name appears in the poem. It sounds like I'm supposed to be sacrificed or something, but it's not totally clear."

Quine chuckled. "Oh, what agony to not know your own poetic fate!"

Matt felt his patience snap and his anger flare up. "It's not funny!"

Quine stopped laughing. "You are right. It isn't funny at all, nor fair."

Matt calmed down a little. "Then will you tell me?"

"No."

"Why not? Don't I have a right to know?"

"If you have a right to know then you'll figure it out for yourself," said Quine. "Children these days. Or any day! They always want a handout. Such entitlement! You never want to *work* for what you want. Well, I'm going to teach you a life lesson I had to teach myself once upon a time. Twice actually. If you want something, then you have to work for it. And there's no time like the present to start working for what you want. Here, I'll be generous and help you get started." Quine's two gloved hands coalesced in midair. One hand picked up the spiral-bound notebook off the ground, while the other zoomed to the other side of the room and rifled through a set of drawers until it found a pen. The two hands came together and held out the notebook and pen to Matt.

"Let's see if you can finish the poem yourself, hmm?" Quine's disembodied hand flipped through the pages of the notebook. Matt could now see about an inch of dark skin at the wrist and forearm. He noticed some darker lines in the flesh, a tattoo Matt was guessing. He was very curious to know what sort of thing a man like Quine would have tattooed on his arm.

Quine opened the notebook to a page that already had some scribbled numbers on it and a sketch of the Obsidian Compass, but still had a blank space toward the bottom half of the page. He held it out to Matt. "Just scribble it down anywhere."

Matt tentatively took the notebook and pen, wincing. With all the burns and cuts on his hand he could barely hold the pen correctly.

"Now," said Quine, "write down what you know, and work from there."

Matt began to scribble the poem on the page with a sloppy hand, but he didn't get two words out before Quine started commentating.

"The Aeternum," he said. "A poem that begins with eternity. Isn't that beautiful irony?"

"Um, yes," said Matt, and he continued.

"'The Aeternum will fix what is broken . . .'"

Quine cleared his throat. "'*Mend* what is broken.'"

"Whatever, same thing," said Matt.

"But it isn't the same at all," said Quine. "Two words may have similar meanings, but they will evoke different images and emotions. You must understand this in poetry, in life! *Fix* is too routine and indifferent for what is needed here.

Mend has a more comforting, holistic connotation. Plumbers fix clogged toilets. A mother's love can mend a broken heart."

"Okay. Got it," said Matt a bit snappishly, crossing out the word *fix* and replacing it with *mend* in cramped handwriting beneath it. He was starting to feel a headache coming on. This Marius Quine was a real piece of work. Maybe that was part of being a poet.

"'The Aeternum will *mend* what is broken. Reclaim what is lost,'" Matt repeated. "The next line is something about taking over the world. 'The world will be yours,'" Matt remembered and wrote it down. "Now this is when some of the words start to get cut off. 'The world will be yours, but it comes at a . . . cost'?"

"Ooh, yes, that's perfect!" said Quine. "I love a clean rhyme. What next?" Now he was speaking as though Matt were the one making all this up, and he was just here to coach on the sidelines.

Matt read over what he'd gotten down so far. The remaining lines would be more difficult to finish. He racked his brain, which was feeling increasingly dull and fuzzy, trying to see the piece of paper from Vincent's office in his mind's eye. "There's something about a sacrifice," said Matt. "'A sacrifice must be . . .' made, I'm guessing. 'To win . . .' To win . . . what? The world?"

"That would be some nice alliteration," said Quine, "but

you already talked about winning the world. Best not to be redundant. My guess is you're trying to express a slightly different idea."

"What do you mean *I'm* trying to express a different idea," said Matt. "This is your poem! Not mine."

"If you like," said Quine.

"What, is this a game to you?"

"A game!" said Quine. "That works!"

"What?"

"For the poem."

Matt looked down. "'A sacrifice must be made to win this game'?"

"Yes, that sounds right," said Quine. "Almost there."

Matt took a breath. The next line was the part that mentioned him.

Bring Mateo t . . .

"'Bring Mateo *to somewhere*'? Or 'Bring Mateo *the something*'?"

"What does it sound like?" said Quine.

"It sounds like I'm going to be sacrificed. Or something like that," said Matt.

"Yes, very good," said Quine.

Matt felt a jolt run through him, like he'd just been shocked by those electrical paddles at the hospital. The pen he'd been writing with slipped from his fingers and fell to the floor. "Wait. So . . . you're saying I *will* be sacrificed? Like, *murdered* kind of sacrifice?"

"I'm not sure *murder* is precisely the right word."

"Then what's the right word?!" Matt shrieked so his voice cracked.

"You know," mused Quine. "I'm not sure there *is* a right word for this. Some things just have to be experienced in the moment."

"What moment? What experience?"

"The moment when you are sacrificed," said Quine, "in order to create the Aeternum."

Matt felt his head spin and his heart drop to his stomach. "What? What are you . . . ?"

But Matt could not finish his questions. Something smacked him hard in the face. He was jerked away so fast he wasn't certain he brought all his parts with him.

22
Family Ties

Matt's eyes flew open. He gasped for breath, and his limbs flailed. He felt like he was falling, but someone was holding him tightly in their arms.

"Mateo," said a voice. His mom. "It's okay, *chéri*. I've got you."

Matt stopped fighting. He looked around, but he couldn't see. Everything was bright white until he blinked a few times and saw the dark silhouettes of several people around him. After a few more moments his vision sharpened, and their faces started to take shape. His mom, dad, Corey, Ruby, Jia, Tui, Chuck, and Annie were all hovering over him like a team of surgeons ready to conduct experiments on him.

His mom still cradled him against her chest. Matt pushed himself away. She reluctantly let go.

"What happened?" he said, his breathing ragged and his head buzzing.

"You blacked out," said Ruby. "You had a seizure."

"A seizure . . . ," said Matt.

"It was scary, bro," said Corey. "You were shaking so much it was like you were flickering in and out like a dying lightbulb."

"I didn't . . . disappear?" he asked. "I didn't travel?"

"No, *chéri*," said his mom, her voice shaking a little. "You only blacked out for a minute."

Matt tried to sort through what had just happened. His head ached. He felt weird, like he was only half here and half somewhere else. "I went to the future," he mumbled.

"The future?" Ruby asked. "How far? What year?"

"I don't know," said Matt. "I saw flying cars and buildings that went in waves and loops. I read poetry. . . ."

His mom and dad shared a concerned look.

"He's probably got a touch of heatstroke," said Annie. "It causes hallucinations and fainting spells. I've seen it plenty at the fair in Chicago."

"He needs water," said Tui.

"Ruby, Corey, get some water please?" said Mrs. Hudson.

In less than a minute they each came back with a cup of water. Mrs. Hudson took the cup from Corey's hands and placed it to Matt's lips, tipping it for him. Some of the water spilled down his face and neck, but he drained the entire cup in five seconds. It soothed his dry throat and smoky lungs.

Matt lifted his left hand to wipe his mouth. His mother gasped.

"What?" Matt looked at his hand. He thought maybe he'd gotten yet another injury, but when he held out his hand he realized he was holding something. The dagger, the one Quine had given to him.

"What is it?" Ruby asked.

"It's . . . ," Mrs. Hudson began, but choked on her words.

"It belonged to her father." Matt held the dagger out to his mom.

Mrs. Hudson gently took the dagger and held it gingerly in her hands. She gazed at it, speechless, her eyes glassy. Matt saw a lump form in her throat. "Where did you get this?" she whispered.

"Quine gave it to me."

His mother stiffened. Her nostrils flared, and her eyes flashed. "What?" she snapped. Matt flinched at the sudden sharpness in her voice. "When? Where?" She looked around, as though Quine might suddenly appear at any moment.

"Just now," said Matt. "When I blacked out I traveled to the future and . . . and I met Quine."

His mom's face flooded with fear and alarm. She held the dagger so tight she began to shake. His dad put a hand on her shoulder.

"But, bro," said Corey. "That's impossible. You never left."

"You were here the entire time," said Ruby. "You only blacked out for a minute, and we were all watching you. You never left our sight."

"Maybe I was only gone for an instant for you, but I had to have gone. How else can you explain that?" Matt pointed to the dagger.

"What happened with Quine?" Mrs. Hudson asked. "What did he say? Did he hurt you?"

Matt shook his head, trying to clear the fog that was still hovering over his brain. "I don't know. We talked about stuff. Cell separation. Poetry. Self-peace."

"Self-peace?"

"It's achievable," said Matt.

"Mateo," said his mom, grabbing his face between her hands, forcing him to look right in her eyes. "I need you to think very carefully. I need to know everything that happened between you and Quine."

"Nothing, really," said Matt. "I was trying to ask him questions about Vincent and the Aeternum, but he wasn't very helpful."

"What did he look like?" Ruby asked.

"I don't know," said Matt. "He was . . . invisible."

"Invisible?" said Corey.

"Except for his hands. Sometimes I could see his hands, though he wore gloves. I think he has some major tattoos on his hands and arms."

Mrs. Hudson's eyes narrowed, her brow furrowed. He could tell she was thinking something, putting together the pieces of a puzzle, but he wasn't sure what.

"Hey," said Corey. "If Matt traveled, then that means his compass works, so now we should all be able to travel, right?"

"I think so," said Matt. "But if Blossom didn't travel too, she probably needs some repairs, I'm guessing. I'd better start checking . . ."

He tried to get up, but his dad forced him down. "How about you take a little break?" he said. "Travel can wait. Let's get you out of the sun. You need to rehydrate."

Matt nodded, suddenly realizing how weak he felt. His arm hurt too. The burns hurt twice as badly as they had before.

His dad helped Matt get belowdecks into one of the dim, cramped cabins. Corey and Ruby brought him more water, and his mom put another wet T-shirt on his burned arm.

"What's this?" she said, tapping his hand, which was clenched into a fist. He turned it over and noticed bits of white paper sticking out between his fingers. He slowly opened his hand, revealing a balled-up scrap of paper. Matt's heart flared. His mom almost reached for it, but Matt quickly closed his fist.

"It's nothing," he said. "Just garbage." He stuffed the paper in his pocket. His mom looked at him suspiciously, but then her face softened. She sighed and shook her head. "Will I ever be able to keep you in one place?"

"I didn't do it on purpose!" he said.

"I know," she said. "But try to stay around for a while,

give us all a break." She leaned over and kissed him on the forehead.

After his mom left, Matt reached in his pocket and pulled out the scrap of paper. He unraveled it and flattened it out with his left hand, revealing a jumble of letters and words written in awkward, sloppy handwriting. It was completely nonsensical on its own, but Matt understood what it was at once. It was the missing piece from Quine's letter, the missing pieces of his poem that Matt had been writing down. He'd ripped it off as he was being torn away in time.

Matt studied the letters and words. He began to piece them together and fill in the blanks.

The next day the whole family and crew were buzzing around like a bunch of worker ants, trying to prepare for travel. Matt and Jia had been all over the boat, inspecting and making repairs. They discovered a slight crack in the engine. Jia said the heat from all the geysers must have caused it. It was a miracle they'd been able to travel at all.

"Can we fix it?" Matt asked.

"That depends," said Jia. "Do you have any peanut butter and bubble gum on board?"

Matt laughed and went belowdecks to rifle through their food supplies. It was kind of a mess. Nothing was very organized. Cans and jars and packets of food were all jumbled together. He finally found a jar of peanut butter. He was guessing bubble gum was going to be a little more difficult to find. Gum, gum, where would he find gum? His mom always kept some mint gum in a small desk drawer. Matt started opening drawers and cupboards. He looked through bins of junk. He found an old-fashioned camera, a few sixties and seventies rock band records, piles of letters, and photos of Chuck hiking mountains and canyons and climbing cliffs, some of them from years past, when he still had dark hair and a shorter beard. Tucked between the photos was the recipe card for tuna and Jell-O pie. Matt glanced at it briefly, marveling at how anyone could make such a disgusting thing, and then his eyes caught on the name at the bottom of the recipe.

MADE WITH LOVE AND LAUGHTER
BY GLORIA HUDSON

That was weird. Did Chuck borrow this recipe from Gaga? Matt turned the card over and found something else weird. A Polaroid of his dad in a tuxedo, his arm around another man in a tuxedo. They looked very much alike. Matt recognized him as his uncle Charles. He rifled through the other pictures again, looking a little more closely at the faces. The more he saw, the more his frown deepened. He jumbled all the pictures together and went above deck.

"Corey had some bubble gum left over!" said Jia, holding

up a pink pack of bubble gum. "Did you find any peanut butter? Matt, what's wrong?"

Matt didn't answer Jia. He stumbled over to where Chuck and his dad were talking.

"Hey, Matty, what you got there?" asked Chuck.

Matt looked down at the photos he was holding, and back up at Chuck.

"Uncle *Charles*?"

Everyone fell silent. Chuck went rigid. His eyes flicked down to the photos in Matt's hands.

"Matt, what are you talking about?" said Mr. Hudson. He walked to Matt, who handed him the recipe card. Mr. Hudson glanced at the recipe, his brow knit in confusion. He turned the card over and saw the Polaroid and grew even more confused.

"How did you get this?" said Mr. Hudson to Chuck. "Why do you have it?"

Chuck let out a long breath. "Because it's mine," he said. "I've always had it, since the day it was taken. It's the last picture we took together before I left." Chuck took off his hat and his sunglasses. Mr. Hudson just stared at him, but Matt could see him twitching a little, the recognition in his eyes as he noticed the unmistakable characteristics—the hairline, the long, straight nose, the laughing gray eyes.

"Charles . . . ," said Mr. Hudson.

"Hey, big brother," said Chuck solemnly.

"But . . . you . . . you can't be Charles. You're . . . too *old*. I'm older than you. Last I checked . . ."

"Yeah, I know," said Chuck. "Time travel can be a little tricky that way."

"Time travel . . . ?" said Mr. Hudson. "When did you . . . ? What happened?"

Chuck glanced briefly at Mrs. Hudson. It must have meant something, because suddenly she gasped, covering her mouth. "No," she said. "Oh no, he didn't!"

"I'm afraid he did," said Chuck.

"Who did what?" said Mr. Hudson, looking between his brother and his wife.

"Sit down, brother," said Chuck. "I'll tell you everything, but I'm afraid you're not going to like it very much."

Mr. Hudson slowly sat down in one of Blossom's vinyl seats, his legs trembling a little. Chuck sat next to him. He ran his fingers through his hair in a way that was so much like Mr. Hudson, Matt wondered how he could ever have missed the connection.

"It was at your wedding when it happened," Chuck began. "Was it 1999? I was twenty-three and going nowhere. Mom kept bugging me to go to college, like you, but I was never as good and smart as you. I was the screwed-up younger brother."

"Word, yo," said Corey, lifting up a hand.

"Corey, be quiet," said Mrs. Hudson. Corey looked at Matt

and smiled, as though he'd just proven his point.

"Anyway," Chuck continued, "at your wedding I got a little tipsy. You probably wouldn't remember that because you were busy celebrating with your beautiful bride, but I snuck a bottle of wine and I had a little too much, I guess. I went into the trees to be sick so Mom wouldn't see, and then there was this man. He was dressed all in black, but kind of weird clothes, some of them sort of old-fashioned, but he had on red shoes."

"That's Captain Vincent!" Corey shouted.

"Shh!" said Ruby. "Let him talk."

"I thought he was part of the band or something. We started talking, and he asked if I was the lucky man of the hour and I said, 'Sure am! I'm the luckiest son of a gun that ever was!' And then everything went dark. I think I passed out, maybe. The next thing I knew, I was inside of some old ship, sailing in the middle of the ocean. And there was Dad."

"Dad!" Mr. Hudson interjected. "You saw *our* dad?"

Chuck nodded.

"Wait. I thought Grandpa Hudson died," said Ruby.

"We thought that too," said Chuck. "We thought he'd died on a hiking expedition in Patagonia, but we never did find a body, and then here he was right before my eyes. He looked exactly the same as the last time I saw him. Hadn't aged a single day. So I thought maybe *I* had died, too, and here I was seeing good old Dad again. He didn't recognize me, of course. I told him who I was, and he didn't believe me until I showed him the scar on my leg where I'd cut myself on the fence that one summer and had to get stitches." Chuck pointed to a white line, just below his knee, that was about three inches long. "Anyway, there was a lot of confusion. I thought I had died. Dad thought it was all some elaborate joke. We demanded Captain Vincent explain what was going on, but all he would tell us was that he had to prevent catastrophic events from happening."

"He thought you were me," said Mr. Hudson. "He was trying to keep Belamie and me from being together. He must have thought Dad was me, too, when he took him, and then when he realized he'd made a mistake he came to take me at the wedding so Belamie and I wouldn't be together, only he took you instead."

"I pieced that together eventually," said Chuck. "But it took a while. Boy, you sure did make him mad, taking his lady."

Matt looked over at his mom. She was covering her eyes and shaking her head, like she didn't want to believe what she was hearing. "What did Vincent do with you then?" she asked.

"He stuck us in a tiny boat and set us out in the water, then started to sail away."

"Ooh, you got discarded," said Corey. "That happened to us too."

"How did you get away?" Ruby asked.

"Dad told me to grab some oars, and we chased after the ship for a while, even started to gain some ground, but then the water started to bubble up around it. Then, inexplicably, a rope dropped down the side of the ship, and someone called down for us to grab hold. Dad told me to jump, to grab on to the rope, said he would be right behind me. He practically shoved me out of the boat. I caught the rope just before the ship disappeared and went for the worst ride of my entire life." He shivered at the memory.

Matt shivered, too, remembering the time he'd time-traveled that way, hanging from the *Vermillion* by a mere rope. He'd never been so utterly terrified in his life.

"I let go of the rope," said Chuck. "I probably shouldn't have, but as soon as I saw a glimmer of light and land, I let go and went rolling. And then when I got my bearings, I realized I was in Tanzania! In 1975, a full year before I was even born! Forget death, I thought I'd gone plumb crazy."

"So what did you do?" Mr. Hudson asked.

"I waited around for a while, hoping that ship might return, but it was gone, so I did what I had to do to survive. I got a job. Made my own way. I traveled the world as much as I could, hoping to find that ship, or Captain Vincent, or Dad, but it was all in vain. And then the time came when Dad was supposed to disappear, and I got a grand idea. I wondered if I could prevent all this from happening."

"Oh no," said Ruby, covering her eyes with her hands.

"Don't worry, I wasn't the reason Dad got abducted in the first place. I got my dates mixed up. I came home a full month after Captain Vincent had already taken Dad. You can imagine my frustration. I threw a bit of a temper tantrum and then Mom found me. She didn't recognize me of course, but she must have seen the desperation in my face and took pity because she asked if there was anything she could do to help me. I realized in that moment what a good, kindhearted woman our mom is, and I felt bad for what a hard time I'd given her all my life. I knew she'd never believe who I was. I was only supposed to be six years old then. But I didn't want to leave. I was home, and I had promised Dad I would look after you and Mom. We both worried Captain Vincent might come after you again, though we still didn't know why.

"I told Mom I was looking for work and asked her if she needed help on the farm, that I was good with plants and land and knew quite a bit about vineyards, which wasn't true exactly, but I was willing to learn. Mom said that might work temporarily, until her husband returned. He had gone away and she wasn't sure when he'd be back, but she could employ me until he did. Well, I knew he wouldn't return, so I said I'd stay until he got back. She asked where I was staying, and I said I mostly lived out of Blossom. Mom never did like Blossom, but she was the most valuable thing I owned. I'd worked for three years straight on the fishing docks to be able to afford her. Anyway, she said I could stay in the little guest cottage by the vineyard temporarily, and I've been staying there temporarily ever since. I worked in the vineyard, and I kept an eye on you and Mom, though I kept my distance. Once my younger self got a little too close, tried to talk to me, and that was weird. I think I caused an earthquake almost. I remember I'd always been a little bit scared of Chuck, the farm manager, as a kid. Weird to think I was scared of myself! It's quite the trip. . . . Anyway, I thought everything was fine, nothing to worry about. And then you two were getting married. You were nice and invited me to the wedding and everything. Of course it was on the vineyard anyway, but I thought, hey now, here's my chance to make things right for myself at least. I could keep that crazy Captain Vincent guy from abducting me. I could at least have a normal life, even if I couldn't save Dad. So when the wedding came, I watched myself closely. Watched myself steal that bottle of wine and get a little too tipsy, and then I saw *him*."

"Vincent . . . ," said Mrs. Hudson.

"I marched right up to him and started shootin' the breeze, told him I liked his shoes, and that buttered him right up, so I asked if he was a friend of the bride or groom. He said groom, but he hadn't seen him yet, and could I point him in the right direction? And that's when it hit me. Someone was going to lose their life that night, and I'll be damned if it was going to be my big brother on the happiest day of his life while loser me was doing nothing more than puking in the trees. So I pointed to my younger self and said, "'There's the lucky man of the hour. Boy, she picked a real winner, didn't she?'"

"You sacrificed yourself?" said Mr. Hudson. "For me?"

"I didn't sacrifice anything," said Chuck. "We both know I was a screw-up going nowhere. This way I actually got to go somewhere. Probably gave me a better life than I would have had if I'd stayed."

Matt couldn't believe this. Chuck. His uncle Charles . . .

"*Why* didn't you tell us?" said Mr. Hudson. "At least Belamie and me. We would have understood."

Chuck shook his head. "You had enough to deal with. I didn't want you to feel responsible in any way. You aren't of course, but I didn't want you to feel that way."

"I'm so sorry, Charles," said Mrs. Hudson, her voice full of emotion. "But also thank you. Thank you for letting Matthew stay."

"Hey, I've never seen him happier than when he was with you. That's not something you can just mess up without it sitting heavy on your conscience. I thought everything would be fine after that, that we'd all just go on with our new wacko-normal. I could accept that, go with the flow, you know? But then Mom told me about the kids getting abducted, and I knew it was happening again, that Captain Vincent still had it in for you. I told Mom, 'Get those kids up here, away from the city and all those kidnappers. They'll be safe here.' And that's just what she did, but I guess even that didn't work."

Mrs. Hudson growled a little and ground her teeth. She looked livid. Mr. Hudson didn't say anything. He still looked stunned.

"So are you, like, our uncle?" Ruby asked.

"I sure am. Your uncle Charles."

"But we've always known you as Chuck," said Corey, "so can we call you Uncle Chuck?"

"You bet."

"Wahoo!" said Corey, lifting his fist into the air. "I have an Uncle Chuck!"

Chuck smiled and gave Corey a fist bump. "You look a lot like your dad, but I have to say you kind of remind me of me as a kid, doesn't he, Matty?" He looked to Mr. Hudson, who nodded absentmindedly. "Now that's a compliment in some ways, but in other ways it's a warning. You behave yourself."

"Hey, I'm not stealing bottles of wine or anything," said Corey.

"Good boy," said Chuck, then he turned to Ruby. "And you're the spitting image of your mom, and I see you're going to be just as fiery and will keep the whole world in line with a sword."

Ruby beamed and blushed.

"And Matty Junior," said Chuck, turning to Matt. "You're

quite the genius. I don't think I'd ever have been reunited with my brother without you. I never felt too lonely. You were all my friends before, but now, because of you and your compass, I feel like I have a family again."

Matt reached for his compass, feeling overwhelmed. Everything that had happened to Chuck, to his family, all because of his compass. Because of *him*. Matt had been the one to make the compass in the first place. None of this would have happened without him.

"What about Dad?" Mr. Hudson asked. "Do you have any idea where Vincent left him?"

Chuck shook his head. "None whatsoever. Looked like we were in the middle of the ocean. Could have been a hundred years ago, or a thousand. I don't know."

"We'll find him," said Mr. Hudson, clearly determined.

"How?" Ruby asked. "We don't have the map anymore."

"I'll find a way," said Mr. Hudson. "We didn't need the map to find Mateo."

"Even if we could rescue him," said Chuck, "you gotta think about the repercussions of that. It doesn't fix things necessarily, and in some ways might make it worse."

"What do you mean?" said Mr. Hudson. "How could it be worse to get him back!"

Chuck put up a hand as though to calm his brother. "Just think it through," said Chuck. "If we got Dad back at the time he was taken, he would be younger than both of us, almost thirty years younger than me, his youngest son. And maybe we could live with that, but what about Mom? How would she handle having her husband come home, unchanged from the day he left, but she's old enough to be his mother? How do you think that's going to go over?"

Mr. Hudson sank down a little. "We could rescue him and take him back to the date when he was taken. Then it will be like he was only missing for a day or so."

Mrs. Hudson shook her head. "You know it won't work like that," she said. "You'd most certainly cause a glitch."

"What if we rescue him but we make him wait?" said Ruby. "We find him when he was discarded, but explain everything that's happened and tell him he has to wait for forty years until he can be reunited with Gaga?"

"Yes!" said Mr. Hudson, pointing to Ruby, but speaking to Mrs. Hudson. "That's a reasonable solution that wouldn't cause a glitch!"

"Yes, in theory," said Mrs. Hudson, "but again, think through the repercussions, as Charles said. You expect your father to put his life on hold for forty years, knowing that his sons are being raised without him, his wife living her life without him?"

"Why not?" said his dad. "Mom never got remarried. She never even went on a date after Dad left."

Mrs. Hudson shook her head. "But your father might act differently, and besides that, a lot can happen in forty years.

Too much has already happened on our end. It would be impossible to thread the timelines back together without causing severe damage in one way or another."

They fell silent. Matt was still letting all of this settle in his mind. He was calculating all the possibilities, any solution, but he was coming up empty.

Mr. Hudson rubbed his head, pulling his hair. "So that's it? Vincent rips *my* family apart, steals my brother's and my dad's lives when they did nothing to deserve it, and there's *nothing* we can do about it?"

Mrs. Hudson put her hand on Mr. Hudson's back and spoke softly. "Matthew, I'm so terribly sorry."

"There is something we can do," said Matt, clutching his compass firmly in his hand. Everyone turned to him. He'd been waiting, allowing the idea to fully form in his brain, checking for any weak spots, any holes. If they were there he didn't see them. "The Aeternum," he said. "*We* are supposed to get the Aeternum."

"What?" said his dad.

"Mateo," said his mom.

"No, listen!" said Matt. "Don't you see? The Aeternum is meant for *us*. For our family, to repair all the damage Vincent has done! That's why *I'm* mentioned. Because I made the Obsidian Compass, and I can take us to Quine who has the Aeternum!"

"But what about the sacrifice part?" said Corey. "What if

one of us has to die or something?"

Matt shivered a little, thinking about what Quine had said to him, but he wasn't about to tell his family about that. "I think the sacrifices in our family have already been made," said Matt. "Mom sacrificed her parents for the Aeternum, and Dad did too. And Chuck. We've all made sacrifices. As for that last line, where it says 'We are on' I think it's saying we're on the same side. We're friends in the future! Or family, I don't know. But somehow we're connected, because at some point I must have given him my compass to give to Mom, and now he wants to give us his Aeternum so we can fix everything that got all messed up with all our time-traveling." Matt's mind was reeling. His whole being felt like it was on fire, telling him he was on the right path. Foremembering. This was what they were supposed to do. He just *knew* it. They would get the Aeternum. They'd go back in time and make it so Captain Vincent couldn't abduct his grandpa or Uncle Chuck, or even them. They'd save his mom's family. He'd fix everything so it was just as it should be.

"I think Matt's right," said Corey, and Matt beamed at his brother.

Ruby nodded, her expression serious. "Me too," she said. "It makes sense."

"Oddly, I do too," said his dad.

"And I," said Tui.

"Me too," said Annie.

Mrs. Hudson looked at her husband like he was crazy. "You can't be serious."

"Belamie, it makes sense," said Mr. Hudson. "It's like everything has been leading us to this moment. To Matt, and Quine, and the Aeternum, for the chance to *fix* things."

"B-but," Mrs. Hudson stammered, grasping for some argument. "But we don't know where Quine is."

"Yes, we do," said Matt. "He's right where you left him when he gave you my compass."

Matt watched understanding seep into his mother's eyes. She paled a little, but he also saw resolve in her expression. It was as if she'd known this day would come ever since that day she'd received the compass. That everything would come full circle eventually. Matt, too, felt as though his whole existence somehow revolved around this moment, and Quine, and the Aeternum. This was his destiny. He'd never been so certain of anything in his entire life.

23

The Sacrifice

1772
Asilah, Morocco

They arrived about a half mile from the shore. Blossom had again taken on the form of a large boat, stretching and widening, with a small mast and sail spiking up from the middle.

Matt thought Asilah looked like something out of a legend, a fairy tale. White buildings nestled on the edge of the sea. When they reached the shore, Mr. Hudson and Chuck jumped out of Blossom and pulled the boat onto the sand.

Matt hopped down, scanning the beach.

It was empty. He saw no one. Perhaps Quine was in the city.

And then he appeared. Formed out of thin air, not just his hands, but his entire body. He was about fifty feet down the beach, just standing there, gazing out at the ocean. His mom drew in a sharp breath. Matt felt a gentle tug in his chest, a tingling in his fingers. He started to walk toward Quine until his mom grabbed his hand.

"Mateo, no," she said.

Matt turned and looked his mother in the eyes. He saw the fear there, and the love. "It's okay, Mom. He's on our side."

"How can you be sure?" she asked.

Matt thought for a moment. "I can just feel it." He knew it wasn't a satisfying answer, but it was the best he could do. He really could *feel* it in an almost physical way. "It's going to be okay," he said.

His mom squeezed his hand, and for a moment Matt thought she wouldn't let him go, or that she would insist on coming with him, but then she nodded and dropped his hand. She seemed to understand that whatever was about to happen, it was supposed to be just Quine and him. "Be careful. Please," she said.

Matt nodded, and then he left his family behind and walked toward the man on the beach. "Mr. Quine?" Matt called when he was about ten feet away.

Quine turned around, muttering something under his breath.

Quine was blurry around the edges, and even though Matt couldn't see his face clearly, there was something familiar about him, as though he knew him from sometime in his past, or maybe his future, like he was foremembering him. Who was this mysterious man?

Matt slowed. All the confidence he'd felt a moment ago had suddenly vanished. The tug he'd felt before suddenly seemed to change, now pulling in the opposite direction.

"Hello, Mateo," said Quine in that familiar yet indecipherable voice that somehow echoed inside his head and reverberated in his chest. Matt focused on Quine's blurry face. It flickered into clarity for just a moment, revealing dark, intelligent eyes that looked familiar and foreign all at once.

Matt thought it was best to get right to the point. "I've come for the Aeternum," he said. "I need it."

"Do you?" said Quine, the blurry line of his eyebrow arching.

"Everything that's happened, it's my fault. I need to make things right again."

"Ah," said Quine. "Yes, to make things right . . . but right for whom, exactly?"

"My family," said Matt. "And maybe other people too." He was starting to feel unsure about this. After he fixed all that had gone wrong with his family, then what? Would he go fix other things? Eliminate wars and injustice, eradicate hunger and poverty, save the whole world throughout time? That would be a good thing, wouldn't it?

The earth began to shake, sudden and violent. Matt stumbled back. What was happening? Had they caused a glitch somehow?

The sea churned and parted. A ship rose from the water, a black flag on the mainmast whipping in the wind. The *Vermillion*. It surged toward them, heading straight for the Hudsons.

"Watch out!" Matt shouted. He raced toward his family, who were now all running toward him as the *Vermillion* careened onto the beach. Sand and water rained down on them. They all fell as the ship bulldozed Blossom, crushing the bus-boat like an aluminum can beneath a foot.

"Oh no!" Chuck put his hands to his head. "Blossom!"

As soon as the ship stopped, a rope was slung over the side of the *Vermillion* and Captain Vincent appeared. He scaled down the rope and jumped to the beach. Brocco came after him, followed by Wiley, and then Albert, who struggled to lower himself and finally fell the last ten feet, rolling awkwardly in the sand.

"Mateo!" called Mrs. Hudson. She scrambled to her feet, but Tui was faster.

"I have him, Captain!" shouted Tui. "Stay with the others!" Tui grabbed Matt and pulled him against her so he was facing outward in an almost hostage-style hold.

Captain Vincent walked toward the Hudsons, swaggering with his sword in hand, eyes blazing. Mr. and Mrs. Hudson stood together, creating a barricade between Vincent and their children. Chuck had hold of Corey. Annie stood in front of Ruby, rifle aimed right at Vincent, but she didn't shoot and Captain Vincent showed no fear of her. He didn't even acknowledge their existence. He strode right past them and went directly to Quine. He stopped a few feet before the blurred man. Tui pulled Matt close to her. He felt her grip tighten on his shoulders.

Vincent bowed to Quine.

"I have done everything you asked me to do," he said, "and humbly ask that you grant me the Aeternum, as you promised."

Matt was confused. *Vincent* had been in touch with Quine? He'd been taking orders from him? Quine was on *his* side?

"You've done very well," said Quine. "But I still need Mateo."

Vincent looked in Matt's direction. He flicked his head, and before Matt could even comprehend what was going on, Tui bent down and flung Matt over her shoulder. He bounced as she ran.

"No!" Mrs. Hudson shrieked. "Tui, what are you doing?"

Matt was dumped before a pair of red Converse. Vince grabbed him. Matt struggled to free himself, but Vincent held him so tight he could barely move.

Matt saw his mother rush toward him, drawing her father's dagger, but Vincent drew his own dagger and held it at Matt's throat, while Tui drew Vincent's sword and pointed it at

Mrs. Hudson. She froze in her tracks. Annie lifted her rifle, aimed for Vincent, but Wiley and Brocco came up behind her, Brocco with a gun in each hand. He pointed them both at Annie's head.

"Drop the gun, Li'l Sure Shot, before I return the favor you paid me the other day." He lowered one of his guns, aiming at her backside. Annie glared, her eyes murderous, but she had no choice. She couldn't possibly move fast enough to disarm Brocco before he shot her, and if she shot Vincent, Brocco would definitely shoot her. She lowered her rifle, dropped it in the sand.

"Tui," said Mrs. Hudson. "Why . . . ?"

"*Why?*" Tui snarled. Her dark eyes flashed with violence. "You leave us behind. No explanations. Nothing. And you ask *why* I am not on your side?"

"But, Tui, I'm your *friend.*" Mrs. Hudson was wild, confused.

Tui spat on the ground. "We are not friends," she growled. "You are not my captain! The day you left us you became nothing more than a weak coward, and I saw that Vincent was always meant to have the compass and the Aeternum. You left us both. Together we planned our revenge. We both sacrificed. I went to that terrible place and waited for you. Captain Vincent said you would find me there."

Matt swallowed, feeling the blade against his throat. Tui had been a spy for Captain Vincent all along. All this time he thought she'd been trying to help them, protect them. . . . He thought back, remembering how adamant Tui had been when it came to finding Captain Vincent. He thought she'd wanted revenge upon him, to stop him, but really she only wanted to help bring the Hudsons to Vincent. Bring *him*, Mateo, to Quine. To sacrifice him so he could have the Aeternum.

"Please, Vince," Mrs. Hudson begged. "Don't do this. He's my *son*."

"He's no more your son than I am your husband," said Vincent. "You have always known this would be the boy's fate, whether it came to your benefit or mine. Now," said Vincent, turning to Quine. "What do you need me to do with the boy in order to get the Aeternum? Spill his blood?"

Matt sucked in a breath as he felt the knife dig into his neck. He was sure it was drawing blood already.

"Oh no," said Quine. "Nothing so gruesome. I only need to touch his hand."

"His hand?" said Vincent in a surprised tone. He clearly was not expecting this. Matt wasn't either. What was so significant about his hand?

"Don't worry," said Quine. "I promise the effect will be *magnificent*. Explosive and mind-boggling. We are a powerful combination, Mateo and I. The joining of our hands will activate the Aeternum, infuse it with immeasurable power, all for your taking. But we cannot touch each other of our own accord. You must force our hands together." Quine removed the glove from his right hand. The blurriness sharpened and pulled into focus, just for a moment, but enough for Matt to see the rootlike tattoo spread over his hand, branching up his wrist and arm until it disappeared into his shirt.

Matt's breath caught in his throat. It wasn't a tattoo. They were scars. Burn scars. Identical to Matt's.

Words and phrases clicked into place inside his head.

A sacrifice must be made

To win this game.

Bring Mateo to me

We are one and the same.

Matt was Quine. Quine was *him*. They were the same person.

"Join your hands," said Vincent. "Simple enough." He grabbed Matt by his scarred wrist, and Quine by his, pulling them together. Matt could feel a buzz in his fingertips, a kind of electrical current running between him and Quine.

"Remember my warning, Vincent," said Quine. "Once you go down this path, there is no turning back. You will be forever changed, and forever is a long, long time. But no time at all, really."

"I believe that is exactly the point," said Vincent, and he forced Matt's and Quine's hands together.

A jolt ran through Matt. Heat rushed down his arm, through his hand and into Quine's. Matt also felt searing heat coming from Quine, rushing through his hand and back up his arm, into his shoulder and through his entire body. Quine was glowing. He almost looked like he was on fire. Was Matt on fire, too? The heat grew, the energy intensified, and just when Matt thought it was too much, that he would combust, he did. Quine did, too. They both exploded, flew into a billion pieces.

Matt still had some awareness, some sense of his physical form, even though he could not control it. He was moving very fast, at light speed. Faster. Where, he did not know. But he could feel Quine's presence as well, moving around and through him, their cells mingling, intertwining, combining in some way.

Matt felt himself pulling back together, his cells communicating with each other, moving back into the shape of him. He felt his heart first, and then blood pumping in veins, lungs expanding with air, bones, muscle, and sinew. When he was fully assembled again, when every cell was back in its proper order, Matt was back on the beach with his scarred, burning hand outstretched and a small black stone resting in the center of his palm. The stone was very familiar to Matt. It looked exactly like the stone from his bracelet, the one that was now in Matt's compass, except this one felt *alive*. It pulsed with warmth and energy in Matt's hand. The symbol etched in the stone was clearly visible now. The markings glowed like the blue base of a flame. It was the Chinese character for eternity. It was the symbol for the Aeternum.

Matt gaped at the warm, glowing stone, unable to speak or move, until Captain Vincent plucked the stone from his hand. Captain Vincent pressed the Aeternum into the center of his Obsidian Compass, as Matt had done before, only this time, with the activated Aeternum, it had a different effect.

The Aeternum clicked into place. Nothing happened for a moment, and then the Obsidian Compass also began to pulse with a bluish glow. It unlocked and unfolded itself. Circles within circles separated from the compass and rotated, transforming it into a sphere. Captain Vincent rose off the ground, feet hovering over the sand. A bluish glow emanated from him. Matt could feel heat pulsing off his skin. Captain Vincent was being altered somehow. The glowing orb in his hand was making him immortal, imbuing him with unimaginable power. The light within the compass grew and grew, brighter and brighter, until it burst with blinding white light that radiated outward in every direction. Matt was certain the entire world was being incinerated, and then the light shot back into the compass in a flash of a second.

All was still. Silent.

Matt looked around. The world had paused. The wind did not blow. The sea did not rush. The waves were frozen, the white crests hovering in a curl. His family, the crew, even Captain Vincent looked like wax figures, very lifelike but frozen in time. Mateo seemed to be the only one awake and able to move. He went to his mother and reached out to touch her hand.

"Do not touch," said a voice. It was Quine's voice. Matt turned all around but did not see him. Then the air began to shimmer. Matt marveled as he witnessed billions of tiny particles form and coalesce, bind and take shape, until Quine once again stood before him, this time clear and fully visible.

"They are suspended in the universe," said Quine, gesturing to his family, Jia, and the crew. "Time has been paused, if you will, and the human existence is intertwined with time. Once time reasserts itself in the world they will be just as they were. Except Vincent. He will be very different."

"What about us?" Matt asked. "Why aren't we suspended?"

"We have always been different. We have different rules."

Matt looked down at his scarred hand, then looked at Quine's. "We are the same person," he said. "You and me, I mean. Aren't we?"

"We were born the same person, yes," said Quine, "but I do not think it is completely accurate to say we are the same person now."

"What do you mean? Did you somehow alter your DNA or something?"

"No," said Quine. "In that regard we are still the same. But a person can't be reduced to just their genetic coding. We are *always* changing. You are not the same person now as when you were born. I am not the same person now as when I was your age. We have grown and changed both physically and mentally. Even the cells that make up our physical bodies are different. But I was once you, and one day you will be me."

Matt studied Quine. Himself. His older self by fifty years, perhaps more. He recognized the eyes, the shape of his features, though his hair was streaked with silver, his face lined and worn by time and the gravity of the world, the burdens of life. Quine had seen things, done things that Matt had not. They were the same and yet separate, and he felt far from comforted with the knowledge. It terrified him. He didn't know who this person was standing before him, even though he knew it was himself. He did not know what he wanted, or what he was working toward, or whose side he was on.

"Something troubling you, Mateo?" said Quine.

Matt hesitated, not certain how to phrase the next question. "Am I good?" he asked. "I mean, are *we* good?"

Quine lifted an eyebrow, his lips parting into a somewhat sad smile. And then he recited a poem.

I celebrate myself, and sing myself,
And what I assume you shall assume,
For every atom belonging to me as good belongs to you.

Matt let the words wash over him. He wasn't sure he fully understood them, but he liked the way they made him feel.

He guessed that was the point of poetry, in the end. To make you feel.

"Did you write that?" Matt asked. "I mean, *we*?"

Quine shook his head. "Walt Whitman. A true poet."

"It's nice," said Matt, "but I'm not sure it answers my question."

"Doesn't it? Do you wish to be good?"

"Of course," said Matt.

"And how would you define *good*?" Quine asked.

"Doing the right thing?"

"What is the right thing? Do you always do it?"

"I . . ." Matt began, and then trailed off. He thought he did, but he suddenly wasn't so sure.

"Me neither," said Quine. "It's something I have been considering my entire life. Many a human has done great wrong in the name of doing what they believed was right. Take Captain Vincent," he gestured to the inanimate Captain Vincent. His arm was outstretched. The spherical compass in his hand glowed blue at the center. "He believes he is right," said Quine. "He is the hero in his own story, but you believe he is a villain."

"Isn't he?" said Matt.

"Perhaps," said Quine. "I don't particularly care for him, but then who am I to judge? My opinion is rather biased. He did hold us at knifepoint, after all, though I guess it's kind of cheating to know that we survive."

"What will happen now that he has the Aeternum?" said Matt.

"A great many things," said Quine. "Prepare yourself. The future will not be easy for you. More sacrifices will need to be made."

Matt swallowed. "Can't you tell me all the things that will happen? Can't you just tell me what I have to do?"

"What's the use of knowing everything?" said Quine. "Sounds boring to me, and if I know anything about you, which I think I do, you hate to be bored. Take care, Mateo." Quine turned as though he meant to leave.

"Wait! Please, I just have one more question."

"Yes?"

"Why did you change our name?"

Quine grinned mischievously. "Another thing I'll let you figure out for yourself. Now I must go. Time is about to reassert itself, and things will move very quickly. It's best if I'm out of the way." He gave Matt a final wink before he disintegrated into a billion pieces. "Oh and one more thing," said Quine, his disembodied voice now hovering in the air. "Hold on to Jia." And then he was gone, his voice carried away on the wind.

Wind. The air had been so still, but Matt felt it begin to stir, brush against his cheek like a whispered omen.

The ground shifted beneath Matt's feet and the world began to move again. But not in its usual order. The waves retreated and melded back into the sea. Mrs. Hudson came alive, but instead of continuing in her path toward Captain Vincent she moved backward, robotically. Everyone else did, too, including Matt. Suddenly he was back in the clutches of Vincent, then holding hands with Quine, the light expanding and retreating. The world was moving in reverse.

Things started to change and disappear in an unnatural fashion. It looked like an invisible slingshot was shooting people, one by one, in random directions. First Wiley and Brocco went, both of them soaring back into the *Vermillion*, and then Albert, his round, pale face shocked and afraid. Next the ship pulled away from the beach and disappeared. Blossom rose from the sand, taking shape like it was being inflated.

Matt rejoined his family. His parents, Corey and Ruby, Chuck, Tui, Annie, and Jia. They were back inside Blossom, who hissed and growled like a cat who'd just had its tail yanked. They traveled backward like a tape in rewind, bouncing through space and time. They were flung back to Nowhere in No Time, to Yellowstone, the geysers sucking back in the lava, then water and billows of white steam. They went back to Chicago, over the fair of the glowing White City, the Ferris wheel, and the huge stadium and tents of Buffalo Bill's Wild West show. It was here that Annie left them. She was sucked out of the window, spinning in the air like a ragdoll, her rifle still clutched beneath her arm.

And Jia.

Matt remembered Quine's last words to him.

Hold on to Jia.

Matt grabbed Jia's hand just as that invisible slingshot seemed to pull her back, ready to fling her into the ether. They clasped fingers, and then there was a battle of forces. Jia was being pulled away, sucked toward the window. She started to scream. Matt held tight, ignoring the pain.

"I got you!" said Matt. "I won't let go." But he started to feel the pull as well, slowly but surely sucking him toward that vortex of space and time.

"You have to let go, Matt," said Jia. "It's okay. I'll be okay."

She started to release him.

"No!" Matt shouted, gripping her fingers as tightly as he could, but he began to shake with the effort.

Matt felt someone grab on to him. He looked over. Corey had his left hand, and Ruby was holding on to Corey.

"We got you, Matt!" said Corey. "We won't let go!"

Mrs. Hudson reached for the twins, Mr. Hudson held on to his wife, and Chuck held tight to his brother. All of them clung to each other, a big, unwieldy family chain.

The universe snapped.

The bus shot back again, over the white and gray landscape of Wrangel Island. Tui was sucked out of Blossom, screaming as she was hurled back into the Ice Age.

The next thing Matt knew they crashed down onto solid

earth and were bouncing over rickety fencing and vines, heading toward a house. Not just any house. Gaga's house!

They were back at the vineyard. Corey was at Blossom's wheel, struggling to get control. Matt saw something big suddenly fall off the side of the bus and roll in the dirt. It was his dad! And then his mom fell off the back. She landed on her feet and kept running. Blossom rattled and groaned as they moved steadily toward the house, right toward the porch.

"Corey, stop!" shouted Ruby. Corey stomped on the brakes, but too late. Blossom crashed into the porch. Metal crunched as wood cracked and splintered. Matt was flung forward and slammed against the front seat, then tossed back.

Blossom gave a little beep, as if to announce their arrival, and then her engine sputtered and died.

24
The Beginning

Something shifted and groaned beneath Matt, and he realized he had landed on top of Jia.

"Sorry!" said Matt, scrambling to release her, but then felt a tug on his arm. He looked down. Their hands were still linked. He'd gripped her hand so tight his fingers were white and numb. Still he did not let go.

"*Nǐ hǎo*, Mateo," said Jia, smiling.

Matt smiled back. "*Ni hao*, Jia."

The door to the bus slid open, and there were his parents. His mom's hair was once again a wild dark tangle. His dad looked pale and dazed. His clothing was torn and dusty, his glasses crooked on his face.

"Are you all right?" Mrs. Hudson asked. "Is everyone okay? Corey? Ruby?"

"We're fine," said Ruby.

Mrs. Hudson pulled Matt out of the car and into a bone-crushing hug. His dad embraced him, too, and then Ruby, and Corey, all of them hugging him so tightly he could barely breathe. He didn't mind a bit.

"Where's Charles?" Mr. Hudson asked, looking inside the bus.

"Back here," said Chuck, lifting up his hand. "Cozy as a kitten." He pushed open the hatch and rolled out, then yelped. "What the beetle juice!"

They all scrambled to the back of Blossom just in time to see little Pike climb out and hop to the ground.

"Where in the universe did you come from?" said Chuck.

Pike paid Chuck no mind and sauntered over to Jia, taking her hand. "How did you get in there?" Jia asked. Pike just looked up at her, expressionless as usual.

"She must have held on tight and found a way to stay," said Ruby. "Just like you did."

The Hudsons all glanced at each other. Corey was the one to say what they were all thinking.

"How can we know that she's on our side and not spying for Captain Vincent?" Corey asked. "I mean, she kind of sold us out before, didn't she?"

As if in answer, Pike produced a folded sheet of paper and handed it to Matt. He opened it, and the rest of the family crowded in as he read.

Forgot to tell you that Pike will be staying with you. She's on your (our) side.
M. Quine

"What does he mean, 'our' side?" said Ruby. "Quine gave Vincent the Aeternum, didn't he? How can he be on our side?"

"Maybe he understands things that we don't," said Mrs. Hudson. "Remember, we still don't know exactly who Quine is. It's possible he really is on our side, and everything he's done has been for good reason." Matt looked up at his mom. She was gazing at him, studying him, and in that moment he knew that she knew. Or at least she suspected.

Quine was Mateo. Mateo was Quine.

But it seemed neither Matt nor his mom wanted to say it out loud. That would open up too many questions, too much doubt and fear. He was not ready to face that yet, and it seemed she wasn't either. Quine had given Vincent the Aeternum. Matt still was not sure what that meant, who or what he would become in the future. It made his head hurt, thinking about it.

Pike gave one of her rare smiles. Matt folded up the piece of paper, slid it in his pocket with the others—the poem, his adoption papers. "If Quine says she's on our side, then she is."

"So we're back home, huh?" said Chuck, gazing around the vineyard. "Looks like a tornado hit this place."

It did look like a tornado had swept through. Aside from the damage they'd done to the porch, windows were broken, and a big branch of the willow had fallen down on the roof, crushing one of the chimneys. The vineyard was destroyed completely. Vines had been torn up by the roots and scattered, and Chuck's little cottage was in splinters. All that remained intact was the toilet.

"Did we do all of this?" Matt asked.

"I don't think I'm *that* bad of a driver," said Corey.

"This isn't your fault, *chéri*," said Mrs. Hudson, her face darkening the more she looked around.

Mr. Hudson stared at the broken windows of the house. "I need to check on Mom," he said, but before he could take three steps, the front door to the house burst open.

"Oh! You're okay!" Gaga cried, clutching at her chest as she ran down the porch. "I was so worried. I saw the kids tumbling around inside Chuck's bus, and then you two running after them, and then I couldn't see you at all. I thought you'd all gotten swept up in the storm and disappeared!" She stopped in front of them, breathing hard and fast, and Matt could see her face was streaked with tears. "Is anyone hurt? Matty, Belamie, kids? Oh, Matty, you look like you got run over by a car!" She assessed Mr. Hudson's torn and dirty clothes, the bruises now blooming on his face. "And Mateo! Your arm! That looks serious."

"We're okay, Mom," said Mr. Hudson. "Just . . . went for a little ride."

"I'll say," said Gaga. "What a storm! It came out of nowhere, ripped out all my hydrangea bushes and broke half the windows and then . . ." She trailed off as she noticed Jia and Pike. "Oh! Hello. Who are you?"

"Sorry, Gaga," said Matt, stepping closer to Jia. "These are our friends, Jia and Pike. They came to visit . . . just before the storm hit."

"How . . . lovely," said Gaga, looking over Pike's pillowcase dress decorated with pins, and Jia's many-pocketed vest bursting with tools and supplies. They weren't exactly your average kids. "I am sorry we aren't in better shape to receive guests. Everything is in such disarray. The plumbing is a mess."

"I can fix it!" said Jia. "I'm very good with plumbing, especially flushing toilets. Do you have any of those?"

Gaga looked startled and perplexed. "Why, yes, we have a few of those."

"Perfect! I'll take a look right away." Jia marched up the porch steps and went inside the house as comfortably as if she lived there. Pike quickly followed.

Gaga took a step toward the house, then paused, like she

wasn't sure what to do. She turned to Matt. "Your friend is very enthusiastic about plumbing."

"She's the best," said Matt, beaming. He was so glad Jia was here.

Gaga gazed toward the ruined vineyard. "Chuck, I'm afraid you've got your work cut out for you with this mess."

"Oh, don't worry, Mrs. H.," said Chuck. "I'll take care of it."

"Thank you," said Gaga. "I don't know what I would have done without you all these years."

Chuck gave a shrug, but Matt could see his face flush. "Matty here would take care of you just fine, I'm sure."

Gaga waved her hand and let out a little *pfft*. "My son has many skills, but yardwork isn't one of them."

Mr. Hudson nodded. "Very true."

"And you'll stay with us, Chuck, for now?" said Gaga. "Until we can get the cottage rebuilt."

Chuck seemed startled by this. "Oh . . . that's okay, Mrs. H. It seems like you have plenty of guests to be dealing with, and you know I can stay comfortably in Blossom."

Gaga sneered at the bus now stuck halfway into her porch. "In that old hunk of junk? No, I won't hear of it."

"He can have our room," Matt suggested. "The kids can all sleep on cots in the basement."

"Yeah!" said Corey. "We'll build a fort."

"Then it's settled," said Gaga. "You'll stay with us."

Chuck nodded, scratched the back of his neck. "All right. Thank you."

"Well, I suppose I'd better go supervise our young plumber." Gaga went back up the porch and into the house. When the door closed behind her, the rest of them stood there in silence.

"Aren't you going to tell Gaga who you really are, Uncle Chuck?" Ruby asked.

Chuck seemed to go a little green in the face. "I'm not sure that's such a good idea."

"But we're going to find Grandpa, aren't we?" Corey asked. "I mean, we can't just leave him behind, not when we could save him. So we'll have to tell Gaga everything."

Mr. and Mrs. Hudson glanced at each other, communicating something in their silent language. "We'll discuss it," said Mrs. Hudson, "but it's complicated. Now that Vincent has the Aeternum . . . it changes things."

"But we're here, aren't we?" said Ruby. "We were sent back to almost the same time we left, and we're all together. Maybe the Aeternum didn't work like Vincent thought it would."

"It's possible," said Mrs. Hudson, though Matt could tell she didn't really believe this. "Only time will tell."

Matt swallowed the fear that continued to rise in his throat. He wondered if that was part of Vincent's game. Let them stay together for now. Let the fear rise in them, at what might happen. It was working.

"I'd better go check out the vineyard," said Chuck, pointing to the wreck of vines and fences. "If there's anything to be salvaged it needs to get back in the ground as soon as possible."

"Want some help?" said Mr. Hudson.

"No, no," said Chuck. "You stick with your wife and kids. I got this."

Chuck walked away, and Mr. Hudson looked after his long-lost brother. It had to be weird, Matt thought. He marveled at how time travel had affected their family. Grandpa Hudson, Uncle Chuck, and his mom, who had been born nearly three centuries in the past. And he had done all of that. For better or worse, Mateo was responsible. The weight of this truth pressed down on him so that his knees practically buckled. He'd already caused so much damage, but it was also why they were all here together now. He wouldn't trade that for anything. Now he just needed to make sure they could all stay together.

"Let's go inside now," said Mr. Hudson. "I'm sure Gaga could use some help."

They all started to file into the house, but something caught Matt's eye before he went in. A square of white on the willow tree by the pond. He went over and found a piece of paper pierced to the tree with a dagger. He recognized the dagger. It was Captain Vincent's. The very one he had just held against Matt's throat.

Matt tore off the piece of paper from the tree. The fear rose up in him again, nearly choked him, as he read the words printed on the page in black ink.

This is only the beginning.

Acknowledgments

The journey continues! I could never have written this book without the help and support of so many smart, kind, and talented people. Many thanks to my agent, Claire Anderson-Wheeler, who always has my back and calls the calm to my storm. Huge thanks to my incredible editors, Mabel Hsu, Melissa Miller, and Alex Arnold. Your enthusiasm, creativity, and smarts have inspired and challenged me, and this book is better for it. Huge thanks to copy editor Jenny Moles and proofreader Dan Janeck. Whoa. You guys are boss. I know this book had a lot of mind benders, and you caught so many snags and helped untangle those truly dizzying timelines. Any remaining mistakes are my own. Thanks to Amy Ryan for the fabulous design, and to Katherine Tegan, Kathryn Silsand, Mark Rifkin, Kimberly Stella, Vanessa Nuttry, Robby Imfeld, Samantha Benson, and all the fantastic team at Katherine Tegen Books and HarperCollins for helping this series grow and find its way into the hands of young readers.

Thanks to my writing pals Brianna DuMont, for speed-reading and offering advice and encouragement, and Kate Hannigan and Amy Timberlake, for always lending a listening ear and helping me talk through the rough spots. Thanks to Elli Dastrup and Ahmed El Shamsy for the Arabic translation and to Daisy Jiang, Jianli Huang, and Dianna Larsen for the Chinese translation. It was just one word in each language, but it was an important word and the internet was no help at all. (What?! You're telling me the internet doesn't know *everything*?)

Thanks to Janie George for making me look fancy online, and to Katie Nydegger for keeping me organized and sane. And shout-outs and love to all my girls for the many, many cups of tea and chats of encouragement. Life would be so dull without you.

To my kids Whitney, Ty, Topher, and Freddy—thanks for all the inspiration. (Yes, Ty, you inspired Corey. Thanks, and you're welcome.)

Finally to my husband, Scott, my champion and true companion—you put up with a lot of crazy while I write these crazy stories, and you do it with grace and good humor. I love you.